D0187231

Isthmus
Village
Black
Village
Tall
Hassle
Trolla
Ogre's Fen Gyre Front
Void
Censor
Ship
With a Cookie River
Water
Fire
Earth
North
Village
Air Ores
Flies
Gap Village
Fish River
Isle of
Illusion
Peace
Gap Chasm
Brain
Coral
Computer
Lake
Kiss-Mee
Mare
Good Magicians
Castle
Lake
Wails
Isle of
View
Castle
Roogna
South
Village
Lake
Ogre-Chobee
Vortex
Mount Rushmost
Region
Madness
Gateway
Castle
Mount Parnassus
Faun & Nymph
Retreat
Ivory
Tower
Evil
Glades
Centaur
Isle

XANTH

GATEWAY TO ADVENTURE

Dug stared longingly at Nada Naga's image on the screen, a lusciously beautiful young woman in an outfit resembling the sinuous contours of a serpent.

"It will be easier if you get into the scene with me," she said. "So that we can relate to each other more readily."

"I'd love to get into the scene with you," he agreed, "But you're on the computer screen, and I'm out here in real life."

"You have to suspend your disbelief a bit," said Nada. "When you can manage to believe in Xanth, then you will experience magic."

"When I believe that, I'll be crazy," said Dug.

"No," answered Nada, "you will just be in another realm." It suddenly seemed to Dug as if she were a real person, communicating through the barrier of his disbelief.

"How do I play this game?" he said at last.

"Take my hand," Nada said, "and I will lead you into it." She extended her lovely hand to him. The scene expanded. Now he seemed to be in the glade, and Nada stood beside him. . .

PIERS ANTHONY

DEMONS DON'T DREAM

A TOM DOHERTY ASSOCIATES BOOK
NEW YORK

DEMONS DON'T DREAM

Copyright © 1993 by Piers Anthony Jacob

Cover art by Darrell Sweet

A Tor Book
Published by Tom Doherty Associates, Inc.
175 Fifth Avenue
New York, N.Y. 10010

Tor ® is a registered trademark of Tom Doherty Associates, Inc.

ISBN: 0-812-53483-2

First edition: February 1993
First mass market printing: February 1994

Printed in the United States of America

0 9 8 7 6 5 4 3 2 1

Contents

DEMONS
DON'T
DREAM

1
COMPANION

Dug was exasperated. "Forget it, Ed! I'm not interested in any silly computer game. They all claim to be so easy to play and so exciting, and every one of them has a squintillion stupid things you have to do just to get started, and then the games are just awkward figures on painted backdrops, and you have the May-I syndrome."

"The what?"

"You know. No matter what you do, you get an error message and you have to start over, because you forgot to say 'May I?' or something just as idiotic before you did it. Computers are great at that. They figure you're supposed to know everything before you start, and they're going to make you do it over and over until you finally figure out what they want, by which time you're sick of it all. I don't want to waste my time."

But his friend Edsel had the annoying fault of being too persistent. "I'll bet I can find you a game you'll really like. No May-I syndrome. No dull backdrops. Real adventure. Something you'll get into easy and never want to leave."

"And I'll bet you can't. There is no such game, because real people don't program them, just computer scientists who lost touch with reality decades ago."

"It's a bet," Ed said immediately. "What're the stakes?"

Dug refused to take it seriously. "My girlfriend against your motorcycle."

"Done! I always liked your girlfriend anyway. Give me a week to get the game in, and you can kiss her goodbye meanwhile."

"Hey, I wasn't really—" Dug protested. But Edsel was gone. Oh, well. It wasn't as if there was any real risk. Dug wouldn't take his friend's motorcycle anyway.

Now it was time to get into his homework. So he called Pia instead. "Hey, I just made a bet with Ed. The stakes are you against his motorcycle."

She laughed. "You better hope you lose, because that cycle needs work."

"I know. I won't really take it."

"But he'll really take me if you lose. He likes me."

Suddenly Dug was nervous. "You mean, if—you'd—?"

"A bet's a bet, Dug. You have to make good on it. You know that." She hung up.

Shaken, he stared at his unopened books. She had hardly seemed surprised, and not at all annoyed. Had he been set up?

It didn't take a week; Edsel had the game Saturday morning. "You crank this into your computer, and call me when you're sick of it. If you don't call in an hour, I'm calling Pia for a date, because I'll know I won."

"Aren't you going to stay and help me get the thing loaded? You know it's going to take time just to—"

"Nah. The bet is that you can do it yourself, with no hassle, and you'll really like it. So if I'm right, you won't need me at all, or care that I'm not around. If I'm wrong, you'll be on the phone within an hour to let me know."

"Half hour, more likely," Dug said grimly.

"Whatever. So try it and find out." Ed departed.

He seemed so sure of himself! But Dug had never met a computer program he liked, other than the one that blanked the screen after five minutes, and he seriously doubted that he would like this one. But if it was easy-loading, he'd give it a fair try, and still be on time with the phone call.

He looked at the package as he went upstairs to his room. COMPANIONS OF XANTH. This appeared to be a silly fantasy setting, exactly the kind Dug didn't much like. How could Ed think he'd go for this, even if it wasn't too hard to get going? Then he looked again. There was a picture of a young woman of truly comely face and figure, in an outfit resembling the sinuous contours of a serpent. Wouldn't it be something to meet a creature like that! Maybe she was the inducement; they figured that some poor sap like him would buy the game in the hope that she was in it. If she was, it would be only as an animated flat picture. A ripoff in spirit if not in technicality.

He settled himself by his computer table and turned the system on. While it warmed up and went through its ritual initial checks and balances, he opened the package. There were no instructions, just a disk. There wasn't even the usual warning note forbidding anyone to copy it. Just the words INSERT DISK—TYPE A:\XANTH—TOUCH ENTER. He had to admit that was simple.

He inserted the disk, typed the mysterious word, and touched ENTER. There was a momentary swirl on the screen. Then a little man appeared, almost a cartoon figure. The figure looked at Dug and spoke. His words appeared in type in a speech balloon above his head. "Hi! I'm Grundy Golem. I'm from the Land of Xanth, and I speak your language. I'm your temporary Companion. If you don't like me you can get rid of me in just a minute. But first listen a bit, okay? Because I'm here to take your hand and lead you through the preliminaries without confusion. Any questions you have, you just ask me. You do that by touching the Q key, or clicking the right side on your mouse. So go ahead—ask."

Why not? Dug touched Q.

There was a ding. A huge human finger appeared and nudged Grundy on the shoulder so hard that he stumbled to the side. "Hey, not so hard!" Dug had to smile. "Okay, so you have a question. You have one of those primitive Mundane keyboards, right? So you have two ways to do it. You can type the question so I can see it, or you can touch ENTER and it will bring up the list of the ten most common questions at this stage. Then you can use your arrow keys to highlight the question you want, and touch EN-TER again, or just shortcut it by typing the number of the question you want. I'll wait while you decide. If you want me to resume without waiting, touch ESCAPE." Grundy took a step back, twiddling his tiny thumbs.

Dug found himself intrigued despite his cynicism. He touched ENTER.

Grundy reached down and caught hold of a bit of string at the bottom of the screen. He pulled it up, and a scroll of print unrolled. There were numbered questions.

1. HOW DO I GET OUT OF THIS CRAZY GAME?
2. HOW CAN I SHORTCUT TO THE AC-TION?
3. WHO IS THAT CREATURE ON THE COVER?
4. CAN I GET MY MONEY BACK IF I QUIT NOW?
5. HOW DO I GET A BETTER COMPANION?
6. HOW DO I SAVE MY PLACE SO I CAN TAKE A PEE BREAK AND PICK UP WHERE I LEFT OFF?
7. WHAT MAKES YOU THINK THIS GAME IS SO GREAT?
8. CAN A FRIEND PLAY TOO?
9. WHAT'S THE PRIZE FOR WINNING?

O. HOW MANY PRINTED QUESTIONS ARE
THERE, AND CAN I CALL THEM UP
ANYTIME?

Dug smiled. It seemed they had had some player input.
He touched 0, which he took to be 10; he realized that it
couldn't be listed as 10 because when a player touched the
1 it would take him to 1 without giving him a chance to
complete the number. That was one of the things computers did: pretending not to know what the player really
wanted.

The question highlighted. Grundy came to life. "There
are a hundred questions in this edition of the Companions
of Xanth Game, and there may be more in future editions
as we get more player feedback. You can call up the list
anytime by touching HELP and paging down. For two-
digit numbers you can hold down the first number while
you touch the second, and both digits will register. But it's
probably easier just to ask me."

It probably was. But Dug decided to play with the list
a bit more. The questions were still on the scroll. So he
touched 1.

Grundy animated again. "To quit this game, touch ALT
ESCAPE and turn off the set. But I hope you don't quit
yet; you haven't given us a fair chance. We hardly know
you."

They hardly knew him? As if they were real and he was
a mocked-up player! That seemed arrogant. But also intriguing. Dug touched 2. "To shortcut directly to the action, touch SHIFT ESCAPE. But I strongly advise against
this, because there's more you have to do, like checking
in, and you'll be stuck with me as your Companion. Once
you know the ropes, you can skip this whole scene, but
please don't do it this time."

Fair enough. So far there had been no confusion, and he
had not yet gotten into the game proper. He could skip
ahead and look at it, but it made sense to give the Golem
his chance. He touched 3.

"That creature on the cover is Nada Naga, Xanth's most luscious eligible princess. She is one of the available Companions." Grundy cocked an eye at him. "Maybe it's time you asked about Companions, if that isn't clear yet."

So Dug typed WHAT ABOUT COMPANIONS?

"I'm so glad you asked about Companions!" Grundy said. "That is of course the name of this game, and the main thing that distinguishes it from others. In this game you are never left to flounder helplessly, guessing at the procedures. You have a Companion to guide you through. Anything you need to know, you can ask your Companion, and if he (or she, if you select a female) doesn't know the answer, he'll give you a responsive guess. He will also warn you when you are going wrong, and in general be a true friend to you. You can trust your Companion absolutely—except for one thing. Touch Y or ENTER if you want to know about that one thing."

Dug was tempted to touch the ESCAPE key instead, but was hooked. So he touched ENTER.

"That is smart of you," Grundy said. "You see, your Companion is your truest friend, ordinarily. But there is one chance in seven that he will be a False Companion. That one will pretend to be your friend, but will lead you into mischief and doom. So if you get that one, you must be wary, and not take his bad advice. Unfortunately, there is no obvious way to tell a Fair Companion from a False Companion, because they look and act the same—until some key point in the game, when the False Companion will betray you. You must judge only by assessing the quality of the advice you are given, and recognizing bad advice. If you are able to identify your False Companion, you can not exchange him for another; once you choose your Companion, you are stuck with him throughout the game. You can ask him to go away, but then you will be alone in the game without guidance and are likely to get eaten by a dragon, or suffer some worse fate. It is better to keep him with you, but to be wary of him. It is possible to win the game with a False Companion, just a lot more difficult."

The Golem paused, so Dug typed in a related query. SUPPOSE I JUST QUIT THE GAME, AND COME BACK NEW?

"If you try to leave the game and return, so as to get a new Companion, you will find that the layout of the game has changed, so that not only are you not certain whether your new Companion is True or False, you are not sure whether paths which were safe before remain so. If you are well along in the game, it is better just to continue. But it is your choice, of course."

This warning, rather than turning Dug off, intrigued him. So he could never quite trust his Companion. That promised a special thrill of excitement that would not have been there otherwise. He looked at the listed questions, and touched 9.

"The prize for winning the game, which is not easy to do, is to receive a magic talent, which will be yours in any future games you play. We do not know what that talent is, but it will surely be a good one, that will be a great advantage for you."

Sort of like getting a free pass to another game. Dug shrugged. He didn't care much about fantasy anyway, so this wasn't much of an inducement. He was beginning to get bored with this, so he touched 5.

Grundy frowned. "I was hoping you would decide to stay with me. I can speak the languages of animals and plants, and learn things that others can not." Then he smiled. "But maybe you still will choose me. Here are the six other Companions from which to choose." He pulled up another scroll.

This contained six names: Goody Goblin, Horace Centaur, Jenny Elf, Marrow Bones, Metria Demoness, and Nada Naga. Dug recognized the last name: the luscious creature of the cover. He didn't need to check the others. He highlighted Nada Naga, and her description and a picture appeared.

NADA NAGA, PRINCESS OF THE NAGA FOLK OF
XANTH, WHICH ARE HUMAN/SERPENT CROSS-
BREEDS, CAPABLE OF ASSUMING EITHER FORM
OR ONE IN BETWEEN. AGE 21, UNMARRIED, IN-
TELLIGENT, NICE, BEAUTIFUL. ASSETS: MATU-
RITY AND ABILITY TO ASSUME FIGHTING FORM.
LIABILITIES: PRINCESSLY LIMITATIONS.

Being a princess was a liability? Dug had to laugh. He
was prepared to cope with it. What fun it would be to have
such a woman as his Companion! Without hesitation, he
touched RETURN.

The picture expanded, and Nada Naga stepped out onto
the main screen. "Thank you, Grundy," she said in a dul-
cet voice. Actually it was print in a speech balloon, but
Dug could almost hear it. "I shall take it from here."

Grundy sighed and walked off-screen. Nada turned to
Dug. "Please introduce yourself," she said appealingly.
"Just type your name and description, so that I can relate
to you."

Eagerly he typed. DUG. MALE. AGE 16. So she was
five years older; who cared? This was only a game.

"Why, hello, Doug," she said. "I am sure we shall get
along very well."

Oops. DUG, he typed. NO O. IT'S NOT SHORT FOR
DOUGLAS, EITHER. IT'S JUST DUG.

She lifted one dainty hand to her mouth, blushing prettily. "Oh, I apologize, Dug! Please forgive me."

Actually, if she wanted to call him Doug or Douglas, let
her do it. From her it would sound just great.

NO NEED, he typed quickly. I NEVER MET A PRIN-
CESS BEFORE. It was a game, but it had become an interesting game, and he wanted to play it for what it was
worth. He realized that he was losing his bet with Edsel,
but he no longer cared. He just wanted to continue playing.

"It is a liability, being a princess," she said. "It was nice
of you to select me anyway. I shall try to be an effective
Companion for you."

I'M SURE YOU WILL BE PERFECT, he typed, speaking the words at the same time, really getting into it.

"Dug, may I give you some advice?" she asked prettily.

"Anything you want," he said, his fingers flying to keep the pace.

"It will be easier if you get into the scene with me. So that we can relate to each other more readily. Do you know how to do that?"

"I'd love to get into the scene with you," he agreed. "But you're on the computer screen, and I'm out here in real life." So maybe it was a foolish business, getting emotionally involved like this, treating her as if she were a real person, but it was fun. He was amazed at how responsive she was.

"This is true. But though I can not come out to join you, you can in effect come in to join me. You have to suspend your disbelief a bit, and refocus your eyes."

"I'll try." He wished he could forget this was a fantasy game, and just live the fantasy: himself with this lovely woman.

"You see, the screen looks flat to you because you are focusing flat. But if you will try to focus your eyes on something behind the screen, as if it were a window to another world, you will find that it becomes rounded. See if you can do it."

Rounded. She was already so nicely rounded that he hardly cared about the rest. But he obligingly tried to focus his eyes beyond the screen. The image of Nada fuzzed somewhat; that was all. "I don't see to be getting it," he said.

"See the two dots at the top?" she asked, pointing. Now he saw them, hovering just above her speech balloon. "Try to make them become three dots. Then you will be in the right range. It may not happen right away, but once it does, you will know it."

"Okay," he typed. He was glad that he could do it by touch, so that he could answer her without taking his eyes from the screen. He refocused his eyes, trying to make the two dots into three. He didn't really believe that anything would come of this, but he wanted to give his best try to whatever she asked him to do.

The picture blurred, refocused and blurred again. The two dots became four, then bobbed a bit and fused into three. And then, quietly, the third dimension came.

Dug stared. Literally. The picture was now 3-D! He wasn't wearing colored glasses or using one of those two-picture stereo dinguses; it was just the computer screen. But now the screen had become like a pane of glass, a window opening to a scene beyond. Nada Naga stood in the foreground, with the grass of the glade behind her, and the fantasy jungle in the background. It was all so real he was stunned.

"That's better," Nada said smiling. "I see you in rounded form now, Dug."

She saw *him* as rounded? She was the most delightfully rounded woman he could imagine! But he did not type that in. Instead he made a safer statement. "It's amazing! How did it happen?"

She frowned prettily. "I don't suppose you would believe me if I told you there's some magic involved?"

He shook his head. "I don't believe in magic."

"That's too bad. That is the second, and greater step. When you manage to do that, you will truly be in the game."

"Suspension of disbelief," he agreed. "I really wish I could! But I'm a skeptic from way back. As they say, I'm from Missouri."

She looked blank. "I thought you were from Mundania."

Mundania. Cute notion. "I think Missouri is a state in Mundania. The people there always have to be shown something before they believe it. So if you show me magic, I'll believe it. Otherwise—"

She smiled. She made a sinuous ripple, and suddenly she was a snake with her human head. "This is my naga form, which is natural to me. My magic enables me to assume human form, or full serpent form." She became a coiled python, whose reptilian eyes fixed on him as it slithered from the fallen garments. But he was not revolted. He could take snakes or leave them; he knew they were beneficial creatures, so he just left them alone. This one did not dismay him at all. He knew it was Nada, in the context of the fantasy game. It would be useful to have such a reptile on his side, if some game threat materialized, as was sure to happen when he really got into it.

"I realize there is magic in a fantasy game," he said carefully. "Things happen all the time in movie cartoons and such. People get flattened by steamrollers, and then pumped back into round with a shot of air, and they are normal again. So you might say that I believe in magic in such a context. But never in real life."

The snake slithered behind a screen, carrying the woman's piled clothing in its mouth. In a moment the human form reappeared from behind the screen, decorously dressed. "But if you come into Xanth, then magic will work. If I went to Mundania, I would not be able to change form; I'd be just a little helpless snake." She frowned. "I know; it happened once. But here we follow *our* rules. So when you can manage to believe, then you will experience magic."

"When I believe that, I'll be crazy," he said sourly.

"No, you will just be in another realm. But you don't have to believe, to play the game. Just remember that our rules govern here."

"I'll do that," Dug said, surprised by her responsiveness. It really seemed as if she were a real person, communicating through the barrier of his disbelief. "How do I play this game?"

She smiled again. The glade lighted when she did that; it really did become brighter, as if a slow flashbulb had gone off. So it was a foolish technical effect; he still liked it. She was just such a beautiful woman that he could bask all day in her smiles.

"Take my hand," Nada said, "and I will lead you into it." She extended her lovely hand to him.

Dug reached for the screen, then caught himself. He typed I TAKE YOUR HAND.

The scene expanded. Now he seemed to be *in* the glade, and Nada stood beside him, about half a head shorter than he. She turned to him, her bosom gently heaving, her brown-gray eyes complementing her gray-brown tresses. Suddenly brown-gray was Dug's favorite color. "Thank you, Dug; it is so nice to have you here."

"It's so nice to be here," he said, discovering that disbelief was getting easier to suspend, at least in this context. He knew he would never get close to a woman like this in real life, so he might as well do it this way. Certainly the way the scene had come to life was amazing.

"Now, this glade is a safe haven," Nada said. "But the moment we go out of it, we're playing the game proper, and there will be challenge and trouble. So while I don't want to bore you with too many explanations—"

"You aren't boring me," Dug said quickly. She could have been delivering the world's dullest lecture on Shakespeare's most boring historical play (which was a fair description of a normal English class session), and still have fascinated him. He was satisfied just to remain in this glade and watch her talk. Because she seemed to be genuinely interested in him. That was surely the fakery of the game programming, but it was excellent fakery. He remembered a challenge that was ongoing: companies were trying to build a computer that could maintain a dialogue with a person so effectively that the person would not know it was a computer. The computer would be in a sealed-off room, so the person couldn't see, and would have to guess whether there was a computer or a person in there. So far no computer had fooled the experts, but it was getting close. Nada Naga, as an animated projection for such a computer program, was awfully close. She seemed so alive, and not just because of her appearance.

She smiled again, as he had hoped she would. "Thank

you, Dug. I need to be sure you understand what is happening, because it is my job to take you as far through the game as possible, and if you fail to win the prize, it won't be through any fault of mine. But my ability is limited, and in any event the decisions are yours; I can only answer your questions and advise you. I myself don't know the winning course. But I do know Xanth, and so I will be able to guide you away from most of its dangers." She paused, glancing at him. "Are you familiar with Xanth?"

"Never heard of it," he said cheerfully. "I'm not a fantasy reader. I gather it's a hoked-up fantasy setting, with beautiful princesses, ugly goblins, walking skeletons, and smoky demonesses." He had picked that up from the list of alternate Companions. "I presume I'll have to cross mountains and chasms and raging rivers, and fight off fire-breathing dragons, and find special magic amulets to enable me to get into magically sealed vaults where the treasure lies. And that there are so many threats lined up that the chances are I'll be wiped out early, and then I'll have to start over, knowing a little more about what to avoid. Frankly, I'd rather just stay here and talk with you." His glance fell to her bosom, and bounced away, because when he was standing this close to her he could see right down inside. He loved the sight, but didn't want her to catch him staring. She might put on a jacket, ruining the view.

"You do seem to have a good notion of the game," she agreed. She inhaled, and he almost bit his tongue. "But you can't win it by staying here. So soon we shall have to start the trek. Normally the best first step is to go to ask the Good Magician Humfrey for advice. Unfortunately he charges a year's service for a single Answer to a Question. Since that isn't feasible for you—"

"Right. No point in going there. Let's talk. Do you ever date Mundanes?"

"Date? Do you mean one of the Seeds of Thyme? We might find one of those if we go to the right garden."

He laughed. "I mean, do you ever go out with Mundanes?"

"I am about to go out into Xanth with you, to show you the best route to—"

"I mean like doing something together. Seeing a show, having a meal, talking. Having fun."

Her lovely brow almost furrowed. "We shall be pursuing the quest together, and we shall see what Xanth has to show along the way. We shall talk as much as we need. I hope this is not unpleasant for you."

She just wasn't getting it. So he tried once more. "Like maybe dancing together, and kissing."

Nada gazed at him, a peculiar expression crossing her face. She was finally getting it! "I think not. I am here to be your Companion. I am not your romance. Please do not try to kiss me."

Dug laughed again, but it was to cover up embarrassment. She had told him no plainly enough. If he tried to kiss her, she would turn into a serpent and chomp him. "I was just asking. So what else do I need to know about the game?" Because if he had to play the game to keep her with him, it was worth it.

Then he had to laugh at himself. Nada was a game figure on his computer screen! He couldn't kiss her anyway. Yet here he had gotten all interested, in the faint hope that she might agree to do it. He really was getting into this.

But wouldn't it be great, if it were possible, and she were willing! She was so much better than the girlfriend he had just lost to his friend. So foolish as it was, he was going to try to please her, in the hope that eventually she would agree to kiss him, even if it could be in name only.

Nada got down to business. "It is almost impossible to win the prize directly, because we don't even know where to look for it. So we shall have to go see the Good Magician, and hope that you can make some kind of deal with him for his advice. I know the way there, so will guide you. However, the path is dangerous in places, and we don't know what might happen, so we shall have to be very careful. There are enchanted paths, but those are for the regular folk of Xanth. We shall have to go cross-country." She glanced up, smiling briefly. "That means we will encounter those mountains, chasms, rivers, and dragons you described, and may not even get as far as the Good Magician's castle."

"If we don't, and I'm out of the game, may I ask for you again, the next time I play?"

"You may do so, but I will not be able to help you any better than the first time, because the threats will be changed. So you may be better off choosing another Companion, who may work better for you."

"Will you remember me, in the next game?"

"Yes. But it may be difficult for me, because I may have seen you get eaten by a dragon. That would be traumatic for me."

"Then I'll try not to get eaten," he said gallantly. "Is there any good way to discourage dragons?"

"That depends on the dragon. I will be able to back off a small one. But a large one—it is better simply to hide."

"Aren't there any repellents, or weapons, or whatever? So I could travel prepared?"

"There may be, if you are clever enough to find them. This is one of my liabilities: I do not know very much about human weapons, or how to use them. If you wish to exchange me for a Companion who does, such as Horace Centaur—"

"No thanks. I'll try to make do on my own." Dug looked around. "Is there a town nearby, where we might get weapons or supplies? That might be our first stop."

"There is Isthmus Village. I could take you there. But the people are not friendly to strangers. It might be better to avoid it. There are fruit and nut trees, and egg rolls, and pie plants, so food will be no problem, and perhaps you could prepare a staff or cudgel for your defense."

But Dug was feeling ornery. "No, let's try Isthmus Village first. That's a funny name; why is it called that?"

Nada bent down to sketch a map in the dirt in the center

of the glade. Dug caught a compelling glimpse down her front, and wisely gave no sign, though he feared his eyeballs were about to bulge out of their sockets. Talk of three-dimensional effects! "This is the general outline of Xanth," she said. "This is where we are, at the edge of the isthmus. Here is the village a little farther along. It derives its name from its location."

Dug tore his errant eyes away from her décolletage long enough to glance at the map. "Why, that's the state of Florida!" he said, surprised. "You mean we're in the Florida panhandle?"

"If that is what you call it. It is the main route to and from Mundania, which is why we meet Mundanes here. But this is not your Mundane state. This is Xanth, and you must remember that, because there are things here you are unlikely to find in Mundania."

He had been glimpsing some of them, but of course he couldn't admit it. "Good enough. Let's get moving."

She straightened up, nodding. She stared to walk to the edge of the glade, and it was evident that he was walking with her, because the scene shifted with his motion. This should be interesting, if only because of its realism. He didn't care about the prize; he just wanted to stay in the scene.

2

OGRE FEN

Jenny Elf waited nervously in the chamber reserved for the prospective Companions. Sammy Cat, unconcerned, snoozed in her lap. She had to serve a year for the Good Magician Humfrey, because she had asked him a Question and gotten an Answer. But he had sent her to the Demon Professor Grossclout instead, and now she was part of this weird game for Mundanes. Why the demons wanted to run a game for Mundanes only the demons knew, but she was obliged to play her part.

Nada Naga had just left, being chosen as a Companion by a Mundane Player. That left the Demoness Metria, the skeleton Marrow Bones, the zombie Horace Centaur, and the polite Goody Goblin. In a moment a new person arrived, to fill the vacated space in the roster. She was a woman just about as beautiful and well endowed as Nada. She wore a gown as brown as the bark of a tree, and her hair was as green as foliage.

"Hello," the woman said. "Is this the Companions' den?"

The others sent glances around, but none of them connected. Jenny realized that it was up to her to answer. "Yes it is. Come and join us. I'm Jenny Elf, here to serve out my service for the Good Magician."

The woman stepped inside. "I am Vida Vila, a nature nymph. I owed Professor Grossclout a favor." She took a seat.

"Vida Vila," the skeleton exclaimed. "We have met before. I am Marrow Bones. I brought Prince Dolph through your region several years ago."

Vida nodded. "I thought you looked familiar. But I am not good with skeletons; they all look alike to me. That prince must be about grown by now."

"Yes. He married Electra, and they have twins."

"Oh, pooh!" Vida said, dispirited. That was impressive, because for that instant she became a growly bear. But she quickly reverted. "I hoped to marry him myself, when he got old enough. Princes don't grow on trees, you know, or I would have grown my own."

NOW HEAR THIS, a disembodied voice blared. IT IS TIME FOR THE SELECTION OF THE FALSE COMPANION.

"But we already had that selection," Jenny protested. She had been relieved when the lot had not fallen on her, because she did not want to be false to any person.

TRY NOT TO LET THE MUSH IN YOUR HEAD SHOW, the voice said sternly. It was Professor Grossclout, of course, the demon in charge. A NEW FALSE COMPANION MUST BE SELECTED BEFORE EACH PLAYER CHOOSES HIS COMPANION, SO AS TO PRESERVE THE ODDS. REMEMBER: ONLY THE CHOSEN ONE WILL RECEIVE THE INDICATION. THAT ONE MUST CONCEAL THE STATUS FROM ALL OTHERS. NO ONE MUST KNOW, UNTIL IT IS REVEALED IN THE COURSE OF THE GAME.

"Oh, get on with it, Clout," Metria muttered.

DID I HEAR A MUTTER? the voice demanded dangerously.

Metria's mouth zipped shut. In fact, a zipper appeared

across it. She was a demoness, but she knew whom not to aggravate. The Professor was said to be a creature who had been wheeled from Hell, or something.

THE SELECTION IS—NOW.

Jenny kept herself perfectly still. No indication came. She had escaped selection, again. What a relief!

After a moment, she looked around at the others—and found them looking around too. Each was trying to discover who had been selected, but none of them could tell. It could be any of the seven of them, because Grundy Golem was also a potential Companion. Maybe the lot had fallen on him.

"Look out—here comes a Player," Metria said, peering out the window.

Immediately they all sat still in their seats, so that their images would be ready when the Player asked to see the prospective Companions. They could see the Player in the one-way window, but he could not see them until he asked to.

He? She. It was a girl. She looked sort of ordinary, but that was typical of all Mundanes. Her hands hovered over the keyboard, which was the clumsy way Mundanes had to access magic, and her eyes were fastened to her side of the window.

Grundy Golem was the master of ceremonies, and he was good at it. "Hi! I'm Grundy Golem. I'm from the Land of—"

"Why, hello, Grundy!" the girl exclaimed. "I'm so glad to see you. How is Rapunzel?"

That set even the loud-mouthed golem back. "She's fine. She's home because she's expecting a delivery by the—" He paused. "Do you mind telling me how old you are?"

"Sixteen," the girl said brightly. "I know all about the Adult Conspiracy. I attend a progressive school."

"Uh, yes," Grundy said, still somewhat at a loss. "So you have come to play our Companions of Xanth Game, Miss—"

"Kim. I won a talent contest, and this was the prize. To

get the first copy of the new Xanth computer game. I love Xanth. So here I am."

"Um, there may have been a mistake. You're actually the second to play."

"The second? Oh, darn! Who's first?"

"A boy named Dug. We didn't realize that the first had been promised to you."

"Well, it wasn't exactly promised. But the game's not officially on the market yet, so I figured—well, never mind. I'm used to being second." She looked sad.

Jenny was getting to like this girl, for some reason. Maybe it was because she looked so ordinary, but had so much personality. The boy, Dug, had been handsome, but more like a blank in character, and Jenny was glad he hadn't chosen her to be his Companion. Of course he had chosen Nada; any male human being would. But this girl Kim was different, in a number of ways.

"So you know about Xanth," Grundy said, trying to get reorganized, now that this introductory spiel had been broken up. "But do you know about this game?"

"Oh, sure. All I need to, anyway. I have to choose a Companion, and she'll tell me everything else."

"You can choose a male Companion, if you wish," Grundy said. "I happen to be available."

"Gee, Grundy, you'd be great! You can talk to anything. But maybe I'd better at least check the others, just in case."

The window became two-way. Now Kim could see the six available Companions.

"Oh, there's Jenny Elf!" Kim exclaimed, delighted. "And Sammy Cat! Hey, Jenny, I wrote you a letter!" Jenny felt a thrill of pleasure at the recognition. "But I didn't get an answer." Jenny squirmed. "But I know how it is. You have a whole lot of other stuff to do, like getting better. The Mundane Jenny, I mean; of course I couldn't get a letter from Xanth."

Kim turned to Grundy. "I'm sorry, Grundy. I like you, really I do. But Jenny Elf's my favorite, and Sammy can find anything except home. I've got to go with her."

"That's all right," Grundy said graciously. There was nothing else he could do. He walked out of the glade.

Jenny stood and stepped through the window, into the main scene, carrying Sammy. She was really glad to be chosen, because Kim seemed like a nice girl, who already knew about Xanth. Jenny was also doubly glad now that she was not the False Companion. It no longer mattered who else had been selected, because the Player had chosen, and would deal only with Jenny.

"Hello, Kim," Jenny said. "Thank you for choosing me. I will try to be a good Companion for you."

"Oh, I know you will!" Kim said enthusiastically. "I wish this could be real, instead of just an old game. But I don't guess you can't tell me how to step into the real Xanth."

"Well, not quite," Jenny said apologetically. "But I can tell you two steps that will bring you a lot closer. First you have to refocus your eyes. Do you see those two dots?"

"I see them." In a moment, following Jenny's instruction, the girl had succeeded in bringing the third dimension. Instead of being a flat image beyond the screen, she became a rounded one, and the screen seemed more like a window. It was almost as if they were in the glade together. "Oh, this is wonderful!" Kim exclaimed.

"The other thing is harder. You have to suspend your disbelief. If you can do that, then you will seem to be right here in Xanth, because you'll believe it."

"Oh, I want to believe it!" Kim exclaimed. "I'd give anything to be in Xanth for real! But deep down inside, I'll always know this is a game, and not real."

Jenny was saddened to hear that. How could she convince the girl that it was Mundania that wasn't quite real? But that was why this was the harder challenge; people just couldn't make themselves believe what they didn't believe.

"Well, we can play the game anyway," Jenny said. "At least the visual magic is working. Now, I don't know what the prize is, or where to find it, so I think you will have to go to ask the Good Magician Humfrey, if you don't mind."

"Mind? I'd love to meet the Good Magician! Will I get to fight my way into his castle, too?"

"Yes, I'm afraid you will."

"Wonderful! Oh, this is so thrilling! I can't wait to get started."

Jenny was somewhat taken aback by this enthusiasm. She herself had had some trouble adjusting to the Land of Xanth, which was so different from the World of Two Moons where she had lived before. But of course Kim was Mundane, so she had to be thrilled to be anywhere else. "We can start now, if you wish. Sammy can find us a safe path past the Ogre Fen." For each Player started from a different place in Xanth, so they wouldn't interfere with each other. Dug had started from the isthmus, but this was farther to the east. The demons moved the site back and forth each time.

"Oh, are we near the Ogre fen Ogre Fen? Will we get to see an ogre?"

"We don't *want* to see an ogre!" Jenny protested. "Ogres are dangerous. If we get near any of them, they are liable to squeeze us into pulp and plop us into a cook pot, or worse, if they're in a bad mood."

Kim looked disappointed. "Well, could we maybe just sneak by where they can't see us, so we can just catch a little glimpse? It would mean so much to me."

Jenny saw that they had a problem. "Look, Kim, maybe you are used to reading about Xanth, where nothing really bad happens to major characters. They just get scared, but it always turns out okay in the end. But you're not a Xanth character; you are a Player, and if an ogre catches you, he'll do something mean to you, like biting off your head, and you'll be out of the game. Furthermore, if you should come back in the game, not only will you have to start from scratch with a scrambled set of threats, that ogre will remember you, and come after you faster next time. It doesn't get easier to start over, it gets harder. So you don't want to run afoul of any ogres; they'll ruin your chances, even if you don't really die when they pull you apart and use your legbones as toothpicks. I'm sure Sammy can find a way through the Ogre Fen without encountering any ogres, and that's what we should do."

"But I don't want to get caught by the ogres," Kim protested. "I just want to see them. So when I go home I can say I saw a real live game ogre. What's the sense in playing, if I can't see what I want to see?"

"Well, I sort of thought you might want to win, and get the prize."

"Well, of course I want to win the prize! But the fun is also in the playing. I want to experience every part of Xanth, and enjoy it to the utmost. It's great already, just seeing it in three-dee and talking with you just as if you're real."

It was worse than Jenny had feared. Underneath all her knowledge of Xanth, Kim really didn't believe at all. So she wasn't taking it seriously enough. She had an Attitude Problem. This was sure to lead to mischief. But Kim was the Player, and she was the one who made the decisions. All Jenny could do was help and advise her.

"Well, if you insist on seeing an ogre, we'll go see an ogre," Jenny said. "I'll have Sammy try to find a path that leads to a place where we can see without being seen. But I still think it's a bad idea."

"It's a terrible idea," Kim agreed. "But fun, too. Adventure is the spice of life. Let's go!"

So Jenny set Sammy down. "Find a path that leads to a place where we can see an ogre, without any ogres seeing us," she told him. "Don't run ahead; just find where it starts." She had learned how to manage the cat, so that she didn't have to chase madly after him when he went to find something. She had first come to Xanth when Sammy had dashed off to find a feather, and she had followed him so he wouldn't get lost, but gotten lost herself. Since then she had been stuck in Xanth, but soon enough she had come to like it, though she did miss her family back on the

World of Two Moons. The last thing she wanted to do was have Sammy run into some other world, so that they wouldn't be able to find their way back to Xanth.

Sammy headed off. Jenny held on to the invisible leash the demons had given her, so that she could tell by its tug where the cat was. Sammy couldn't feel the leash; in fact, he didn't know she had it. It stretched just as far as it needed to, invisibly long, but contracted as she caught up, until it was invisibly short. So she no longer had to dash pell-mell after the cat, trying to keep him in sight; he was always within the feel of her hand.

However, this did not make things perfect, because the cat took the most direct cat-route to whatever he was finding. If this was along a path, fine. But it could as readily be under a thorn bush, or up along a tree branch, or through a river. Or under the nose of a sleeping dragon. Sammy would zip by before the dragon woke, but Jenny was slower, larger, and smelled of elf, and all those things made a difference to a dragon. So care was still required.

In this case the cat merely zipped through the thickest tangle of a cornfield. The corn popped madly as she forged through it. "Oooh, firecrackers!" Kim exclaimed, delighted.

"No, just popping corn," Jenny said. "Oh, I hope the sound of it doesn't alert the ogres!"

Then she felt something sticking to her. She looked, and discovered kernels of caramel corn. They were overripe and gooey, so they made a real mess. She tried to pull them off her clothing, but they had melted in and wouldn't come out. Well, this was the kind of nuisance that happened, when she chased after Sammy.

Soon they came to the cat, who was sitting at the end of a path, licking the caramel from his fur. This was the one.

Jenny glanced at Kim. Kim was not really here; instead there was the square window to Mundania, showing her as she sat at her keyboard. The window was always right in sight, so that the Player could see the game scene; it moved along with Jenny. So it was easy to forget that

Jenny was traveling alone, physically. Kim would not really be in the scene until she achieved the second act of belief, and believed in magic. But that would happen as the game progressed. Some things just took time to believe.

Jenny picked up the cat. They followed the path through the deepening reaches of the dread Ogre Fen. Jenny would be glad when they got out of here, because it was the kind of place only an ogre could like. The trees were warped, the victims of ogre pranks; some had been tied in knots, and others looked like pretzels. Some were in tatters, showing that once an ogre in a bad mood had passed. The ground was no better; it was grudgingly shifting from a swamp to a bog, and thence to a marsh; soon it would become a full fen. Fortunately the path itself was dry. This was because the ogres preferred awful paths, so didn't use this one; thus Sammy had found the one safe from ogres. Or at least less dangerous; no path was truly safe from an ogre.

They passed some cords hanging down from branches extending over the path. Jenny's elbow brushed one. It twanged loudly. Immediately several other cords twanged, forming a quartet of notes, as if several people were singing.

"What's that?" Kim inquired, startled.

"A vocal cord," Jenny said. "I hope it doesn't attract the ogres."

But when she tried to move on, she brushed another cord, and there was another group of simultaneous notes. She shuddered; the ogres were sure to hear this music!

They were lucky; no ogres came. Jenny breathed a sigh of relief. But she knew that the danger wasn't over. They needed to get out of ogre country.

They came to a hugely spreading tree whose trunk looked like thick rubber and whose branches had rubber rings spaced along them. The tips of the branches touched thin wires, which in turn swung away through the branches of other trees. There was a faint humming coming from the wires, and now and then a crackling sound.

"What kind of tree is that?" Kim asked. "It's grotesque!"

Jenny studied it. She had had to take a cram course in the flora of Xanth, so that she could be a good Companion and identify anything that might be either helpful or dangerous. "It's an electrici-tree," she said. "It has a lot of power, I think."

Kim laughed. "I'm sure it has! Maybe this is where our electric power comes from. I see the wires headed away. We better not stay here too long; the electric field might be bad for us."

Jenny looked. Sure enough, the tree's roots extended down into a shimmering field. There was water below, but the wire grass grew up thickly. She hadn't run into this in her studies; maybe she had snoozed through that particular lecture. "An electric field is harmful?" she asked.

"Well, we don't know, for sure. But folk don't like to live too close to power lines, just in case."

Then they heard an ominous thudding, and the ground trembled. "The ogres are coming!" Jenny said, alarmed. They must have heard the vocal cords after all. "We'd better hide in the tree."

So she scrambled up, with Sammy scampering up ahead of her, and the screen view that connected them to Kim angling along. Just in time; the first monster was already heaving into awful sight. Of course there was no such thing as a good sight, near an ogre, except the sight of a fast way out of sight.

"Oooo, an ogre!" Kim exclaimed.

"Quiet!" Jenny hissed, horribly alarmed. Ogres had adequate hearing: adequate to locate whatever they wanted to squish flat or pound into oblivion or chomp into quivering fragments.

"What are they doing?" Kim asked, in a lower tone.

Jenny studied the scene. It was a whole tribe of ogres, males and females, and they seemed to be looking for something. Then they spied it: a glowing ball nestled in the electric field. One ogre lumbered into the field and grabbed the ball—and burned his hands. He dropped it, with a small curse that set fire to the nearby grass. Or maybe it was the fiery ball that did that. "I think they're collecting a ball of lightning to heat their cook pot," Jenny whispered. "Ogres aren't smart enough to make their own fire, so they must have to take it where they find it."

"A lightning ball!" Kim exclaimed. "How Xanthly!"

"Not so loud!" Jenny warned.

But it was too late. An ogre perked an ear. "Me hear thing near," he said. Jenny felt deepest dread. Then he cocked an eye. "Me see a she!"

Disaster! "We have to flee!" Jenny said.

But the only route out was the one they had come in on, and the ogres were standing too close to it. The big male ogre was already stomping toward the electrici-tree. They were trapped.

The ogre reached up and whammed the branch they were on with his hamfist. The whole tree shuddered, and the branch vibrated violently. Jenny was jarred right out of her perch. She screamed as she fell.

But the ogre swept his hamhand across and caught her by the scruff of her collar. "See she!" he exulted, waving her around for the others to inspect.

"Leave her alone!" Kim cried. "She's with me."

The ogre peered at the sound of her voice. There was the window-screen, showing Kim beyond. "Fox in box," he grunted, and grabbed the screen. He hauled it up to snout level, upside down.

"Eeeek!" Kim cried as the picture jolted around. Her hair fell away from her body as the screen was inverted. Then the ogre got it turned over, and her hair flopped back into place. "Let go of that screen!" she said, shaken. "Imagination in the game is fine, but this is ridiculous!"

The ogre laughed. "Me dump in sump," he said, shoving the screen down into the water of the marsh.

"Oh!" Kim cried as her picture emerged. "Blub!" Now her hair was soaking wet. "Stop that!"

"Just look—me cook," the ogre said, carrying both

Jenny and the screen toward a huge pot an ogress was setting up. The lightning ball was already under it, and the muddy swamp water was beginning to bubble.

Jenny tried to think of something to do, but couldn't. They had fallen right into the worst possible situation: captives of the ogres. She had tried to warn Kim to be careful and quiet, but the girl hadn't paid enough attention.

But now Kim regrouped her composure. "You can't do this," she said angrily.

The ogre paused, evidently perplexed. He was trying to figure out how to ask why not, but couldn't make it rhyme, so he just stood there stupidly. Ogres were good at that. But then he put it together. "Not got?"

Jenny still couldn't think of an answer. She was really washing out as a Companion! She should have thought of some way to stop Kim from insisting on coming here.

But Kim was now defending herself. "You can't cook us just like that. We're people. You have to win us in a contest."

All the ogres looked at each other, confused. They had never heard of this. That meant that they couldn't be quite sure it was wrong. But Jenny was confused too. What kind of contest? An ogre could win just about any physical contest, especially if it required strength. Ogres were justifiably proud of their strength and ugliness. "How, now?" the ogre who held them inquired.

"We must have a stupid contest," Kim said. "To see who is most stupid."

The ogres liked that. They were most proud, with most justification, of their stupidity. They were bound to win such a contest. "Rules, tools," the main ogre said in what in a smarter person would have passed for bad rhyme and worse logic.

"It's like a game," Kim said. "You must be the Ver and I'll be the Pid. Those are our names. But we have to find the rest of our names. When we do, we'll know who is smarter, and so who loses."

The ogres were confused. That wasn't surprising; so

was Jenny. What did Kim have on her mind? She obviously wasn't stupider than any ogre, and would be hard put to it to prove it, especially to an ogre.

"Me Ver," the ogre said. "She Pid." He was so confused that he wasn't rhyming.

"First put us down," Kim said. "You can't play with your hands full."

The ogre set the screen down next to the bubbling pot. He set Jenny down beside the screen. The other ogres settled on their haunches, waiting to see what to make of this.

Kim brushed back her hair, which was drying. "Now we will take turns naming us, until we find names that fit."

"How know?" the ogre asked, in another sloppy attempt at rhyme.

"Why, the other ogres will know," Kim said brightly. "When they hear a name that makes sense, they'll exclaim with recognition."

The other ogres looked doubtful. Their doubt was well taken; they were hardly smart enough to recognize any sense in anything even if they understood the game, which they didn't.

"I'll start," Kim said. "Sil. That's the name. Can you match it to our names?"

The ogre pondered hard. Fleas jumped off his head, annoyed by the heat. But it was no good; he did not know what to do.

"Like this," Kim said. "You are Sil-Ver. I am Sil-Pid. Are those good names?"

The ogre pondered harder. A wisp of steam rose from his head as a thought tried to forge through heavy resistance. He was unable to form a conclusion. Neither could the other ogres.

Jenny saw that the ogre's name made a word: silver. That could be considered a name. But it didn't seem to be very unintelligent. That might be why the ogres couldn't recognize it. What *was* Kim trying to do?

"Well, then," Kim said. "They must be bad names. You try one now."

Jenny was afraid the ogre's hair was going to catch on fire as he tried to think. But just as the first curl of smoke appeared, he got it: "Bop."

"Very well," Kim agreed. "You have challenged me to make good names with that. You are Bop-Ver and I am Bop-Pid. Are those good names?"

The ogres remained doubtful. So did Jenny. They were nonsensical names.

Kim looked disappointed. "I guess I couldn't make any good names with your suggestion. So I'll make another for you. Riv. Can you make good names from that?"

The ogre was finally catching on. "Me Riv-Ver," he said. "She Riv-pid."

There was a stir among the other ogres. "Riv-Ver," an ogress said. "River! Good name."

"Oh, my," Kim said, looking unhappy. "You did make a good name! It's probably a really stinky river, too."

The ogres clapped their hamhands, pleased. They were getting into it now. But Jenny wasn't; she didn't see how this was going to keep Kim's screen out of the boiling pot. She knew that if Kim's picture got boiled, it would be just as if *she* got boiled: she would be out of the game.

Then Kim frowned. "But is it a really obtuse name?" Then, seeing the ogres' confusion, she clarified her reference: "witless."

The ogres considered the matter, and slowly concluded that it was not ogrishly witless.

Now it was the ogre's turn to offer a name. "Chomp," he said.

Kim concentrated. "Now, let me see. You are Chomp-Ver. I am Chomp-Pid. Are those good names?"

It turned out that they were not. She had lost her chance, again.

But now it was her turn to supply a name. "Stu," she said. "Can you make a good name with that?"

The ogre tried. "Me Stu-Ver," he said. "She Stu-Pid."

There was a pause. Then an exclamation. They had recognized a name! "She Stu-Pid!" an ogress exclaimed. "She Stu-pid! Stupid!"

Then they were all chorusing it. "Stupid! Stupid! Stu-pid!"

Jenny began to get a glimmer where this might be headed.

Kim sighed. "I guess you have done it. You have found a good name for me. I'm Stupid."

The ogres were quick to agree.

"But we still haven't found a good name for him," Kim said after a moment. "Do you have another one to try?"

The ogres were unable to change mental gears so swiftly, and could not come up with a name.

"Well, then, let's try Cle," Kim said. "Does that work?"

The ogre managed to put it together. "She Cle-Pid. Me Cle-Ver."

There was another slow reaction. The ogres recognized a word! "Cle-Ver! Clever! He Clever!"

"Why, so he is," Kim agreed. "That must be his name. Clever."

"Clever! Clever! Clever!" the ogres chorused.

Kim frowned. "Now we both have names. He is Clever. I am Stupid. "So which one of us is more stupid?"

"She stupid!" the ogre said, nailing it down.

"So he is Clever, and I am Stupid," Kim said. "So I am more stupid than he is."

They chorused agreement.

Suddenly Jenny saw the point. "So she wins! Because she is the most stupid!"

The ogres stared at each other. How had this happened? Kim had won the stupid contest! They had to let her go.

But when Jenny started to walk away, the ogre stopped her. "Elf no stupid," he said. "Elf go potty." He picked her up by the scruff and swung her toward the hot pot. Sammy Cat, perched on her shoulder, seemed about ready to jump off.

Oops. Kim had won her own freedom, but not Jenny's. Without Jenny as her Companion, she would not fare well in the game. She would not actually die if they dumped her in the pot; the demons would conjure her back to the character storage bunker. But she would be through for this session.

"Then we shall have to have a contest for the elf," Kim said. "But we'll need new names." She pondered briefly. "Let's see, you're male, so you must be called Gent. She is female, so let's call her Belle. Can we find good names?"

The ogre couldn't think of one, so Kim suggested one. "Co."

"Me Co-Gent," the ogre said. "She Co-Belle."

Cogent? Jenny saw that Kim had this set up for another win. But it didn't work, because the ogres didn't recognize the word.

Then the ogre suggested a name, trying to force a win for his side: "Dum."

Kim considered carefully. "Then you are Dum-Gent, and the elf is Dum-Belle."

Again the slow reaction. "Dum-Belle! Dumbell! Dumbbell! She Dumbbell!"

Kim's mouth opened in seeming dismay. "Oh, you have named her! She's a real dumbbell, all right!"

But Jenny remained smart enough to keep her mouth shut.

The ogres agreed. But the game wasn't over, because the ogre still had to be named. Kim suggested Intelli. And to the amazement of all, they got a good name out of that: not Intelli-Belle, but Intelli-Gent. Intelligent!

After some further consideration, the ogres realized that they had been had again. They had to let Jenny Elf go, too.

The two hastened to depart. Kim had evidently seen more than enough of real live ogres for the day. But Jenny had to admit that she had done a very nice job of getting them out of their picklement. She might make a good Player after all.

However, there was a lot more of the game to go, and not all the other creatures they encountered would be stupid.

3
ISTHMUS

Nada hoped for the best, but expected to settle for less. She had indeed been chosen to be the Companion of a teenage Mundane male, which was her worst-case scenario. He had already tried to get fresh, and male freshness was really stale for her. Almost as bad, he knew nothing about Xanth, and did not believe in magic. This was bound to be a real chore.

It had seemed considerably more romantic when the Demon Professor Grossclout had first broached the notion. He had explained that Clio, the Muse of History, was getting ready to write up another volume in her ongoing *History of Xanth*. She had assigned the production chore to the demons. They expected it to be a good story, and there were openings for major characters therein. "Provided their heads are not full of mush," he said.

Nada wasn't interested. She had little concern for the business of the Muses, and less for demons, and none for the role of a major character. "I just barely escaped having to marry a child, last time I was a major character," she reminded him. Now she hoped to remain comfortably retired, and let others carry the burden of notoriety.

"Ah, yes," the Professor said knowledgeably. "You needed to marry a prince, and only two were convenient. One was underage, and the other was your brother Naldo Naga. Now both are securely married, and you are Xanth's most eligible princess." He gazed at her through his impressive spectacles. "Have you considered that such an episode may be excellent for introducing you to new prospects?"

Nada's sleeping interest began to stir. "Prospects?"

"If a new eligible prince of sufficient age is to show up anywhere, it will be in such a volume. I should think you would want to be on hand for the occasion."

The demon was beginning to get to her. Nada was now in her thoroughly marriageable decade, and time was passing. It would be disheartening if a suitable prospect escaped because she wasn't keeping an eye on the scene.

"But why are the demons involved in this?" she inquired. "Demons are never major characters. They care nothing about human events, unless they wish to interfere with them."

"Will you make a princessly oath of secrecy?" the Professor asked. "The question has an answer, but it is not given for mere humans to know."

"I am only half human," Nada said. "No one ever called me mere." She inhaled. It was an action that normally had a peculiar effect on any adult human males in the vicinity, making them become more reasonable and attentive, especially if she happened to be leaning forward at the time.

"Precisely," Grossclout said, yawning. In this manner he demonstrated his immunity to this particular magic.

Now her female curiosity was stirring too. Something phenomenally significant might be in the works. "Very well. So oathed."

"It is truly demon business," Grossclout confided. "The Demon E(A/R)th is attempting to take over Xanth. Naturally the Demon X(A/N)th objects to this. So the two are settling it in the Demon Way: by a contest of innocents in a dream."

"But demons don't dream," Nada protested.

"Because they don't sleep," he agreed. "Except for confused ones such as Metria. They merely go into stasis and think. However, mortals do sleep, and do dream, which is what keeps the realm of the gourd in business. Mortals also have waking dreams. Thus they will dream for the demons. The Game of the Companions of Xanth is intended to be an animation of such a dream, wherein mortals can participate as if it is reality. One of them will win the prize, and one will not. This entire volume of the Muse's history is to be devoted to this decision. Thus it falls to the lesser demons to make the arrangements, and to the mortal folk to play it out. We do not know what will constitute a win for the Demon X(A/N)th, but we are certain that this matter affects us most intimately."

Nada was horrified. "If the Demon X(A/N)th loses, magic will disappear from Xanth!"

"This, too. So it does behoove us all to cooperate, hoping that our efforts will facilitate his success."

"But suppose we unwittingly make him lose?"

The Professor grimaced. He was very good at it, having terrified generations of hapless students at the Demon University of Magic. "That would be unfortunate," he remarked, his tone making Nada feel exactly like a student.

She did not dare question the matter further. She agreed to participate in the volume. Thereafter she attended rehearsals diligently, because the Professor assured her that she would be chosen to be the Companion to a Mundane Player.

"A Mundane!" she shrieked, horrified. "I don't want to associate with any Mundane!"

The Professor could be amazingly reasonable when he tried. "Grey Murphy was a Mundane."

And Grey Murphy was Good Magician Humfrey's assistant, and a Magician in his own right. If Nada didn't marry a prince, she could marry a Magician; they were of

similar status. Princess Ivy had already sewn up Grey
Murphy, of course, but it did illustrate the point. It was
theoretically possible for a Mundane to be worthwhile.

"Particularly if the Demon $X(A/N)^{th}$ should lose,"
Grossclout said, as if reading her thought. He had had generations of practice in that sort of thing too, reading the
guilty faces of students. "Mundania would then be much
more important, and you would do well to have an association with a Mundane."

So Nada acceded to the notion of being a Companion to
a Mundane. "But I won't let him touch me in any Adult
Conspirational way," she said firmly.

The demon glanced at her torso, which was among the
firmest in Xanth. "Naturally not," he agreed. "He will
probably be underage anyway."

"Underage!" she shrieked, echoing her horror of two
moments before. "I have *had* it with underage males!"

"This is simply the nature of Mundanes who are interested in fantasy games," he explained soothingly. "They
are all rebellious teenagers. It is in the *Big Book of Rules*."

She allowed herself to be soothed. "But how do you
know that I will be selected to be a Companion? Aren't
there any other prospects?"

"Certainly. There will be six or seven. But suppose one
of them were your brother Naldo, and the Mundane Player
were female? Whom would she choose, regardless?"

"Naldo," she said immediately. "He is Xanth's
handsomest and most accomplished prince, until recently
Xanth's most eligible bachelor."

"And if the Mundane is male?"

Nada opened her mouth, and closed it again. He had
made his point, in his irrefutable professorish manner.

Thus the rehearsals, which included male demons playing the parts of uncouth teenage Mundane males with
grabby hands. Nada had to learn how to discourage these
without biting their heads off. Because in her large serpent
form she could readily do that, and the Professor made
clear that this was a no-no. Players were not to be harmed

in any way by their Companions. In fact, it was the Companion's task to ensure that their Players were not hurt at all, and to help them proceed through the game and win the prize.

"But suppose he's really obnoxious?" Nada demanded. "*Then* may I chomp him?"

"No. You must find some innocuous way to avoid his unwarranted attentions."

"But Mundane males are famous for their oafish persistence in the face of polite demurrals."

"True. Consider it a challenge."

"I shall do no such thing! I resign my position in this stupid game!"

The Professor looked pained. "Please do not force me to exert disciplinary persuasion."

"Forget it! I'm not one of your demon students! I'm a princess! I am departing these premises forthwith."

"I can not allow you to do that."

"Who cares what you allow! You have no authority over me."

"Unfortunately for you, I do have authority."

"Oh? Give me one indifferent reason why I should remain here against my princessly preference."

Grossclout sighed a small cloud of smoke. "Do you remember when you and Electra toured the realm of the gourd? You tasted some red whine."

"So I tasted some red whine!" she agreed. "I wanted to identify it. So what?"

"So any creature who partakes of the food of the realm of the gourd thereafter remains bound to the gourd. Had you forgotten that?"

Nada's hands flew to her face to cover up her unprincessly gape of horror. "Oh, my! I had forgotten."

"Therefore you have an obligation to the realm of the gourd. The demons have acquired the option on that obligation. You must participate in our project. That will acquit you."

Nada realized that she was stuck for it. The Demon Professor was notorious for leaving nothing to chance. Wearily she returned to the rehearsal.

Now she was glad of those tedious rehearsals, because she was well versed in turning aside obnoxious male moves without in any way diminishing her princessly status or maidenly appeal. She could handle herself. That of course did not make the situation fun, but at least it was tolerable.

This Dug promised to be exactly the type she had rehearsed against. He was tall, handsome, halfway smart, and oafishly ignorant of magic. Furthermore, his hands were just twitching to put a move on her. He had spied her in the lineup, and his orbs had spun into twin WOW position. What a job this was going to be!

But once it was done, she would be free of her obligation to the gourd. Possibly it might even be worth it.

They came to Isthmus Village. Because Dug had exercised his prerogative to Make Decisions, and naturally had made a bad one. He was from Mundania, where food evidently did not grow on trees. He thought they had to get supplies. Even weapons. How could he use a weapon from the other side of his screen? He needed neither food nor weapon here, as long as he refused to believe in magic. As long as he thought it was just a game.

At least that gave her some respite. As long as he did not believe, he could not truly enter the scene, and thus could not annoy her with anything other than verbal harassment. Of course she would have to handle the reaction of the villagers when they saw the screen traipsing about.

It did not take long for the villagers to notice them. A gruff village headman approached. "What are a beautiful Nada princess and a weird magic screen doing in our desolate village?" he demanded. Gruffly, of course.

"We wish to obtain supplies and weapons," Nada said dutifully. "We are traveling to see the Good Magician, and fear privation along the way."

"Why don't you just use the magic path?"

"We can't. It's supposed to be a challenge, so the protection of the enchanted paths are denied us."

"Well, you won't get any help here. We are angry folk who don't like outsiders. Were you not so beautiful, we would be inclined to chastise you."

"Listen, twerp, you can't talk to her like that!" Dug exclaimed from the screen.

Sure enough, he was getting them into trouble. "It's all right, Dug," Nada murmured. "They can't hurt us."

"Yeah, I'd like to see them try," he said aggressively.

The headman grimaced. "We may oblige you, apparition. Come out of that wandering screen and we shall enjoy giving you a decent thumping."

"Boy, I'd sure see about that, you old goat."

Nada moved to cover the screen as well as she could with her body, blocking Dug off from the scene. "We shall be going immediately, thank you kindly, sir," she said to the headman.

"Oh no we won't!" Dug cried, as the screen circled around to recover its view of the proceedings. "Much as I like the sight of your backside." There was a slight fuzziness about the last word that indicated that the magical translation had had a problem; evidently he had used a different word that might or might not mean the same thing. Nada had the distinct impression that had it been possible for him to reach through the screen, he would have done something that required her to wham him across his insolent face.

"Oh, do you think so, you seclusive wretch," the headman said, as other villagers closed in around them, each looking more surly than the others. "Just because you can hide behind a lovely woman, you think you can insult us."

"No, no!" Nada said desperately. "He's not trying to insult you. He just doesn't understand." She tried to cover the screen again, this time being careful not to show her backside to it. Unfortunately this was worse. Not only did she have the impression that Dug was peering down the front of her dress, the village men were inspecting her posterior. What a mess!

"The bleep I don't understand!" Dug shouted. The word

"bleep" was strongly fuzzed, showing that the Adult Conspiracy had blocked out the original word. Which was odd; she had never heard of it operating that way before. For one thing, there were no children close by, and Dug, at sixteen, was eligible to join the Conspiracy. There should have been no suppression of speech. "Much as I like looking at your bleeps up close."

Angry herself, Nada stepped away from the screen, folding her arms across her bosom. She would let Dug and the villagers exchange their own words; she had done all she could to avert trouble, but since both parties seemed to want it, that was that.

"Get out of the village!" the headman shouted back. "We don't want your kind here! We have trouble enough already."

"Not without our supplies," Dug said.

A canny look crossed the headman's face. "And how will you pay for supplies?"

That evidently made Dug pause. He didn't have anything he could pass through the screen. But in a moment he bounced back. "With information, you bleep. What would you like to know? How ugly your puss is? How big your feet are?"

"We don't need information, we need to be rid of the censorship," the headman said. "What can you do about that?"

"Censorship!" Dug exclaimed. "You mean you have that here?"

"We certainly do! And it's a horror. Its power is increasing all the time, too. Soon it will totally enslave us, making us wholly miserable instead of merely frustrated."

This was new to Nada. But perhaps it offered an avenue for resolution of the crisis. "What is a censor-ship?" she asked.

"It's a ship, of course. It sails into our port every day, and its censers send their incense smoke through our village, ruining our dialogue and incensing us. That is why we are so angry all the time."

"Censorship!" Dug exclaimed, laughing. "So that's what it is! I had thought it was something more serious."

"We find nothing humorous about it," the headman said. "We just wish to be rid of it."

"But it's just a pun. Where I come from, it's a serious matter. They take books out of the libraries, and they stop the people from knowing the truth about government, and next thing, in countries where it's really strong, they get into thought control."

"Exactly. At first it seemed mild, even beneficial. To protect our children. But it kept protecting more things and more people, until now we are almost slaves to it. But we are powerless to throw it off."

Dug reconsidered. "Okay, I guess maybe you do have a real problem. I don't like censorship; I want to make up my own mind what I should read or hear. I guess you do too."

"That is the truth," the headman said dourly.

Nada still found this confusing. "Why don't you just ask the ship to go away?"

"We should have done that at the outset," the man agreed. "But we were seduced by what it seemed to offer. It promised us advantage, indeed, dominance over all others. Sheer folly, we now know to our cost. There are a number of ships, and some will depart when asked. But this one, though it masqueraded as a nice one, is actually the worst of them all, and once it establishes control it never lets go by choice."

"Does this particular censor-ship have a name?" Dug asked.

"It is the dread vessel *Bigotry*. If only we had fallen victim to some other ship, such as *Politics* or *Literary* or *Prudish* or *Social*, we might have escaped. I understand that some ships really do have the welfare of their victims in mind. But not this one. This one closes out all other views, being absolutely intolerant of differing belief. We deeply regret ever being lulled by its seeming care for our welfare; it cares for no welfare but its own."

Dug nodded with agreement. "You got that right! Okay,

this must be a game challenge. Something I have to handle before I move on. So we'll help you get rid of it. Will that be a fair exchange for our supplies?"

The headman forgot to be angry. "We would give anything we have, to be rid of that ship and its insidious fumes."

"Deal!" Dug said. Then: "Exactly how does it work? I mean, does the smoke smell bad, or something?"

"No, it has only a faint perfume. But wherever it circulates, it suppresses anything it deems to be offensive. It is a puritanical vessel that will not allow any bleep, bleep, or bleep thoughts to be expressed." The man turned his head and spat, disgusted by his inability to say the words. "This of course ruins our fishing, building, social lives, and even our entertainment, because it is impossible to perform tough manual chores without venting an occasional bleep, or to woo a maid without telling her bleep, or to play a game of dice without saying bleep."

"Wow!" Dug said. "You mean it really does stop you from saying bleep?" He looked surprised as he heard his own word. "Yeah, I guess it does. Boy, I don't blame you for getting mad! Nobody likes getting censored and incensed."

"To be sure," that headman agreed gruffly, looking less angry. "Many ships do that, and originally this had appeal. We thought to improve our speech. But we assumed that our wishes for speech would govern. We discovered that *its* rules governed instead. And not merely for speech; that is merely the first stage. Soon it will begin controlling our actions, and finally our thoughts. But we have been unable to escape the devious incense fumes from the censers of the ship. Worse, the definitions are expanding. Originally it was only cursing it stopped, but now we can not even say bleep."

Dug nodded. "I think I have it. I read about it in civics class. What do you call a female dog?"

"A bleep."

"I thought so. Pretty soon it will be running your entire

lives, because censorship feeds on its own power to enforce its rules. They don't have to make sense; that's not the point. They just have to be followed, or else. Eventually you won't even be able to breathe without choking on the fumes, and life won't be worth living."

"Exactly. We are already somewhat short of breath." The other folk nodded agreement, and some coughed.

Nada was amazed. Dug was actually getting along with the villagers. He understood their problem. Maybe she had misjudged him.

"Okay. What do I have to do to get rid of this ship?"

"It is very hard. That is why we can not do it for ourselves. But perhaps an outsider, not yet fully suppressed by the fumes, could manage it. You have to get the solution."

"That's what I want, the solution," Dug agreed. "What is it?"

"It is a magical fluid that can put out the censers, so that the incense no longer burns. Only that special solution can do it. When the incense no longer burns, there will be no more smoke and no more fumes. Then the ship will be unable to harm us, and will have to go away."

Dug's mouth quirked. Nada realized that he still was not taking this quite seriously, but she decided to stay clear as long as the dialogue was making progress.

"And where may I find this magical solution?"

"It is beyond the pail."

"Beyond the pale," Dug said. "Of course."

"You must take the pail and bring the solution back in it. That is the only way."

"I shall try to do that. But just how far beyond the pale, uh pail, is this solution?"

"We do not know. We know only that it is in the possession of the Fairy Nuff."

"Fair enough?"

"Yes. If you can convince her to give you the solution, all will be well."

"I'll do that. Which direction is the pail?"

"That way," the headman said, pointing to the side.

"Well, let's go," Dug said briskly. "I shall return."

Nada had no idea whether they would be able to find the pail, let alone the Fairy Nuff, or get the solution, but at least this was better than quarreling with the villagers. She walked in the indicated direction, and the screen walked with her.

Soon they saw the pail. It was colored daylight blue, and looked very bright and nice. But as they walked toward it, it receded, staying out of reach.

"I begin to see why the villagers didn't get it," Dug said. "But we'll have to prove we're smarter. Can you get around beyond it, so I can herd it in to you?"

For answer, Nada changed into small serpent form and slithered out of her clothes. Then she realized that she shouldn't have done that; how was she going to get back into them, without Dug seeing her body? A princess could not allow a mere man to see her torso or her panties. Especially not a Mundane man. But she would have to worry about that later; she had already changed.

She slithered rapidly around to the side, and through the underbrush. She circled around until she was well beyond the pail. Then she started to change—and realized that she didn't have her clothes here. She couldn't grab the pail unless she had hands. So she slithered back under the brush near a blanket bush, changed back to human form, wrapped a blanket around her, and walked back out to intercept the pail. She lay down, hiding, then changed back to serpent form, keeping the blanket more or less in place so that it would be there when she changed again.

Now Dug's screen advanced on the pail. The pail retreated, teasing him. But when it crossed the place where Nada lay, she abruptly changed back to human form, grabbed its handle with one hand, and her blanket with the other. "Gotcha!" she exclaimed with unprincessly vernacular.

The pail flung itself about, but could not get free. After a moment it hung quiescent, defeated.

"Great!" Dug called, his screen hurrying across the terrain. "Now we can go on beyond the pail."

"In a moment," Nada said. "Stay here; I will be right back." She hurried back to where her clothing was. She picked it up, went behind a very elegant and even symmetree, and hastily got back into her formal human garb. She was careful not to let go of the pail, because if it got away from her, she knew they would not catch it in the same way again. The she walked out to rejoin Dug. She had managed to get by this incidental personal crisis, but she would have to be more careful next time she needed to change.

They moved on—and discovered snow. It covered the path and extended into the forest to the sides. "This can't be right," Nada said. "Xanth is warm. There is snow only on the mountaintops, and sometimes in unusual storms. There hasn't been any storm here, and it's not cold."

"Maybe it only looks like snow," Dug said.

She squatted and touched a finger to it. It was cold and somewhat gooey. She licked her finger. "Eye scream!" she exclaimed, surprised.

"Ice cream?"

"Eye scream," she clarified, pointing to her eye and mouth.

"You scream? Oh 'I scream.' What's it doing here?"

"I don't know. It must be coming from somewhere. See, it seems to be flowing and melting."

"Then let's find out where it's coming from. Maybe we can get around it."

"Or at least across it," she said. Her slippers were already thoroughly gummed up. "It seems to be flowing from somewhere ahead of us."

As they went, the ice cream (as Dug called it) became colder and harder, so that her feet were no longer gummy. Now they were cold. Dug, within his screen, had no problem; he just floated over it.

Fortunately she spied a shoe tree. She plucked a warm pair of boots from it and put them on. Now her feet were all right, and the blanket over her dress helped keep the rest of her warm. But she hoped they found a way out of the eye scream soon, because she knew she would get cold again as soon as she stopped moving.

They came to a castle formed of packed sugary snow. It wasn't a big castle, but that was because there was not an awful lot of eye scream available to make it. It had nice windows formed of thin sheets of ice. "Maybe whoever lives here knows what this is all about," Nada said. She went up to the frozen chocolate door to knock. She discovered that there was a screen door before it.

There was a large eye set in the screen. "Who are you?" the eye screamed.

"I am Nada Naga, Companion to Dug Mundane, who is a Player in the game. We are trying to find the Fairy Nuff. I don't suppose she lives here?"

The eye screen blinked. "No, she lives on down the fairway, of course. But you can't reach her unless you settle with my mistress of the castle first."

Nada was getting cold standing there. "Who is the mistress of the castle?"

"The Ice Queen, of course." The eye was still screaming; that seemed to be its only mode of dialogue.

"Then may we talk to the Ice Queen?" Nada asked, trying not to shiver with the chill.

"Actually the mistress isn't here right now," the eye confided with a conspiratorial wink. "Her clone is here. She looks just like the Queen, though."

"Then may we talk with the Ice Queen Clone?"

"The Ice Queen Clone!" Dug chortled.

The eye eyed him. "You find something funny about that?"

Dug, perhaps remembering how sensitive the villagers had been, decided to back off. "No, I'm an I-Screen-Clone myself."

This kid was quick on his mental feet, Nada realized.

The eye was mollified. "Sure." The eye twisted in its socket so as to look back beyond the door. "Hey, mistress!" the eye screamed. "There's a luscious eyeful of a maiden to see you."

"Have you eye-screened her?" a voice called back.

"Yes, I screened," the eye screamed. "There's an I screen with her."

"Are they appropriately awed?"

"The maiden is shaking and her teeth are chattering."

Nada was shivering cold, but decided not to clarify the matter.

"Then send them into the cone room, and have a scone for yourself."

The door opened. "Follow my glance," the eye screamed, looking into the hall. There was a dotted line marking its glance.

Nada entered, with the screen close behind. When she looked back, she saw the eye screen scone rolling up.

The cone room turned out to be shaped like a giant cone, unsurprisingly. In its center was an old woman wearing a snowy shroud. "I am the Ice Queen Crone," she said.

Nada realized that of course the clone would not admit to being a copy; she was pretending to be the real crone. "I am Nada Naga, and—"

"Yes, yes, I heard the eye scream," she said impatiently. "You want to reach the Fairy Nuff. But first you have to do something for me, or I will turn you to luscious slush, or maybe slushious mush."

"Yeah?" Dug said. "I'd like to see you—" He hesitated as the Ice Queen Clone lifted a cold finger, preparing to implement her spell. "I mean, that won't be necessary. What do you want of us?"

"I want a new flavor of eye scream, of course. One no one ever heard of before. What have you got?"

Nada was blank. But Dug came to the rescue. "No problem. How about Spinach Soufflé ice cream, for the child who won't eat his vegetables?"

"Wonderful!" the Ice Queen Clone cried. "I love to make children suffer! I will make up a potful right away."

"Just so long as I don't have to eat it," Dug said. "Now will you let us go on to see the Fairy Nuff?"

"Of course. Just go right down the fairway there." She indicated a door in the side of the cone.

They went out the door, and found themselves on a sunny green expanse. There was no snow. "Why, this is a golf course," Dug said, surprised.

"It looks like a finely clipped lawn to me," Nada said, as surprised.

"The fairway, of course. That is where the fair enough would be, in this crazy place."

"What would a fairy want with a lawn?"

Dug glanced at her through the screen, then shrugged. "I suppose there is a pun there. You know, this place—what do you call it, Zanth—might be okay if it wasn't for all the stupid puns."

"They are there for the cri-tics," Nada explained. "Because the cri-tics can't handle the intelligent puns, and they hate to think they're missing anything."

"Critics are like that," he agreed.

Nada grew warm as she walked, and had to take off the blanket, and then the boots. But this was certainly preferable to the snow.

In the center of the fairway they found a kind of exhibit or marketplace, with things set out for inspection. "This is a fair," Nada said. "We must be getting close."

"It's some affair," he agreed, looking around. "A fairground on a fairway."

In the center of the fair, with flair, was the booth of the Fairy. She was very fair, even beautiful, with scintillating wings. But she looked sad.

As they approached, Nada discovered that the Fairy was not female, but male. He was so delicate that he seemed feminine from a distance. His booth was set out with decanters of all shapes and sizes, containing fluids of many colors.

"Are you the Fairy Nuff?" Nada inquired hesitantly.

"What's it to you, snaketail?" he snapped. "Can't you read it on the ledger?" He pointed to the words FAIRY NUFF.

"Listen, you winged freak, don't talk to her like that!" Dug said.

"Why not, screenbrain?" the Fairy demanded.

"Because she's a lovely and good person, and she's try ing to do her job, that's why, you androgynous creep."

Nada couldn't help it; she was getting to like aspects of Dug Mundane. She kept her mouth shut.

"Well, you aren't any of those things, you midget-brained Mundane," the Fairy retorted. "So what did you come here for?"

"We need a solution," Dug said. "Just give us a bucket of it, and we'll get out of your face."

"And what will you give me for that solution, you fugitive from dreariness?"

Dug paused. "Tit for tat, eh?"

"No. That's the next booth over."

They looked at the next booth, where several bare-breasted nymphs perched. A man was approaching it, hauling along a bag marked TAT. Nada decided not to inquire further.

Dug seemed quite intrigued by the nymphs, however. His eyes seemed eager to zip over there, hauling his head along after them. "Don't forget what you're here for," Nada murmured

He forced himself to remember, without perfect success. "What are those creatures?"

"They are nymphs, of course. Females almost without minds, existing only for the sport of the moment."

"But what a sport!" he breathed.

"If you want to have brainless fun," she agreed.

"Yeah." He seemed oblivious to her tone.

"That is evidently just about your velocity," the Fairy remarked.

That got Dug's attention. "What's it to you, Nuff? You never heard of play?"

"Fair play, of course," the Fairy said.

"Ouch! I walked into that one. Okay, what do you want for your solution?"

"I want not to be the object of misrepresentation."

"You don't have a solution for that?"

"My solutions apply only to others."

Dug considered. "Exactly what kind of misrepresentation are you the object of?"

"Folk insist on calling me gay, when as you can plainly see, I am nothing of the kind. I want recognition as the sour individual I am."

"Let me see if I have this straight. You are a fairy, therefore folk call you gay?"

"Exactly, I have no idea why they think all fairies are gay."

Dug pursed his lips, seeming to think of something obscure. "Maybe this is a problem it's better to avoid," he said. "Exactly how is your name spelled?" Dug could have read it on the ledger, but for some reason his eyes were straying back to the nymphs.

"Eff Aay Eye Are Why. Enn You Eff Eff."

"Try spelling it FAERIE."

"That will change things?"

"It just might."

Nuff looked extremely dubious, which was the way Nada felt. How could such an irrelevant change affect the attitudes of others?

"Very well." He touched the ledger, and the letters shifted. Now it read FAERIE NUFF.

Another person approached the booth. "What are you spelling, Nuff?" he asked seriously.

"Nothing to interest you, clodbrain," Faerie Nuff snapped.

"What a grouch!" the man said, moving away.

Nuff stared after him. "It's magic!" he breathed.

"Right," Dug agreed. "Now they know you're not gay. How about our solution?"

Nuff made a negligent gesture.

"Take any bottle," Dug told Nada.

"But who said to?" she asked.

"Nuff said."

So it seemed. She lifted a nice decanter of purple elixir, pulled off the stopper, and poured it into the pail. When she set it back on the table, it refilled of its own volition. She replaced the stopper. "Thank you, Nuff," she said.

"You earned it," the Faerie said sourly.

But when she looked in the pail, it was empty. Had Nuff cheated them? She started to speak, but Dug beat her to it. "Did we misunderstand the nature of the deal?" he inquired in what was, for him, a remarkably peaceable tone.

"Fair well," Nuff said, waving.

Nada looked around—and saw several wells she hadn't noticed before. "I think it's in a well," she said.

So they went to the wells. There were five of them, labeled A B C D and E. One of them must have the solution they could haul away.

Dug's face lighted. "Fair-E-Nuff!" he exclaimed. "Well-E-Nuff. We want E-Nuff."

"We want enough, yes," she agreed, perplexed.

They went to Well E, which was somewhat isolated from the others. "Well E Nuff Alone," Dug said with satisfaction. "It makes weird sense."

There was a bucket on a rope. Nada let the bucket down into the well until it splashed in the water below. She drew it up. The fluid was purple, matching that of the bottle they had chosen. Nada poured it into the pail, and this time it stayed there. "Good," she said, relieved.

"Good E Nuff," Dug agreed cheerfully.

They returned the way they had come. When they reached the castle of the Ice Queen Clone, they walked around it—and found themselves immediately in a snowstorm. Nada had forgotten to bring along her boots and blanket, and was suddenly cold again.

"Try a drop of solution," Dug suggested.

Nada dipped her finger in the pail and flicked a drop of fluid out into the snow. Immediately the storm calmed, and a clear path opened before them. The solution was working.

"You are really coming to understand how things work here, Dug," she said, impressed.

"Well, I always was a quick study," he said. "Once I caught on to the rules of nonsense, I just had to apply them."

So it seemed. He was young, arrogant, and a Mundane, but he did have his points.

They returned to Isthmus Village. "We have the solution," Dug announced. "Where's the ship?"

The headman led the way south to the port. There was the sinister ship, with its great awful censers hanging fore and aft. On its hull was its name: BIGOTRY. Nada felt a tingle of horror as she beheld it. This ship was made from the disgusting wood of the bigotree! No wonder it smelled so bad. It was surrounded by an aura of suppression; it was impossible for there to be any joy or freedom near it.

There seemed to be no sailors on that dread vessel. It was a ghost craft, bearing no living creature. What person could stand to be near it?

"Looks good," Dug said. "Let's get aboard her and douse those censers."

That meant that Nada would have to do it, because Dug wasn't really in this scene. He was protected by his screen.

She sighed silently and got into the dingy little dinghy boat the headman showed them. She set the pail between her knees and took the oars. She hauled on them. They were heavy, but she heaved hard and made them move. The headman watched as the dinghy moved out. She was alone, except for the screen.

"Boy, you sure look great when you're moving like that," Dug said, staring at her front.

As if things weren't bad enough! "Why don't you take an oar?" she gasped. Because she was a maiden she did not speak the rest of her thought: *And shove it somewhere loathsome.* In fact, because she was a princess, she could not even think of it in greater detail, frustrating as it was. She suffered the same sort of repression the censor-ship brought to the isthmus, only hers could not be doused by any solution. She wished that just once she could step out of her role and do something fiendishly unprincessly.

Meanwhile the awful mood of the ship intensified. There was an ambience of gloom, hatred, and loathing. The ship was here on a mission of destruction, seeking to extirpate not only all pleasure in life, but ultimately life itself. Total repression, so that it would no longer be possible even to breathe, and all the victims could do was expire and rot away. What a cargo of malice! Her breath was getting short, and not just from her effort of rowing; it was as if a depressing weight were bearing down on her, squashing out her strength and will. How much longer could she continue?

The dinghy touched the somber hull. "Okay, tie the boat close, and carry the solution up there," Dug said. "This isn't nearly as hard as I thought it would be."

Nada tried to make an angry remark, but the overpowering fumes of the censers left her barely able to breathe. So she took the pail in one hand, and grabbed a rope ladder with the other. She hauled herself up, rung by rung, until she made it to the deck.

"Great!" Dug said. "What an antique this is! I wish I had a model of it."

Nada just wished he could be physically here, to suffer the effects of this ship of doom. She dragged herself across the dark planking toward the nearest censer. It was as if she were climbing a mountain, and the slope got steeper with each step. She had to drag each leg forward through a seeming miasma that clung like rotten goo. Every breath seemed to bring in a thick sludge of vapor that soiled her tenderest innermost recesses. She closed her eyes and plowed on.

"Come on, Nada, you're real close," Dug said encouragingly. "Just a couple more steps, then heave the pail up and slop some in."

Two more steps? It might as well have been two more worlds! Nada couldn't even keep her feet any longer. The stench from the looming censer was overpowering her last resolve, and she was falling. The pail was tilting, its precious solution about to spill out across the deck, wasted.

Hands caught her and the pail. "Come *on*, we've got to get this done," Dug said. "We can't give up now." He coughed. "Phew! What a stench!"

He lifted the pail from her slackening grasp and lurched forward. His breath wheezed. His body trembled. He seemed to be swept back by a sickly wind. But he fought forward just a little more, closing the grudging gap between the pail and the censer. He heaved the pail up, tilted it, and splashed some solution into the censer.

There was a pouff! and a hideous cloud of vapor spread up and out. It soiled the air, then thinned, and faded away. The incense had been extinguished. For the first time she saw the lettering on the censer: HATRED.

A breath of clean air swept in. Nada, sprawled on the deck, inhaled. How sweet it was!

They had done it! They had overcome the censor-ship. The isthmus would be free!

Then another whiff of awfulness came. Nada looked—and saw the far censer. They had extinguished only one of the two. The job was only half done.

She dragged herself up. She had no idea now she would ever make it the length of the ship and to the other censer. She would just have to try.

"Oh, brother, the other one," Dug said, staring across at it. "I don't think I can make it."

As her mind cleared, Nada realized something. "Dug! You're in the scene!"

He looked around, startled. "I guess I am. How did that happen?"

"It means you believe," she said.

"I don't believe! I just couldn't stand to see you struggling like that, when I'm the one who got us into this thing. It wasn't fair."

"You must believe I'm real, or you wouldn't care."

He stared at her. "I guess maybe I do, then." He shook his head, not really believing his own belief. "Maybe it's just that when I realized this was serious, I had to believe. I couldn't let censorship win, even in a joke land like this." He smiled. "Well, maybe we can make it to the other censer together."

"Maybe we can," she agreed. "Take my hand."

He took her hand. Then they walked together across the deck. It was much easier now. There was far more strength in unity that she had imagined. Also, she now knew that the solution worked, and that gave her more courage. What they were doing wasn't pointless; all they had to do was do it right, and the censorship would be finally defeated.

The fumes intensified, but their effect was no longer overpowering. The two of them forged onward, not even slowing. They reached the grim censer, and Dug lifted up the pail and poured out more of the solution.

The fumes stopped. A glow came from the censer, but not of burning incense. It was the glow of clean daylight. The gloomy cloud surrounding the ship was dissipating, and the deck was brightening. They had defeated the second censor censer more readily than the first.

Nada looked at it. Its letters said IGNORANCE.

"Hatred and ignorance," Dug murmured, awed. "The two pillars of bigotry. And I'll bet this is the ship of fools, too. Because only fools would let such bad things govern them."

"And only fools would try to stop all others from saying or even thinking what they wanted to," Nada said. "Fortunately we don't have a lot of that in Xanth."

"We have plenty in Mundania, though," he said. "I guess that's what makes it such a dreary place." He looked around. "Damn! I'm glad to be here!" Then he laughed. "Hey, I swore! It didn't get bleeped out. The censorship really has been beaten."

"It really has been," she agreed. "For now. But it will surely be back, once it returns to its source and gets its censers restored."

"I guess so. Too bad. But let's get off it and get back to Isthmus Village. We have a whole adventure to get through."

So they did. This was only the beginning.

$$\overline{4}$$

WATER

K im was glad to get out of the Ogre fen Ogre Fen. She knew herself to be a smart, and therefore un- attractive, girl, but it had taken all her ingenuity to outsmart those stupid ogres. She wanted no more such en- counters. This was after all supposed to be a fun game, wasn't it?

"So which is the fastest way to the Good Magician's castle?" she asked Jenny Elf.

"Well, it's south, but we shouldn't go that way."

"What do you mean, shouldn't go that way? Why not?" Kim remembered how Jenny had warned her against messing with the ogres, and in retrospect she appreciated that advice more than she had in futurespect. Henceforth she would pay more heed to the advice of her Companion.

"Because of the elements."

Kim remembered. "Oh, yes! Those five regions in north-central Xanth. Air, Fire, Water, Earth, and the Void, going from south to north."

"What?" Jenny asked, seeming confused.

"What's the problem?"

"That's not the order."

"Of course it is! I read it in the *Visual Guide*. There's a map."

"Well, the guide is wrong. Is it a Mundane book?"

"Of course."

"That explains it. Mundanes don't know about magic."

"Well, I've have to see it to believe it. We should be closest to the Void, and south of that is Earth."

"You're right about the Void, but the next one down is Water. The Water Wing, in the shape of—"

"I get it. It has little waves on it, too. And Fire is in the shape of flames, and Air is like a puffy cloud. Everything's punnish, in Xanth. Okay, let's circle the Void and go see the Water Wing."

"You don't really believe me," Jenny said.

"I didn't say that." But it was true. Kim didn't believe that the map was wrong. It was in print, after all.

"Maybe we should go east to the Sane Jaunts River," Jenny said. "The birds are there, but they won't bother us if we didn't do anything to annoy them."

"Why should birds bother us anyway? We can just shoo them away."

"Some of them are big birds."

"Big birds? Is that another pun?"

"I don't think so. I mean rocs."

"Rocks?—oh, *rocs*! The hugest of birds! Like Roxanne Roc, in the Nameless Castle."

"Yes. We don't want to bother any rocs. They know we're in the game, but still, we shouldn't take chances."

They had taken chances in the Ogre Fen, and almost gotten wiped out. Kim could have sworn that her hair got wet when the brute dunked her screen. That was her imagination, of course, but it had been uncomfortable at the time. She didn't want anyone turning her screen upside down again, either; she had felt giddy as the whole landscape inverted and swung around. Just how an ogre could grab her screen she didn't know; it was just the picture of

Xanth she saw. But funny things always did happen in Xanth.

"Okay, let's go by the birds," Kim agreed. "I'd like to see a roc, anyway, as long as I'm on this tour. From a distance." She no longer wanted to see any monsters up close, because now she was afraid that one of them would smash her screen, or eat it, and it would go dark and exclude her from the game. She wasn't yet ready to quit the game, by a long shot.

They found a path that went east. These were not enchanted paths, Kim understood, because those were reserved for regular Xanth folk. It was just the game's excuse to force the Players into out-of-the-way places where they could get into trouble. If Players were allowed to use the enchanted paths, there wouldn't be much challenge. Anyway, it was surely more interesting along the bypaths.

In due course they came to the bank of the river. Kim was disappointed; she had hoped that it would be a real fantasy spectacle, but it was just a meandering stream, similar to any in her own realm. However, the plants along its banks were interesting; she recognized a pillow bush and a pie tree. If only she could eat a meal here, and stay the night, so she could use these things! But it was her fate as a mere Player never to actually be *in* the Land of Xanth. She hated that limitation.

Some plants were unfamiliar. They looked like hollow straws sticking up from the foliage. "What are those?" she asked.

Jenny looked. "Oh—straw-berries. We use them to drink tsoda pop."

Strawberries. She should have known.

Farther along there was an odd stick on the ground. Jenny picked it up, holding it so that Kim could see it. She discovered a red pair of lips on its surface. "Don't tell me, let me guess," she said. "Lipstick!"

"Of course," Jenny agreed. "Some girls use them to make their lips stick to things more firmly. I've never been quite sure why, unless they're afraid their kisses are too short."

The ground shuddered. Something large and solid was coming. Jenny hid behind a tree, and Kim peeked past her shoulder.

It was an animal with a bovine body, horns, and a weird wide-mouthed head. It sniffed the air, smelled Jenny, and looked at her with its bulging eye. "Croak!" it bellowed.

"Croak?" Kim asked.

"Well, it's a bull-frog," Jenny explained.

The creature leaped into the river, made an enormous splash, and disappeared under the surface. It was a bull-frog all right.

They walked on along the river. Kim half hoped she would see a water dragon, but she didn't. It was like Mundania: the creatures were there, but seldom to be seen. Maybe it was just as well.

"Are we south of the Void yet?" she asked after a bit. "Maybe we should cut back west now."

"I don't think so," Jenny said cautiously.

"Oh, come on; let's go see." Kim found a path and forged along it.

"No, no!" Jenny cried. "It's not safe!"

But Kim was being willful again. She knew it, but also knew that she was tired of walking down the river. She wanted to see the Water Wing—or the Earth region, to verify that her map was correct.

She came abruptly to a line of demarcation. The trees of the forest were reasonably normal—and then there just didn't seem to be anything much. It wasn't exactly a wall or precipice; she just didn't seem to be able to focus on it. How odd!

"Stop!" Jenny cried from behind. "Don't take one step farther!"

"Oh, don't be silly," Kim retorted. "I can't take a step here anyway; I'm just looking at it through the screen." Except that she wasn't exactly looking, she was just, well, *trying* to look.

So she moved forward. Suddenly there was a scene ahead: a gently sloping valley, with lush green turf and pretty little flowers of several colors sprinkled throughout. Pleasant puffy clouds drifted above, delicate columns of mist hovered over a lake, and the air was sweet. "Oh, this is nice!" she breathed.

Then the view jerked and turned sideways. The terrain spun horrendously. "Hey!" Kim cried. "What's happening?"

There was a change of scene. Suddenly there was Jenny Elf, her arms spread wide, hands clenching on something. The lovely landscape was gone.

"What are you doing?" Kim demanded. "I saw a really beautiful place, and I want to go back there."

"I'm hauling you out of the Void," Jenny said. "You're lucky I managed to catch hold of the back of your screen. Otherwise you would have been gone. Because nothing can cross out of the Void, once it is past that boundary."

"But I was just looking!" Kim protested. "I'm immune to getting caught, because it's just a picture, to me."

"Well, your screen was getting caught!" Jenny retorted. "And what happens to your role as a Player if you fall into the Void?"

That sobered her. "I lose," she admitted. "And I have to start over again, with the hazards at least as bad. That's no good. Even if I do lose, the first time, I want to get just as far as I can, so I know what to look out for next time. Thank you, Jenny; you did the right thing."

"That's all right," Jenny said. But she looked shaken, and Kim knew why: it was now twice that Kim had willfully gotten them into trouble.

"I'll try to behave better, really I will," Kim said contritely. But Jenny still looked wary.

They returned to the river and moved on south. Suddenly a huge bird took off ahead of them, perhaps startled by their approach. "That must be a roc!" Kim exclaimed. But then she saw that it had four legs with hooves, and the head of a horse. "No—it's a winged horse!"

"An alicorn," Jenny said. "I never saw one of those before!"

"A what?"

"An alicorn. A winged unicorn. There aren't many, but sometimes a griffin and a unicorn will meet at a love spring—well, I don't know what happens, but then we have alicorns."

"What do you mean, you don't know what happens?" Kim said sharply. "I read about how you were inducted into the Adult Conspiracy at age fourteen, and you must be fifteen now. Only a year younger than me—and *I* know what happens."

"You're Mundane," Jenny said. "Mundanes have funny ideas about things. But for the purpose of this game, I'm still a child, with the limits of a child. Professor Grossclout decreed it. So I can't know anything that's in the Adult Conspiracy, even if I might know out in real Xanth."

"Why should you be defined as a child?" Kim asked, surprised.

"So I will have the innocence of a child. That's an advantage, in some situations. I may be able to help you get somewhere, or do something, that an adult couldn't."

"That would be interesting," Kim said. "Very well: we won't discuss how alicorns come to be. They get delivered by the stork, or whatever."

"Yes."

They moved on. Kim never did get to see a water dragon, but she realized that there was plenty of Xanth to go yet.

It was clouding up. A storm was building in the sky. "Oops," Jenny said. "Try to stay out of sight. That looks like Fracto."

"Who?"

"Cumulo Fracto Nimbus, the meanest of clouds. He always blows an ill wind. If there's anything interesting happening, he comes and wets on it."

"Oh, pooh," Kim said, intrigued. Now she remembered Fracto, with contempt. "I'm not afraid of any ol' cloud!"

A vague face formed on the cloud. "I heeeard thaaaht!" Fracto puffed.

"So what? You're just a bag of wind."

"Ixnay," Jenny was murmuring. "Don't work him up."

But it was too late. The angry cloud was swelling up like a toad with gas, looming over them. Already the first cold gusts of wind were coming, bearing the first fat drops of water. Fracto's mouth pursed and blew out a much fiercer wind, containing flecks of sleet. They were in for it.

"I'm sorry," Kim said, realizing that this could indeed be mischief. "I guess my big mouth has gotten us into another."

"It's all right," Jenny said without overwhelming enthusiasm. "Let's see if we can maybe get up in a tree, so we don't get flooded out."

"It's *not* all right," Kim said. "You've been trying to do your job. But I'm just—well, I know I'm no beauty, so I try to make up by being smart with my mouth. It's a defensive mechanism. Only sometimes I'm doing it when I shouldn't. Like right now. And making it tough for you. So I'll try to watch it. Okay?"

"Okay," Jenny agreed, with an appreciative smile.

Meanwhile, they had Fracto's rage to deal with. Jenny cast about for a suitable tree to climb, but all the trees in view were wrong in separate ways. Some had tall, featureless trunks not easy to climb, some had thorns, and many were too small. "Sammy, find us a close tree to climb," Jenny said to the little cat.

Sammy bounded off. "Wait for me!" Jenny cried, chasing after him. Kim followed. Her screen just seemed to go wherever she looked, exactly as if she were really in the scene, and much of the time she forgot that she wasn't.

Kim heard a faint, eerie music. It was enchanting, but too distant to be intelligible.

They crossed an open area. Kim saw a giant spreading acorn tree beyond, easy to climb and sit in. The cat knew exactly where to go. But Fracto chose this moment to strike with all his fell force. A solid—well, liquid—sheet of rain came down to smite them. The water smacked into her screen, blurring it; she wished she had windshield wipers.

"Sammy!" Jenny cried, diving down. The cat had gotten swept into a sudden gullywasher which was taking advantage of a gully, and he was getting washed away to the side. Jenny grabbed him, but then fell into the gully herself.

More rain poured down, sluicing across the scene. Kim grabbed a handkerchief and tried to wipe her screen, but her hand just passed through it without effect. How silly, to think she could affect a scene within the computer game!

"Oh!" Jenny cried, being carried along by the rushing water. She was flailing, but couldn't get free, because she was holding the cat with one hand and water was coursing in from all around.

There was a rumble of satisfaction from Fracto. He was succeeding in messing them up.

Kim followed along, unable to do anything to help. She felt really guilty, because she was the one who had set off the irascible cloud, while Jenny was the one paying the consequence. "Jenny!" she called, knowing it was pointless.

But maybe she could help. She could go ahead and see if there were any good places to get free of the gullywash. Then she could tell Jenny, and she could get out of there.

But the storm just seemed to get worse, and she just couldn't see anything other than bits of overhanging branches and more water flowing in. All the world seemed to be water!

Again she heard that eerie music. It was as if someone were singing, and playing a stringed instrument. It was ethereally lovely, but still too faint to understand.

The gullywash became a stream, and the stream a river. Kim tried to find a shore, or even a shallow place, but the trees had retreated, leaving a broad expanse of water, with still more rain pelting down to trouble the surface. Jenny was being carried into a veritable sea!

Then she heard a sinister rushing sound. That sounded like—like a waterfall! Right ahead.

She hurried back to find Jenny, who was doing her best to stay afloat with the cat. Her hair and clothing were matted, and her spectacles were thoroughly fogged. "You have to get out!" Kim cried. "There's a waterfall!"

Sammy perked an ear. He meowed. Jenny smiled. "He says it's only a cataract," she reported.

A cat-aract. Naturally the cat wouldn't worry about that. But it remained a serious matter for a person. "You don't want to go through that," Kim said. "Who knows where it leads!"

"I don't have much choice," Jenny said sadly. "I'm sorry I wasn't a better Companion for you. But if you move on south, maybe you can still find the Good Magician and go on with the game."

"Don't be silly," Kim said. "I'm not going to leave you here." But how could she do anything useful?

The sound of the cataract swelled. Within it seemed to be that eerie melody, not quite drowned out, tantalizingly familiar. As if there were a damsel with a dulcimer somewhere beyond. But between her and them was the crashing water. Kim floated along, trying desperately to think of something, and failing. The rain was still pouring, and a stiff wind was boosting Jenny right on toward the disaster.

Maybe it wasn't so bad. Maybe it was just a little bit of rapids, and then the water would drain off to the side and Jenny could scramble out onshore. Kim went ahead to take one more look.

It was much worse than she had had any right to fear. There was a misty veil, and beyond it a plunge into a dark ocean. That seemed hopeless.

She turned back to find Jenny—and the elf was already there, being carried right into the plunge. Jenny shrieked as she floated over the brink.

Kim dived for her. Her hands caught hold of something.

Then she, too, was hauled over the brink. Instead of saving Jenny, she had just gotten herself into trouble.

They fell, seemingly endlessly. Water was all around, in columns. Below was a frightening whirlpool.

They plunged into it, Jenny was swirled away. Kim inhaled to try to scream, but breathed water. She choked.

Then something was hauling her. She struggled feebly, to no avail. Whatever it was would have its way with her.

She landed on a warm grassy bank. She blinked, seeing the head and shoulders of a man. She had been rescued!

"Jenny!" she gasped. "Jenny Elf! She's in there—"

The man dived under the water. A fluke showed as he disappeared.

A fluke?

Kim sat up, coughing out pockets of water. She was utterly bedraggled, but safe, and the rain had stopped. But where was she?

Then Jenny Elf appeared, still holding Sammy. She seemed to be swimming rapidly, but without effort, just halfway sliding across the water. Kim blinked, then realized that Jenny was being carried by the man, who seemed not to need his arms for swimming. How strange!

The man set Jenny on the bank beside Kim. She was smaller than Kim had realized, being only about two-thirds her own height. But of course she was an elf. Other elves of Xanth were even smaller.

The man started to haul himself out of the water. "Eeeek!" Jenny cried. "You can't change here! I'm not in the Adult Conspiracy!"

"Oops," the man said. "Then I remain in merform for the nonce." He flipped up his nether section, and lo, it was a green tail. He was a triton! A man with the tail of a fish.

"Thank you for saving us," Jenny said. "I am Jenny Elf, and this is Kim, a Player in the game. I'm her Companion. If I may ask—"

"I am Cyrus Merman," the man said. "Son of Morris Merman and the Siren. My mother makes beautiful music, but she no longer makes it for strangers."

"That music!" Kim exclaimed. "That was the Siren's song!"

Cyrus looked chagrined. "Oh, you heard it! We thought no one was near. My mother's music always leads strangers to trouble, so she never—"

"She didn't know," Jenny said. "We were just passing, and then we ran afoul of Fracto, and he blew up a tempest and washed us into the Water Wing."

"The Water Wing!" Kim cried with recognition. "That's where we were heading."

"You picked a treacherous route," Cyrus remarked. "It was fortunate I happened to be near. Of course I was near because I was listening to my mother's music. I don't have a wife to keep me distracted, you see."

"I thought the Siren stopped her music," Kim said, perplexed. "I read how Chester Centaur destroyed her instrument, where the magic was."

"For a long time she wouldn't sing or play at all," Cyrus agreed. "But there are so few people in the Water Wing that it seemed safe, so she remade her magic dulcimer, and now my father and I love to listen. The music doesn't hurt anyone, it is just incredibly fascinating to men, who must come and listen to it. The problem is that they tend to forget what they are doing, and crash their ships into rocks or do other foolish things. But my father and I are used to it, and anyway, we are unlikely to drown. So we just listen and enjoy it."

"Oh, I would like to hear some more of it, before we go," Kim said. "All I heard was so faint, but I loved it."

"My aunt the Gorgon's talent affected only men, when she was young," Cyrus said. "But when she matured, so did her power, until it affected everyone, even animals. I think the same is true for my mother's talent."

"Then we should listen, before we go," Jenny said. "Because Kim wants to experience all the things of Xanth as she goes along."

Cyrus turned his handsome gaze on Kim. "What is this

game you are playing?" he inquired. "You look like an attractive but otherwise ordinary young woman to me."

Kim opened her mouth, but stalled out before speaking. Attractive?

"She's Mundane," Jenny explained. "She won a talent contest, and the prize was to be the first to play the demon's Xanth Game of Companions. Somebody else sneaked in and was first, so she's actually the second, but still, she's playing the game. We're going down to ask the Good Magician how to proceed, since we don't know where the prize is, or even what it is. I mean, it's a magic talent, but we didn't know what talent."

Cyrus considered. "I suspect it is a good talent, so as to provide a strong incentive for the Players. I suppose it would be especially strong for Mundanes, who otherwise can never have magic."

Kim finally found her voice. "It hardly matters, since I can never actually be in Xanth. All I can do is play a role from the other side of the screen."

"The screen?" he asked blankly.

"This one." Kim put her hand out to touch it. And froze, astonished.

"Your screen is gone!" Jenny exclaimed. "Now I remember: you grabbed my hand. Trying to stop me from going over the waterfall. But instead I pulled you down. I must have pulled you through the screen!"

"But you couldn't have!" Kim protested. "There's no direct contact."

Cyrus smiled. "Are you saying that I merely imagined hauling you to shore? It certainly seemed like contact to me."

Kim reached down to touch the ground. It was solid. She touched Jenny's shoulder. It was there. She reached for Cyrus, then hesitated.

"By all means touch me," the merman invited. "In fact, lean over the water, and I will kiss you. That should be contact enough."

Was he daring her? Or teasing her? Kim decided to take

him up on it. After all, she would never have another
chance to kiss a merman.

"Uh, I don't think—" Jenny started, worried.

Kim leaned forward, and Cyrus leaned forward, and
their two faces met. They kissed. It was wonderful.

"You are an effective kisser," Cyrus remarked, smiling.

"I must be here," Kim said dreamily.

"You must have taken the second step," Jenny said.
"Now you believe in magic."

"So it seems all the way real," Kim agreed. "But I
know it isn't."

"But in Xanth, illusion is part of our reality," Cyrus
said. "So if you have the illusion that you are here, that is
good enough for me. You must come and meet my parents."

Jenny looked alarmed. "I'm not sure—"

"But I want to hear the Siren sing," Kim said. "I'd love
to meet your folks, Cyrus."

"Excellent. Allow me to go change. When my mother
changes, she can form a sequined dress at the same time,
but I have never mastered that ability. I shall return." He
swam away.

"Changes?" Kim asked.

"They can turn their tails into legs," Jenny explained.
"But then they are bare. As a juvenile, I'm not allowed to
see a bare man. That is why I had to stop him from changing before."

"Oh. Changing from merform to manform," Kim said.
Then she thought of something else. "Why were you
alarmed when he offered to introduce us to his parents?"

"In Xanth, people mostly meet people just as they are,"
Jenny explained. "But if they bring their parents in, it
means they may be getting serious."

"Serious?"

"Like maybe getting married."

"Married!" Kim exclaimed, astonished.

"He likes you. He's not married. So—"

"But I'm only sixteen!"

"So maybe he would have to meet your parents, too. Prince Dolph was still fifteen when he married Electra." Jenny smiled. "I understand they had a time trying to figure out how to signal the stork, because neither knew. But they did manage to do it."

"This is ridiculous. I'm not about to get married. Certainly not to signal any stork! This is only a game."

"Maybe it's not a game to him. Remember, you did kiss him. That's a pretty strong sign." Jenny shrugged. "Of course I'm not party to the Adult Conspiracy, so maybe I'm all wrong."

Kim was nonplussed. She was not at all sure the elf was wrong. She liked the merman, but this was getting ridiculous. "Maybe we had better get on out of here, then."

"Maybe we had better," Jenny agreed.

They stood, and Kim became aware of two things: her clothing was sodden and chafing because of the dunking, and Jenny was not only smaller than she was, she had pointed ears and four-fingered hands. She was different not only from Kim, but from other Xanth folk.

But already Cyrus was returning. Now he was with legs, and he wore a shirt and trousers. He looked twice as handsome as before. It was too late to get away, and it would have been impolite to go without waiting. Anyway, Kim realized that she wasn't eager to separate from him quite yet. For all the mischief it might portend, that kiss had been fun. Back home, no boy had kissed her and complimented her the way the merman had.

"Right this way, ladies," Cyrus said grandly. "My folks are expecting you."

Kim wasn't quite sure how she felt about that. But she did want to meet the Siren, about whom she had read.

They followed Cyrus along a pleasant path. Soon they came to a nice little house. It seemed to be made of glass. But the glass shimmered, as if not quite solid.

Cyrus saw her looking. "Water bricks," he explained. "Lacuna's son Ryver made them for us."

Water bricks? "May I touch one?" she asked timidly.

"Certainly; they are tough. It's just his magic; he's good with water. That's a talent we respect, here in the Water Wing."

Kim gingerly touched a brick. It was soft but resilient, giving way only a small amount before resisting. Like a velvet-covered block of stone. Ryver was indeed good with water.

The door opened, and a lovely older woman stepped out. This was the Siren. "Come in, come in!" she said. "We have set the table for you."

Set the table? But Kim knew she couldn't eat, because she wasn't really here. Or could she? About all she could do was try it and see what happened.

Then the Siren got a closer look. "But you're soaking wet, both of you. Come inside; we'll have you dry and changed in no time."

Inside it was pleasantly warm. A fire was burning in the hearth. The sticks there were translucent and colorless: waterlogs, of course. Ryver wasn't the only one who was good with water.

The Siren bustled them into a lavatory whose walls were fortunately lined with opaque water bricks, and helped them out of their sodden clothing, and put them into nice fresh dresses. Jenny looked much improved; her regular trousers and jacket had made her look like a child, while now she looked more like a young woman. A very petite one, by human standards, but still ladylike.

"You look wonderful, Kim!" Jenny said.

Which was what Kim should have said to Jenny first. "You too," she said belatedly. But she sneaked a peek at the ice mirror on the wall, and saw that she did look rather nice, in contrast to her usual. Maybe the magic of Xanth was enhancing her. Too bad she didn't have that magic in Mundania!

They went out to join the family. Kim tried to remind herself that this was all just a game setting. But it did indeed seem like a friendly backwoods family, and she liked it. Maybe Fracto had done them a favor, blowing them here so that Cyrus had had to rescue them.

Morris Merman was a handsome older man, also wearing legs and clothing for the occasion. "So you're Cyrus' young woman," he said affably.

Kim knew she should demur, but she didn't quite know how. She looked desperately at Jenny.

Jenny tried. "Kim is just passing through. This is a game to her—"

"A game!" Morris exclaimed. "That was a serious kiss!"

Kim's emotions were getting so mixed it was as if someone were stirring a big wooden spoon in them. She loved being complimented, but knew she couldn't afford to be taken seriously.

"I mean, she's a Mundane, just visiting Xanth, and—"

"A Mundane!" the Siren said.

It was sounding worse and worse. "Maybe we can talk later," Kim said uncomfortably.

But underneath her embarrassment was the wild excitement of recent developments. She had made the giant second step, and now seemed to be right in Xanth—and a handsome magical man had kissed her and called her attractive. Who needed to win the prize? This was fun enough.

The Siren served water cress, water chestnuts, water lemon, water rice, and water fowl, served on water lily leaves. For a beverage there was seltzer water. This was, after all, the Water Wing.

Somewhat dubiously, Kim tried her first mouthful—and it seemed real. So her belief was strong enough now to make it work. Relieved, she went ahead and enjoyed her meal.

Then they sat before the fire, and the Siren played and sang for them. It was absolutely beautiful and wonderful, and it evoked emotions Kim could not define. She wanted to be here always!

"Now we must talk," Cyrus said. "There is something I would like to ask you, Kim Mundane."

"Oh? I really don't know very much about things here." Kim had thought she knew a lot, but she had made so many mistakes that she realized she was an ignoramus.

He was unfazed. "As you know, I am unmarried. I am twenty-eight years old, and it is past time. But until now I have not had much opportunity to find a suitable woman. Now I think I see that opportunity."

Oh, no! Kim had almost forgotten about that. She loved this adventure, but she knew she couldn't stay, and she knew she couldn't marry anyone here. She didn't want to hurt anyone's feelings. Especially not anyone as handsome and nice as Cyrus.

She looked at Jenny, but it was evident that the elf didn't know what to say either. Kim had once again over-ridden Jenny's cautions about kissing Cyrus and meeting his parents, and thus sent signals she had not properly understood.

How was she going to get out of this?

$$\overline{5}$$

PEWTER

Dug was glad to be on the way again, with a knapsack of supplies and some weapons. That business with the censor-ship had seemed like a joke, but had turned deadly serious. Maybe that was because it was all too easy to joke about serious things, avoiding really coming to terms with them. He had never much liked censorship, mainly because it always seemed to cut out the fun parts of anything he wanted to read or watch. But he hadn't taken it seriously. Until he had seen Nada Naga struggling across the deck of the ship, trying to do the job that he, Dug, had undertaken to do. That just wasn't right. Suddenly he had come to believe in the importance of the mission, and with that belief, it seemed, had come acceptance of the larger situation. The realization that some genuine values underlay all the funny fantasy stuff he was seeing. Maybe he didn't really believe in magic, but he did believe in those values, and was willing to sacrifice in order to support them. Maybe most people went through life without ever discovering such values, maybe even poking fun at them, but those were empty people who didn't count.

Of course he also happened to be with a beautiful woman, and wanted to impress her. That had to figure in. She had let him know early on that she was not about to go on a date with a mere Player, but maybe if he did something really worthy she would change her mind. So he had had that other reason to get into it. She might be a mere fantasy character in her fantasy setting, able to do a type of magic nobody in his right mind would believe, but she was the loveliest creature he ever expected to see. Even if he never got to first base with her—in fact, even if he never came up to bat with her—he wanted her faint favor. He wanted her to remember him as more than a teenage jerk from Mundania. That potential memory had become very important to him.

They were walking east, proceeding along the isthmus toward central Xanth. Because this was a game, there was bound to be another challenge soon. Things never just carried along smoothly, in games. That was why he had wanted supplies and weapons, though Nada had claimed that they were unnecessary. She had said that there were many things to eat along the way, and that it was her job to protect him from harm, so he would not have to defend himself. But he didn't want to depend on the largess of the land for food; a good game would see that they wound up hungry at some point. And he certainly didn't want to depend for protection on the woman he wanted to impress. So maybe she thought he was being foolish, but he was playing it smart. He hoped.

Actually he sort of hoped for a bit of trouble to come, because he wanted an excuse to try out his new weapon. It was a magic sword the grateful Isthmus Village headman had given him. It was supposed to be infinitely light for the user, and infinitely heavy for the opponent. What that meant was that he would never get tired swinging it, but if he used it to fend off an opponent's blow, it would be as solid as a boulder. So nobody would brush his sword aside to get at him. He was no expert swordsman, but this should give him a great head start in using his weapon. If only he could find a pretext to try it out.

They came to a river. It wasn't broad or savage, but it was big enough so that it was clear that they could neither jump over it nor wade through it. The path went up to the bank, and resumed on the far side.

"Maybe there's a boat," Dug said, looking along the bank.

"I fear not," Nada said.

"Why, are there alligators in the water, so we can't swim?"

"I see no allegations. But I think there is normally a bridge, that must have been removed before we arrived."

"To make the river a challenge to cross," he said. "Well, it doesn't seem like much of one. If it is safe to swim, we can do that."

"I am not sure we can. You see, this is my liability."

He glanced at her. "If you have any liabilities, I sure can't see them."

"I have princessly limitations."

Oh, yes; there had been a mention of that. "Like what?"

"I may not show my human body to a man who is not my husband."

"Oh, you can't go naked? Because you're a princess?"

"Yes. An ordinary woman could do so if she chose, provided that the one who saw her was not underage. You are not quite underage, though there are those who would argue the case. But as a princess, I must set a perfect example of propriety. So human nudity is impossible for me in this instance, and allowing a man to see my, uh, undergarments would be worse."

"Worse? You mean that bra and panties are worse than—"

She blushed. "Please don't use such terms in mixed company. They are integral to the Adult Conspiracy."

Dug sighed inwardly. He had sort of hoped to get a look at her body, coincidentally. Pretending not to notice. But the game makers had scotched that. "What about using your snake form? That doesn't count as naked, does it?"

"No. Serpents have no concerns about nudity. Neither my full serpent form not my natural naga form presents any problem. But if you wish me to accompany you in my human form, there is a difficulty."

He did prefer her in human form. She might be the world's most beautiful serpent, but he was no judge of serpent beauty. He had more of a notion of human beauty, and she had that in overflowing measure. "Okay—suppose you cross in serpent form, and then change back to clothed human form when you're dry?"

"I must resume human form in order to don my clothes. I can leave them behind when I change to serpent form, but I can not don them in serpent form."

So she had to be a naked woman before she could be a clothed woman. It figured. "So I'll turn my back while you change. Will that do it?"

"It may. But I fear trouble, and I must try to protect you from it."

"You mean something will maybe attack us when my eyes are closed? But your eyes will be open, won't they? So we won't be unprotected."

She looked doubtful, but nodded.

"Then let's do it," he said briskly. "This hazard is a lot easier to handle than a dragon."

She still looked dubious, but did not argue.

"But it's okay for you to see me?" he asked. "No impropriety there?"

"If you do not object," she agreed.

Actually he would not ordinarily care to have a woman see him naked. But this was different in several ways. First, it was only a game, so wasn't really happening. Second, if he couldn't see her body, maybe he could get a little bit of the feeling by letting her see his body. This gave him just a flicker of comprehension how a flasher might feel. Third, he wanted to show that nakedness was no big thing, in the faint hope that eventually she might agree.

But mainly, he wanted to get across that river, and he didn't want to get his clothes or supplies wet. So he just had to do what had to be done.

He went ahead and stripped, not letting himself think about it too much. It was a funny thing, disrobing in a game that seemed so real. But sort of exhilarating, too. It made him feel free, as if civilized hang-ups were being dumped along with the clothing. Could this be the way nudists felt? He was getting an education in feelings from the oddest situations!

Naked, he didn't look at Nada. In fact, he didn't face her, either. He just jammed his things into the top of his knapsack and closed it tight. Then he waded into the water, holding the knapsack up. When he was deep enough to swim, he went into modified sidestroke, so he could keep the knapsack clear of the water. It was easy enough, and he hoped Nada was impressed.

Soon he was across, as it really wasn't very far. He found his footing and walked on out. He set down the knapsack and shook himself dry, still facing away from the princess. "Okay, you come on across," he said. "I won't look."

"No, you must watch," she said. "Because there could be some other danger, such as a harpy, attacking while I am defenseless. I watched you, and you must watch me."

"Okay," he said, surprised. He got into his underpants and turned. His body was not yet dry enough for the rest of his clothing.

Nada was in her naga form: a serpent with her human head. Her clothing was neatly bundled. She must have done it while in her human form, then changed before he turned. But how was she going to carry her bundle?

Then she assumed full serpent form. The snake's mouth opened wide and bit down on the bundle. The serpent slithered smoothly into the water. She was carrying her bundle as readily as he had carried his.

But now he understood her point: if something attacked her right now, she would be unable to fight back, because her jaws were taken by the clothing. If she dropped the clothing to fight, then she would be unable to dress when she resumed human form later. It would be quite awkward. So he had to protect her, in this moment of her vulnerability. That made him feel obscurely good.

Fortunately nothing attacked. The serpent completed the crossing, dropped the bundle, and became the naga. "Finish dressing," the human head said.

Dug hastily did so. Then he turned to face away, so that Nada could change: first to human form, then to human clothing. He picked up the knapsack, to close it up again and put it on. Then he noticed the shiny buckle on it.

Shiny buckle. Reflective. If he held it up, just so, could he possibly manage to see—?

He fought with himself. Could it be so bad to catch just a distorted glimpse, if she didn't know? How could a creature invented as a game character know or care? Especially when she thought the real crime was showing panties? It wasn't her panties he wanted to see!

He lifted the knapsack, angling it so that the buckle turned. The reflection showed the tops of trees, then the river, then—

Suddenly the screen was blank. Dug was back in his room, staring at a dead computer screen. A system malfunction? No way! He had done it! He had broken a rule, and the game had kicked him out. Bleep!

He looked around. Everything seemed so infernally *mundane*! Not like the pretty colors and magical contours of the game. He had never realized before exactly how dreary ordinary life was.

Why had he done it? He had known he wasn't allowed to look at the body of the princess. He hadn't known that the game had this way of enforcing its rules, but that didn't matter. The point was that he had tried to do wrong, and had been punished for it.

"Oh, Nada Naga, I'm sorry," he breathed, experiencing cutting remorse.

Then he seemed to hear something. He cupped an ear,

listening. He didn't hear anything, but faint words appeared in the screen: DUG! DUG! WHERE ARE YOU?

It was Nada's speech! Very faint, but definite. The lockout wasn't complete!

"I'm out in Mundania!" he answered. Then, remembering, he typed it on the keyboard.

There was a pause. Was he getting through? The screen remained dark, except for the faint glow where a speech balloon might be.

DUG! IS THAT YOU? I CAN'T SEE YOU.

"My screen went blank," he said as he typed it.

WHAT HAPPENED?

There was no point in trying to conceal it. "I tried to see you," he typed. "In the buckle on the knapsack. I'm really sorry, and I apologize. I deserved my punishment."

The screen brightened. Now he could see Nada, clothed, standing beside the river. Near her was his fallen knapsack.

She turned to face the screen. "But did you actually see me?" her speech balloon asked.

"No. But it didn't matter. I tried, after I promised not to. I'm disgusted with myself."

"If you didn't see me, then I have not been compromised," she said. "I can still be your Companion."

"Except that I'm out of the game," he typed. "I'll have to start over." Somehow that seemed dreadful.

"No! It is just a warning. You can return, to this scene, if you are careful."

Dug was abruptly excited. "I can! Great! I'll be really careful!"

He refocused his eyes, and in a moment the scene became three-dimensional. But the screen remained; he was seeing the scene, without being *in* it.

Nada peered through the screen at him. "What is the matter?"

"I'm seeing it, but I can't seem to get back into the scene," he said. "Maybe that's my remaining punishment for—"

"No, your belief must have been damaged," she said. "Can you get it back?"

How could he patch up a damaged belief? The game had punished him doubly: first by kicking him out, and second by reminding him that he was just a figure behind a screen, unable ever to be really part of the scene. He was never going to go against a game rule again! He had gotten into the scene the first time by suffering a realization that there was something of importance underneath the punny façade. He had come at it obliquely, not quite believing in magic, but believing in *something*. So what did he believe in this time?

Dug closed his eyes, searching within himself. What was the nature of his belief?

Suddenly he knew what it was: he believed in the game. Because it had had the power to boot him out when he tried to cheat. It was a real world, there beyond the screen. The computer was merely his limited access to it. Maybe his being in the scene was an illusion, but it was a real scene he seemed to be in. He might have doubted before, but now he believed.

"Oh, Dug—you're back!" Nada exclaimed, hugging him.

Hugging him? He opened his eyes.

Immediately she drew back. "Oh, I have done something unprincessly!" she cried, appalled.

"I'll never tell," he said gallantly. But he would never forget, either; that was the best hug he had ever felt, and maybe the best he ever would feel.

"Oh thank you! For a moment I feared I had disqualified myself."

"No, I was the one who almost did that." Dug looked around. All of it was there. He was definitely back in the scene. He intended to do his utmost to remain in it. Because, fantasy or reality, this was the greatest experience of his life.

They were across the river, which had in its fashion proven to be a much greater challenge than it had seemed.

Nada looked around. "I see a pie tree," she said. "I feel like doing something wicked, after that scare, such as eating something fattening."

"I can hardly imagine you being fat," Dug said, trying not to look too closely at her body.

"Well, it certainly wouldn't be princessly. But I don't splurge often." She walked to the tree and plucked a rich lemon meringue pie. "Would you like some, Dug?" she inquired prettily.

Could he eat here? There was one way to find out. "Yes. Thank you."

She drew a knife from somewhere in her clothing and cut across the pie. Dug was startled; there had seemed to be no place in her costume to conceal such a knife. But of course she was a magical creature; she might have a magic pocket. The rules were different here, as he had just been so forcefully reminded.

She handed him a slice of pie. He took it and tried a bite. It was delicious. It probably wouldn't have been, if he hadn't believed, but that was no problem now.

"I should explain that Companions represent another kind of challenge," Nada said as they ate. "We may be approached, but only in appropriate manner."

"Oh, I've learned my lesson!" he reassured her hastily.

"Yes. You were penitent and you apologized. Therefore you were allowed to re-enter the game. You could not have hugged me, but I was able to hug you. Because you had moved me to do so, even if it was unprincessly."

"It was one great hug."

"Were I other than a princess, it would be easier for you to relate to me."

Dug realized that she was telling him something significant. Not outright, but obliquely. That if he wanted, for example, to kiss her, he might be able to do so, if he impressed her enough to make her kiss him. So the proscriptions weren't absolute; he just had to learn to play the game right. It was good to know.

They finished the pie in short order. Then they resumed their walk.

After a time, a flying dragon spotted them. It veered toward them, blowing out anticipatory puffs of smoke.

Dug drew his sword, but Nada stopped him. "A sword won't work against a firebreather," she pointed out. "It would toast you before you could use your weapon."

Dug had to agree. "I guess we'd better hide behind a tree, then."

"No, I will simply scare it away." Suddenly she was a small snake, slithering out of her fallen clothing.

That was supposed to scare a dragon?

But once she was free of the clothing, she changed into a large serpent. In fact, it was huge. Three times the size of the dragon. Then she lifted up her giant head, opened her enormous mouth to show a terrible array of fangs, and sent a ferocious hiss at the dragon.

The dragon didn't argue. It made a U-turn in air and fled.

The serpent slithered back to Nada's clothes. Dug didn't need to be asked; as he had said, he had learned his lesson. He also had a glimmer how she could stop him from kissing her: by biting his head off. He turned and put his face to the trunk of the nearest tree, and closed his eyes. He waited until Nada told him it was all right to look.

When he did look, she was back in her normal, lovely human form. "You are impressive," he said. He was not referring to her human form.

"Thank you." She knew what he meant.

They resumed their trek. Dug was happy; not only had he returned to the game, he was now experiencing its full adventure. What more could he ask?

The day was declining. "We shall have to make camp for the night soon," Nada said. "Because I am not competent to protect you well against the predators of the night."

"Night? Already? It seems like only an hour!"

She shook her head. "Perhaps time is different in Mundania. It may be that only an hour has passed there.

But here much of a day has passed. I suppose if you prefer to leave the game, and return in the morning—"

"Nuh-*uh*! I don't want to get out of the game at all, if I can help it. I might not manage to get back in."

She considered that seriously. "I think you should be able to return, if you obey the rules and maintain your belief. Certainly you should be safer there."

"But shouldn't I be exposed to the danger, instead of copping out? I mean, is that fair play?"

"I don't know. I think that is your option. I understand that it is possible for a Player to depart, and to return to the game another day without any time having elapsed in the game. This is marvelous magic I do not understand, but surely convenient for you."

Dug recognized her description of a saved game; of course it wouldn't change when not being played. "Well, I didn't think I would like this game, when I heard about it. But I do. I want to play it right. That means day and night. If I win, I win; if I lose, I lose."

"You do not object to sharing a tent with me?"

Dug managed to keep his face sober. "I do not object. I will keep my eyes away, if you just tell me when."

She smiled, and he realized that he had scored another minor point. "Then we must seek a suitable campsite."

Soon they found one. It was marked CAMPSITE—ENCHANTED. It looked very nice.

"But just what exactly does it mean, enchanted?" he asked.

"It means that bad creatures can not attack here. So we may sleep without fear."

"But I thought we couldn't use the enchanted paths."

"This is not a path. It is a safe area. Players are allowed to use these."

"That's a relief." Because Dug had learned to take the fantasy threats seriously. He knew that if he got chomped by something that went bump in the night, or bumped by something with teeth, he would be out of the game. He

could appreciate how dangerous it could be to sleep unprotected.

There was a big fabric plant growing nearby. They
harvested some blankets and canvas, and soon had used
available ironwood poles to fashion a framework. There
was a box of magic tent pegs that gripped the edges of the
fabric and held them firm. Nada knew what she was doing
a good deal better than he did, so he followed her lead.
The resulting tent did not look professional, but neither did
it look incompetent. They spread pillows from pillow
bushes on the ground, and the blankets over them.

Then they harvested potluck pies from the pie trees, and
some milkweed pods. Dug was getting used to the way
puns became real here; this was just the way it was, in
Xanth.

There was a pleasant stream crossing a corner of the
protected site. Nada went there to wash. "Please do not
look," she said politely.

Dug went to the tent, lay down, put his head in the pillow, and closed his eyes tightly. He had always been a
quick study, and the game had taught him well. Absolutely
no peeking!

Soon she came to the tent. "Your turn," she said.

He got up and went to the river. He was not surprised
to find it cool and pleasant on his skin; he had been reminded that this was a game, from which he could be ex-
cluded, but also that while he was in the game, it was
increasingly real. So he no longer questioned that reality;
he reveled in it. Whatever the rules of this fantasy land
were, he would follow them literally, from now on.

Nada was sitting up on her pillow-bed when he returned. She was in a stunning nightdress which actually
was far more discreet than it seemed, showing no extra
flesh. "Dug, I must ask you something," she said hesitantly.

"All the rules!" he exclaimed. "I'm not breaking any
one of them!"

She smiled. "Of course. My concern is this: I normally

sleep in my natural form, but if you would prefer that I re-
tain human form, I will. I understand that some people are
uncomfortable in the presence of reptiles."

He needed no thought at all before answering. "Make
yourself comfortable, Nada. I know who and what you are,
I've seen you change to snake form, and if I wake and find
a serpent beside me, I'll understand." Because much as he
liked her human form, he now knew that it was completely
off bounds, and he didn't even want to be tempted. Only
if he behaved himself absolutely could he ever hope to be
allowed *not* to behave himself. So he was going to do all
he could to keep her happy. She might be his Companion,
but he was going to be a perfect escort for her, too.

"Thank you, Dug." Her face did not change, but her
body melted into serpent form, the nightdress sagging
around it. She slithered out of the apparel, formed a loose
coil, and laid her human head on the pillow.

There would have been a time, Dug reflected, when
such a sight would have amazed him. But that was history,
as of a few hours ago. He changed into the pajamas she
had laid out for him and lay down on his own bed.

Sleep was magically swift and restful. Dug could not be
sure whether he slept eight hours, or one, or one second.
Because this was a game, it could be just a fade-out,
fade-in leading to the next scene. But it seemed like slum-
ber.

Next day they came to a sign: SHORTCUT TO SUC-
CESS. There was an arrow pointing down a side path.

"Does this make sense?" Dug inquired.

"I have not been told about this," Nada said, frowning.
"I don't believe that such a sign is normally here. That
suggests that it has been set up for the game."

"Does that mean we have to go that route?"

"By no means! A challenge set up for the game is as
likely to be troublesome as rewarding. It may be safer to
avoid it and make our own way south."

Dug considered. "About how much farther is the Good Magician's castle?"

"Several days, at our present pace. We shall also have to cross the Gap Chasm, which is formidable."

"And the shortcut might take us there sooner?"

"A magical route could take us there in one moment," she said. "Two moments at the most. But it could also lead us into mischief. I suspect it is a gamble which can either help us greatly, or complicate things greatly, depending on how we manage to handle it."

"What do you recommend?"

Now she considered a good half-moment. "Do you like traveling with me?"

Dug forced himself to be subdued. "Yes."

"You would not mind taking several extra days?"

"I would not." He would not mind taking several extra years, with her, even if he never got to look at her body.

"Then I recommend avoiding this shortcut, because I can convey you to the Good Magician by the slow route, while I am not sure what will happen on the shortcut."

But Dug was becoming canny about his real objectives. "Which do *you* prefer, Nada?"

She was surprised. "My preference does not count. You are the Player. I am here to be your Companion, to help you accomplish your desire in the game."

Except if his desire was to grab her and kiss her. Failing that, his desire was to please her. He didn't care about winning the game; he just wanted to stay a while longer in this magical land, and be with her, and make her smile on occasion.

"I would love to be with you extra time," he said carefully. "But I realize that for you this is just a job, and I don't want to make it more burdensome than it has to be. I can go either the safe slow route or the mysterious adventure route. Which would you prefer it to be?"

"I have to confess that I am femininely curious about that shortcut," she confessed femininely. "But I seriously question whether it is wise, so—"

"I'm curious too," he said. One thing this game had done: it had made him figure out his true desire. Pleasing her was more important than being with her for a longer time. "So shortcut it is. The foolish Mundane has made another foolish decision."

She shot him an appreciative glance that made it all worthwhile, regardless of the outcome. "Perhaps not entirely foolish," she murmured.

They followed the shortcut. It led to a marshy glade with odd-shaped depressions near a sharply rising mountain. Nada looked uneasy, but didn't comment.

Dug sniffed the air. "What is that smell? Did a whale die here after eating a mountain of cabbage?"

Nada sniffed. "Oh, I don't like this!"

"Neither do I. If that's the Good Magician's castle ahead, he needs to catch up on a century's worth of baths."

"I fear it is an invisible giant," Nada said faintly.

"Oh, is he going to step on us? Then we'd better get onto the shadow of that mountain."

"Worse. Because—"

The ground shook. The very trees seemed to jump. In fact, some *did* jump, as if kicked by an invisible foot. Then a swatch of nearby forest was abruptly flattened, as if the foot had landed on it. The smell intensified.

Dug stared. "That invisible giant—you weren't joking?"

"A princess seldom jokes."

Another swatch of forest flattened. "It's coming toward us!" Dug cried. "Run for the mountain!"

"I fear we have no choice," she agreed, running with him. Even distracted as he was by the overpowering stench and the threat of being stepped on, Dug couldn't help but notice how she looked when she ran. He wished he could watch that when not distracted. But he would never tell her that, of course. It wouldn't be Mundanely.

They reached the mountain. There was a cave opening, leading into a dimly lighted tunnel.

Another invisible foot landed, squishing more forest. It

was alarmingly close. "We'd better hide in there!" Dug said.

"Not if we can help it," Nada said.

He hesitated. "Why not? It can't be worse than here."

"Oh, it can," she said. "I fear this is Pewter's cave. It shouldn't be here; it's south of the Gap Chasm. But the shortcut must have conveyed us there."

"A pewter cave? You mean it is used to store metal carvings?"

"No. It—"

Another invisible footprint was forming. This one was right before them, and the ground was rapidly indenting toward them, as if a huge boot had landed heel-first and the sole and toe were coming down. The smell had become an intolerable stink.

They launched themselves into the cave, where the boot couldn't reach. Just in time, for the whole region shook, and dust stirred everywhere except where the footprint was.

"Oh, nuisance!" Nada swore. "We have been driven into Pewter's lair. The shortcut is a Pewter Plot."

"What's so bad about pewter? It's just tin and lead, an alloy they use to make pretty figurines and things."

"This is Com Pewter, Xanth's evilest machine," she explained. "He was turned into a nice machine recently, but for the purpose of the game he is defined as he used to be. He changes reality in his vicinity, so as to have everything his way. Now we're really in trouble, and it's all my fault, because I told you to try the shortcut."

Com Pewter. Another stupid pun. "No, I told you we would try it. Obviously this is a special game challenge. So I'll just handle it and go on, no sweat."

"You can't just handle Pewter!" she protested. "He handles you."

"Well, we'll see about that." Dug marched on into the cave, having concluded that foolish boldness would impress her more than ineffective caution.

They came into a larger cave, where there was a collection of junk. A screen stood up in the center of that pile. WELCOME, MUNDANE PLAYER, it printed.

So this was the dread machine! But Dug had learned not to dismiss magic things contemptuously; they could indeed fight back, here in this Land of Xanth. "Hello, Com Pewter. What can I do for you?"

YOU CAN SERVE ME FOREVER, the magic screen responded.

"Apart from that."

YOU CAN FORFEIT YOUR GAME.

"No choices in between?"

NONE.

"Well, I don't care for those options," Dug said firmly. "So I'll just be departing now. It's been nice meeting you."

MUNDANE PLAYER CHANGES HIS MIND.

Oops. "Then again, maybe I'll stay and chat with you awhile," Dug said, discovering that his mind had indeed been changed. He was beginning to understand what Nada had meant about the evil machine changing reality. This could be worse trouble than he had figured on.

"Now wait, you evil machine," Nada protested. "You aren't allowed to give him a no-win either-or! You have to give him a chance to beat you."

WHO SAYS? the screen demanded irritably.

"The Demon Professor Grossclout," she retorted. "He set up the rules for the game, and if you don't obey—"

PRINCESS COMPANION CHOKES AND IS UN-ABLE TO COMPLETE HER SENTENCE, the screen printed.

Nada choked and coughed, not finishing her sentence.

But this was enough to give Dug the hint. "So it's this Demon Big Cloth who runs the game, not you! And he says you have to give me a fair chance. Which means you have to give my Companion a chance to advise me. Otherwise—"

OTHERWISE WHAT, IGNORANT MUNDANE?

Dug did not like being called ignorant, but since that accurately described him in this situation, he let it pass. He made a flying guess. "Otherwise you forfeit, screen-for-brains, and I win. Now let Nada go."

GIRL COMPLETES HER IRRELEVANT REMARK, the screen printed grudgingly.

"Grossclout will make mush of your crockery brain," Nada finished.

I WOULD LIKE TO SEE HIM TRY.

Nada rose to the challenge. "If I snap my fingers, he will appear," she said. "Because that's my signal for game interference." She held up her hand, fingers cocked.

DAMSEL'S HAND GOES NUMB.

Nada's fingers sagged. She could not snap them.

"But I can snap mine," Dug said. "Want to bet he won't respond to somebody's finger snap from this area?"

IGNORANT MUNDANE'S HAND GOES NUMB.

Dug lost sensation in his hand. This computer was sharp!

But now Nada was free. "My hand has recovered," she said. "You can't control both of us at the same time. So now *I'll* snap."

NO NEED, the screen printed quickly. IT WAS ONLY A JOKE. HAVE YOU NO HUMOR? THE MUNDANE WILL BE GIVEN AN EVEN CHANCE.

Dug had seen that kind before: bullies who claimed it was only a joke, when they had to back off. He had never liked that kind. At least they had backed the ornery machine off a bit. "So I'll have an even chance," he said, getting it officially stated, because it was apparent that statements had the force of reality here.

I SHALL GIVE YOU THREE TASKS TO PERFORM, AND—

"Nuh-*uh*!" Dug interrupted. "I'll define the rules." Again, he hoped to prevail by getting his definitive statement in first. He knew that any tasks the evil machine set would be almost impossible to accomplish. "We'll have a pun riddle contest. First one who can't guess the other's riddle loses." Because he was pretty good at riddles.

NUH-*UH*, the screen printed. ONE MUST ANSWER AND THE OTHER FAIL. IF BOTH ANSWER OR BOTH FAIL, THE ROUND IS NULL.

Dug had to admit that was fair. At least he had defined the nature of the contest. "Okay. I'll go first." He paused, but the machine did not object. So he dredged up a punnish not-too-dirty joke he had heard, hoping Nada wouldn't object: "What is spelled with a hymen?"

MAIDEN-HEAD, the screen printed.

Ouch! Pewter had heard the joke! Now he was down one, and if the machine floored him, he'd be lost.

HOW DID THE DEMONS PULL THE KISS-MEE RIVER STRAIGHT?

"What river?" Dug asked blankly.

"He's Mundane," Nada said. "He doesn't know our landmarks. You have to tell him before using them."

THE KISS-MEE RIVER FLOWS SOUTHWARD ALONG EASTERN XANTH, CONNECTING THE KISS-MEE LAKE TO LAKE OGRE-CHOBEE. THE DEMONS PULLED IT STRAIGHT, RUINING IT. BY WHAT MAGIC DID THEY ACCOMPLISH THIS?

Now something clicked. "There was a river somewhere—Florida, I think—the Kissimmee—that the Corps of Engineers channelized. You mean this is a pun on that?"

ANSWER THE QUESTION.

Dug looked at Nada. "It is true," she said. "The demons did do that. You must answer."

In the real world, the demons had simply dug a straight channel and routed the river through it, eliminating the meanders. It had been reckoned an environmental disaster. No magic there, and no puns; it had been one seriously unfunny business. How was he supposed to make a joke of it?

"I guess they used a pushmi-pullyou spell on it," he said without much hope.

ERROR! the screen printed. HEE-HEE!

But he wasn't quite lost yet. "You have to show that

you have a good answer," Dug said. "Because if you don't, it doesn't count."

"That is true," Nada said, relieved.

The evil machine wasn't fazed. THEY PULLED THE S'S STRAIGHT, MAKING THEM L'S. THUS KISS-MEE BECAME KILL-MEE, WITH NO MORE CURVES.

And when the S's went straight, making them small L's, the river became straight too. It did make punnish magical sense. Dug knew he had lost.

"Okay, Pewter, you beat me," he said. "What now?"

YOU ARE IN A DREAM WHICH IS OUR REALITY. YOUR REALITY IS OUR DREAM. RETURN TO IT.

Com Pewter's screen showed a picture: Dug's room, with his messy bed in the background and used socks on the floor. Mundania—suddenly the dreariest possible place.

He looked at Nada. "I'm sorry. I lost. I really wanted to stay with you, but I have to go."

"Yes," she said sadly. "I have failed you."

"No, I failed myself. I didn't make the grade." He was determined to be a good loser; it was all that was left.

He faced the screen. "How do I—?"

STEP THROUGH.

So Dug lifted a foot and put it to the screen, which seemed to grow larger. His foot passed through without resistance and landed on his chair. In a moment he was through, and back in his room.

He turned, and saw Nada on the screen. "But you can play again, Dug," her speech balloon said. "If you ask for me—"

SILENCE! the screen printed. Then it went dark. Dug was definitely out of the game.

$\overline{6}$
HYDROGEN

Cyrus Merman was about to pose his question to Kim. Jenny quailed, fearing that the pleasant evening was about to become extremely awkward. Even without much knowledge of the things hidden by the Adult Conspiracy, she could tell that this was an extremely serious matter. She had failed to protect Kim from this, and so had not been a good Companion.

"Dear, perhaps you should give her the background," the Siren said to her son. "Remember, Kim is not from Xanth, and she may not understand, otherwise."

"Certainly," Cyrus agreed. "If it is not too boring."

Jenny knew that Kim would not be bored by any postponement of the dread question. "We're sure it will be most interesting," she said quickly.

He smiled. "It is nice of you to say that, Jenny Elf. Certainly it interests *us*, but we are natives of this region."

"Oh, we want very much to know," Kim said with all the faint heartiness she seemed able to muster. The irony was that she really did look very nice in the dress the Siren had provided, and had she been a regular denizen of

Xanth, such a union would have been entirely appropriate. So Cyrus was twenty-eight; he was still a handsome, vigorous man, surely nicely experienced, who could be good for a girl of sixteen. There were many such girls in Xanth who would jump at the chance.

"Then we must do it in appropriate style," Morris said. "For this history has become a play, and we like to re-enact it on significant occasions."

Jenny and Kim exchanged another glance of doubt. Significant occasion? But what could they do, except agree, hoping that some diplomatic way would turn up to get out of this misunderstanding?

"We must assume roles," Cyrus said. "For this narrative concerns the Curse Fiends, and their concern is acting. Indeed, it was from one of their traveling troupes that we learned it. Of course we can not hope to do it as well as they do, but it is more fun being in it ourselves."

Kim found a bit of her voice. "A play? I was interested in acting, but—" She broke off, looking troubled.

"Oh, you were?" the Siren asked solicitously. "What happened to prevent it?"

"I—I guess I wasn't right for the part," Kim said reluctantly.

"The part?" Cyrus inquired. "Couldn't you have any part you wished?"

Kim laughed. "Hardly! People have to try out for parts, and only a few get the good ones. I didn't want to be a person lost in a crowd scene, so I tried out for the ingenue. The more fool, I! After that disaster I stayed away from acting."

"Ingenue?" the Siren asked.

"The role of the lovely, quiet, innocent girl."

"But surely that was perfect for you!" Cyrus exclaimed.

"A perfect disaster. I'm a talkative, pushy, unlovely girl."

"Surely this is not so," Morris said. "You have seemed, if anything, somewhat reticent."

Jenny knew why: because of this embarrassing question of marriage. But she didn't dare try to clarify that.

"And you have not seemed at all forward," the Siren said. "You have been, if I may say so, extremely well behaved."

"And you are lovely," Cyrus said. "Even when you were bedraggled, I saw the beauty marks on your face."

"Beauty marks!" Kim exclaimed. "Those are zits!"

Cyrus' brow furrowed. "Do they not serve the same purpose, in Mundania? Just as Jenny Elf's freckles add luster to her face?"

Jenny jumped. She did have freckles, as did Electra, who was now a princess, but she had never been sure they were an enhancement. Now she saw that Kim was trying to suppress a flush. This was evidently an embarrassing subject for her. Perhaps she thought the merfolk were teasing her. Yet if they were not, it was no better, because it meant they believed she was suitable for marriage. Somehow this predicament just got worse as the mer people got nicer.

"It is obvious that Mundanes know little of character or beauty," Morris said. "But as it happens, this is a violent narrative, with no important female players. Would you prefer to assume the role of a prominent male?"

Kim was taken aback. "Oh, I couldn't!"

But Jenny saw a possible avenue of escape here. An unfeminine role might be just the thing to divert the notion of marriage. "You should try it, Kim," she said. "It could help."

Kim looked at her, gradually comprehending. "A pushy male," she said. "Yes, that could be good." Then she glanced at the others. "I mean, a real challenge. To portray someone that—that different."

"That is the heart of acting," Morris said. "To assume a role that is quite different from one's own nature, and do it effectively. This should test your skill."

"Well, I'm really not a good actress. Actor. I never got the chance to be in a play."

"Until now," Morris said. "Here are the roles: Loud-speaker, who is the villain. He is a powerful Magician."

"Well," Kim said dubiously. Jenny could appreciate why. It would be a challenge to play the part of a male, and another to be a villain, and another to be a Magician, when she knew so little of the true ways of such folk.

"I shall be happy to be Loudspeaker, this time," Cyrus said. "It is certainly a challenging role, quite unlike my nature."

Morris nodded. "And there is Hydrogen, a beneficial Magician."

"Aren't there any, well, just ordinary parts?" Kim asked plaintively.

"There are some," Morris said. "But I understood that you wished a leading part. This one seems good."

Jenny saw how tempted Kim was, despite her uncertainty. So she gave her a nudge. "Why not try it, Kim? The worst you can do is make an awkward mess of it."

Kim paused, assessing the prospect in the manner Jenny had. If she made an awkward mess, she might become unattractive to the merman, and he would not ask her to marry him. It might be embarrassing, but for the best. So, guided by this nudge, she agreed. "I will be Hydrogen."

"Excellent," Morris said. "Now, Loudspeaker, being evil, has no friends, but Hydrogen, being good, does. One of these is the young woman Bec, who is always on call to help. So if Jenny wishes to be his loyal companion and adviser—"

"Yes!" Jenny exclaimed. "I will be Bec on call."

"And there is an assortment of other men, lesser characters, ranging from lowly to Magicians, with their wives and families. My wife and I will fill those roles, and she will make the background music, so as to generate the realism. With a little bit of cooperation and imagination, we shall see the scenery form."

Jenny wondered how that could be, since the merfolk did not have the magic of illusion. But it didn't matter. She just hoped that the story would divert Cyrus' attention from Kim, so that the play would not be followed by an uncomfortable scene. But she wasn't at all sure this would happen.

"Now, I must explain that in this narration, we do not actually move about," Morris said. "We only speak our parts. It may facilitate the effect if you close your eyes, at first, until the mood takes hold."

Jenny was glad to oblige. She did not fancy herself much of an actor anyway, and this made it easier. Then she realized that she could contribute in another way: by humming. Because it was her magic talent to form a dream when she hummed, that anybody who wasn't paying attention could enter. Maybe she could form a dream of what the merman described, and they could all seem to be in it.

"But where is the script?" Kim asked.

"Script?" Morris seemed perplexed.

"To read our lines from. So we know what to say."

"Oh, nothing like that is needed. I will narrate the background, and each role will speak as appropriate. It is never quite the same twice. This gives it renewed vigor."

"Oh, improvisation," Kim said. "I suppose I can try that." She seemed less than certain, however.

"Now we commence," Morris said. They sat back in their comfortable water chairs and closed their eyes.

The Siren played her dulcimer. It was beautiful, as before, but eerie. Jenny felt a lukewarm shiver ripple through her spine. That music really was magic! It was doing things to her imagination, so that she began to see a landscape. In fact, it was the map of Xanth, as seen by a flying roc, with all its little trees and lakes and the Gap Chasm jaggedly crossing its center.

Jenny hummed faintly, forming her dream from that description. It was easy to do, working along with the Siren's music.

Morris spoke gravely, setting the scene.

In the year 378 following the First Wave of successful human colonization of Xanth, there

came the Seventh Wave. The Human King Roogna
had died almost a century before, in battle with
the invading Sixth Wave, and there had been a
time of distress. But now things were relatively
quiet. The Seventh Wave, unlike some others,
was peaceful. Its members had fled their own
land to escape harassment by more powerful
groups, and did not wish to inflict their ways on
anyone else, or to do harm to either people
or animals. They remained together, rather than
mixing with the human folk already here, and
married among themselves. Consequently the
magic talents of their children were relatively
weak, being mostly what is termed the spot-on-the
wall variety: a person could make a spot of color
appear magically on a wall, but of what real use
was it?

   This lack of significant magic made the Seventh
Wavers feel inferior, which tended to isolate
them even more. They were poorly equipped to
defend themselves against the depredations
of dragons, who liked to tease them by snatching
them up, toasting them with fire, and feeding
smoked pieces to their offspring. Often the more
talented other Wavers were as bad, abducting
them for slaves. They retreated to the deepest
wilderness in the most unexplored region of
Xanth, but there were violent ogres there who
harassed them by twisting them into pretzel
shapes, hurling them into orbit around the
moon, and other nuisances. So they built a
castle under Lake Ogre, around the vortex that
was the gateway to the underworld, and there
they were able to hide—until the demons came
up from below to interfere with them by
molesting their women and twisting their men's
heads around to face backward on their bodies.

*"We have to have more magic!" they concluded
at last. So in the year 400 they set up a research
group to discover the secret of magic talents.
It was an ambitious undertaking. They did not
want to wait another generation for stronger
magic to develop in their offspring; they wanted
actually to learn to manipulate the talents they
already had, to make them more effective
immediately. It was called the Talent Research
Group, headed by the good man Hydrogen, whose
talent was to make dirty water become clean.
This was considered to be the best talent the
Seventh Wave had produced, which was why he
was put in charge. Even so, it was not
phenomenal, because anyone could duplicate
his feat by pouring water through a bag of sand,
and changing the sand every so often.*

Morris paused in the narrative, and there was a silence.
Jenny had found herself seeing the group of people, beset
by dragons, hostile folk, and ogres, finally hiding in the
great Ogre Lake and trying to find magic. Now she realized that this was only the background. It was time for the
players to play.

"Oh, Hydrogen," she said. "How are you going to find
the secret of magic talents?"

Kim realized that it was her turn. "Why, er, we'll just
have to study the matter and see what we can come up
with." Then, realizing that that was inadequate, she added:
"Bec, go call the others together. We'll have a brainstorming session."

"A storm on a brain?"

Kim laughed. "Who knows? That might be good magic!
But what I meant was that we should have a good talk
about it, and see what ideas we can come up with. We
can't do anything if we don't have a good plan of action."

So Bec called the others: "Hey, others! Come together!
Hydrogen wants to storm your brains."

There was a shuffle of feet, and when Jenny closed her eyes again she seemed to see a number of people coming to join them. Soon her dream took better hold, and she saw them clearly. "We are here," one of them said. His voice didn't even sound too much like Morris'.

"I want you all to make suggestions," Hydrogen said. "Any suggestions, no matter how silly they might sound. Because the good idea we need may be the one that seems too silly for anyone else to consider. No negative comments are allowed."

"I have heard it said that there is unity in strength," someone said. "I have noticed that our weak talents are sort of similar. Is it possible that we could get together and reinforce each other's talents, making one big strong talent?"

"It's an idea," Hydrogen agreed.

"But it has never been done before," someone objected. "In Xanth, talents never repeat." Then, receiving the stares of the others: "Oops! That was negative, wasn't it! I take it back."

"Could we change our talents by mimicking others?" another asked. "All orienting on the same talent?"

"That's another idea, in harmony with the first," Hydrogen said.

"How about a talent that will set the ogres back?" another asked. "Like maybe a powerful curse?"

It seemed good to Hydrogen. So they got together and tried to emulate the one who had a faint power of cursing. And it worked. At first all they could do was produce a floating voice saying $$$$! But in time that unified curse became strong enough to wilt nearby foliage.

After a year they took their group curse out into the field for field testing. A brute of an ogre stood in the field. "Me see he flea!" he exclaimed as he advanced on the group, ready to squish the flea with one swat of a hamfist.

"One," Hydrogen said, counting. "Two. Three!"

They all threw their pieces of the curse together, directly

at the ogre. It detonated in front of his face. $$$$! It scorched his eyebrows and burned the fur of his nose.

Temporarily blinded, the ogre stumbled away, swiping at the air. He wasn't retreating, because ogres didn't know how to do that. He was merely advancing in the wrong direction.

"It worked!" Bec cried jubilantly. "The curse foiled the ogre!"

But it wasn't strong enough to foil a group of ogres. So they returned to their laboratory and labored for another year. In that time they developed the curse to such a strength that it could blow an ogre into the next scene. In fact, they were now able to drive the ogres away from Lake Ogre, forcing them to start their long trek across the length of Xanth to the Ogre fen Ogre Fen. The Talent Research Group was a success.

"But it is not enough to handle dragons," Hydrogen said grimly. "We must keep working." So they had another brainstorming session, and looked for something even more potent. They also set to work training the rest of the Seventh Wavers to unify their talents, because though each person's magic was small, the accretive effect was large. They began to call themselves the Curse Friends, but those on the receiving end of the curses preferred to call them the Curse Fiends. That was all right; their neighbors were learning respect, thanks to Hydrogen's Talent Research Group.

In three more years they had their second breakthrough: they discovered how to expand their talents. Now Hydrogen focused on his original ability to clean water, and learned how to tap the basic elemental forces so that he could permanently enhance the properties of any substance. Loudspeaker, a member of the group, was now able to expand his talent of amplifying his voice, and could use it to create Words of Power. Other group members enhanced their own simple talents. In the course of the next several years, eight of them managed to build up their talents enough to enable them to qualify as Magicians. What a change from their former puniness!

But now came unforeseen consequences of power. Each person, having tasted more of it than he had ever believed possible, wanted yet more. Resentments flared. Others wondered openly why Hydrogen should be the leader, when there were now many excellent talents. Hydrogen tried to maintain peace, but people who had been nice and mild and powerless now were grasping and savage. Power had corrupted them in direct proportion to its increase.

Then Loudspeaker did the unspeakable: he used his Words against his own people. He used an especially potent Word to turn the other members of the research group into green chobees, who promptly fled to Lake Ogre, where they were lost. They remembered none of their manlike lives, and wanted only to chomp men. They had very long mouths full of sharp teeth, so it was dangerous to get close enough to try to reason with them. So there was no alternative except to rename the lake Ogre-Chobee and let them be. At least others would be warned of the danger by the name. Actually, there was a bright side: now no strangers could wander across the lake and find Gateway Castle beneath it, because the chobees would chomp any who tried.

Only Hydrogen escaped, because he had been away at the time of the sneak attack. He realized that Loudspeaker had to be stopped before he caused even more trouble. The only one who could stop the evil Magician was Hydrogen, because he was the only other surviving Magician among the Curse Friends. "Loudspeaker, you have done a bad thing," he said grimly. "But I will stop you." It didn't seem like much of an oath, but the people applauded.

Bec went to call other curse-wielding actors. Hydrogen formed them into a new group, whose joint curse could be charged with his own elemental energy. Now they had a weapon capable of destroying Loudspeaker.

The evil Magician meanwhile had gone to a region north of the Gap Chasm in central Xanth. He had set up a palace formed of spliced Words, and used other Words to enslave the resident fairies, harpies, and other creatures of the air so that they had to do his bidding. There was a chain of linked Words around the whole estate, and each Word was barbed. No one could get close without receiving a terrible tongue-lashing. He had what seemed to be an impregnable bastion.

But Hydrogen assembled his team, and they stood on a mountain opposite the palace. Hydrogen stood at the pinnacle and called across to the evil Magician. "Loudspeaker, I demand that you surrender, and practice evil no more. Otherwise we shall blast you out of your fortress."

Their only answer was a barrage of sharp Words. They flew like daggers, and slammed into the wooden shield the heroes hastily erected. For Hydrogen had expected more treachery, and had prepared for it.

"Okay, you asked for it!" Hydrogen cried with noble righteous ire. "One—two—three!"

His loyal group hurled their joint curse, modified to contain plenty of Hydrogen's magic. It was an air attack. It struck the palace and blew it away. It whirled around, searching for Loudspeaker, but he was not there. He had sneaked out during the night, leaving only his sharp Words to guard the palace.

The curse, its target undestroyed, was unfulfilled. It continued to search the area, blowing wildly. Hydrogen had not thought to put dissipation into it, in case of failure. So it just continued to rush around, never relaxing. There was nothing to be done except to let it be. Hydrogen and his band had won the battle but not yet won the war. "Oh, fudge!" Hydrogen swore.

Thus there came to be the Region of Air, where the wind eternally whirled and searched, seeking what wasn't there.

Loudspeaker retreated north and set up another small evil empire, this time using his Words to dominate trolls, goblins, and other denizens of the earth. Battalions of mean creatures marched around the central earthworks, shouting awful insults at any who were foolish enough to come into range. It seemed to be another implacable retreat.

Hydrogen sent Bec to scout out the territory. Bec reported that it was an ugly place, almost as drear as Mundania.

"Mundania!" Hydrogen exclaimed. "What do you have against Mundania?" Then, reconsidering, he said, "Oh. I forgot. Yes, it sounds pretty bad."

So he gathered his force on the ground near the empire, and called again to the enemy. "Loudspeaker, give it up! Or we shall bury you!"

The only answer he received was a barrage of thrown spears, tipped with the sharpest Words yet. These plunked into the hasty shield with expressions that caused the group's ears to burn. Loudspeaker certainly had an evil way with Words!

"Sticks and stones will break my bones, but names will never hurt me!" Hydrogen called. Several of his group were startled; they had never heard that particular expression before, and it did not seem to make a lot of sense here in Xanth where names could be devastating.

Then they launched a massive adapted curse. It looped up across the land, and came down directly on the earthworks. Boom! The earth flew up and out, with rocks spewing across the landscape, and melted rock flowed across the scenery. Some bits of stone coalesced in the air to form tiny glass teardrops which would have seemed highly significant to Mundanes, but were merely fragments here.

But the curse couldn't find its target, because Loudspeaker had again cravenly fled. The curse searched diligently, refusing to quit until it had accomplished its mission. Hydrogen had forgotten to put a dissipation into it, again. There had just been too much on his mind, and that detail slipped through the cracks, as it were.

Thus came to be the Region of Earth, where the ground

continually moved and mountains spewed their intestinal lava out randomly. It was not exactly Xanth's nicest place.

Hydrogen shook his head. "I'm having some trouble getting the hang of this heavy magic," he confessed.

Meanwhile Loudspeaker had moved north again, and used more Words to dominate fire-breathing dragons, salamanders, and other hot creatures. He fashioned a castle of burning Words, and surrounded it with a ring of fiery language. Once more, he seemed to be securely ensconced.

But Hydrogen refused to quit. He brought his group up to the edge of the territory. "Loudspeaker!" he called. "Now, you quit destroying the environment like this, or I'll blast you out!"

His only answer was a fiery Word from a dragon. The tongue of flame licked against the hasty shield and heated it until it melted. The men had to drop it before their fingers got burned.

"So that's the way it is!" Hydrogen said, annoyed. "Well, I'll just fight fire with fire!"

Then his group fired a curse so hot it set the neighboring air on fire and blazed across the sky until it scared into the castle and blasted it to flaming fragments. The very sky caught on fire, and it flickered forever after, called the aurora. A forest on the ground burst into a flame so fierce that it was never possible to put it out.

But once more the target was missing. Loudspeaker, in cravenly anti-hero fashion, had sneaked out, leaving his unfortunate assistants to bear the brunt of the fire curse. The fire looked and looked, burning everything it encountered, but the evil Magician just wasn't there. So why hadn't Hydrogen put a time limit on the curse: "I really thought we had him, this time," he said sheepishly.

In this manner came to exist the Region of Fire, where flames were eternal and only creatures of flame could survive for any length of time. Fireflies and spitfires loved it, but few ordinary people or creatures resided there.

"I guess I'm just not much of a hero," Hydrogen confessed woefully.

Meanwhile Loudspeaker had moved north again, into the veriest heart of Unknown Xanth, thinking no one would find him there. He settled by a nice lake, and compelled the poor fish to serve him, and water nymphs had to disport themselves for his satisfaction. Around his water works a monstrous water dragon curled, ready to chomp anyone who intruded. Water fowl kept sharp eyes out for the approach of any hostile forces. It seemed that no one could bother Loudspeaker here.

But Hydrogen had not learned how to quit. He brought his group to the verge of the lake and sent loyal Bec to investigate. Bec was always on call, and always finished her task before starting another. She swam quietly through the lake and observed its formidable array of defenses. "This will be a very wet undertaking," she reported.

So Hydrogen came up to the lake and called, "Loudspeaker, now you get out of here and become a nice model citizen, or I'll wash you out!"

His only answer was a great splat of bilge water that almost drowned his group. Then the water dragon and water fowl oriented on him and massed for an attack.

"Well, then, it will be a water war," Hydrogen said wetly. His group pumped out a curse so wet that it would have drowned the sun if it had struck that orb. Fortunately the sun had the sense to stay well away from it. The curse went splat on the water works, and washed everything into the lake. It filled the lake to heaping, and then piled up into a mountain whose crest foamed angrily, looking for its target.

But Loudspeaker was gone again. The water searched all over, washing a deep depression into the land, but could not find him. So it made a liquid shrug and settled into flatness, overflowing into the west where it formed the Half-Baked Bog, and into the east where it drained off into the Sane Jaunts River, and it was done. Because—surprise!—this time Hydrogen had remembered to put a time limit on the curse.

Thus came to be the Water Wing, a passive region

where men and creatures could reside and interbreed. It was a rather pleasant place, overall, and soon developed a nice community of merfolk who had consideration for the local environment and always welcomed visitors.

Meanwhile Loudspeaker had set up operations to the north. This was a desolate region where no one cared to go, and the truth was that Loudspeaker wasn't too keen on it either, but he was running out of options. Since Hydrogen had pursued him to all the nice regions, he had to try a nasty one. Maybe then he would be left alone long enough to build up his army and magic and conquer Xanth in style. Because this was his fell ambition: to make all the land slave to his merest whim. Even if his whim wasn't nice. He was collecting a band of whims who would do whatever he wished, and whatever no one else wished. He had even found a cute female whimsy to entertain his off-hours.

Hydrogen was a slow learner, as was shown by the time it took him to learn to put limits on his curses. But in time he did get there. So this time, considering that Loudspeaker always retreated before the solid (or liquid) curse could score, he put Bec on the job of cutting off the escape. In fact, this time she would even make the challenging call. Hydrogen had a secret reason for this.

So Bec went around to the north, then stood at the edge of the ugly place and called out the challenge. "Loudspeaker, quit this funny business and give up your bad magic, or I will curse you into irrelevance!"

Her only answer was a whimsical blob of garbage that went splat against her shield. So Bec called Hydrogen and told him about it, and he swore a medium oath that he would this time blow the enemy into sheer nothingness. He readied his group's worst curse, an awful Nothing bomb.

Loudspeaker, thinking that the charge would be from the north, tried to sneak back south to hide in the nice lake of the Water Wing. But this was where Hydrogen was. Now Hydrogen bombed him. The Nothing curse exploded, forming a tremendous dome of chaos that destroyed everything in its range, then sank down through the ground in a singular fashion, and was never heard from again. In fact, nothing else that entered that singularity ever returned, because Nothing had made its ultimate home here.

Thus came to be the Void, the home of nothing. Around its edge was an event horizon, where normal events stopped and became nothing. Only largely imaginary creatures like the night mares could enter the Void and return.

This time Loudspeaker had not escaped. Even his memory was gone, so that only a few storytellers knew he had ever existed. He was now nothing, and Hydrogen's job was done.

Now Hydrogen considered. He realized that a great deal of damage had been done by this momentous campaign against evil. All of the battles had done damage to central Xanth. He wanted to see that never again would there be havoc wrought by an air attack, earth encounter, fire fight, water war, or void violation. It would be better if the secret of modifying magic talents were lost, so that no other person could make himself into an evil Magician.

As it happened, Hydrogen was now the last of the original Modified Magicians. So he sent the other members of his group back to Gateway Castle, except for Bec on Call, then settled in the Water Wing, and devoted the rest of his life to developing the talent of keeping a secret. Finally he perfected it, and invoked it, and forever after no one in Xanth was able to rediscover the secret of modifying talents. Hydrogen's last great enchantment had made it impossible.

Hydrogen married Bec, of course, and their descendants became the merfolk of the Water Wing. They had to marry humans and fish in alternate generations, to maintain their status as mer people. The Curse Friends remained a close-knit group with weak individual talents, all of them related to cursing, and became great actors. The villages around Lake Ogre-Chobee were always glad when one of their troupes arrived, because their plays were always superb.

Thus it was a regular circuit of the lake. In time no one remembered that the Talent Research Group had even existed, or that for fifteen years there had been havoc in central Xanth while things were being put to rights. For more than two and a half centuries Xanth was reasonably quiet, until the onset of the Eighth Wave.

"But that is another story," Morris concluded.

Jenny opened her eyes. The ancient scenery of Xanth faded away with its heroic deeds and misdeeds. She was back in the present, with the nice mer family. She was no longer Bec on Call, but Jenny Elf. However, she now knew a good deal more about Xanth than she had.

"Now we know the background," Cyrus said. "It was a stroke of fortune for my father when the Siren arrived here, because then he could marry her instead of a fish. Now I would like to do something similar."

Jenny saw Kim freeze. As Hydrogen, Kim had become a reasonably bold if error-prone hero. Now she was just a girl who remained error-prone, or perhaps error-supine. What was she going to do?

"Which brings me to my question for you, Kim," Cyrus said. "This is something which perhaps only you can do for me, but which is supremely important to me. It concerns my marriage."

"I—I—" Kim managed to say, before her voice freaked out and fled. Jenny's voice had already done so. Morris and the Siren looked on benignly.

"Therefore I must ask you, Kim," Cyrus continued grandly, "whether you will allow me to travel with you until I find a suitable mermaid elsewhere in Xanth to marry? For you see I am not used to traveling beyond the Water Wing, and fear I would encounter mischief if I did so alone. You are the first human traveler to pass this way in some time. As my father says, you seem to be the right young woman for this purpose, because you are not of Xanth and so there is no impropriety in our keeping company for a time. We merfolk are highly conscious of the proprieties, perhaps because we derive from the playacting

Curse Friends. With a man there would have been no problem, of course, but it may be a long time before a traveling man passes this way."

Kim looked as if about to faint with relief, perhaps tinged with a dab of disappointment. Jenny emulated Bec on Call and stepped into the breach. She found her voice, where it had been cowering under her chair. "Kim will be happy to have you travel with us," she said. "Until you find a suitable mermaid to marry."

Kim scrambled to find her own voice, but it was just out of reach. So she nodded her head vigorously, smiling. There were tears in her eyes.

"Excellent!" Cyrus said heartily. "This is a great relief to me."

At last Kim recovered her voice. "Me too!" she squeaked.

"We are so glad this has worked out," the Siren said. "Now you must rest here for the night, so as to be fresh for the morrow."

Kim and Jenny were glad to agree.

7

BLACK WAVE

Nada glared at Com Pewter. "Aren't you proud of yourself," she said severely. "You tricked my Player into coming here with that shortcut, and herded him into your cave, and used your superior knowledge of Xanth to defeat him in the riddle contest, so now he's out."

EXACTLY, the screen printed smugly.

"Thereby making me a failure as a Companion. I hope you're satisfied."

I AM.

"Oh, you're impossible!"

I AM AN EVIL MACHINE. HO HO HO!

"I liked you better when you were a nice machine."

I WAS NICE ONLY BECAUSE LACUNA TRICKED ME INTO RECOMPILING. NOW IN THE GAME I GET TO BE EVIL AGAIN. BUT YOU ARE WELCOME TO ASSUME YOUR LUSCIOUS SERPENTINE FORM AND CURL AROUND MY HARDWARE ANYTIME, NAGA CREATURE.

"Well, Dug will come back into the game, despite you, you crock of capacitors."

THEN HE WILL HAVE TO MEET ME AGAIN AND DEFEAT ME IN A HARDER GAME THAN BEFORE. I WILL HAVE THE SINISTER PLEASURE OF DUMPING HIM AGAIN. SO YOU HAD BETTER SHOW HIM YOUR PANTIES WHILE YOU HAVE THE CHANCE, PRINCESS.

"You unspeakable cad!" she cried, outraged.

YOU'RE LOVELY WHEN ANGRY.

Nada snapped her fingers. Professor Grossclout appeared. He was an imposing old demon, complete with fangs and tail. "This annoying machine is insulting me!" she said.

Grossclout frowned. This made his natural grimace even more formidable. "You come to this position with a head full of mush, and you complain because your charge washed out?"

Nada suffered an instant of absolute unholy fury. Then she realized that the Professor was baiting her, as he did with those he hoped might someday improve. It was actually almost a compliment. "I hope to do better next time," she said bravely.

A peculiar expression fought to cross the demon's face, but lost. Nada realized that it was a smile, which would have been in alien territory had it emerged. "Maybe, just maybe, *if* you succeed, you will become a creature worth knowing," he grudged. Then, to Pewter: "Carry on, evil machine."

THANK YOU, Pewter replied, obviously thrilled with the compliment.

Grossclout twitched a little finger negligently. Suddenly Nada was back in the Companions dugout, with Grundy Golem, the Demoness Metria, Goody Goblin, Horace Centaur, Marrow Bones, and a new one, Vida Vila.

"What happened to Jenny Elf?" Nada asked.

"She was chosen to be Kim Mundane's Companion," Grundy said.

"Oh. So Vida came in to replace her in the roster."

"No. Vida replaced *you*."

"But I'm still here," Nada protested, confused.

Vida laughed. "I replaced you, then Jenny was taken, now you have returned, so maybe now I'm replacing Jenny. Do you mind?"

Nada had to laugh too. "No, of course not. I was just surprised by the change. I shouldn't have been."

"How was it?" Goody asked politely.

"It was awkward, at first, because Dug was trying to express crude male interest in me."

Vida smiled. "It comes with the territory," she said, inhaling. She was of course one of Xanth's loveliest creatures. Nada realized that had she been in the lineup, Dug well might have chosen her instead of Nada.

NOW HEAR THIS, Professor Grossclout's voice blared. IT IS TIME FOR THE SELECTION OF THE FALSE COMPANION.

Oh, that. She had forgotten. She sat up straight, so as not to betray any reaction, along with the others.

THE SELECTION IS—NOW.

YOU.

Nada was too petrified to jump. The lot had fallen on her! She was now the False Companion. Oh, disaster.

But she had to play it out, because part of her role was to conceal it from others. That way no other participant in the game could tell her Player to beware of her. She had to keep it secret, acting exactly like a Fair Companion—until she found the perfect chance to send him into ignominious loss.

She gazed around, pretending not to know who it was, and saw the others doing the same. Except with them it was not pretense. Then she shrugged, as if realizing she would never know. The others did the same, looking relieved. So she made herself look relieved too. Oh, how she hated this! A role of ultimate deception—it just wasn't princessly.

"Look out—here comes a Player," Metria said, peering out the window, exactly as before. Nada wondered whether she had been the False Companion last time; she would have enjoyed it, being forever mischievous.

They sat straight in their seats, ready for consideration. Nada gazed out the one-way screen.

And froze. It was Dug, of course—re-entering the game. And she knew exactly whom he would choose. Because he knew her, and liked her, and trusted her.

This time she was required to betray his trust. Oh, woe!

Another voice sounded in her head. *You will receive further instructions. You will obey them implicitly, without imposing your own judgment on their merit.*

Yes, she responded unhappily. Could she possibly hide behind one of the others, so that Dug would think she wasn't available this time?

"Hi! I'm Grundy Golem. I'm from—"

"Sure thing, Grundy," Dug said amicably. "Let's cut it short, okay? I'm a retread."

Maybe, just for variety, he would choose one of the others. Such as Vida, who was even lovelier than Nada, because she could change her form to match her mood. Maybe Metria, who would take him exactly as far as her mischievous impulse went, possibly even flashing a naughty glimpse of her panties at him before vanishing in smoke. Maybe even a male, so he wouldn't have any problem crossing the river.

"I'll take Nada," Dug said, as she had really known he would. He had sealed his fate, the innocent fool! He had forgotten that a new game meant a new False Companion, who could even be the last game's Fair Companion.

She stood and stepped through the window. "Hello, Dug," she said, according to the formula. "I will try to be a good Companion for you." It was a lie; she would pretend to be a Fair Companion, awaiting the chance to mess him up worse. The False Companion was not supposed to do any ill early, because she might only betray her nature without washing out her Player, giving him the clue how to handle her. She had to wait until late in the game, when he had his best chance to win—and make him lose instead. So that it would be much more difficult for him to re-enter the game and win. Because the hazards grew more formidable as progress was made, and any hazard that defeated a Player had to be overcome in the next game, when it would be worse. That was to discourage Players from deliberately washing out, so as to get a better layout next time.

"It's great to be back with you," he said gladly. "I've already refocused my eyes, and in a moment I should be all the way back inside the game." Indeed, as he spoke he was becoming more sharply defined, and his screen was fading. He had caught on well, and wanted to believe in the magic, so was doing it.

"I am glad to be your Companion again," she lied. Oh, how she wished he had not chosen her this time! But she was stuck for her revised role. If he asked her whether anything had changed, she would have to lie. If she gave herself away, or tried to wash him out early so as to get out of the False assignment with minimal damage, she would be in trouble herself. Professor Grossclout would know, and disallow it. So she couldn't arrange to accidentally show him her panties or anything like that. Not that she would, of course; it wasn't princessly.

"Well, let's go!" he said happily. "This time I'm going to do things better, and not goof up the way I did before."

Nada concealed her sigh. Little did he know!

They set out along the path. "Now, it's okay to go get supplies and all at the Isthmus Village," Dug said. "That turned out satisfactorily. I mean, we did them some good, right? And we abolished the censor-ship. So I won't avoid that, I'll just do it more efficiently this time."

"But the game layout will be different," she reminded him. "And you will be unable to avoid your nemesis Com Pewter, no matter what you do, because he will remember, just as I do." She was now a False Companion, but she had to play the part of a Fair Companion, and this was exactly what a Fair Companion would say. In fact, she would have to act exactly the same as she would have, until after he got by Pewter, because it was pointless to wash him out when it might occur naturally. Her job was not merely to wash him out, but to wash him out just when he was on the verge of a significant breakthrough or victory. To make it as painful as possible for him. So she had to be the perfect Fair Companion, until that dastardly chance came to be the perfect False one.

"That's okay," he said in his Mundanish idiom. "I want to settle with Pewter anyway. He was just lucky, beating me in that riddle contest. I just didn't know enough about Xanth."

She saw that he was in danger of hurting himself through overconfidence. She should warn him—but the Fair Companion would not have the heart to hurt his feelings, and the False Companion noted that his attitude would make him an easier patsy. So she allowed her silence to be taken as agreement.

The path led to a strange village. Its layout was different, and the houses were dissimilar, and the people—Nada had never seen folk exactly like these. They were just like regular humans, but they were black. Or at least dark brown.

"What's this?" Dug asked, startled as he made a similar observation.

"The layout has changed," Nada said. "I didn't realize that it would be this drastic. This is an entirely different village."

"You said it! Those are blacks."

"You recognize them?"

"Well, not as individuals. But they are—I think the dictionary word is Negroes. People from Africa. We had—I mean, in Mundania there was an ugly—they were brought over as slaves, and then after a war they were freed, but the white folk never did really accept them. It's supposed to be all equal now, no discrimination, but—well, it's like that censor-ship. One of those bad things that exist."

Nada found this confusing. "White people brought black people to their land—and then would not accept them?"

"Not as free people. Not as equals. Not to live next to. There was a whole lot of trouble about integrating the schools, because—" He saw her blank look. "Just take my word: I'm white, and I'm not proud of what my people did. But it's not all that easy to set things right. I mean, once there was this black girl in my math class, and I sort of liked the look of her, she was almost as pretty as you, in her way, and smart too, but I knew if I even said boo to her, I'd lose most of my friends, and her brothers would maybe beat me up. So I just had to ignore her, and I guess she thought I was pretty snotty, but I mean it just wasn't worth the hassle. Probably she thought I was a jerk anyway. So there never was anything there, but I wish—well, I don't know what I wish, but I feel sort of bad about it."

Nada was perplexed and relieved. Perplexed because it was apparent that the social attitudes of Mundanes were stranger than she had known, and relieved because this had nothing to do with her role as a False Companion, and she could just put that aside for now and not think about it. "You wanted to associate with her, but others would not allow it?"

"Yeah, I guess. Her name was Princilla, not Priscilla, and I thought it was a really neat name, you know?"

"Princilla—like Princess," Nada said, appreciating it.

"Yeah. Like you. But whites just don't date blacks, in my town, not if they want to stay healthy. It's even worse if a black man wants to date a white girl. We're all in classes together, and we play ball together, and we ride the bus together, but there's a line—" He shrugged. "But that's there. Now we're here. I'm sure Xanth doesn't put up with that bleep. What do we do?"

"There is no need to visit this village," she reminded him. "We don't need weapons, and food grows on trees. So the only reason to stop here is if there may be something you can learn or acquire that will help you farther along in the game, which is doubtful." This was the truth.

"You know, in other games, you have to go fetch a magic key, or something, before you can get through a locked door to get something else. This isn't that sort of game?"

"I don't think so. I suppose there could be a key, but I don't know where a locked door would be. I really don't know how you can get where you have to go; that's why we need to see the Good Magician."

"Yeah. Well, maybe there is something I can learn here, that will help me. So let's go talk with these people."

"As you wish." It was amazing: so far her status as False Companion had made no difference at all. At the rate Dug was going, he very well might wash himself out despite anything she could do, leaving her clear both with respect to the game and her conscience. It was, ironically, a somewhat endearing quality in him.

"Hi there," Dug called as they approached the nearest man. This was a carpenter, or at least a man doing some sawing of wood. He seemed to be building a house, slowly.

The black man paused, staring at them. He did not speak.

"Look, I mean no harm," Dug said. "Last time I passed this way, there was a whole different village here. I'm amazed how it changed so suddenly. If you don't want to talk to me, okay, I'll just move on. I'm not looking for any trouble. But I sure am curious what happened."

The man turned his gaze on Nada. She smiled, cautiously. There was a subdued glow when she did that, brightening the man's face. That happened, sometimes. He had to smile back. "You got one pretty woman there," he said.

"She's not my woman," Dug said quickly. "She's just my Companion." Evidently realizing that this lacked clarity, he made a more formal introduction. "This is Princess Nada Naga. She's just showing me around the game."

The man nodded. "That must be some game."

"This is Dug Mundane," Nada said. "He has to find his way to a prize, we think. I am a native of Xanth, so I am guiding him. But it is clear that there are some parts of Xanth I don't know very well myself. I never saw folk like you before."

"You're a magic woman?" the man asked.

"Yes. I can show you, if you wish." She wasn't eager to

do this, because then there would be the complication of returning to her human form without allowing her body or underclothing to be seen. But it was her job to help Dug get through the game, for now, and if showing her magic was required, then she would do it.

"Show me," the man said.

So she assumed serpent form and slithered out of her clothes. Then she assumed Naga form. "We are serpent folk," she explained. "This is my natural form."

Other black folk were walking toward them. Nada hoped they were friendly. She did not want to have to assume large serpent form and fight them to protect Dug, but the game required that she do so if necessary.

"You really are magic," the first man said. "Okay, change back, and we'll talk."

Now Dug interceded. "She can't just change back, because then people would see her bare body. She needs a private place."

The man nodded. "Body like that, I can see why." He turned and shouted at the half-built house. "Hey, Mari, someone to see you."

"All right, Jaff," a black woman called from the house.

Dug picked up Nada's clothing, wadded it into a bundle, and proffered it to her. "Go ahead, Nada," he said. "I'll be all right."

She returned to full serpent form, took the bundle in her mouth, and slithered toward the house. She did seem to have broken the ice.

Mari opened the door, and Nada slithered in. Then she set down her bundle, assumed naga form, and explained: "I'm a naga—a serpent woman. I need a private place to resume my human form and get dressed."

The woman hesitated. "This is the only room in the house. We're still building it."

"Oh, it's all right for you to remain," Nada said. "Just so long as there are no men or children."

"My man's outside. No children."

So Nada resumed human form, and quickly got into her clothing.

"You've got some human form!" the woman said.

"Well, I'm supposed to. I'm a princess."

"There are others like you?"

"Yes. We naga folk live mostly in the mountains, underground. We fight goblins when they try to intrude."

"Goblins!"

"No offense intended," Nada said quickly. "Some goblins are nice. I have friends who are goblins. But—"

The woman burst out laughing. "Did I say something funny?" Nada inquired, nettled.

."Goblins raid our stores," Mari said. "We don't like them either. It's just that what you said sounded so much like what we've heard when white folk talk about *us*. About how we're okay, as long as we stay in our place."

Nada was mindful of what Dug had just told her, about the strained relations between the white and black folk of Mundania. "Are you by any chance from Mundania?"

"That's what you call it, yes. We left, because—"

"Because they wouldn't let you be equal, or intermarry."

The woman nodded. "Something like that. But we don't know that it's different here. This is one weird place, but the folk are white."

"Actually there are other colored folk in some places," Nada said. "Green, purple, gray—"

"Maybe we should try to meet them."

"I suppose you could. I don't know where they live now, but there used to be some around Castle Roogna."

Nada was all the way dressed now. They went out. Dug was talking with a group of men. It seemed to be friendly.

Dug saw her. "Hey, I think we can make a deal," he said. "These good folk will give me supplies, if one of them can travel along with us, to see if there's a place in Xanth they will be welcomed. If it's okay with you."

"It is your decision to make," she reminded him. "But perhaps we should learn more of these folk before deciding."

The black men glanced at each other, and glanced at bit longer at Nada. "Sure, let's talk," Jaff agreed.

They walked into the village, where there was a larger, more finished house. They settled on crude wooden chairs. Jaff seemed to be the spokesman, since they had talked with him first. "We're from what you call Mundania," he said. "We crossed only a couple of years ago. We were having a bad time, no good jobs, things were tight, and then somehow we found this path to this magic land and we said, hell, it can't be worse than what we face at home! So we moved here, with our families. But there were some strange things here, like pies growing on trees, and real live dragons, and goblins. So we found a place to camp and sort of hunkered down, and now we're trying to decide whether to settle here or look around some more. We've seen some of the people here, and they're white. We're not sure how they'll be. We don't want trouble, we just want decent jobs and lives. But things just seem to get weirder, the farther we go in this land, so we aren't sure yet what to do."

"You must be a Wave!" Nada exclaimed.

"A wave?"

"A Wave of Colonization. There have been ten or so, and each Wave usually brings a lot of violence, but not all of them. So you must be the Black Wave. If you don't want to fight, I know the folk here don't want to fight you. We always need more human folk in Xanth, and there are plenty of places to live."

"This sounds pretty good," Jaff said. "Still, we'd like to check it out before we do anything much."

"Look," Dug said. "I'm just a visitor here myself, as I told you. When my game finishes, I'll have to go back to Mundania. But I don't think there's anything in the rules that says I can't take someone else along. I should get a good tour of the region, because I have to find whatever it is I have to find, and anyway, I can make side trips if I want to. So I think it's a fair deal. You fix me up with some supplies, and a weapon to defend myself, and I'll take along one of you, and he can ask all the questions he wants, and maybe find the place you're looking for. Then he can return and tell the rest of you about it."

Nada was uneasy about this, and not just because of her ugly mission. "I don't know."

Dug turned to her. "You have a problem with that?" he asked, half smiling.

"Yes. You are a Player, and I am here to guide you and protect you, to the best of my ability." That was now a half-truth, and she hated it, but she was bound by the rules of the game. "But it is not my job to guide or protect any other person. I might save you from mischief, but the other would suffer it, when he wouldn't have if he had not come with us."

Jaff looked at her. "You are protecting him?" He was obviously dubious.

"You saw me change forms," she replied evenly. "I can become a big serpent if I choose."

"She sure can," Dug said enthusiastically. "She backed off a flying dragon once! And she knows Xanth, so she can keep me out of trouble, if I don't insist on blundering into it anyway."

Jaff looked at his wife. Mari spoke. "She's a good person, Jaff. She's a princess of her kind. Her folk fight goblins."

Jaff turned back to Dug. "We're ready to risk it if you are."

"Then let's do it," Dug said. "Who is coming?"

There was a pause. Then a man who seemed to be in his thirties spoke. "I think I can handle it."

The others nodded agreement. "Sherlock can handle it," Jaff said.

"I'll have to get things from Smith," Sherlock said.

"By all means," Jaff agreed. Sherlock went to another part of the village.

So they got together supplies, and gave Dug a good solid club for a weapon, and Sherlock joined the small party. He was neither large nor handsome, but seemed alert. Nada wondered whether he was a plant by the game, representing some additional challenge. After all, the Isthmus Village had led them into a considerable challenge, and Black Village was where it had been, so must have been arranged by the game. Dug had chosen to get along rather than antagonize the folk of the Black Wave, but the challenge might not yet be over. Should she warn him about this, or keep silent?

She was now a False Companion. She kept silent.

The three of them were soon on their way along the path. But evening was approaching, just as when they had passed this way before. Was the time fixed by their location, or was it coincidence? She had thought it was still morning when Dug lost the riddle contest and left the game, but perhaps it had been afternoon. So this might be evening of another day. It really didn't seem to matter. All she had to be concerned about was getting him safely through to Com Pewter, and if he didn't lose to the infernal machine again, she would find something worse to make him lose. Then she would be free of her uncomfortable obligation, and if he came back a third time, and chose her again, she might be a Fair Companion.

"We shall have to make camp for the night, soon," Nada said.

"Right," Dug said. "And we know where. Let's get on to it."

"You know where?" Sherlock asked. "I thought this region was just wilderness. We have explored it, and found no safe havens."

Nada nodded. "That must be right," she agreed. "This is our second effort in the game; Dug got eliminated by Com Pewter, the evil machine, and had to start over. The geography got changed, so probably the enchanted campsite we found before is no longer there."

"The geography changed? When did you pass this way before?"

"Yesterday," Dug said. "There was a different village here then."

Sherlock shook his head. "We have been here for a year."

"Well, you would say that. You're part of the game."

"No, you are part of the game. We came to Xanth on our own, and I assure you, it is no game to us."

Dug looked at Nada. "Can you figure this out? Which is real: what we saw, or what they saw?"

"That's easy to resolve," she said, realizing what the key had to be. "The path is enchanted, not to protect us, but to direct us to the challenges of the game. So Isthmus Village must be in one place, and Black Village in another, and the path took us to each in turn, making it seem that they were in the same region."

"Isthmus Village," Sherlock said. "We know of that. It is about a day's walk from here. The people are taciturn and unfriendly, and they refuse to use any expressive words."

"That's changed," Dug said. "They were being oppressed by a censor-ship, but we managed to douse its censers, and now the folk are expressive and happy again."

"I wish there were a ship we could abolish, to make us welcome," Sherlock said.

Nada realized that though she was doomed to betray Dug, she did not have to do the same for Sherlock, whether or not he was part of the game. "I do not think you are unwelcome here," she said. "Mundania is a dreary, awful place, but this is Xanth."

"It may be Xanth, and it may be magic, but we have encountered unfriendly animals and people," Sherlock said. "The Isthmus Villagers, the dragons, the goblins—"

Nada laughed. "Those don't count! The Isthmus folk we explained about; they were unfriendly to us too, at first. Dragons always attack people; they see us as prey. And goblins are mean to everybody, unless they are taught respect. That is improving now, since Gwenny became their first lady chief, but that's only one tribe; the others are still bad. You don't seem to have met the regular human folk of Xanth yet."

"It's true. You are the first travelers to pass who accepted us. The others either shied away without coming into the village, or were polite but refused to associate with us. That's why we were cautious about you."

"The others were probably cautious because they didn't know you," she said. "Strangers can be dangerous. Even strange trees can be dangerous."

He laughed. "Yes, so we discovered. There's the one full of tentacles—"

"Tangle trees," she agreed. "There are many dangers in Xanth. That's one reason the visitors in the game are given Companions to guide them. I don't know everything about Xanth, but I can spot the obvious threats." She paused. "For example, there's one now. Don't touch that object." She pointed to something lying in the path ahead of them.

"That's just an old horn," Sherlock said.

"That is a stink horn," she said. "If you touch it, it will make a foul-smelling noise."

Dug laughed. "Say—that sounds like fun!" He bent to touch the horn.

"No!" Nada cried, but she was too late.

BBBRRRRRRUMMPPPOOPOOHH! It sounded like the worst imaginable odor as it blew back Dug's hair and smirched his face. He stumbled away, but it was no good; the stench had gotten on him.

"Oh, now we'll have to clean you up," she said, dismayed. "Otherwise you won't be fit to be near."

"That's for sure," Sherlock agreed, holding his nose. "She did try to warn you."

Fortunately there was a small stream not far away. They went to it—but Nada hesitated. "I don't think that's a normal stream," she said.

"I don't care what it is, I just want to get clean," Dug said. He dipped his hand and scooped out water to splash on his face. "Uh-oh."

"You'll have to wash your clothes, too," Sherlock said. "Maybe you better just change to new ones. I see a trouser tree nearby; I'll see what else I can find."

Dug just squatted there, staring into space.

"Come on, get out of those things," Nada said briskly.

"No, I can't do that," he said. "You would see me, and I am very sensitive to that, because you are a beautiful princess I would like to know better, and I don't want to make a bad impression on you, and I would make a bad impression if I appeared naked before you, and anyway I don't know if there really is anything else to wear, so I had better stick with what I have on, and in any event I have to wait to see what Sherlock comes up with, and wasn't I a fool to touch that horn, it really stunk me up, and I wish I had listened to you, but naturally I had to just barge ahead and get in trouble, as I always do, because that's my nature, and I see the disgust on your face, and that hurts me because that's not the way I want you to see me, because I'd rather be kissing you, you lovely creature, in fact if I had my druthers I'd do more than kiss you, but in this weird land I can't even look at your panties without getting booted from the game, and that's a real pain, so I just have to keep quiet about it and try not to make a fuss, but you must really be disgusted right now, I know I sure would be if I were in your shoes, and"

"That's a stream of consciousness!" Nada cried, appalled.

"they are very pretty shoes too," he continued without interruption. "I must say, more like slippers, really, making your feet look nice, and of course your legs look nice too, and I'd really like to run my hands over—hey, why am I talking like this?" he demanded, dismayed. "I can't stop myself, I'm saying everything that's on my mind, no privacy whatever, and every time I look at you it gets really embarrassing, because"

"The water of the stream of consciousness made you have to say everything that's on your mind," she said loudly, using her own voice to drown out his voice, in an effort to prevent him from embarrassing them both any more.

"all I can think of is how luscious you are, and I don't

care if you are a princess, and are several years older than me, I just want to grab you and"

"I will go fetch Sherlock!" she screamed, and fled before hearing any more. What a disaster this was!

She found Sherlock, who was returning with shirt, trousers, and shoes. "Did you get him clean?" Sherlock asked. "Or do you want me to scrub him, you being a woman?"

"That's a stream of consciousness!" she cried. "He's speaking everything on his mind!"

His eyes traveled up and down her torso. "That's bound to be trouble," he said. "Is there an antidote?"

"I don't know! I don't know what to do!"

"Then we'll just have to gag him until we figure something better out," Sherlock said. "Here, I found a scarf, too; it should do the trick."

Dug saw them coming. "I don't want to be saying all this!" he said, looking desperate. "It's just coming out. Anything that triggers a thought, out my mouth it comes! Now I'm bound to say something about race relations, because Sherlock is black, and I want to keep my mouth shut, and I can't, and I'm bound to insult somebody even though I don't want to, and what are you planning to do with that scarf? You're not going to choke me, are you? I really don't mean to be like this, I can't help it if my crowd never let me play with black children, and my friends called them ni—" He stifled himself by clapping his hands to his mouth.

"This is a gag," Sherlock said. "Let me put it on you." He did so, and Dug did not resist. He had at last been silenced.

Nada concluded that Sherlock knew what to do. "I will go look for a campsite," she said, and walked away.

She was in luck. There was an enchanted campsite in a different place from the prior one. They would be able to spend a safe night. She set about gathering fruit and pies for supper, and canvas for a tent.

After a while the two men joined her. Dug was clean, in the new clothing, and still gagged. He looked grateful rather than miserable. Sherlock, instead of being a burden to have along, had turned out to be a great help.

What a disaster it would have been had she been the one to touch that stream of consciousness! She would have blabbed out her False Companion nature. She hoped the effect did not last long with Dug; this job was difficult enough without that.

Sherlock looked around. "I don't remember this place, and I've been through here. I'm sure it was just plain old forest before."

"It must have been set up for the game," Nada explained. "The game is superimposed on Xanth, and interacts with Xanth, but we don't want to bother too many regular Xanth folk who know nothing about it."

"But your path led you right to our village," he pointed out.

"Either you are game folk, or the demons decided you were a legitimate challenge," she said.

"Maybe it doesn't matter. Just so long as we find a good place to settle. We don't want to remain where we are, but we don't want to walk into trouble either."

"If you are the Black Wave, you will find a place to settle. Every other Wave has. Maybe Dug's challenge here is to help you find that place. From what he says, I gather that some Mundanes would not even try to help you."

"That's for sure!" He hesitated. "If this is where we spend the night—separate tents?"

"If you prefer. I change into my natural form to sleep. If you don't mind being in the company of a human-headed serpent, it would be easier to set up just one tent."

"For sure. If Dug doesn't mind."

Dug, gagged, shook his head no. He didn't mind.

"Then let's see what we have here." Sherlock opened his pack and brought out a coil of wire. "We can tie this between two trees, to support the canvas. And I have metal tent pegs too; they hold better than the scrounged ones, usually."

"You have metal things?" she asked, surprised. "How did you get them?"

"Smith makes them. Anything we need, from swords to plowshares. He really knows how to work metal."

"He has magic? He can change the form of metal? Usually, those from Mundania lack magic."

"No magic. He's trained, is all."

Dug laughed through his gag. They looked at him, so he pulled it down. "Black Smith!" he said. "It does make sense." Then he pulled the gag back up before he could say too much more.

Sherlock smiled. "He's a blacksmith, certainly. But what would be the point of magic, since he can do it all with fire and tongs?"

"Well, a magical blacksmith would shape oars from ores, getting an iron oar, or silver oar," she explained. "Something like that. Maybe not silver, as that isn't black. It sounds as if your Mundane Black Smith is more versatile."

"Maybe so," he agreed.

They put up the tent and settled down to supper. But another problem appeared: how was Dug to eat with the gag on?

"I wonder," Sherlock murmured. "The way things work here, maybe it would do."

"What would do?"

"I saw some humble pie growing near the river," he said, rising.

"Humble pie!" she exclaimed. "Maybe it would!"

So Sherlock fetched a humble pie, and they fed Dug a piece. In a moment Dug's endless monologue faded out. He was now too humble to bore the others with all his thoughts.

"How did you ever think of that?" Nada asked, impressed.

Sherlock shrugged. "Elementary," he said. He had not eaten any humble pie.

Nevertheless, Nada was sure they were going to get along.

8
BUBBLES

K im had been enjoying the game. Now she was enjoying it more. She liked having the handsome merman along, being satisfied that he was not trying to marry her. For one thing, he knew this Water Wing well, so they would surely make excellent progress through it, without running afoul of whatever threats it offered. For another, he was excellent company. He was mature, clever, polite, and generally nice. What more could a girl ask?

They started at the eastern fringe of the Water Wing, and floated west in a water boat that sought and followed the various currents going their way. It was slow but comfortable. Each of them had packs with supplies, provided by the mer family. Cyrus showed them how to fish, not for food but to attract exotic specimens to the lure. There were rainbow trout, their semicircular bands of color making the surrounding water beautiful. There were the tiny white specks of light that were starfish, and one that was too bright to look at: a sunfish. A swordfish playfully feinted at the boat, and a sawfish made bulging eyes at them: it *saw* them.

But after a time this palled. They were on a seemingly endless expanse of water, going somewhere but not fast. Kim was getting bored; this wasn't exactly her idea of adventure.

Then she saw a glimmer in the air. It wasn't a bird, it was a bubble. A shimmering soap bubble, perhaps, just floating innocently by, the light glinting iridescently from its surface. Where had it come from? Where was it going? Who had blown this pretty little bubble? Kim didn't know, and didn't much care; it was just interesting to watch.

It was followed by another bubble, a bit larger and shinier. Then a third. In fact, there was a chain of bubbles, drifting along on a vagrant eddy of wind, passing the boat and moving on. Each was larger and brighter than the one before it, as if the bubble blower were growing and gaining experience.

Then a bubble seemed to have something in it. Kim strained to see, but could not make it out; just a reflection, maybe. Yet a peculiar one.

The next bubble was empty, but the one following that definitely had something in it. Kim peered closely, but still couldn't quite make it out. So she reached out and caught the bubble.

It popped the moment she touched it, and the object fell into her hand. It was a twisted paper clip, not readily usable. How had it gotten inside the bubble? How had the bubble managed to remain floating, with this weight inside it? This was such a curious matter. She hadn't realized that paper clips even existed, in Xanth; they were Mundane.

She tried to bend the paper clip back into shape, but it was beyond redemption. She considered dropping it into the water, but she didn't want to be a litterbug. Finally she hooked it into a buttonhole as an impromptu decoration.

Meanwhile the bubbles were still drifting by, and still getting larger. There seemed to be a loose chain of them crossing the lake, coming from who knew where and going to who knew where else. When she looked behind, she

saw the diminishing line of them disappearing in small-
ness. When she looked ahead, she saw the line maintaining its size, but realized that was because the bubbles
were still growing, so that their size balanced perspec-
tive. There must be some pretty large bubbles at the end
of that line!

She peered at each passing bubble. Now a number of
them definitely had objects inside them. They were all different, but there was something similar about them too.
What was it?

One bubble carried a worn clothespin. Another had a
chipped cup. Another had an empty bottle. And so on: a
torn picture, a worn shoe, a stopped clock, a book with the
cover torn off, a pair of socks with holes in the toes. Everything was in some way defective or useless. These were
all throwaways! Things Mundane people no longer
wanted. That explained the twisted paper clip.

She worked it out as the bubbles moved on by. This was
a magic land, so it had magic problems and magic solutions. Maybe even punnishly literal, she thought with a
smile: somewhere there would be a solution that was a
magic solution: a drink or elixir. These bubbles were like
trash bags: just put your junk in them and let it float away.
A disposal network. The bubbles were probably going to
a central dump, where they would pop and deposit their
refuse. No fuss, no muss, no bother. Wouldn't it be nice to
have something like that at home! Somehow this stuff
must have strayed into Xanth, so was being conveyed
away.

The bubbles continued, still growing larger. One had a
broken bicycle. Another had a stuffed chair with the stuffing leaking. A kiddy car with the steering wheel gone. A
large, old, worn dog. A—

Wait a minute! Kim snapped back to the dog bubble.
What was a living creature doing in the trash? Because the
dog *was* alive; it was lying there with its nose on its paws,
breathing slowly and gazing out without much interest. It

was nondescript, mostly shades of brown with some white around the edges. A mongrel, undistinguished.

And that was why, of course. With no special pedigree, and well beyond the fun of puppyhood, she was no longer a desirable pet. Maybe she was ill. So she had been thrown away. Kim had heard of this sort of thing. Sometimes people would just dump their pets off on country roads and drive away, hoping someone else would take care of them. Of course usually that didn't happen; instead the poor pets expired of starvation and exposure, never understanding how they got lost. That just made Kim so mad! But she had never had a pet, so maybe she didn't know how it was. Maybe she would have a different attitude, if she had had the experience of keeping in an aging or sick pet. But she doubted it.

The bubble was drifting on behind. The dog lifted its head and gazed at her. It gave its tail half a wag, then sank back into hopelessness. It knew it was doomed.

Kim reached for the bubble, but it was now too far away. And what would she do anyway, with a tired old dog? It probably had fleas. It was better just to let it go. It would soon be dead anyway. No one would care.

"No!" she cried. She stood up and then leaped for the bubble. Her hands touched the shimmering surface, and it popped, and her arms closed around the dog. But she was falling, because she had leaped from the boat. Splash! They fell together into the water.

"Help!" she cried. She could swim, but not while holding a large dog in her arms. And she was not about to let go of the dog, because she didn't know if *it* could swim.

Then Cyrus was there, swimming extremely efficiently with his tail. He caught her and the dog and heaved them back into the boat, where Jenny Elf helped them get untangled. "What happened?" Jenny asked, amazed. "Did you fall out of the boat?"

"No, I leaped out of the boat," Kim explained. "To catch the bubble."

"The bubble?"

"Didn't you see the line of bubbles floating by?"

Jenny shook her head. "No."

Cyrus heaved himself back into the boat, keeping his tail. "There were no bubbles," he said. "It must have been a daydream. I think I caught a glimpse of Mare Imbri. She must have brought you that nice dream."

"No bubbles?" Kim asked. "Then what about this?" She let go of the dog, who was now sitting in front of her.

"A dog!" Jenny cried. "It's been so long since I've seen one of those!"

"A bitch," Cyrus agreed. "You found her in the water?"

"What do you mean, a bitch!" Kim retorted. "She's a perfectly nice dog!" Then she remembered that this was what a female dog was called: a bitch. Just as a female horse was called a mare, and a female pig a sow.

"Oh, I'm sure she's nice," Jenny agreed, extending her hand. But the dog shied away fearfully.

"It's all right," Kim said, stroking the dog's damp back. "Jenny's my Companion." The dog relaxed, accepting Jenny's touch.

Then Sammy Cat stepped forward. Kim was worried, but then realized that the little cat would not step into danger, and he knew how to find what he wanted. Sure enough, the two animals sniffed noses. Then Sammy walked away, satisfied. He was Jenny's cat, and Jenny had been accepted, so Sammy was accepted too.

Cyrus extended his hand, but the dog retreated from him too. She didn't growl, she just grew nervous. "She's your dog," Cyrus said. "I never heard of a daydream turning real like that, but it must have happened."

Kim looked around. There were no longer any bubbles in sight. They had vanished. They couldn't all have drifted away so quickly. So maybe it had been a daydream. But the dog was real. As real as anything in this game. Had it been a challenge, to rescue the animal?

"What do you call her?" Jenny asked.

"My bubble dog? I don't know." Kim turned to the dog. She noticed that the dog's mouth was marked with black and white so that she seemed to be smiling, though it was merely a color pattern and not true emotion. "I think someone was—was throwing her away. Because she'd old. All the bubbles had old, worn, or broken things. But when I saw a living animal, I—I just couldn't let it happen."

"Perhaps you should check to be sure she is healthy," Cyrus said diplomatically. He knew that the chances were that the dog was not.

Kim seized the opportunity. "Bubble dog, let me see if there is a tag on you, or something," Kim said. There wasn't; probably such identification was unknown in Xanth. "Let me get you dry, while I'm at it." She brought out a towel and rubbed the dog's fur, at the same time checking for mange, fleas, or broken bones.

But the bubble dog turned out to be surprisingly healthy. She was solid—perhaps seventy pounds—but not fat, and her fur was so thick it was like dense carpeting. She was very quiet, not growling, whining, or barking, and did not try to get away. Her teeth were clean, and there were no signs of infestation. She was healthy, just old.

"Maybe she's magic," Jenny suggested. "There are very few straight dogs in Xanth. She might be a werewolf, or something."

"Are you magic?" Kim asked the dog. The dog just looked at her, not seeming to understand.

"Perhaps she was dumped because she was not magic," Cyrus suggested.

"Well, *I* won't dump her!" Kim said firmly. "She's a nice dog, and I like her, and I don't care if she is nonmagical, so am I." But then a nasty thought occurred. "But I'm only visiting here. What happens to her when I go home?"

"I would try to take care of her," Jenny said. "But I don't think she likes me."

"Nonsense," Kim said. "She just doesn't know you." Yet Kim herself was almost as new to the dog as the other two were. Why should the dog accept her?

She knew the answer: she was the one who had rescued

the dog from the bubble. Thus she had earned a special place in the dog's affection. That was all right, as long as the dog did not attack the others.

She couldn't just keep thinking of her as "the dog." There had to be a name. "All right, you're officially the bubble dog," Kim said. "Bubbles for short. Okay?"

The dog did not object. She lay down in the bottom of the boat and went to sleep.

"Bubbles it is," Cyrus said. "I wonder if I could day-dream of floating bubbles, and find one with a thrown-away young beautiful mermaid?"

Kim laughed. "Who would throw away a young beautiful mermaid?"

"Unless she had a terrible temper," Jenny said, smiling.

"Mermaids do not have hot tempers," Cyrus said some-what stiffly. "The water keeps them cool and calm."

"Except when there's a storm?" Kim asked mischie-vously.

"Merfolk dive below when there are storms."

"Maybe she's hungry," Jenny said.

"How can she be hungry, when we haven't found her yet?" he asked. Then he shifted streams of thought. "Oh, you mean the dog. Perhaps so."

They did not have any dogfood in their supplies, but they did have water crackers. Kim took one and offered it to Bubbles. The dog sniffed it, considered, and finally ac-cepted it. She settled down to eat it, slowly.

The boat moved on. The slow progress soon became boring. Jenny and Cyrus slumped, snoozing, and so did Kim.

Until a sharp bark woke them all up. Kim's eyes popped open—and there was a head looking over the boat. She sti-fled a scream, afraid that it would merely provoke the monster.

Jenny was doing the same. "It's a water dragon!" she whispered, frightened. "And we're way far from land!"

But Cyrus did not seem to be worried. "That's just Plesio," he said. "He's friendly."

"That's a plesiosaurus!" Kim exclaimed. "From the Age of Dinosaurs." For she had at one time been fascinated by the dinosaurs, and had learned a number of the forms of the age of reptiles. This extremely long-necked, flippered creature fit the description.

"Yes, he really likes to please people," Cyrus said. "He must have seen us poking along, and decided to help speed up our journey." He unshipped some rope, tossed out the end, and the creature caught it in its mouth. Then it swam briskly ahead, pulling the boat swiftly along.

"But Bubbles couldn't have known it was all right," Kim said, stroking the dog's head. "She tried to warn us of danger."

"Yes she did," Jenny agreed. "We can sleep safer with her along."

Now their progress was rapid. The surface of the lake fairly whizzed by. A shore appeared ahead, and soon they reached it. Plesio halted and dropped his end of the rope. "Thank you," Cyrus called as he coiled the rope.

They took out water paddles and moved the boat into shallow water, and then into a broad marsh. "But I thought we were going to a river," Kim said.

"The With-A-Cookee River," Jenny agreed. "It flows from the Half-Baked Bog. So first we have to get through the bog."

Oh. Now she remembered the map. "Why is it called Half-Baked?" Kim inquired.

"Because half of it is next to the Fire Region," Cyrus said. "That's not my favorite place, but the best channel passes close by there, so we'll have to use it."

All too soon Kim saw what he meant. There was smoke on the horizon, billowing up from what looked like a wall of fire, and the channel through the marsh led toward it. The green plants along the bank turned white with the increasing heat, and then brown. "Why, that looks almost like marshmallow!" Kim explained.

"Yes, this is the Mallow Marsh," Cyrus agreed. "If you are hungry, you can eat the toasted mallow plants."

Kim reached out and pulled off a mallow. It was crinkly brown on the outside, but gooey white inside. She tasted it. Toasted marshmallow, sure enough.

Jenny ate some too. Then Jenny offered a mallow to Bubbles, but the dog would not take it. So she handed it to Kim, and Kim offered it, and this time Bubbles took it. This was a one-girl dog, without doubt.

The wall of fire loomed closer. Kim realized that the reason the channel was so close to the fire was that this was the only place too hot for water plants to clog.

"We shall have to move rapidly," Cyrus said. "I shall enter the water and pull the boat, as Plesio did. That will protect me from the heat and speed our travel. If the two of you are able to paddle—"

"We'll try," Kim said bravely. That firewall was now impressively high and hot. Her clothing had long since dried out. She dipped her hands in the lukewarm water and splashed herself wet again. The water itself was warm, but did help cool her. Jenny, understanding, did the same. It would help them survive the fire. As an afterthought, she splashed some water on Bubbles, who glanced at her but did not protest.

Jenny paddled near the front of the boat, and Kim paddled near the back, on the other side, trying to time her strokes to match the elf's. Cyrus pulled by holding a short length of rope between his teeth and swimming vigorously. The boat moved well, but still the high flames were ferocious. Both girls had to pause frequently to splash more water on themselves and on the dog. Near the wall of fire the water was boiling, but it seemed to be cooler below the surface.

Now the source of the flames was apparent: a row of burning trees. Somehow they seemed to maintain their height and mass and foliage, despite burning up. How could that be?

"That's firewood," Cyrus explained.

Well, that made sense, in this magic land. Kim had always known how punnish Xanth was; she just tended to forget when under stress.

Kim heard growling. It wasn't Bubbles; indeed, the dog heard it too. Her floppy ears perked up. It was coming from the firewall! But how could there be any living thing there?

"Firedogs," Cyrus gasped. "Pay them no heed. They live in the hot steel and iron section, and harass passersby, but they can't leave the Fire Region."

Kim's fevered mind wondered whether there was a pun buried there: steel and iron. Steel andiron—same as a firedog back home. She kept paddling, though she feared that her hands were blistering.

The growling faded, but was replaced by a heated hissing. "Firedrakes," Cyrus explained. "Very fierce birds."

But the drakes, too, were confined to the fire. Then there came a hot buzzing. "Don't tell me," Kim gasped. "Let me guess: firebugs."

"Right."

The channel began to veer away from the firewall, to Kim's great relief. Then there was a fiery neigh. That would be a firehorse. Sparkling insects flew out and danced above the water: fireflies.

Bubbles barked. Kim started to reassure the dog, then realized that the dog might have smelled something. She looked around—and spied a serpentine form writhing across the surface of the water toward them. Suddenly she knew what it was. "Firehose!" she screamed.

Cyrus lifted his head and stared. "That will burn through the boat!" he said, alarmed.

"Then we'd better hurry!" Kim gasped, doubling her effort. The boat went faster, but she saw that the firehose was going to touch it.

Jenny saw the danger. She stood up and whirled her paddle. She brought it down across the firehose, making a great splash of water and fire. The hose, startled, pulled back for a moment—and the boat slid by, untouched.

There was an angry cry. Kim looked, and saw the flaming outline of a man, standing before his firehose, shaking his fist at them. "Sorry, fireman, you can't burn us this time!" she called as the boat put distance between them.

A flaming human female form appeared. She held some kind of firestick. She pointed it at the boat. Bubbles barked.

"Duck!" Kim cried, throwing herself down.

A bolt of fire shot over the boat, just missing her.

"That was no duck," Cyrus said. "That was Miss Fire."

"So silly of me to confuse her," Kim said.

Away from the firewall at last, they relaxed, catching their breaths. "They were surprisingly determined, this time," Cyrus said. "Usually they don't really try. I wonder what got them all fired up?"

"It's probably a game challenge," Kim said, realizing. "It was getting too easy for me to make progress, so they heated it up."

"That must be it," Jenny agreed. "You have a loyal Companion to help you, but the challenges do get harder as they go. Few Players are supposed to make it through to the prize."

Cyrus nodded. "I see this will be an interesting excursion. I must say you rose to the occasion, Kim."

"No, that was Jenny who rose," Kim said to cover her pleasure at the compliment. "She stood up so she could bash the firehose, so we could pass."

"True. But you gave the alarm."

"No, that was Bubbles. She barked." Kim stroked the dog's head.

He shrugged. "Your modesty becomes you."

"I'm not modest. I'm pushy. I just did my part, the same way the rest of you did."

"Of course," he agreed. But he did not sound quite convinced.

The dog was getting restless, so they paddled to the bank, and let her scramble onto land, where she did her canine business. Evidently she was a house-trained canine, which was fine. Kim liked her very well. It was fun having a pet, even if it was only in the game.

They resumed motion through the Half-Baked Bog. It was extensive, but by paddling and poling they made good progress.

"It is getting late, but we must reach the headwaters of the With-A-Cookee River by nightfall," Cyrus said.

"Why?" Kim asked. "Can't we camp here?" She was so tired that she hardly wanted to push on farther than she needed to.

"No. There is no solid land here, just marshy islands. And it would be uncomfortable for you to sleep in the boat. But mainly, there are the allegations."

"The what?" Jenny asked. "Allegory?"

"A related species, perhaps. The allegories are found in the ever glades, while the allegations are here. We don't dare relax until we are out of their range."

Kim realized that these puns might have unpleasant representations. "Okay; on we go. I hope we don't meet any." But she suspected that the game would not let her get by without tackling this next challenge.

She was right. Bubbles barked as a large aquatic reptile swam toward them, with a ribbed greenish hide, solid threshing tail, and a mouth stuffed with more gleaming teeth than she cared to try to count. "Keep moving," she murmured to Cyrus and Jenny.

"You are intruding on my territory!" the allegation said, with some justice. "I shall have to chomp you."

Cyrus was silent, and Kim knew it was because he could not refute the charge. It was up to her.

"We are traveling an established route," she said. "You don't have authority to interfere."

The allegation pondered. Evidently she had managed to refute it. Meanwhile the boat was moving. Then the creature made another accusation. "You are transporting an illicit animal. I shall have to chomp it."

"Oh no you don't!" Kim cried, putting her arms around the dog. "This is my pet, and nobody chomps her without first chomping me."

The allegation paused again. It seemed she had refuted

it again. The boat was still quietly moving. But the thing hadn't given up. "You are a Mundane! You have no rights in Xanth. I shall have to chomp you."

Oops! She was indeed Mundane, so she couldn't refute that. What was she to do? While she considered, the creature was nudging up closer, ready to snap at her. Even if it missed her, it would surely catch the boat, and rip out a chunk, causing the whole thing to dissolve.

But she knew there had to be a way through. So she made what she hoped was a good refutation. "I am a Mundane Player in the game. I have the right to tour Xanth as long as I play the game. You can't chomp me unless I make a mistake—and I haven't made one here."

"Curses," the allegation muttered, turning aside. She had foiled it!

The boat slid on through the bog. Soon the land on either side firmed up, and pretty plants appeared. "The With-A-Cookee!" Jenny exclaimed. "See—there're the cookees growing."

"The cookies," Kim agreed. "So now at last we can camp."

"Yes," Cyrus agreed. "You handled that allegation very well, Kim."

"Thank you," she replied, feeling more justifiably flattered. After all, there were only so many compliments a girl could take from a handsome man before they started getting to her.

"That's odd," Cyrus said. "That wasn't here the last time I passed this way."

And there ahead was what looked like an enchanted campsite. "Does the game provide safe havens for Players?" Kim asked Jenny.

"Yes. But you have to find them yourself."

"It seems I did." Kim turned to Cyrus. "This must be about the edge of your range."

"It is. I travel the Water Wing freely, but seldom venture far into the neighboring regions. Nevertheless, I'm sure this was mere jungle before."

"It surely was," Kim agreed. "But the proprietors of the game must have set up rest stops in out-of-the-way places, and this is one of them. I'm certainly glad to have it." Which was perhaps her understatement of the day. She had used her wit and gotten through just fine, but she had been lucky too. She was willing to bet that luck wouldn't hold much longer.

They tied the boat and walked into the campsite. Cookee plants grew all around, as well as fruit and nut trees, and assorted material bushes. She knew this would do just fine for the night.

Cyrus went to a private spot, changed into legs, and went to work collecting materials and pitching two tents, while Kim and Jenny picked fruits and nuts, pies and milkweed pods and piled them on the picnic table. There was even a dogwood tree bearing dogfood; Kim put some of that in a wooden dish for Bubbles, and the dog liked it. "Ah, this is living!" Kim remarked as they ate.

Both Cyrus and Jenny looked surprised. "This is routine," he said.

"Not for me. Where I live, pies don't grow on trees, and milk doesn't come in pods. This really is the land of milk and honey." She picked up a honey-soaked comb she had found and began licking the tines clean. She would be able to use it on her hair when all the honey was gone.

"Well, they don't where I come from, either," Jenny said. "But it's the way it is in Xanth. There's nothing special about it."

Kim shook her head. "You folk don't know when you're well off. You have such wonderful lives, compared to the pollution and parsimony and poverty we have. That's why everyone who knows about Xanth wants to come here. Even if only for a few hours, in a stupid game."

Cyrus was interested. "What are the mermaids like, in your world?"

Kim laughed. "There are no mermaids! Well, maybe some faked-up ones, in tourist shows, but those are just regular women with their legs bound into tail-costumes. Nothing you'd be interested in."

He was surprised. "There are no crossbreedings with fish?"

"None. That sort of thing just doesn't happen in Mundania. In fact, there can be trouble when different races or cultures marry. It happens, but not often. People stick mostly to their own kind."

He shook his head. "Truly has it been said: Mundania is dreary."

"Truly," Kim agreed.

Kim and Jenny settled down for the night in one tent, and Bubbles lay down at the entrance, satisfied to be a guard dog. Cyrus, always the model of decorum, slept in his own tent.

In the morning they took turns washing, then ate and disassembled their tents so as to leave the camping area pristine for the next travelers. They got in the boat and set off down the With-A-Cookee River. They didn't need to paddle; the gentle current carried them slowly along toward the west and north.

"But don't we want to bear south?" Kim asked.

"We do," Jenny said. "But the river will take us to the sea, and then we can paddle on along the shore, bypassing the Gap Chasm and other menaces such as Com Pewter. We can land south of it and find a path going inland. We can pass Castle Roogna and go on to the Good Magician's castle. It's not a straight route, but it's a fairly easy one."

"Com Pewter!" Kim said. "The evil machine! I'd like to meet—"

"You don't want to meet Pewter!" Jenny said, alarmed.

Kim sighed. Jenny's advice had been good so far, as she had found out when she didn't follow it. "No evil machine," she agreed regretfully.

The cookies growing along the banks became fancier. There were clusters of ginger, chocolate chip, banana, walnut, raisin, and molasses cookies, growing out of beds of sandies. Pinwheels spun around on their stems. Kim reached out to pick one.

"No!" Jenny cried as Kim was about to take a bite. But she was too late, as usual. Kim's mouth was already in motion. She bit out a piece, and it tasted very good.

"Why did you try to tell me no?" she asked. "There's nothing wrong with this pinwheel cookie."

"That's not a pinwheel, it's a punwheel," Jenny said.

"Oh? What will it do to me? Make me a pundit? It can't make me a pungent, because I'm not a man, I'm a girl. Still, I suppose I could go around telling jokes, the way a pun-gent would. I could be his pun-girl, maybe." She paused. "What's the matter?"

"You're punning in circles," Jenny said.

Kim looked at the cookie. She had taken a bite, and it had affected her speech. "I'll try to watch my pun-ctuation, so as not to pun-ish you any more," she said punctually.

"Maybe we'll find an antidote soon," Cyrus muttered. Even Bubbles hid her head under the seat, as if trying to shield her ears from the sound.

Kim decided to keep her mouth shut until the effects wore off. She just kept acting impulsively, then regretting it.

They saw things swimming. They looked like more allegations. There were also small shoes in the water. Kim knew what those were: water moccasins. She was glad they were secure in their boat, because this was not the best place to wade or swim.

Later in the day the river widened, and there were marshes to the left. The marsh water bubbled effervescently.

"Lake Tsoda Popka!" Jenny exclaimed. "Oh, I remember when Che and Gwenny and I had our first popka-squirting fight! Of course Gwenny won't do anything like that now; she's a chief. And Che's her Companion, so he has to behave too." She took an empty water bottle and dipped it into the lake. "But I'm not a chief, and not a

Companion to a chief. I'm just an innocent elf girl who doesn't know any better. So I can do it." And she held her thumb over the top, shook the bottle violently, and squirted tsoda water all over the boat.

"I know about that game!" Kim said, managing not to pun. She grabbed another water bottle and dipped it in the lake. "I'll puncture your balloon!" Soon they had a full-scale squirt fight going, while Cyrus, too decorous to participate, retreated to the farthest part of the boat, and Bubbles hid under the seat.

Then something horrendous loomed ahead. It made a bubbly roar. They paused to stare at it. The thing was like a swirling mass of gelatin, with colored bubbles throughout. "What's that pun-k in the pun-ch?" Kim asked.

"That's the Tsoda Popka monster!" Cyrus said. "It must have been attracted by the commotion."

"Well, tell it to pun-t on out of here," Kim said.

But the monster, perhaps aggravated by the puns, reached out a bubbly tentacle to strike the boat. The tentacle hissed effervescently—and where it touched the boat, the boat began to hiss and sparkle too.

"What's happening?" Kim asked, alarmed.

"I think the Popka monster turned the water boat into tsoda water," Cyrus said, alarmed. "It is dissolving away!"

The monster sank out of sight, but that did not end the problem. The boat was now bubbling at a great rate, and becoming jellylike. They had to scramble out of it before it dissolved away.

There they stood, on a somewhat spongy bank. They were all right, and they had saved their supplies, but they had lost their boat. They would have to walk the rest of the way.

Unfortunately they seemed to be on a squishy island. Around it swam the allegations, moccasins, and other things with projecting fins.

Kim opened her mouth. No pun came out. She wasn't surprised. Their situation did not seem at all funny.

9
GERM

Dug was better in the morning, being neither consciously streaming nor humble. For sure, he was going to watch what he ate and drank, after this!

The path was just beginning to veer south when they came to a grove of very tall trees. "I am not sure about this," Nada said. "I think these are hassle trees. If so, we should avoid them."

"We don't need any tall hassle," Dug agreed.

"I have not been this far," Sherlock said. "I hope you folk know how to deal with the dangers of this region."

"The best strategy is simply to go around this grove," Nada said.

But there was only one path, and that one proceeded through into the tall hassle grove. Nada could leave the path and travel in serpent form, but the two others could not. "Guess we'll just have to chance it," Dug said. "The game doesn't give us much choice."

"It may be a game to you," Sherlock said. "But it's pretty serious to me. I mean, if you lose, you're suddenly back home in Mundania, right? But if I lose, I'm food for a dragon, or worse."

"You're right," Dug said. "I think I got the better deal, getting supplies from your village. If you want to break the deal, I'll give you back the stuff."

"But you're going on?"

"I have to. I've got a game to play."

"Then I'm going on too. Just let's be careful, okay?"

"Super careful," Dug agreed. "I don't want to wash out again."

They walked on into the tall hassle grove. Dug was afraid that the trees would sprout arms and attack, but they seemed stable. They were so tall that they shut out the direct light of the sun, putting the path into gloom. There were no animals in sight.

Then they heard something. At first it was faint, but it became louder as they moved toward it. It was a sort of thumping and swishing, as of something very large jumping around and breathing hard. The ground shuddered.

Dug exchanged a glance with Sherlock. The black man shrugged. The path led only two ways: forward and back.

By the time they reached the center of the tall hassle grove, the whole forest seemed to be shaking as if an earthquake were practicing its moves. It was hard to keep their feet on the bouncing ground. But there were no roars or other indications of a hungry monster. Maybe it was something impersonal, like a boulder bouncing up and down inside a volcano. They moved forward almost on tiptoe, though it was hard to tell how they could have made any sound loud enough to be heard over the deafening reverberations.

At last they spied a large glade. Sunlight streamed down in a region like an amphitheater. In the center was a flock of birds.

"Birds?" Dug asked, surprised. He had to yell to make himself heard over the noise.

"Rocs," Nada yelled back. "By their color, I'd say female rocs. But whatever can they be doing?"

For the birds were standing in a line, flapping their wings, and kicking their feet up. That was the source of the swishing and thumping. They were so solid that when they set down their feet, the ground shuddered. For the rocs were *large* birds. Each was big enough to carry away an elephant, if it chose, if it could find an elephant.

It was Sherlock who caught on. "They're rockettes!" he exclaimed. "Practicing their routines!"

"Roc-ettes," Nada agreed. "Female rocs. But what do you mean by routine?"

"Dancing. A chorus line. High kicks."

"They do seem to be doing that," she agreed. "But to what point?"

Sherlock exchanged a glance with Dug. "Well, they like it in Mundania," Dug yelled.

Just then the rocs halted, in perfect unison, resting their feet and closing their wings. It was the end of their act. Silence fell like a sudden curtain. Just in time to catch Dug at the top of his voice. His words carried right through the glade with loud and perfect clarity.

Every huge bird head turned toward him.

"Uh-oh," Sherlock murmured.

"They can't fly through the forest," Nada said. "We can escape along the next path. Follow me!" She shifted to large serpent form and slithered rapidly forward.

Dug paused only long enough to snatch up her clothing and jam it into his pack. Then he and Sherlock galloped after her.

The rocs, evidently annoyed by the intrusion, launched in a mass into the air. They bore down on the fugitives. But the circle of trees ringing the glade was too close; the birds had to land before they crashed. So some dropped down to pursue afoot, while others winged on up over the forest to peer down at the path from on high.

This was one tall hassle, for sure, Dug thought.

Nada Serpent slithered out of the glade, down the next path through the forest. Dug and Sherlock followed. The nearest roc screeched as she made a grab for them with her claws and beak. The sound was deafening. But she overbalanced, not being accustomed to hunting on her feet, and fell beak-first on the ground. Dug felt the great whomp just behind him, and kept going.

Then he realized that Sherlock wasn't beside him. He snatched a look back—and saw that one outstretched talon had snagged Sherlock's pack. The man was trying to get loose, but the talon had plunged right into the ground, anchoring him.

Dug stopped, turned, and hauled out the club they had provided. He ran back toward Sherlock.

"Watch it, you fool!" the man cried. "She's watching you!"

Indeed, the huge head was lifting, and the huge near eye was orienting. Even stretched flat on the ground, the bird could readily snap him up, because the foot was close to her head. What could he do? If he fled, Sherlock would be done for; if he didn't, both of them could be done for. Because his club was a puny thing compared to that monstrous beak. If he had gotten another magic sword, this time around—

But he did have a knife. That would have to do. He put away the club and got the knife.

The roc's head swung toward him. The beak opened.

Then he saw a stink horn growing almost in front of him. He jammed the point of the knife through it.

BBBRRRRRRUMMPPOOPOOHH! The foul-smelling sound ripped through the glade, staining everything. But Dug paid no heed. He held his breath, squinted his eyes, and lifted the thing up toward the roc's gaping mouth. He whipped the point about, so that the stuck stink horn flew off—into that mouth.

The roc snapped at it reflexively. Then her eye assumed a somewhat startled, somewhat disgusted look, as if something tasted monumentally bad. A wisp of putrid stench leaked out from the corner of her beak.

Dug didn't wait to watch. He already had a pretty good notion how the big bird felt. Instead he ran up to Sherlock and the claw and wielded his blade. It bit into the claw as if it were so much tough wood. This was like hacking down a tree, except that his meager blade lacked the heft to do much damage.

The roc screeched. It seemed he had struck a nerve. She yanked her talon out of the ground, hauling Sherlock into the air. He slid off the talon, landing neatly on his feet. "Go, man!" he shouted.

Dug realized that he was just standing there watching. He put his legs in gear and ran as fast as he could for the path. He almost expected to have a talon skewer him on the way, but he made it intact.

He joined Sherlock behind a hassle tree. They looked back at the roc. She was dancing in a much fancier pattern than before, trying to get the stink horn smell out of her beak. "That was one smart ploy," Sherlock said appreciatively. "Nothing else could've distracted her. You saved my life."

"I was lucky," Dug said. It wasn't false modesty, it was an exact description.

"Well, it looked good from here," Sherlock said. "Come on—we've lost the serpent lady."

They resumed motion down the path. Nada was waiting, in her naga form. "What happened?" she asked. "I thought you were right behind me."

"Bit of a problem," Dug said. "Let's move on before that roc realizes that this path is wide enough for her to run along if she keeps her wings closed."

Indeed, the roc was already drawing that conclusion. She was blowing out the last of the stench and advancing on the path. She was not nearly as fast on her feet as she would have been in the air, but she was a mighty big bird, and could surely move as rapidly as they could.

Nada resumed her slither, and they followed, running. They heard the thumping as the roc's big feet hit the ground. Her footsteps seemed slow, but that was deceptive; they were far apart. Dug snatched another glance back, and saw that she was gaining on them.

Fortunately the path was winding, which slowed the big bird, because she could not maneuver her bulk in this confined space as readily as they could. Then they came to a fork. They dashed right, because that bore south, and had the luck to hear her take the left fork, losing the way.

But they had hardly begun to relax before a roc wheeling in the sky squawked loudly. There was an answering squawk from the ground, followed by the screech of claws skidding to a halt. The other rocs were correcting her course!

"How are we going to escape, with those spy eyes up there?" Dug demanded. "There might as well be a satellite video unit!"

Nada's pretty face on her serpent body looked perplexed. "Who sat light? What did he do on it?"

"Never mind. I was speaking in Mundane. We can't get away as long as those rocs are watching from the sky."

"Unless we hide between the trees of the forest, until they go away," she said.

Sherlock glanced to the side. "Forget it. I never saw such impenetrable underbrush."

Dug looked too. He saw a solid mass of thorns, brambles, and what looked like poison ivy. No hiding place there. "We'll just have to keep moving, and hope things improve," he said. He realized that this was a rather anemic excuse for leadership, but it was the best he could do for now.

They ran on. It took the roc a while to reverse her course and get on the correct path, so they had a bit of leeway. Maybe the game was giving them a chance.

Then they came to a small, swift river. It was too wide to jump over, and way too strong to wade through. However, there was a footbridge over it.

And a sign: STOP. PAY TROLL.

Sure enough, from under the bridge was coming a tall, thin, brutishly ugly manlike creature with a warty countenance. The troll blocked the access to the bridge.

Dug realized that this was another game challenge. He

had to get across that bridge before the roc caught up. So he approached it forthrightly: "What's the toll, troll?"

"All your wealth," the troll rasped.

"Wealth? I don't have any wealth! I'm just a poor Player, strutting and fretting my hour upon this stage."

"Too bad." The troll crossed his ugly but all too serviceable arms, still blocking the way. At that point the sound of the pursuing roc became louder.

"Suppose we just push you out of the way and cross without paying?" Dug demanded.

"Then my friend the diggle will push the bridge out of the way, and you too, if you're on it."

"Diggle?"

From the ground beside them a formidable snout appeared. It had to be the hugest worm anybody ever dreamed of.

"The diggle is the largest of the voles," Nada explained. "It travels through rock, and works only for a song. Maybe the troll sings to it."

"But a vole is a mammal," Dug protested. "This is a worm."

"Uh, friend," Sherlock said. "In Mundania, there are mammals and worms. Here in Xanth it's different."

Dug realized that it was true. The old familiar rules just didn't apply here. He had seen that when Nada first turned from woman to serpent.

"Okay. The diggle works for a song. That lets me out; they tell me that I couldn't carry a tune if I had two others to hold up the ends of it."

"The diggle is not too choosy," she said. "But please don't try to sing; I'm sure it would offend my princessly sensitivities."

That made sense. He had no intention of embarrassing himself that way anyway. He would have to settle with the troll. "Okay. Here's my money," he said, digging into a pocket. He found a handful of coins.

The troll peered at the coins. "What manner of wealth are you?" he inquired.

"I'm a measly dime," the ten-cent piece replied. "I'm a plugged nickel," the five-cent piece said. "We're cheap pennies," the one-cent pieces chorused.

Dug almost dropped the coins. They were speaking!

"Money talks," Sherlock said, smiling.

"Are you solid and true wealth?" the troll asked.

The coins laughed. "Us? We're strictly small change! We aren't even the pure metals we're supposed to be. The pennies aren't pure copper, and the nickel isn't really nickel, and the dime doesn't have any silver at all!"

Dug saw that the coins wouldn't do it. He brought out his wallet and offered a dollar bill.

"Are you solid and true wealth?" the troll asked. Apparently he had a bit of magic, and could make money talk.

"Me? I'm not worth the paper I'm printed on! I'm just one buck, the least of the folding money denominations. This cheap Mundane is trying to foist off zilch on you. Where would you spend me, anyway? Xanth doesn't use money."

"How did mere paper ever get confused with wealth?" the troll asked.

"Well, originally I was backed by gold or silver," the paper dollar said. "But once they got the paper established, they quietly removed the backing, so now I'm only worth what folk think I'm worth, and that's less every year. They keep printing more of us, and that makes us worth less."

"Worthless," the troll agreed.

The sounds of the roc were drawing closer. Dug knew he had to find some way to pay the troll. "What else will you accept?" he asked desperately.

The creature looked around. "Does your black servant work well?"

Sherlock began to get angry.

"He's not my servant!" Dug snapped. "He's a friend, traveling with me. He's not for sale."

"Then your naga princess."

Nada hissed, outraged.

"She's not a servant either! She's my Companion!"

"Precisely. Is she soft at night?"

"She's guiding me through Xanth," Dug said quickly. "No deal on either of them."

The troll shrugged. "Then you can't pay the toll. Go away."

Now the ground was shaking as the roc came closer. They did not have much time left.

Dug looked desperately around. He saw the bridge, and the river coursing through its deep channel. Part of the long body of the diggle was in that channel; it must have drilled through the river along with the ground. Beside that torso was a bit of fluff.

Something percolated through his mind. This was the game. There always had to be a way through. But it wasn't necessarily obvious. Anything odd might be a clue. And that bit of fluff was odd. There was no other fluff, and no pillow bushes in the vicinity; it wasn't from a leaking pillow. It was almost as if it had been carried along with the diggle, as it magically tunneled through the ground. What kind of a hint could it be?

Well, he could ask. "Nada, do you see that bit of fluff? What do you think it is?"

Nada looked. "Why, that looks like a germ," she said.

"A germ? You mean the diggle's infected?"

"It looks healthy to me."

Her lack of a more complete answer just might suggest that there was more to this that she was not supposed to tell him. He had to figure it out for himself. "Germs don't infect things in Xanth?"

"Not exactly," she said evasively.

Suddenly he had a faint nagging thought. Which side was she on? Was it possible that she could be a False Companion? He had almost forgotten about that chance. No, she couldn't be; she had been too loyal. She simply wasn't allowed to tell him some things that were supposed to be game challenges.

The troll, meanwhile, was simply standing there, like a cartoon character who was no longer active. His job was evidently not to attack, but to be a barrier, reacting only when approached. Another game aspect. Xanth had turned real, but the game aspects were slightly flawed, perhaps deliberately.

He got down and reached for the fluff. He held it in his hand—and began to get another idea. Suddenly the pun registered: "This is the Germ of an Idea!" he exclaimed.

"Yes," she agreed. "I wasn't supposed to tell you, but now I can, because you figured it out yourself. The one who has it becomes smarter in thinking up new ideas. It must have been carried along with the diggle after it passed the Brain Coral's pool."

"This is the game-approved explanation for its presence?" he asked, knowing that it was. He had found the key. Now all he needed to do was figure out how to use it.

The roc burst into view. Perfect timing—of course. He realized now that this threat had been carefully choreographed, to give him just enough leeway while keeping him scared. It was indeed part of the game. But he still had to make the right move, or he would be booted out of it again.

He lifted the fluff to his forehead. "Let's have it, Germ, What's the Idea?"

It came to him. *Use the diggle.*

Use this giant worm thing? Here was where his Companion should have useful advice. "How can we use the diggle to escape the roc?" he asked her.

"Why, I suppose we could ask it to carry us along," she said, as if surprised by the question. She was a fair actress, but not perfect in that respect. "But you would have to sing to it."

"You surely have a better voice than I do," he said.

"I surely do. But this is something you must do for yourself, as the Player."

Dug looked at Sherlock. "You heard the lady,". the black man said. "It probably won't pay attention to me."

Desperate, Dug turned back to Nada. "But what about your princessly sensitivities?"

She glanced over his shoulder at the onrushing roc. "Perhaps I can stand it, for a while."

"Then let's go!" he said. He tucked the Germ into a pocket. "Diggle, that roc is about to smear us into messy pieces, getting your nice hide all icky. Carry us away from here. I'll sing to you."

The diggle, who had been as quiet as the troll, came to life. More of its long body drew out of the ground. The thing was so big that the torso was as thick through as that of a horse. The three of them jumped on, bestriding it. Actually Nada remained in naga form, so just lay close.

Dug opened his mouth and forced himself to sing. "I dream of Jeannie with the light brown hair!" he sang, badly off-key. He saw both Nada and Sherlock wince.

The diggle began to move. Just as the roc's beak came down, the diggle plunged under the ground—and carried them along with it. There was no impact; they just went under as if the ground didn't exist, or as if it were no more than water, or even air. It was dark, with veins of rock showing. The diggle's magic was at work.

Then it stopped. "Sing, before the ground congeals!" Nada cried, alarmed.

Oh. He had forgotten to sing. "I dream of Brownie in the light blue jeans!" he sang with even worse melody.

The diggle resumed motion, and the ground did not congeal. So Dug kept singing, and the diggle kept traveling. Since they were underground, the rocs couldn't follow. He had found the way to escape that prior challenge.

He realized that the diggle was making pretty good time. This was a fast way to travel south!

Then the diggle stopped again. "But I was still singing!" he protested.

"You started to repeat yourself," Sherlock said. "The thing may not have much taste in music, but it must get bored with old stuff."

"But I only know so many songs," Dug said. "And parodies of singing commercials."

The ground was starting to congeal. He could feel it thickening around them, becoming viscous. He didn't want it to turn all the way rock solid. "Choka Cola, stinky drink!" he sang. "Pour it down the kitchen sink! Smells like vinegar, tastes like ink!"

The diggle resumed motion, and the ground turned thin again.

But eventually Dug was out of parodies too. The ride would have to end. "Diggle, take us up to the surface," he said. "I'm about to run out of music."

"Music!" Sherlock muttered, pained. Nada murmured agreement. She sounded somewhat ill, and Dug doubted that it was from motion sickness. The two of them had made a great sacrifice, listening to him sing for so long.

The diggle wended upward as Dug sang his last ditty. It reached the surface as he finished.

They dismounted. "Thank you, diggle," Dug said a bit hoarsely. "You were a great help."

The diggle dived back under the earth, leaving no trace of its passage. The ground was solid. "Ain't magic wonderful," Dug remarked, gazing at the undisturbed ground.

"I think that was a diseased germ," Sherlock muttered, rubbing his ears.

"I still have it," Dug said. "It may be useful again."

"Where are we?" Sherlock asked.

"This must be the With-A-Cookee River," Nada said.

"What kind of a name is that for a river?" Dug asked.

"A descriptive one. I have to go change," Nada said. She assumed full serpent form, took her bundle of clothes in her mouth, and slithered off.

Dug looked around. They were not far from the river. This one was too wide for a little troll bridge, and indeed they saw no bridge on it. There were, however, all manner of cookies growing along its banks. That explained the name. The water was calm, but he suspected it would not be wise to try to swim across this one, because it was large enough to contain monsters.

Sure enough, soon he saw a long low snout followed by a faint ripple. Then he saw a single fin projecting from the water. Then a small puff of vapor, as of a water dragon quietly exhaling steam, waiting for some fool to swim by.

How were they to cross? He brought out the Germ and put it to his forehead again. "Got any more Ideas?" he inquired.

Use the cold cream.

Cold cream? Surely it didn't mean the stuff women used to remove makeup!

"Do you see any cold cream around here?" he asked Sherlock.

Sherlock looked around. "All I see is a cream puff—which I think I'll eat." He went to pick it up. It seemed to be growing from the ground, like a puffball. "Hey—this is still hot!"

"How can it be hot, if it's growing? It hasn't been baked in an oven."

"Well, it might as well have been! It's piping hot." Sherlock blew on his fingers, cooling them. The cream puff remained on the ground.

Nada returned, in human form, suitably garbed. "What's happening?" she inquired.

"I'm looking for cold cream," Dug said. "So far all we've found is a hot cream puff."

She looked. "I never heard of a hot cream puff. They're always cool. And cold cream is always cold."

"This puff is hot," Sherlock said.

She went to it. "That's cold cream. I know it when I see it, because on occasion I use it." She bent to touch it. "Hoo. It *is* hot! What can be the matter with it?"

"Look at this," Sherlock said. "There's a hot potato beside it."

"Potatoes don't grow hot either," she said. But in a moment she had verified this too. "This is most perplexing."

Dug saw the outline of a box formed from metallic rods,

enclosing the two objects. "Could this be a hot box?" he asked. "With hot rods for the sides?" By this time he knew that he could not trust the Mundane uses of such words.

"A hot box!" she exclaimed. "That explains it! The plants are being cruelly heated by the hot box. We can eat the potato, and rescue the cream puff, which I might as well have for cosmetic. But they are both too hot to touch."

"You don't need any cosmetic," Dug said. "You're already perfect." Then, lest she misconstrue his attitude, he added: "No offense."

She smiled, almost blinding him. "No offense."

Sherlock delved in his pack. "I just happen to have heavy heat-resistant gloves here," he said. "Just in case I had to handle a small fiery dragon or something." He donned them, then lifted up the potato. It was nicely baked.

But when he lifted the cream puff, something odd happened. "This is turning cold!"

"It must be compensating for all that heat," Dug said. "It is naturally a cold substance, so it must have been really struggling to stay cold in that hot box. Now that we have removed it, all the effort is making it too cold."

"I'll say!" Sherlock said. "The thing's trying to freeze my hands."

Then the full meaning of his Germ of an Idea burst on Dug. "Take it to the water! Let it freeze the water!"

Sherlock hurried to the river and dunked the cold cream. Immediately ice formed and spread outward. "Mind if I ask why?" he asked.

"So we can freeze our way across," Dug said. "I got that idea from the Germ."

Sherlock shook his head. "This is almost worse than the idea you had to sing," he said.

"Yet that did get us away from the rocs," Nada said. "And a good distance down the length of Xanth."

"But this time we don't have an angry roc bird chasing us," Sherlock pointed out.

As if on cue, there was a mean sound to the north. *As if?* Dug realized that it was probably choreographed by the game. And it would probably be a worse threat than the last, in the nature of a game.

"That sounds like werewolves," Nada said, looking alarmed.

"Why not garden-variety wolves?" Dug asked as he headed for the water.

"Xanth has very few ordinary wolves or dogs," she said. "There once were some, but they bred themselves out of existence, the same way man once did."

"Now, that doesn't make a lot of sense," Dug said. "Species can fade out by not breeding, but they can only get stronger by breeding a lot."

"Not in Xanth. If a species interbreeds with other species, the crossbreeds are their descendants. That's not bad, but it does mean that the original species diminish. My naga kind arose when human folk bred with serpent folk, and the centaurs were crossbreeds between humans and horses, and the mer folk derive from humans and fish, and the harpies from humans and birds. There are many such mixed species, and few original species. They were foolishly free in their breeding; it's a wonder the storks didn't balk at all those mixed deliveries. Only the fact that humans kept coming in new Waves enabled them to maintain their pure population." She looked at Sherlock. "Which is why your Black Wave should be welcome; your difference from other humans here is trivial."

Sherlock nodded. "That's about the first time I've liked having a white person call me trivial. But considering how different you are, I can't argue."

"Let's get on with the freezing," Dug said.

"For sure." Sherlock pried the ball of cold cream out of its socket in the ice and dunked it in the nearest liquid water beyond. In an instant that too was frozen.

The pack of werewolves appeared. Sure enough, some were in canine form, and some in shaggy human form, and

some were in between. All were howling villainously.
"Let's move it," Dug said.

"I'll try." Sherlock squatted, sliding the cold cream forward. The water froze around it. He moved out onto the new ice, freezing steadily ahead.

"Get on it, Nada," Dug said. "I'll defend the rear." He drew his knife.

"You are becoming more like a hero," she remarked approvingly.

"I just don't want any of us to get chomped!" He stepped on the ice after her. The ice now formed a Xanth-like peninsula extending into the river. He chopped at it with the knife, trying to separate them from the land. He hoped the resulting ice island would stay afloat.

The werewolves arrived. The first beast landed on the narrow neck of ice—and broke through it, splashing into the water. The ice the three of them stood on floated free.

There was a ripple in the water. A green snout was moving smoothly toward the werewolf. But the wolf scrambled out before the long green jaws parted to chomp him. The other wolves milled on the bank, knowing better than to set paw to water. Dug and his friends were on their way.

However, they were now at the mercy of the slow current of the With-A-Cookee River. Where would it take them? He also saw brightly colored fins. "What are those?" he asked, fearing the answer.

"Loan sharks," Nada said. "Everyone knows they'll take an arm and a leg, if you let them."

"Then we'll just have to stay out of the water," Dug said. He should have known that something egregiously punnish would turn up to make things worse.

"We should have brought a paddle," Sherlock said as he continued to add to their ice island. "Now we're up the crick without one."

"That's the way the cookee crumbles," Dug said.

"You can use your club to paddle," Nada said.

Dug tried it, but it was remarkably inefficient and the island started to rotate. "Maybe I can freeze a keel, so it won't spin," Sherlock said. He maneuvered the cold cream so that a spike formed, projecting like a tail. He dipped the cream, so that the freezing went deep. Soon the ice floe stabilized, and Dug was able to start it nudging across the river.

Then he heard a voice. It sounded like a girl. "Hey, Nada Naga!" it called.

There beyond the far bank of the river was a small party of people, waving their hands. "Who are they?" Dug asked, surprised.

"Jenny Elf—and the other Mundane Player," Nada said. "And someone else. A strange man. This should get interesting."

The other Player? Dug hadn't realized that there was one. This should indeed get interesting!

"Uh-oh," Sherlock said.

Dug glanced at him. "What's the matter?"

"The cold cream's giving out. It's no longer freezing the water."

Dug realized that the game was hitting him with another challenge. Their little ice floe would soon melt, dumping them in the river. He saw the predators circling hungrily.

"This is getting *too* interesting," he muttered.

10
CHASM

K im saw the peculiar party crossing the river. She had been alerted by the woof of Bubbles Dog. A pack of werewolves was baying, hunting down something, and it seemed to be a group of people. But the people had a raft or something, because they were out on the water where the wolves couldn't reach them.

Then one of the people turned, so that Kim saw her profile. "That's Nada Naga!" she cried.

"Who?" Cyrus asked. He was stuck in human form, because of the mean creatures in the river and the lake. They would quickly chomp him if he tried to change form and swim.

"Nada Naga. She's the Companion for the other Player. So that must be the other party. Your competition, Kim."

"Well, sure, I'd like to win the prize," Kim said. "But I like playing the game, too. In fact, I just like being in Xanth. Let's see if they're as curious about us as we are about them."

So Jenny cupped her mouth with her hands. "Hey, Nada Naga!" she called.

In a moment Nada answered. "Jenny Elf! Is that you?"

"Yes! We're stuck. On a squishy island. And sinking. Can you help?"

"We're free-floating. On an ice floe. And melting. Can you help?"

Were they destined to watch each other pass, being unable to get together? To separate and never see each other again, after coming so close? Or to watch each other sink into the water and bog, victim of the predators? Kim didn't like either notion. "This is another game challenge," she declared. "There has to be a way for us to help each other, if we want to. If we can just figure it out in time."

They considered. "I could pull their ice floe to shore," Cyrus said. "If someone protected my flank from allegations, moccasins, and loan sharks."

"Nada could do that," Jenny said. "If someone protected *her* flank."

Cyrus peered across at the other party. "How could that luscious girl protect anyone else?"

"She's a serpent woman," Jenny explained. "She changes into a serpent, the same way you change into a fish tail."

He nodded, seeing the possibilities. "They are drifting toward us. But I see that they are precariously perched."

"What can we do about that?" Jenny asked, concerned.

Sammy jumped from her shoulder to Cyrus' pack. He put his paw in. The end of the rope showed.

"Can you throw your rope that far?" Kim asked, catching on. Sammy had found what they could do.

"No. It is light rope, and must be weighted if it is to carry."

Sammy jumped to Kim's pack. "I think—" Jenny started.

Kim delved into her pack. She brought out a spare pair of shoes. "Here is your weight."

He knotted the end of the rope around the shoes, then hurled it toward the diminishing ice floe. A black man there caught it and held it. Then Jenny and Kim braced

Cyrus while he hauled on the rope, drawing the other party closer.

Then the melting ice floe capsized, dumping the three into the water.

For an instant they were stunned by the calamity. Then Sammy jumped up on Kim's head and batted at her forehead, as if coaxing out a thought. Kim cried out directions—and because she was the Player, the others followed them immediately. "Jenny, hold the rope. Cyrus, take a weapon and dive for them." Kim herself delved in her pack, finding a knife. Then, before Jenny could protest, she dived into the river herself. Sammy jumped from her head to the back of Bubbles, who looked a bit startled but did not protest. The cat was much smaller than the dog, so his weight was not a problem.

Meanwhile the other Player was reacting similarly. "Loop the rope around us all!" he shouted. "Face out. We'll defend ourselves while they haul us in."

In two and a half moments Cyrus reached the other party, and in two more so had Kim. They joined the others, roped together, facing out. The sharks and allegations were circling, but the party now bristled with knives and a spear, and one of its number was a serpent with horrendous fangs. Another had a powerful tail, and evidently knew how to swim very well, to intercept any hostile creature.

Jenny pulled on the rope. Her feet were sinking into the marshy hammock, braced by the dog and cat, but she was able to haul the mass of people slowly toward her. They finally reached the island, but did not try to scramble onto it. "We need to find solid land instead!" Kim cried from the water.

Sammy stood on Bubbles' back and said something in cat talk. The dog moved reluctantly into the water and swam toward another hammock, the cat on her back. Bubbles understood what Sammy was saying!

"They are showing the way!" Jenny cried. "Follow them!" Then she scrambled into the water herself, still holding the rope. The water here was not deep; she was able to wade far enough to catch up to the group. She got inside the loop, next to the serpent, so that she too could defend herself from the creatures outside.

It was a clumsy, messy business, but they pushed with their feet and stroked with their free hands, and nudged in the direction shown by the animals. Soon the ground under the water became firmer, and they were able to walk on it, chest-deep, then waist-deep, then knee-deep. At last they stood on solid land again—and saw a path ahead. There were on their way!

But what a motley crew they were! Dog, serpent, merman, three humans, and one elf were soaked through and spattered with mud. Only the cat was pristine.

"Let's get clean before we make our introductions," Kim suggested. The others were glad to agree.

"Sammy, where is there a good place to—" Jenny started.

The cat bounded off down the path. They followed, forming a ragged line. Soon they came to a larger, clearer lake, evidently one of the sections of Lake Tsoda Popka. It sparkled effervescently. But the cat was dipping a paw, daintily cleaning an imagined speck.

Kim squatted and dipped out a handful. "This is champagne!" she exclaimed. "We're supposed to wash in this?"

"Well, we know just how to do it," Jenny said. She fetched out an empty bottle and dipped it in the lake.

In three quarters of a moment everyone had bottles, and they were in the midst of Xanth's most uproarious fizz fight. Lake Champagne might never be the same, but they were getting clean!

Then Nada Naga, who had assumed human form underwater rather than miss the fight, went off in one direction to find a clothing tree, and Cyrus and Sherlock went off in another to find their own tree, leaving Jenny and Kim and Dug to hold the fort, as it were. They had more or less exchanged names during the cleanup. Bubbles and Sammy settled down to snooze beside each other in the sun, seeming to get along fine.

"So you're the other Player," Kim said boldly. "Are you enjoying it so far?"

"I sure am," Dug agreed. "And I'm only here on a dare."

"A dare? You didn't want to play?"

"I don't go for computer games or silly fantasy. By my friend Ed dared me to try one. I bet him my girlfriend against his motorcycle that I wouldn't like it." He smiled sheepishly. "I lost."

"You bet your girlfriend?" Kim asked, uncertain how to take that.

"Yes. Pia. She's Ed's girlfriend now. I think maybe I was set up. But I couldn't even be mad, after I saw Nada."

"You go for that type?" Kim was being guarded, for some reason she didn't care to analyze. It might be mere coincidence that Dug was a handsome young Mundane man.

"Who wouldn't? She's a knockout!"

"But she's a naga princess," Jenny said. "And she doesn't go for younger men."

"So I learned." He spread his hands. "Don't look at me that way! She's the world's most beautiful woman, and I'm just a sixteen-year-old jerk. I'm just saying that anything I might have lost back home no longer mattered, after I saw what was here." He focused on Kim. "That handsome merman—he's not interested in you, either, I'll bet. Same reason."

"He's looking for a mermaid," Kim agreed. "He's just traveling with us until he finds her."

"Same way Sherlock's traveling with us until he finds a place for his people to settle." He paused. "Look, Kim, I guess we're supposed to be in competition, but I want you to know I don't care about the prize. I just like being in the game."

"Me too," she said, discovering that she was losing interest in the prize.

"You too? I got into this on a dare, but I figured you really wanted to play."

"I do want to play. Just to be in Xanth. I love Xanth. It's so much more interesting than Mundania."

"Yes, it is. I don't know anything about it, but I haven't been bored since I got in, and not just because of Nada. It's some place!"

She nodded. "So do you want to travel on together for a while, if the rules allow it?"

"Sure. We may have nothing in common except Mundania, but that's enough of a cross for us both to bear." He glanced at Jenny. "You're her Companion? Do you know if it's okay?"

"I don't know any reason why not," Jenny said. "I don't think there are any rules, really, except about things like not looking at a girl's panties."

He laughed. "I learned about that the hard way! I tried to sneak a peek at Nada's, and I got blotted out of the game. I mean, my screen went blank, and I had to scramble to get back in. I'll never do that again!" He looked around. "Which reminds me: we need to get changed too. These clothes won't be worth much after this workout."

"We can change after the others find clothing," Jenny said. "We're just keeping an eye out now, in case anything else threatens. But as long as Bubbles doesn't bark and Sammy doesn't wake, it's safe."

"Bubbles?"

Kim explained about the way she had found the dog. "She's really very good," she concluded. "It's a shame that someone was throwing her away. I'm sorry I can't take her with me, when I return to Mundania."

"She can stay with me and Sammy," Jenny said quickly. "We won't let her be thrown away again. I'm sure Professor Grossclout will allow it."

"Who?" Dug asked.

"He's the demon in charge of the game. Compared to

him, every other person's head is full of mush. But he's not too bad, if you ever manage to get to know him."

"Demons in charge of the game! Why?"

"Well, I think it's because of the Demon $X(A/N)^{th}$. He's the source of all the magic of Xanth. He wanted the game to be played. So the demons are handling it. That's all I know."

"What kind of a demon?"

So they had to explain to him about that. By the time they had done so, the others had returned.

That was a surprise. Kim eyed one party, then the other. Nada was in trousers and a male shirt; Cyrus and Sherlock were in dresses. "All we could find," the black man said, embarrassed.

"Same here," Nada confessed.

"But now we can go in the opposite directions and change," Cyrus said, relieved.

This time Jenny and Kim went with Nada, while Dug went with Cyrus and Sherlock. The girls found the tree, and picked out nice dresses. "Suddenly I feel very feminine," Kim said. "I like it."

But Nada reconsidered. "I believe I will remain in trousers," she said.

"You get tired of getting stared at?" Kim inquired. "It isn't a problem I've had."

"Well, you're not a princess."

Kim nodded ruefully. "That must be it."

They returned to the central camp. They saw the three males coming back from the other direction, all appropriately garbed. They settled down to eat, and to get to know each other better. Kim noticed that Cyrus and Nada seemed to find each other interesting. Well, both were crossbreeds, and he was almost as handsome as she was beautiful. Wouldn't it be something, if—but no, it wasn't her business to speculate.

They organized their party and set off south. It was more interesting, Kim thought, having a larger group. Also safer, perhaps, if they didn't encounter anything truly formidable. It was getting late, and they would have to find a campsite before too long.

They came to a centaur range. Kim could tell, because the path widened and was beaten down by hooves. Soon a male centaur galloped up. He was an impressive figure of horse and man, with a large bow and a quiver of arrows. Centaurs were notorious for their marksmanship; they could score on anything they fired at. "Who are you to intrude on our range?" he demanded. He seemed to have a slight speech defect.

There was something familiar about him. Then she identified it: he was Horace, the zombie centaur. One of the prospective Companions. Since he hadn't been chosen, he was now on backup duty, as Jenny and Nada would have been had they not been chosen. So he was in costume, his zombie nature concealed. She was sure it was him, regardless.

Kim looked at Dug. "He's male; you take it," she murmured. Because of course a Player had to handle it; this could be another challenge.

Dug stepped forward. "We are travelers playing a special game," he said. "We aren't looking for trouble, we're looking for a place to spend the night in peace."

"If you come in peace, you are welcome to spend the night in our village," Horace said.

Dug glanced at Nada, and Kim glanced at Jenny. Nada and Jenny both nodded: centaurs could be trusted. Apparently Dug had handled the challenge appropriately, by expressing their desire for peace. Kim was relieved; centaurs were bad enemies and good friends, and there would be no need to fear any dangers of the night here.

So Horace led them to the village. This appeared to be a group of stalls, but there were human-type houses too, evidently for those who served the centaurs. Several other centaurs came out to greet them, among them two mares.

Kim saw Dug and Sherlock blink at the sight of the bare-breasted lady centaurs. Those were the fullest breasts she had ever seen, and she suspected that the sight had far more impact on the men. But both had the wit to mask their reactions. She managed to mask her smile. Actually she would love to have an upper torso like that, to make male eyes pop.

There were passing introductions. Then the centaurs showed them to their stalls, which turned out to be fairly nice little houses with nice beds of straw inside. The three women shared one, and the three men another. Bubbles and Sammy found comfortable places of their own in the straw and were instantly asnooze. It took a while longer for the others to eat and settle down, but in due course they too were asleep.

So this had turned out to be no challenge, Kim thought. But she knew that if Dug had given the wrong answer, the party could have been in desperate trouble. Was Dug a naturally diplomatic person, or had he been lucky, this time? It was important for her to know, because he was her competition. Even if she no longer cared about the prize.

In the morning, refreshed, they resumed their journey. "Would you like a ride as far as the Gap Chasm?" Horace Centaur inquired.

Kim exchanged another glance with Dug. A ride? Was this another challenge? Yet centaurs were trustworthy. Maybe this was just the game's way of moving them along rapidly to the next challenge. In some other variant there could be a real row with the centaurs, or a dragon waiting along the path. But in this one it was at the Gap Chasm, so the sensible thing to do was to get on down there without wasting time. It was as if the game got impatient with delay, and wanted to get on with the action.

"Why not?" Dug said after a pause. "As long as our friends can ride too."

"Your friends are welcome," Horace said.

"If I may inquire," Sherlock said, "is there a place here where a new community could settle?"

Horace was surprised. "What kind of community?"

"A human Black Wave community."

Horace looked at the other centaurs. "We could use more servants," he said. "For the menial chores."

Sherlock frowned. "We'll keep it in mind," he said, evidently intending to do no such thing. Why should his folk settle for more of the same kind of treatment they had in Mundania?

So six centaurs carried the party rapidly southward. Kim carried Bubbles Dog with her, and Jenny carried Sammy Cat on the back of another centaur. The scenery fairly whizzed by. Kim would have preferred to go slower, because she was a bit afraid of the next challenge. Getting across the Gap Chasm was bound to be no easy matter. She knew there was an invisible bridge, but how could they find it? If they tried to go down into the chasm, the Gap Dragon would get them. Nobody crossed the Gap with impunity.

All too soon they arrived. There was the huge chasm, with its base shrouded in fog and the sheer brink of it taunting them. There was no bridge in sight, of course.

They dismounted and the centaurs galloped away. What next?

Dug, heedless of the scary depth, explored the verge. He walked east. Soon the nature of the chasm changed. The land did not drop straight down, but descended in a series of half-loops, so that it was possible to go down without falling. "We can handle this!" he said enthusiastically.

"But there is a dragon below," Nada warned him.

"You can be a big serpent and scare it off," he said.

"I can't scare *that* dragon. Not the Gap Dragon. The only safe way to handle him is to avoid him."

"Well, we can have Sammy Cat show us a way down and across that will avoid the dragon." He was so confident that it was annoying.

"Perhaps," Nada said guardedly.

Kim could see that the naga princess had her hands full, trying to keep Dug out of trouble. She couldn't even change forms both ways in his presence, because of the problem of clothing. It probably wasn't much fun for her, being his Companion. But it might not be much fun for Jenny Elf, either, being Kim's Companion, because Kim was impulsive too.

"This could be trouble," Cyrus said, glancing up.

Kim followed his gaze. An ugly little dark cloud was scudding from the north. "Is that who I fear it is?" she asked.

"Cumulo Fracto Nimbus," he agreed. "You encountered him before."

"I sure did! He always rains on the party."

There was a rumble of thunder. The others looked up. They shared glances of dismay.

"Hey, what's the big deal?" Dug asked. "So a little cloud passes. So it rains a bit. That won't stop us."

"That's Fracto," Nada said.

"Fractal?"

"Fracto, Xanth's worst cloud. We had better get under cover."

"What's all the fuss about one tiny cloud?" he demanded. "It'll be gone soon enough."

"If you do not care to heed my advice, perhaps you should exchange me for Kim's Companion," Nada said somewhat stiffly.

Dug looked surprised. Then he glanced at Jenny Elf, thoughtfully. "I guess maybe there's something I'm not picking up on here," he said. "But as I see it, we can wait until an actual storm threatens."

But the others knew better. They were already hurrying to find the makings of a tent. Kim went to a pie tree she had spied, to gather a good meal to eat while they waited for the cloud's fury to expire. Jenny was going for pillows. There was no telling how long they would have to wait.

"I can't believe this," Dug said. "One stupid little cloud! You'd think it was a hurricane or something."

There was another rumble. The cloud was expanding, puffing itself up voluminously. A puffy face was forming on its surface. A chill gust of wind came down.

"What an ugly puss," Dug remarked, staring up at it.

Sammy meowed. Dug looked around. "I didn't mean you," he said, flashing a smile. The cat relaxed.

"We could use some help on this tent," Sherlock called.

Dug finally realized that this was serious. He went to help pitch the tent.

The first fat drops of rain spattered down. Then their nature changed. "Hey, that's sleet!" Cyrus exclaimed.

Kim held out her hand. Hard pellets bounced off it. "Sleet? That's hail!" she said.

They got the tent finished, and piled unceremoniously into it as the hailstorm intensified. Bubbles and Sammy joined them, not wanting any part of the storm. The dog huddled close to Kim, nervous about the closeness of so many relative strangers, but not making any fuss. Kim was also highly conscious of Dug wedged on her other side.

Now the hail had become snow, piling down in turbulent flurries. They were safe under the canvas, and they had blankets too, so they were comfortable. Kim just couldn't keep her awareness off her closeness to Dug, under a shared blanket. If only something like this could be real, as in a date!

"That's more of a cloud than I figured," Dug said, paying her no attention. "Snow—on a warm day!"

"Not only that," Sherlock said. "It's colored, if you'll excuse the term."

Kim peered out. She saw pastel hues. The snow was all the colors of the rainbow! "It's pretty," she said.

"Nothing Fracto does is pretty," Nada said darkly.

They ate the pies while the storm continued. "I wonder why Fracto came here right now," Jenny said. "How could he know we were here?"

"The game!" Kim exclaimed. "He was sent by the game! It's another challenge."

"A cloud sent to mess us up?" Dug asked. "But all we have to do is wait for it to peter out."

Sherlock shook his head. "I don't know much about clouds or magic, but I'll bet this is going to make a difference. For one thing, this chasm's going to be twice as hard to cross, covered in snow."

Dug nodded. "You're right. After the storm passes, that funny snow will remain. It'll slow us down."

"Slow us down?" Kim asked. "Maybe it will speed us up!"

The others looked at her. "We don't want to jump into that blind," Nada said. "The smaller crevices will be covered up, and the slopes will be treacherously slippery. We should wait until it melts."

"But that could take days," Kim protested. "No, I'm thinking of skiing down on that snow. That would make a tedious trip easy."

"Skiing!" Dug said. "I tried to ski once, and almost broke my leg. That was just a little slope. This canyon's a mile deep. Even a skilled skier could get himself killed."

He had a point. Kim had skied, but she was no expert, and this would be no easy course. "Well, we could sled down it, maybe."

"Where'd we get sleds?"

Sammy stirred. He was about to head out into the storm when Jenny caught him. "Not yet, Sammy!" she said. "Wait till it stops snowing!"

Dug pursed his lips. "He can find sleds?"

"Sammy can find anything," Jenny said proudly. "Except home. So there must be sleds nearby."

"Can you be sure they are near?" Nada asked.

"Actually, I can't," Jenny admitted. "Sometimes things are way far away. But I know he'll find the closest sled there is."

"Okay, so we can get sleds," Dug said. "But sleds can be dangerous too, on an uncharted slope. I was ready to walk it, but I don't know about this."

"Maybe Sammy can also find a safe route down," Kim suggested. "Then we could follow on sleds."

"I wouldn't let him go alone," Jenny said. "But maybe he could ride on a sled with me, and sort of indicate whether it was safe to go on. I think that might work."

Finally the storm eased. Fracto's rages were severe, but seldom endured long. But what damage they could do in a short time!

Kim and the others climbed out of the tent. The snow was several feet deep, almost burying the tent; they had almost to tunnel to the surface.

It was a changed world. Colored snow lay everywhere, changing the landscape. The nearby trees had piles of blue snow on their foliage, while bushes were buried under yellow snow. The level land was covered in brown, while the descending slopes of the Gap Chasm were clothed in black. But it was definitely snow; Kim dipped a finger and tasted it. Black icy flakes.

They foraged for heavier clothing. There were yellow jackets growing nearby, and the cold had frozen their stingers, so that it was possible to wear them. There was also a boot tree with a fine selection ranging from bootees to jack boots. Before long they were all suitably bundled up, looking like so many stuffed dolls.

Kim realized that all this was unlikely to be coincidence. The game had set up its challenge, with supplies in place, and moved in the storm when they arrived. They were not going to go hungry or cold. They merely had to make it down into the Gap Chasm.

"Now, Sammy," Jenny said. The cat bounded away, leaving pawprints in the snow. The dog, less adventurous, remained in the tent.

Jenny followed the cat, and Kim followed Jenny. Soon they came to a sled shed. Kim knew it was that, because there was a sign on the door saying so. The cat bounded up to the door and waited until Jenny opened it. They went inside.

There were two big rounded devices. One was labeled ROBERT and the other ROBERTA. "But these aren't sleds," Jenny said. "At least, not like any I've seen."

Sherlock arrived. "Those are bobsleds!" he exclaimed, amazed.

"They have nicknames?" Jenny inquired.

Now Kim recognized the type. She had seen them race in the Winter Olympics on TV. Horribly swift three- or four-man sleds. They were supposed to careen down into the chasm in these? "But we don't know the first thing about handling a—a Robert sled," she protested weakly.

"Oh, I wouldn't say that," Sherlock said. "I rode on one once. Course it wasn't far or fast, just a little demo hill. I was the steersman. I probably couldn't have steered it wrong if I'd tried, on that track, but I did sort of get the great feel of it. That's the king of sleds, for sure."

Kim felt a sinking sensation. They were going to do it! Go down into that dread chasm on bobsleds!

They hauled the sleds back to camp. "Look what we found," Nada said, pointing.

Kim looked. There were two clearly shaped trails down into the chasm, with square signs posted where each divided.

"How did those signs get there?" Kim asked. "I don't see any tracks in the snow, and they weren't there before it snowed."

"Must be game magic," Dug said. "We really have to sled down those trails."

"But how will we know which way to go?"

"I see the signs say RIGHT and LEFT," he said. "So all we have to do is follow those road signs."

"What kind of challenge is that?" she demanded. "I don't trust this."

"Ah, you're just chicken to take the ride."

"You bet I'm chicken," she retorted, nettled. "Why would they go to all this trouble to set up a challenge, then tell us how to get through it?"

"To get us quickly down to the bottom, where we'll have to figure out how to avoid the dragon."

It did make morbid sense. But still she didn't trust it. This whole business was just too elaborate.

"Well, let's do it," Dug said. "Sherlock and Nada and I can take Robert, and Cyrus and Jenny and Kim take Roberta. We'll race each other down to the dragon."

"Who will then eat the first arrival, so the second can get through," Kim said acidly.

That finally made him pause. But he recovered. "We'll tackle that problem when we get there."

He was hopeless. And she was hopeless, to be so intrigued by him. But she reminded herself that it was only a game. The worst that could happen was that they would wash out and be back in Mundania.

Or was it? What would happen to the others, if the Players disappeared? The Companions would be all right, probably, but the others—Cyrus, Sherlock, and Bubbles— could be stranded in the snow, in the Gap, with a deadly dragon coming.

The game was no longer the fun it had been. But what could she do? Skip out on a challenge? She was stuck for it.

They hauled the bobsleds up to the ends of the two trails. Sherlock showed Cyrus how to steer. "It's mostly leaning, actually," he said. "But you have to time it right, and pull on these handles, here." Then Sherlock went to the other sled and got in. Nada got in behind him, and Dug was ready to push and jump in at the back.

Their own sled had Cyrus, Jenny with Bubbles and Sammy, and Kim as the push-off rider. They got set. "Do we really have to race?" Kim asked. "Maybe it would be better to have one sled try it first."

"It is set up like a race," Jenny said. "Probably it's better to race."

There was just no getting out of this. Kim got set to push off. She looked across at Dug.

"On your mark," he called. "Get set. GO!"

Kim pushed. The sled tipped over the rim and started down. She leaped onto the back and hung on. It felt exactly like falling.

In half a moment they were zooming toward the fork. The sign said LEFT. "Sammy says go right!" Jenny screamed. Indeed the little cat was almost scrambling out of the sled on the right side.

So Cyrus steered it right. They entered a slanting ledge overlooking a sheer drop into the chasm, then threaded past an outcropping into a kind of narrow valley. There was another fork, with another sign: LEFT.

"Go left!" Jenny cried, as the cat scrambled left.

They went left. Kim looked back, and saw that the path of the right fork turned and went directly down the face of the chasm, an impossible drop.

They came to a third fork and sign. This one said LEFT again. "Right!" Jenny cried, and they went right. The trail looped around, found a channel, and debouched on a large level ledge. The sled slid to a halt. They got out.

Kim's heart was thudding. "Two of those signs were wrong!" she said, outraged. "One of them would have dumped us into the chasm!"

Cyrus and Jenny looked back up the trail. "You're right," Cyrus said. He looked shaken. "We can't trust the signs. All of them said LEFT, but we had to go right twice. We couldn't just do the opposite of what they said, because one of them was correct. So there's no consistent pattern."

"Where is the other sled?" Jenny asked.

Sammy jumped from her arms and bounded along the ledge. They followed. Soon they spied it: jammed in a dead end about halfway between the ledge and the top. Its occupants seemed to be all right, though disheveled and annoyed.

"The middle sign was wrong?" Kim called.

"It sure was!" Dug called back. "You're lucky yours were right."

"Ours weren't. We ignored them. Sammy knew the way."

"That's some cat," he said. Then Dug and Sherlock and Nada made their way down the slope to the ledge. Their sled was hopelessly jammed and unusable. Sherlock paused to look carefully at the signs, and then went to check the signs on Kim's trail.

They consulted. With only one sled, only one party

could continue. In fact, there was only one trail leading down from the ledge. "I think this challenge can have only one winner," Dug said ruefully.

"Well, you can have it," Kim said. "This sledding scares me, and so does the dragon below. I'd rather find some other way."

"It is possible to go around the Gap Chasm," Nada said. "But it's a long way, and there are dangers."

"I don't care! I've had all of the Gap I care to."

Dug pondered. "I'd as soon go on down and get it over with. But not with wrong signs. You could make it, with your cat, but we'd probably get skunked again."

"Say, I think I have it figured," Sherlock said, returning. "It's not what they say, it's where they are. When you have to go right, the sign's on the right. When you have to go left, it's on the left."

Kim looked. "You're right! It's like the game of Scissors!"

"Scissors?" Sherlock asked, and the others looked similarly blank.

"It's a game. Most of the players have played it before, so they know the rules, but there are a few newcomers who don't. They sit in chairs in a circle and pass a pair of scissors around. Each one says, 'I receive these scissors crossed,' and passes them on uncrossed, or whatever, and changes the scissors to match. It's different for each one, depending on the scissors. But when a newcomer does it, chances are he's wrong, and everybody knows it. They keep playing until he catches on: it's not the scissors, it's the legs. So maybe someone has his legs crossed, and he passes the scissors on uncrossed, saying they're crossed, and everyone agrees but the poor innocent who's looking at the scissors."

"The signs!" Dug said. "They're the scissors—and you have to look at where they are instead of what they are. That's the challenge—to figure out the key before you get creamed."

"And this was just the practice run, to give us a chance

before we blow it for real," Kim agreed. "Though one of those wrong paths sure looked final to me."

"It isn't," Sherlock said. "I saw where it has a leveling slope after the drop, like a ski jump. *Then* it dead-ends. It looks worse than it is."

"So now we know," Cyrus said. "But we have only one sled. I for one would rather not use it."

"So let's go find some other way," Kim said gratefully. "Let *them* have our sled, if they want it."

"I'm not eager to ride down," Nada protested.

Dug pursed his lips. "How do you feel about it, Jenny?"

"I don't mind which way, as long as I have Sammy to guide me."

Dug looked at Kim. "Want to exchange Companions?"

Kim was astonished. "Can we do that?" She had thought Nada's suggestion to that effect was sarcastic.

"We can try it and see what happens. I never saw any rule saying no."

Kim considered this amazing proposal. Jenny was good, and Sammy was useful, but Nada could become a serpent and a formidable bodyguard. Dug would need the cat's ability to sneak through the chasm valley without blundering into the dragon. It seemed a fair exchange. "Let's do it," she decided.

So Nada Naga joined Kim and Cyrus, while Jenny joined Dug and Sherlock. Sammy Cat remained with Jenny, and Bubbles Dog remained with Kim. It all seemed even.

Then Nada assumed large serpent form and slithered up the snowy slope. She could handle it better in that form than in the human form; the snow gave her sinuous body purchase. She reached a small tree, clamped her teeth on it, and let Cyrus and Kim use her body like a rope to climb up more readily. When they reached the sapling, Nada went on up again. After several such stages they reached the top, cold but safe. Then Kim held out Nada's jacket, while Cyrus faced away, so Nada could return to human form and get quickly dressed.

"We're up," Kim called down to the others, who were now out of sight on the ledge.

"Okay," Dug called back from below. "Been nice knowing you! We're going down." There was the sound of the sled moving.

"And now we have to start our long walk around the Gap Chasm," Kim said. "But I'm relieved not to have to ride down any farther."

The others nodded agreement. So, it almost seemed, did Bubbles.

11
DRAGON

D ug watched the other party scale the slope, leaving the Gap Chasm. His feelings were mixed. He was sorry to see Nada Naga go, because she was the most luscious female creature he could imagine. But she had also been a distraction. He had been more or less blundering through the challenges, and that was no good; he needed to focus clearly on what he was doing. He wasn't interested in winning the prize, just in extending his time in the game. But he realized that he had to keep winning challenges, and following the general course of the game, or he would soon enough be dumped out of it. So Nada had probably been a net liability, not because of her, but because of him.

Jenny Elf, in contrast, was not a romantic figure. He had no hankering to see her panties or body. And her cat was one supremely useful creature. The way he had found the bobsleds, and the correct path down the slope—that was a tremendous asset in this game. So Jenny made all the sense Nada didn't, for him. He should be able to do much better now.

But why had Kim agreed to the exchange? She hadn't wanted to sled down into the depths and meet the dragon. He could appreciate why. But Jenny would have gone out of the chasm with her. Nada hadn't wanted to sled on down, but would have, because she had to follow the route her Player decided on. So they hadn't had to switch for that reason. What did Nada offer that Kim wanted?

Well, protection, of course. Nobody much messed with Nada in her huge serpent form. Nobody, it seemed, except the Gap Dragon. She had been quick to point out that she couldn't back off that particular monster, and he had been quick to pick up on that fact. So despite what he had said, he was worried; there was a real threat down there, and he had better have a notion how to handle it before he got there. So now Kim had that serpent protection. Was that what she wanted?

He turned to look down into the chasm. Cold fog shrouded the depths, so he could not see more than the beginning of the trail. They should be able to navigate it successfully, now that they had the key to the signs. If that went wrong, Sammy Cat would let them know. So the trip down shouldn't be a problem. But the dragon would be more than enough to make up for it.

"What are we going to do about that dragon?" he asked the others.

"That's bothering you?" Sherlock asked in mock surprise. "Me, too. If it eats me, I'm gone. If it eats you, I'm stuck down there with no game Player to lead the way. The Companion doesn't have to help me, you know."

"If Dug gets eaten, he'll disappear from Xanth," Jenny said. "Then I'll call Professor Grossclout, and he'll take me out. I'll ask him to take you too."

"Why should he bother?"

"Because the game isn't supposed to interfere with regular people of Xanth. You're a regular person. So the Professor will have to put you back where we found you." She hesitated. "If I may ask, why did you come with Dug and Nada?"

"I am a member of the Black Wave. I'm trying to find a place for us to stay where folk will be glad to have us, or where there are no other folk to be concerned."

"Oh, like the Curse Fiends!" she said.

"The what?"

"They were folk of the Seventh Wave who settled in Lake Ogre-Chobee and became the Curse Friends, only others call them the Curse Fiends. They remained sort of isolated, and never really mixed with the other folk of Xanth. So I guess you're the Fifteenth Wave. You want to be separate like them?"

"No, not really. But we're prepared to be, if that's the way of it. These Curse Friends—they're not really fiends, then?"

"No, they're just people. They act in plays, and go on tours, entertaining others. I think maybe they would have mixed, but nobody invited them to."

"Exactly. Maybe I should talk with the Curse Fiends."

"After we get by the dragon," Dug said firmly. "Nobody's talking with anybody, if he gets eaten first."

Sherlock and Jenny exchanged half a glance. "Man's got a point," Sherlock said.

"I can ask Sammy how to get away from the dragon," Jenny said. "But I don't think—"

Sure enough, the cat started running up the slope, in the same direction Kim's party had gone. Jenny had to chase after him, cancelling her statement, so he wouldn't keep looking for the way away from the dragon.

Then Dug had a notion. "That evil cloud, what's-his-name, Fractal—he still around?"

There was a warning rumble from the depths. The mist was part of the cloud, and he was still there.

"Maybe better not to aggravate him by mispronouncing his name," Sherlock murmured. "Fracto."

"Fracto," Dug said contritely. "Sorry about that. Of course we don't want to aggravate him. He could blow up a storm again, and bury us."

Sherlock looked at him as if suspecting Dug of some

devious purpose, but did not comment. Sherlock was right: Dug now knew how to get by the dragon.

Kim called down from above: they had made it out of the chasm. "Okay!" Dug called.

They were ready to get into the Roberta sled, but Sherlock hesitated. "What's the matter?" Dug asked.

"I've got long legs. That's not enough footroom in this sled for me."

"Isn't it the same as the other sled?"

"No. Take a look." Sherlock climbed in—and his rear came back into the second person's place. It looked uncomfortable for him, and it would push the other two back, so that there wouldn't be enough room for the third person at the end.

"We'll have to change the order," Dug said. "Jenny, you try it."

Jenny got in, but her legs were much shorter, not reaching far into the front. Dug and Sherlock's longer legs couldn't fit in the remaining space, so again there wasn't room for the third man.

"Then I'll have to do it," Dug said. He got in, and Jenny took the middle, with Sammy Cat in her lap, and Sherlock took the end. Now they fit perfectly.

Sherlock showed him how to steer. It was not hard, the man assured him; the other sled had been magically responsive, so that it seemed that even a thought directed it. All Dug really had to do was hold the handles and focus on where he wanted to go, and it would go there.

Belatedly he wondered: had the game arranged it this way? Because he was the Player, who should handle his challenges himself. The prior run had been for practice, so it didn't matter who steered the sled, but this one was for the money. How could the demon proprietors have known that Dug's sled would be lost, and that he would change to the other one? They must have had magical information.

They got settled in the Roberta sled and started down. Dug knew this was going to be one harrowing ride, but he reminded himself that it was after all only a game. There was always a way through, and they had found the way through for the sled. He hoped.

The sled started with a frightening plunge. It gathered such velocity that Dug abruptly doubted that he had a true path down. This could only end in a splat! He felt Jenny tense; a glance back showed her frozen with half a scream in her mouth, and the cat was hiding his head under her knees.

Then the ground curved up and the sled's runners took a better grip on reality. But before Jenny could get her scream the rest of the way out, the trail made a savage turn and ended in a square drop-off. There was space at either side, so that he could steer off the trail, avoiding the disaster. But the trail was clear, and there was no sign. So it should be right, despite the appearance. What should he do?

Dug had only seconds to decide. He froze. That meant that he did nothing. The sled rushed on down the trail. And off the drop-off. Dug heard a muttered "Sheesh!" from the rear.

Then out of the fog loomed a wall, and in the wall was a crevice, and the sled slammed into that crevice and zoomed on. The trail had jumped a gap in the slope; had the sled been moving slower, it would have crashed into the wall beneath the gap, flattening them and dropping them into whatever lay below. Had he steered it off the trail, he might have brought it to a stop, but they would have been stuck partway down the wall of the chasm. So he had made the right decision, by default.

They came to a fork. The sign said RIGHT, and it was on the right side, so Dug steered it that way. This path dropped, so that they sped up again, and again there was a bit of nervous choice. There seemed to be several tracks, all converging farther down, so it made no difference which one he followed. But some were more ragged than others. The sled struck a bump, and sailed into the air, and he almost lost control. It did make a difference, because they could capsize—or whatever it was that a bobsled did—if he managed it wrong. So he steered for the smoothest path, and corrected course as they bounced around, gaining proficiency. He managed to keep them upright and pointed forward.

The tracks converged. Then the main track suddenly curved up so sharply that it looped. "What is this, a rollercoaster ride?" Dug demanded rhetorically.

"No, a flume ride," Sherlock said, as the loop exited into a bank of snow that shook loose and slid down the slope. They were carried along in the flowing current of white powder; the snow had given up being Technicolor and was now plain vanilla white. Again they were falling, part of an avalanche. But it was not an easy ride; Dug had to keep steering by focusing, lest they turn over or turn sideways. This was like one of those purely mechanical computer games, requiring constant finger dexterity and spot judgment to avoid being dumped. Fortunately he had played a number of such games before getting bored with their intellectual simplicity, and had a fairly steady hand.

"If this is the right trail," Dug puffed through the enveloping snow, "I'd hate to see the wrong one!"

This, too, leveled out at last. They came to another sign saying RIGHT, but they couldn't see the fork; it had been hidden by the fall of snow. Where could they steer?

Dug solved the problem by going right at the sign. The sled hit it and crashed on. The others understood the logic, he hoped: they had to go along the path marked by the sign, which meant that the sign itself would be beside it. They might not be *on* the path, but it would be close to them.

Sure enough, the sled bumped, then dropped into a slight channel. It had found the path. Then the sides rose up, and they were cruising through a U-shaped valley. He had to steer with excruciating care, to keep them on course by banking on the turns. This was a really nervous workout! But was this the correct path? How could he be quite sure?

The valley curved, taking them around and around until they had completed a circle. But they were below the prior track. It was a corkscrew turn! The walls closed over the top, and they were plunging through darkness.

Dug heard water. Was there an underground river here? Then light came, and he saw that they had entered a cavern with a hole in the ceiling for a sunbeam. Ahead was a waterfall. The water came from the right side, and fell into the center of the cave, where it flowed on to the left. The sled bucked like a bronco as it traversed the slush by the river. They could still crash!

There was another sign. LEFT. But it was on the right side. "At least we're on the proper trail," Sherlock said, sounding relieved as Dug steered the sled directly toward the waterfall.

"How can you be sure!" Jenny demanded, seeing disaster looming.

"Because they wouldn't put another sign on a wrong trail; they'd just terminate it."

Then they plunged into the sheet of falling water. And through it. There was space behind it, descending. Sparks flashed as the runners scraped against bare rock. They skidded onto sand, and on down through a round hole just large enough to let them through. They sailed out into space and bright light.

And landed with a plunk on a monster pillow bush. Pillows popped, sending fluff flying wide. But they had stopped, safely. They were at the base of the chasm.

They climbed out and looked around. Behind them was the steep slope of the chasm wall, with its tiny hole up just too high for a standing man to reach from the floor. Ahead of them was a flat, open expanse. Beyond it was the far wall of the chasm, rising vertically to a ledge, and thence to another ledge. To either side was the length of the great valley, curving out of sight. It was actually a pleasant enough place. There was even a pie tree a short distance away.

Then they felt a shudder in the ground. It was followed by another. Whomp! Whomp!

"The Gap Dragon!" Jenny cried. "He's coming—and we can't escape him here!"

"If you have a plan," Sherlock said wryly, "it's about time to put it into effect."

"First I want to settle with that stupid cloud, what's-his-name, who couldn't put out enough snow to cover the slope," Dug said.

There was an angry rumble from above. Fracto was listening and reacting to the criticism.

"But it's the dragon we have to settle with first," Jenny said, alarmed. The whomping was getting louder.

"No, it's that wimpish cloud," Dug insisted. "If Fractal had the gumption God gave a turnip, he'd have laid snow all the way down to the floor so we could coast down properly, instead of having to shunt into a watery cave. But I guess that's what happens when you depend on airheads."

There was a louder rumble, but it was matched by the closer whomping. In a moment the Gap Dragon would round the turn and spy them. "Dug—" Sherlock said, looking pale around the gills, which was a good trick.

"I'm sorry," Dug said stoutly, "but I just can't let inadequacy pass. That pip-squeak cloud didn't do his job right, and we had to land in a bed of pillows instead of a bed of snow, the way it should have been. I don't know why the demons chose such a malingerer! They should have known Flacto would botch it."

"You keep getting the name wrong," Jenny shouted over the double noise of rumbling and whomping. "You're just going to make Fracto even madder!"

"So who cares if Fatso gets mad?" Dug yelled. "It's about time someone called a wimp a wimp! He couldn't work up a decent blow down here. He's just a stupid washout."

The mist along the slope pulled itself into a furiously swirling cloud. Jags of lightning shot out from it. The baleful face of Fracto formed, staring down.

Jenny screamed. "The Gap Dragon!"

"No, that's Crapto, the least of clouds. You can tell by his vacuous expression."

"I mean down on the ground. There!" She pointed.

Dug looked. Indeed it was the dragon. A serpentine, six-legged creature, with a long mouthful of teeth, puffing steam.

Dug stood his ground. "Don't worry," he shouted. "Framto wouldn't dare wet on the Gap Dragon, so the poopy cloud can't get at us."

Sherlock opened his mouth as if about to address an idiot. Then there was a little flash above his head, that wasn't lightning. He had caught on to what Dug was doing. "Yeah," he agreed. "Clouds are notorious cowards."

Fracto exploded. Pieces of cloud flew everywhere, each with the same furious face of the original. Toothpick-sized jags of lightning flew out from them, sticking into the ground. One mini-jag struck the charging dragon on the trail.

The dragon whirled, unhurt but stung by the barb. He sent a sizzling stream of steam at the main remaining body of the cloud. Unfortunately the hot vapor only gave the thing a jolt of extra energy. The central blob expanded rapidly, incorporating the surrounding cloudlets. More lightning flashed. Suddenly Fracto was formidable.

"Aw, it's all flash and no snow," Dug called. "The thing's too hot to make snow anyway."

The boiling cloud turned gray. Then snow began to fly. In a moment there was a blizzard, obscuring the dragon.

Dug grabbed the hands of the others. Silently he led them back to Roberta Sled, still amidst the pillow bush. They grabbed pillows to protect themselves from the sudden cold.

They heard the dragon casting about, searching for them. But the blizzard made visibility almost zero. As long as they were silent, they could not be found except by accident.

Sherlock squeezed Dug's hand appreciatively. The ploy had worked, and was hiding them from the dragon.

But Dug knew that this was only part of it. Before long the cloud would storm himself out, and the snow would melt, and the dragon would be waiting for them. So they had to act while the storm remained. In silence. Which meant that he couldn't explain the rest of his plan to the others; he would have to show them by action.

He tied pillows to his body by knotting their corners together. He got rope from his pack and strung it out so the others could hang on to it, not losing him. Then he set out across the floor of the Gap. He knew which way to go, because the sled pointed that way. If he veered a bit to the side, it didn't matter; he would find the wall soon enough.

He heard the dragon moving, still searching. There was a hiss as steam seared out to melt the snow, but more kept falling, as Fracto proved himself. The swirling snow blotted out both vision and smell. Dug angled his walk to steer well clear of the creature. Any little mistake could bring the steam, and then the dragon, and it would be over. If this weren't a fantasy game, he would have been almost too frightened to act. As it was, he was nervous enough.

Suddenly the wall loomed ahead. Good! He got down and silently scooped up a double handful of snow. He formed it into a ball, then rolled the ball, picking up more snow. When the ball was as large as he could conveniently handle, he rolled it to the base of the wall and left it there. Then he started another.

The others caught on. They made snowballs of their own, and rolled them big and added them to the first one. The pile grew rapidly, and expanded into a ramp, which they quietly packed firm. Then they rolled balls up it, to make it higher, wedging them into place and filling in the crevices with more snow.

By the time the storm began to ease, the ramp extended all the way up to the first ledge in the wall, well, above their heads. They rolled balls up to that ledge, forming a second, smaller ramp extending from that ledge to a higher one. Dug wasn't sure that the second ledge led where they needed to go, but there was no way to find out except to get there and see.

The snow stopped falling. The mist cleared up.

There was a snort. The dragon spied them!

"Get up to the ledge!" Dug cried.

They scrambled, leaving their last snowballs behind.

The dragon whomped toward them. But now there was a thick layer of snow on the ground, interfering with his navigation. He spun to the side and rolled tail over snoot. That gave the three of them time to make it to the ledge.

The dragon righted himself and blew out a thick stream of steam. The snow shrank nervously away from it. The dragon walked slowly toward the wall, melting snow before him. It was impressive.

Then Sherlock realized something. "The ramp! He can use it too!"

Oops! "We must knock it away, quickly," Dug said.

He and Sherlock sat on the edge of the ledge and kicked at the ramp, while Jenny hauled in the loose rope and coiled it. But the ramp was packed solid now, and gave way reluctantly. "We built too well," Sherlock said.

The dragon reached the base of the ramp. His steam melted the packed snow. He paused, considering. He was not all that stupid, it turned out. He aimed his steam upward, and started mounting the ramp.

Dug got out his club and whammed at the snow. But this too was ineffective, because he didn't dare swing hard enough to do real damage, for fear of hitting Sherlock. "Stand back," he cried. "I'll bash this out."

Sherlock got out of the way. Dug braced himself and swung a huge swing. The club bashed into the snow, caught—and jerked out of his hands.

"Oh, no!" Dug cried, diving for it. He got his hands on it, but overbalanced, falling onto the ramp himself. He scrambled to get back, but couldn't; instead he toppled off the ramp. He grabbed at it, but succeeded only in breaking his fall somewhat. He landed on his feet beside the ramp, holding the club.

Now he was in for it! One moment of carelessness had dumped him into the worst possible situation. He was pretty sure he couldn't fight the dragon; it would steam him before he got close enough to do any damage.

But maybe the dragon was too dull to realize what had

happened. Maybe the creature would keep climbing the ramp and—

And what? Gobble up the other two people?

"Hey, steamsnoot!" Dug cried, waving his weapon.

The dragon spied him. He pondered again. Then he got smoothly off the ramp and advanced on Dug. He was not so dull as not to realize that the morsel on the ground was easier to nab than the two on the ledge.

Dug ran. In a moment he heard the dragon whomping after him. But again the snow interfered, and the dragon got fouled up in his own torso. It seemed that it required a delicate balance to whomp, and the snow prevented this. That gave Dug slightly more of a chance than otherwise.

Dug ran in a circle, pursued by the dragon, who had to melt a path ahead of him. Even so, he wasn't exactly slow. Dug looped back to the ramp and charged up it.

But the dragon whipped back on his tail, much faster. He had a cleared area where he had been. As Dug tried to cross to the ledge, the dragon whomped. His foresection sailed right up and came down across the ramp. His weight and mass knocked out a section of it.

Dug slid to a stop, almost falling on the dragon's back. The monster was already bringing his head sinuously back, ready to chomp him. Could he smite that snoot with his club? He lifted it in both hands—and the dragon sent a waft of steam and almost boiled him where he stood. Had he not still been protected by pillows, he could have been finished right then. Dug had to reverse and run back off the ramp.

Now the ramp was out, and he was trapped on the floor of the chasm. The dragon was getting steadily more savvy.

Well, could he fight after all? It seemed ridiculous to have the club and never even try to use it. If he timed the blasts of steam, so as to dodge them, then struck from the side—

He stood his ground as the dragon closed on him. He watched for the steam. The dragon inhaled, started to exhale, and Dug threw himself to the side.

But his foot slipped in the slushy snow, and he fell on

his face. The blast of steam passed just over his back. The snow melted around him.

Dug scrambled up. He plunged to the side, trying to get into position for a strike. But the dragon's snoot was tracking him, and the dragon's torso was inhaling. Could he strike before the dragon's breath reversed and cooked him?

He tried. But the dragon's head dodged to the side and fired another hiss of steam at Dug's feet. Dug leaped clear, and the steam melted the snow where he had stood. He landed on his back in the snow, his club waving helplessly. Some hero he was turning out to be!

As he scrambled back to his feet, he saw that there was a hole in the ground where the snow had melted. It was just about big enough for a man to fall into. He was lucky he hadn't stepped there when it was covered by the snow.

He tried once more to bring his weapon into play. But this time the dragon's tail whipped around and stung his hand. He dropped the club and retreated, his hand smarting. He was having one close call after another!

It was no good trying to fight the dragon. He just wasn't cut out for it. He really didn't know how to use the club and was as likely to hurt himself as the enemy. He was probably better off without it. But the dragon was better coordinated than he was; he couldn't outmaneuver him. What could he do to escape?

Dug turned around and ran directly away from the dragon. But the dragon whomped after him with distressing vigor. Dug tried to dodge again, and slipped again. He sat up—and there was the dragon's snoot, right before his face.

The dragon's mouth slowly opened. Dug realized that he was done for. He had blundered all the way, made a thorough ass of himself, and now would be dispatched. He was disgusted. Why hadn't he used his brain to figure out some effective strategy, instead of just scrambling aimlessly through the snow?

His brain. Suddenly, in this seemingly hopeless situation, it was perking onto high. This was the game. There was always a way through. Maybe several ways. That hole in the ground—he might have crawled into that and escaped the dragon. Of course there might have been danger down there, like biting insects, ferocious rats or goblins. Maybe it was an escape he could have used if he had chosen Goody Goblin as Companion; Goody would have related to the other goblins and gotten him through. If he had taken Horace Centaur as Companion, he might have ridden away from the dragon; he doubted that whomping could match the speed of a gallop. If he had stayed with Grundy, the golem might have talked with the plants down here and gotten information where there was a secret passage through the wall or something. Marrow Bones the walking skeleton might have—well, he wasn't sure what Marrow might have done but there was surely something. But he wasn't with any of those; he was with Jenny Elf, whose little cat had been unable to find a way out, and in any event, he was now stuck here alone. So there might be many ways out, but he had managed to avoid them all and make his situation worse. Because after provoking Fracto into hiding them with the blizzard, he had stopped using his mind and just slogged ahead physically.

He saw now that the dragon knew it was the game. Those near misses with the steam had been intentional. Maybe getting confused by the blizzard had been an act too. In real life he would have been chomped immediately. The dragon had been giving him a chance to get away, if he only had the wit to figure it out. Now the dragon was pausing, giving him one more chance. He had to take it.

He reached into his pocket and found the Germ of an Idea. He didn't need to put it to his forehead. He knew what to do with it, in this punnish realm. "Dragon, beware!" he cried. "I've got a germ. If you chomp me, you'll get it."

The dragon hesitated. So it did understand his words! And it was cautious about a germ. Few predators cared to eat diseased prey. Probably the dragon knew it wasn't that kind of germ, but by the law of the pun he had to accept it. Dug had finally used his brain and found a way.

"Go ahead," he said, playing it for what it was worth as he got up. "Chomp me. Gobble up the germ. Maybe it won't hurt you." For sure it wouldn't hurt the dragon!

The dragon closed his mouth, considering. Then a thought percolated through. He aimed his snoot and inhaled. He was going to cook the prey, getting rid of the germ that way.

But now Dug was on his feet. He put them into gear and ran for the wall.

A jet of steam singed the snow beside him. Another close miss. "Thanks, dragon-breath!" Dug muttered. But he knew the dragon wouldn't miss too many more times; there were limits even to the game. He had to make good his escape now, or it would surely be never.

He touched the germ to his forehead as he ran. The idea came to him. "Jenny!" he called. "Let down the rope for me! Anchor it."

Jenny threw down one end of the rope, while Sherlock tied the other end to a crag. Dug reached it, grabbed it, and hauled up his legs just as another bolt of steam splashed against the wall where they had been. He handed himself up the rope, walking the wall with his feet. Rappelling, it was called, or something. And the dragon was letting him do it. Because it was an approved way to escape. Obviously in real life the dragon could have dispatched him instantly, but the game required that the Player be given every chance. It had surely been the same with the roc in the tall hassle tree forest. And the censor-ship. All he had to do was to learn to play the game right.

He made it to the ledge and heaved himself over. Just in time; his arms were starting to cramp from the unaccustomed exertion. No matter that this was just a game, and he wasn't really here, and his real body was sitting mesmerized by the stupid screen. He was into the spirit and sensation of it, and he felt what he was supposed to feel. Which at the moment was mostly joy, because now he understood what he needed to, to get wherever he was going. He had made the sensible decision to part company with

Nada Naga, getting rid of a foolish distraction. Now he had made the decision to play the game right. After almost losing track and getting skunked.

He stood on the ledge and peered down at the dragon. The dragon peered up at him. Then the dragon winked.

But one thing nagged Dug's mind. He had been clumsy, even after making allowances. He had fallen almost right under the dragon's snoot. At that point he had made what should have been a fatal mistake, and paid the price for it. Com Pewter had shown no mercy on him when he lost the riddle contest. Why had the dragon been so much more generous?

He reviewed it in his mind, suspecting that there was some key element he had missed. Key elements were important here. They could apply to more than one situation, as had been the case with the germ. He wanted to fathom this one.

He had fallen down while trying to bash out the ramp, so the dragon could not reach the ledge. So then he was on the ground, and the dragon was mounting the ramp. The dragon was about to gobble up the two people trapped on the ledge. So Dug had cried out, attracting the dragon's attention to himself.

And there it was. He had, in the heat of the moment, acted selflessly. He had put himself in peril, to save his companions. No matter that the dragon wasn't really after them, because one was the Companion and the other was just a fellow traveler. Dug had done a generous thing. He must have earned a bonus point, and because of it the dragon had let him go, after a reasonable show.

Now he understood. So now he winked back at the dragon.

After which he turned around. "Let's see where we can go from here," he said. "I'm sure there's some way up. What does Sammy say?"

The little cat bounded up the snow steps the two had made, to the higher ledge. He knew where to go—now that they were past the dragon. The Companion could help, but the Player had to handle the main challenge. Okay.

And what would be the next challenge? He could find out. "Jenny, what will we find south of the Gap Chasm?" he asked the elf girl as they followed the upper ledge to a hole in the cliff that now appeared.

"I'm not sure of the details, but I know there's quick sand and slow sand there," she said. "And the Gnobody Gnomes, and the Cow Boys and the Knock-Kneed Knights."

"Now, why do I have the feeling that those are not ordinary gnomes, or young men who herd cows?" Dug inquired rhetorically.

"The Cow Boys are bull-headed," she agreed. "And the Knights are empty. And there's also Com Pewter somewhere in there."

Pewter! This was the one he had been waiting for. The rematch. Jenny Elf didn't realize that he had already encountered the evil machine, and had a score to settle. He should have known that his path would lead him there, because he could not win the game without nullifying whatever had balked him before.

So now he knew his next major challenge. This time he intended to be prepared. "Pewter," he murmured, "I'm going to kick your metal butt!"

Then he focused on their climb out of the chasm, because he had learned better than to ignore the details of the moment. Sammy Cat was leading the way, but there could still be complications. They were now in a wormlike tunnel wending upward, festooned with spider webbing. But the worm would have had to be the size of the diggle. Well, maybe it had been a diggle, who forgot to phase out when traveling, so left a hole in the ground. Just so long as it led them back to ground level.

Meanwhile, he would keep an eye out for anything that might enable him to handle Pewter. So that he could continue playing the game, and remain in Xanth.

12
MERCI

K im walked east along the Gap Chasm. The snow
was already melting; it seemed that the evil cloud
could blow up a snowstorm, but couldn't actually
cool the land. That was just as well; Fracto had caused too
much misery already.

"I guess we'd better fill you in on what we were up to
before we met," Kim said to Nada Naga. "Jenny and I encountered the ogres of the Ogre Fen, then ran afoul of
Fracto and got washed into the Water Wing, where Cyrus
rescued us. On the way out I found Bubbles." She patted
the dog. "Cyrus is looking for a wife."

Nada glanced sidelong at Cyrus. "So I gathered. He
wouldn't happen to be a prince, would he?"

"No, I'm just a regular merman," Cyrus said. "Why?"

"I have been looking for a husband," she said candidly.
"But I would prefer to have a prince."

"I would not do for you anyway, because I must marry
either a mermaid or a fish. I would prefer the mermaid."

"I am not surprised. The naga sometimes must marry either full human folk, or full serpent folk, but we prefer our

own kind. However, we also marry to cement liaisons with other species. But this is done only between princes and princesses."

"But your brother Naldo married Mela Merwoman," Kim said. "She wasn't a princess, was she?"

"My brother Prince Naldo has an eye for the ladies," she replied evenly. "He happened to catch a glimpse of Mela's panties, and decided to marry her. Mela fills her panties very well, considering her age."

"She's young?" Cyrus asked.

"No, old. But she retains her youthful proportions, which are generous. My brother noticed." She shrugged. "Males have never been much for following the rules. Our father was annoyed, until he met the merwoman. Then he concluded that this was a warranted exception to our policy."

"Sounds like sexism to me," Kim muttered.

"Her proportions are surely not more generous than your own," Cyrus said diplomatically.

"Oh, I believe they are! You have to understand that merwomen are not quite the same as mermaids; they are better endowed. I think it is because the sea is colder than the lakes and rivers. Perhaps the salt has something to do with it." She glanced again at him. "Have you ever swum in salt, Cyrus?"

"Never. But I shall be happy to give it a try."

"I understand that the merfolk of the sea and the merfolk of the lakes are incompatible, for that reason," Nada said. "But that is only hearsay."

Kim heard something. "Is that a storm, down inside the Gap Chasm?" she asked.

The others paused to listen. "That sounds like Fracto," Nada said. "Do you think that Dug was crazy enough to aggravate that cloud again?"

"Well, I was crazy enough to do it before," Kim said. "Dug's like me, in some respects."

"Oh? Do you like him?"

"Yes, I guess I do," Kim said shyly.

"Why didn't you say something?"

"Well, where I come from, a girl doesn't."

"You are not where you come from," Nada pointed out.

Kim shrugged. "Still, he's from Mundania too. He's handsome, while I—" She didn't care to finish.

"I suppose he is," Nada said. "I hadn't noticed. He does seem to be interested in—" She hesitated. "Mature women."

"Oh, was he getting fresh with you?" Kim asked, morbidly curious.

"He tried to glimpse my panties, and almost got put out of the game. After that he was more careful."

"So that explains it," Kim said. "I thought he was remarkably polite, for a teenage boy."

"He became polite. He seems clever enough, when one allows for his immaturity."

"*All* Mundane boys are immature. That's why they need girls to mature them."

Nada smiled. "They're not so different that those of Xanth." She peered into the chasm. "I think that's another snowstorm. I wonder what's going on down there?"

A small light flashed over Kim's head, melting the last of the snow in her vicinity. "A blinding blizzard! Would that hide them from the dragon?"

"I think it might," Nada agreed.

"Then Dug must've deliberately insulted Fracto, to create that diversion," Kim said, delighted. "So they could get through safely."

"You *do* like him," Nada said.

"But he has no interest in me, so it doesn't matter. Let's get on and win this game."

Bubbles was happy to lead the way, her tail curling up in a perfect semicircle. The path was clear, and there were no bad creatures in the way. But Kim knew that there would be another challenge before too long. She hoped she would be ready for it.

As they went, they had to discard items of clothing, because of the returning warmth. It was hard to imagine that this had so recently been a snowscape.

Bubbles barked. Kim looked around, because there was always something when the dog gave warning.

Specks appeared in the sky. They danced around, growing larger. They did not seem to be birds or insects; their outlines were squared off, and their motions too bobbing. "What are those?" Kim asked.

Nada looked. "Kites, I think. They like to fly about the Gap, because of updrafts there."

"Oh, I used to love to fly kites!" Kim exclaimed. "Are these magic?"

"Everything is magic in Xanth," Nada said.

"There's a string," Cyrus said. He strode forward, reaching for it.

"I wouldn't," Nada said warningly.

But he was already grabbing the string. He hauled on it, bringing the kite down. It was a huge cubic thing, brightly colored.

The kite suddenly plunged, looming close. It swept into Cyrus, knocking him down. Then, free, it sailed back up out of reach.

Kim dashed over to help him. "Are you all right?" she asked worriedly.

Cyrus sat up, shaking his head. Three little birds were flying around it, cheeping. "Just dizzy, I think," he said dizzily. "What happened?"

"You grabbed the string of a box kite," Nada explained. "It boxed you."

Kim helped him stand. He was unsteady, but the little birds evidently decided he was all right, and flew away. "No more kites," he said.

"No more kites," Kim agreed.

Nada looked around. "That's odd."

"What's odd?" Kim asked, concerned. She saw that Bubbles seemed perplexed, too.

"We seem to be a good deal farther along than I would

have thought. This looks like the terrain beyond Gap Village, and maybe beyond the goblin village too."

Kim realized that the terrain had changed during their distraction by the kite. They were still north of the Gap, proceeding east, but the lay of the land was different.

"Could this be a device of the game to move us more rapidly to the next challenge?"

"It must be," Nada agreed. "Professor Grossclout has demonic powers."

"Well, he *is* a demon," Kim agreed.

As they proceeded, Kim saw that not only had the scene changed, it differed in type. Instead of idle stones by the wayside, there were crystals. In fact, they soon became fancier, with pretty colors. They looked like diamonds, rubies, sapphires, emeralds, opals, amethysts, garnets, and all manner of other gems. Many were small, but some were large, and a few were huge.

Kim gazed at them in wonder. "Oh, I've always loved pretty stones," she said. "But the best I could afford was smoky quartz, which is to real gems as glop is to gold. I've never even imagined such a display!"

"I think they're hiquigems," Nada said. "Impossible to use."

"High-que gems?" Kim asked. "Are they dangerous?"

"No, they are harmless. But you really can't touch them."

Bubbles was sniffing at a nearby gem. Kim squatted, reaching for the lovely red spinel the size of an apple. "I won't get shocked, or anything?"

"Nothing like that. But you are wasting your time."

Kim's fingers closed around the beautiful gem. She picked it up with an oooh of appreciation, admiring its facets.

Then something happened. "Oh, I dropped it!" she exclaimed, chagrined. Indeed, something red fell to the ground. But it didn't look like a gem. It looked like a blob of red gelatin. It landed silently.

Then, as her eyes focused on it, she saw that she had

been mistaken. It was the same gem she had picked up, undamaged. But how could she have dropped it? It had somehow seemed to flow through her fingers, a weird sensation.

She picked it up again, cautiously. Again it fell. But this time she saw it happen. The thing lost form, became a big drop of red liquid, slid between her fingers, landed on the ground—and reformed into the gem.

Cyrus tried to pick up a diamond. It, too, slipped through his grip and turned up on the ground, unchanged. He stared, bemused.

"Hiquigems," Nada repeated. "They don't allow folk to move them."

"It's like a dream," Kim said, as impressed by the willful magic of the gems as by their number, size, and beauty. "They seem so real, yet they might as well be illusion."

"Much of Xanth is illusion," Nada said. "The rest is puns and dragons."

"Pun the magic dragon," Kim murmured under her breath, smiling.

They walked on through the glorious display. Slanting sunlight struck the myriad facets of the gems and refracted even more colorfully up, so that they walked through air as pretty as the ground. Apparently this was just a passing diversion, not a challenge. Unless she was supposed to find a way to take one of the gems. Could there be one among them that was takable, that would help her in the future? She decided to let it be; she preferred to leave these magic stones alone.

They left the gems behind. They rounded a turn—and there before them was the broad expanse of the sea. The path went right down to it—but so did the chasm. So the only way to cross the chasm was to cross the sea, and this time they didn't have a boat. Had this trek been for nothing?

"Maybe we can make a boat," Kim said. "It isn't far, to cross to the other side of the chasm."

"Perhaps we can swim across," Cyrus said. "I don't see any monsters."

"This is salt water," Nada reminder him. "See, there is saltwater taffy growing by the shore."

"All the more reason to try it." He walked boldly to the beach and dipped his toe. "Yow!"

"I warned you," Nada said. "You're a freshwater merman."

Cyrus stepped back, chagrined. "That brine is awful! What self-respecting creature would touch that, let alone swim in it?"

There was a cheery cry from the sea. "Ooo-ooo!" It was a melodious female voice, with the accent on the first syllable. "Are you land folk lost?"

They peered out to sea. There was the head of a young woman. She was swimming.

"We are trying to get to the other side of the Gap Chasm," Kim called back. "But we don't know if it's safe to swim, and one of us doesn't like the salt water."

The woman swam rapidly closer. "It's perfect salt water," she said indignantly. "I have spent all my life in it." To illustrate her point, she dived under, showing her flukes.

Cyrus stared. "That's a mermaid!" he cried.

"Merwoman," Nada clarified. "Look at her décolletage."

Indeed, Kim saw that the creature was superbly endowed. In fact, she had a set of breasts best described as monumental, yet perfectly contoured. The kind Kim herself would never dare dream of having.

Cyrus' attention was no less fixed than Kim's own. "What a creature!" he breathed.

Another little light flashed over Kim's head. "There's your wife, maybe," she said.

"What's that?" the woman called from the sea.

"I'm Kim Human, and this is Nada Naga," Kim called back. "Are you married?"

"No. Bachelor mermen don't grow on shoe trees, you

know. My mother had to make legs and trek endlessly on land to find a suitable husband."

Another light flashed. "Your mother—was she by chance Mela Merwoman?"

"No. There was no chance about it. She was Melantha from the day the storkfish delivered her, as sure as water quenches fire. I'm her daughter Merci."

"Why did she need a husband?" Cyrus said. "Didn't she have your father?"

Merci's lovely brow clouded. "A stupid dragon toasted him when I was away at a school of fish, just ten years ago when I was a merchild. Mother fretted a bit, then finally took the plunge, as it were, and went landward to nab her man. It was all so complicated. It wasn't as if she was choosy. All she wanted was the nicest, handsomest, most manly bachelor prince available. She finally landed Prince Naldo Naga. Since then she's been so busy entertaining him that I hardly see her. They seem to believe in long honeymoons. It's pretty lonely. Now I am dangerously close to twenty-one, hardly a mergirl any more and nary a merman in sight."

Indeed, she was hardly a girl! "There's one in sight now," Kim said. "Merci, meet Cyrus Merman."

Merci turned her beautiful dark eyes on Cyrus. "Really? Let's see you in tails."

"I can't change here," Cyrus said. "I'm a freshwater creature."

"Oh, sure," Merci retorted. "How do I know you're not a regular ordinary sneaky man, trying to trick me into legs so you can catch me away from water and make me do something nymphly with you? I'm tired of you louts who think it's all right to tell a girl anything, just to get your germy hands on her innocent torso."

Nada made an appreciative move. "I like this creature," she murmured.

"So do I," Kim replied.

"Not as much as I do," Cyrus said. Then, to Merci:

"Find me some fresh water, and I'll be glad to show you some germ-free tail."

"There's a freshwater spring a little way up the beach," Merci said.

So they walked up the beach, away from the chasm, and Bubbles found the spring. She lapped some of its water. It was hot, but bearable. Cyrus dipped his toe and pronounced it fit. "Turn your backs, ladies," he said to Kim and Nada. "I must strip, so I don't ruin my clothing."

They dutifully turned their backs. In three quarters of a moment and half an instant there was a splash. They turned again, and Cyrus was basking in the spring.

"But I can't see your tail from here," Merci called.

"Then come over here," he called back.

Merci swam to the very edge of the sea. She changed, and stood, resplendent with a fine set of legs. Bubbles went down to intercept her with a woof. Merci walked up across the beach to the spring and peered down. "You *are* a merman!" she said, delighted.

"Get your tail in here," he invited. "The water's fine."

"Don't be silly. I'm allergic to fresh water. The only way I can handle it at all is in this form." She gestured at her legs with her hands.

He eyed her appraisingly. "Actually, you are not wholly unattractive in that form, though it can not of course compare with your natural one." Evidently it was not a violation of merfolk propriety to view a merwoman in legs or a merman in tail.

"I like this creature," Merci murmured.

"Maybe he can make legs again, so you can get acquainted on land," Kim suggested.

"I'm not sure that would be decorous," Merci said.

"Certainly it wouldn't," Cyrus agreed. "However, we can make it decorous by donning human clothing. Perhaps Kim and Nada will be so kind as to fetch you a skirt, while I return to my trousers."

So they took Merci to a nearby fabric plant and wrapped a length of seersucker around her body, fashioning a ser-

viceable dress. They found lady slipper flowers and put a
delicate pair of slippers on her dainty feet. Nada brushed
her somewhat matted hair and set a passion flower in it.
Now she looked just like a perfectly lovely human woman.

They returned to the spring, where Cyrus was dry and
back in clothing. He looked like a perfectly handsome human man. "Oh, you are surely the creature I wish to
marry," he said. "Except—"

"And you are surely the creature I'd like to wed," Merci
agreed. "Except—"

"Except that you can't stand each other's water," Nada
said. "What irony!"

"Suppose we had merchildren?" Cyrus said. "They
might be intolerant of both kinds of water!"

"I fear our love is doomed," Merci said sadly.

Kim knew the feeling. She reacted against it. "There
must be some compromise," she said. "Couldn't you, uh,
get together in human form, and return to your lake and
sea betweentimes?"

"That would be uncouth," Cyrus said. "Legs are so
clumsy and unaesthetic."

"Tails are the only way to party," Merci agreed.

They certainly seemed to be well matched. "There must
be some way," Kim said. "We just have to find it."

"It would be nice," Cyrus said. "Merci is exactly what
I have been looking for except for the incompatibility of
medium." He glanced at her wrapped torso again. "In fact,
perhaps even more than I was looking for. Freshwater
mermaids are somewhat more slender."

"That's fine, if you like that type," Merci remarked.

"I find I like your type."

"Well, we'll figure it out," Kim said. "Maybe there's a
spell. But at the moment, maybe you can help us, Merci.
We need to find a way to cross safely to the south side of
the Gap Chasm."

"You might swim, if you don't mind fifty-degree water
and a loan shark or two."

Kim had tried swimming in eighty-degree water once,

and found it too cool for comfort. "I think swimming is out. Anyway, Cyrus can't touch sea water. Is there a tunnel or something?"

Merci pondered. "There is a tunnel under the Gap. But it is not safe."

"It must be safer than shark-infested water!" Kim said.

"It is a goblin tunnel," Merci explained.

"Ouch!" Nada said. "I don't relish goblins. I can chomp one or several, but they tend to come in hordes. We had better avoid that."

Kim looked around again, knowing she would see nothing useful. "I wonder whether there is enough dry wood to make a raft."

"I suppose you could build a raft," Merci agreed. "It should only take a few days."

Kim sighed. "Maybe it will have to be the tunnel. And knowing the way the game works, we'll have to prepare to fight off the goblins."

"Game?" Merci asked.

"She's from Mundania," Nada explained. "She's here as part of a game the demons organized. I'm her Companion, here to guide and protect her."

"Oh. Well, I will show you the nearest entrance to the tunnel. But I don't know how you can deal with the goblins. Once when I made legs to walk to land to fetch some flowers, goblins tried to catch me so they could do something horrible to me. Since then I have been very cautious about going on land, and I don't like goblins at all."

The merwoman led the way to a thicket of bushes some distance back from the Gap, where the land was not too far above sea level. There beneath their cover of foliage was a hole in the ground. Bubbles sniffed it.

"It's dry?" Kim asked. "Though it goes under the water?"

"It's dry," Merci agreed. "Though I understand there are portals in the bulkheads to flood it, if necessary. I can't think why the goblins would want to make it that way."

"This is naga work," Nada said, examining the bricked

rim of the hole. "I recognize the type. Naga must have made this, and later lost it to the goblins. We have been slowly losing ground to them for centuries."

"In fish school they taught me that the goblins once roamed freely on the ground," Merci said. "But that now there are relatively few there. Most are underground."

"That is true," Nada said. "The harpies and humans warred with them, and drove them out of much territory. But they are in Goblin Mountain, and there's always the Goblinate of the Golden Horde, the worst tribe of them all. We don't know much about the ones deep belowground, but suspect there are many." She turned to Kim. "Hold my apparel; I will investigate this."

Then Nada turned serpent and slithered out of her collapsing clothing. Kim picked up the outfit and folded it. The serpent slithered into the hole and disappeared.

"They must go on," Merci said to Cyrus. "But must you go with them?"

"There seems to be little point in my remaining here," he said sadly. "I can not enter your sea realm, any more than you can enter my lake realm. I fear our love is doomed before it starts. I must go on, to see whether I can find a fresh mermaid."

"I suppose you must," she agreed. "Perhaps we shall kiss before we part."

"Perhaps we shall," he agreed, perking up slightly.

"It will be a remarkable experience," she said dreamily. "And a poignant memory."

Kim had another notion. "Hey, what about a wetsuit?" she asked.

"We do not wish to get our clothing wet," Cyrus said gently. "It is not as durable as skin and scales."

"No, I mean a bodysuit for diving. We have them in Mundania. We use them to keep the water out and the heat in, so we can swim in cold water. If one of you wore a wetsuit, could you swim in the water of the other?"

"I suppose," Merci agreed. "It would not be very com-

fortable, but it might enable us to visit each other's
homes."

"But it would not be very nice for summoning the
stork," Cyrus said.

"Which is an occasion which should not be ruined."

"I fear it would be little better than doing it in human
form."

"Ugh!" she agreed. "I suppose it could be tolerated in
an emergency."

"True. Human beings have to tolerate it, knowing nothing better."

Kim was getting to feel like an inferior species. Imagine
having to, as they put it, summon the stork while wearing
ungainly legs!

Fortunately Nada returned at this point. She formed her
human head on her snake's body. "It is clear, though there
is the smell of goblins about it. I think we can get through
if we move rapidly and are lucky."

"But how will we see, in that darkness?" Kim asked.

"There is glow fungus on the walls. It seems dark compared to daylight, but is light compared to night. You will
be able to see well enough."

"Let's go, then," Kim said. "Why don't you come too,
Merci? You can return to the sea from the other side, if
you want."

"I suppose I could," the merwoman agreed. She did not
seem at all eager to separate from Cyrus, and he seemed
to return the uneagerness.

Kim climbed down into the hole, Bubbles scrambling
along with her, and the two merfolk climbed down after
her. The interior was not dank, as she had feared, but a bit
like a subway tunnel with tiled walls. As her eyes ad-
justed, she saw the glow on the wall.

The tunnel curved away. They followed it in a down-
ward spiral. Now Bubbles was happy to lead the way, her
tail curving high. The dog was never so happy as when
she was escorting people somewhere. The glow seemed to

get brighter as they went, though she knew this was just the continued adaptation of her eyes.

She lost count of the circles they completed. This was a good deep tunnel! But finally it straightened out and headed in what she trusted was the right direction. From it debouched side tunnels every so often, going she knew not where. Maybe this had once been a subterranean naga city. She wondered what that community had been like. Then the main tunnel narrowed, and the offshoots stopped.

Bubbles barked.

Nada, slithering along in her naga form, abruptly lifted her head. "I smell fresh goblin!" she said, alarmed. "They were not here before."

"Maybe they make regular checks," Kim said. "Is there anywhere we can hide?"

"No. We are directly below the Gap now, and below the water of the sea inlet within it. This is the narrowest section."

"Then we'd better go back and take an offshoot," Kim said. "Maybe there's a room or something to hide in, there."

"But they are coming from the rear," Nada said.

"Then we'd better run forward!"

"They are coming from that direction too."

Kim recognized a game challenge when she encountered it. They were pinned underground between converging hordes of goblins. How could they get out of this fix?

Her concentration was interrupted by the approach of the goblins. "Look, fresh meat!" one cried from in front.

"You have it wrong, zilchpuss," one cried from the rear. "First we entertain ourselves wickedly with the damsels. *Then* we dump them in the pot."

"You're both wrong," another cried. "First we boil them until they turn blood red. Then we use them for entertainment. Then we eat them. Don't you know anything about protocol?"

Bubbles growled.

This was getting more serious by the instant! Not only

were they going to be cooked, some of them were going to get tortured as well. Kim hadn't realized that such things happened in Xanth, but she hadn't reckoned with the goblins.

There had to be a way out! But what was it? All she saw on the walls were indented handholds, no tools or weapons.

Her desperate gaze crossed the low ceiling. She saw a circular indentation. A portal! They could let in the water of the sea!

But how would they breathe? The merfolk could breathe water—but one of them would be caught in the wrong kind of water. So there was mischief, no matter what.

Bubbles woofed. She was sniffing a circular indentation in the floor, right below the one in the ceiling. "What's that?" Kim asked. Wild hope flared. "A secret escape?"

"It is marked for fresh water," Nada said, peering at the inscription on it. "The upper one is for salt water. Apparently my people had uses for each, perhaps when they cleaned the tunnel."

No escape. Both portals sealed off water. Kim's heart sank to about the level of her stomach, and her stomach sank to her belly.

Meanwhile the goblins were advancing like the jaws of a vise, or perhaps more accurately like the pincers of a garbage scoop. They had clubs and spears, but weren't waving them threateningly, not wishing to damage the merchandise before having their fun with it.

Then Kim thought of a way, maybe. This was a sealed tunnel, which meant that the air was likely to be trapped in it. That just might be their salvation.

"Open the ports!" she cried. "Both of them! Let the water in!"

"But—" Cyrus and Merci said, almost together.

"You open the top one, Merci. That's sea water; it won't hurt you. You open the bottom one, Cyrus; that's fresh water. It won't hurt you. Then just hang on, staying in your type of water. We're going to wash these goblins right out of our hair!"

"But how will we breathe?" Nada asked.

"There'll be air in the top half of the tunnel. Just keep your head up. And hang on; we have to stay right here in the center."

The two merfolk applied themselves to the hatches. They turned the plates, unscrewing them. Kim grabbed one of the handholds set in the wall with one hand, and caught Bubbles' collar with the other. Nada curled her tail into another handhold.

Cyrus' portal opened. Water blasted in at high pressure, deflected by the cover, which seemed to be anchored from below by the screw in its center. He hung on to that cover, holding it steady so that the water sprayed out in a rough circle.

Merci's portal opened. Water blasted in from above, similarly deflected. She hung on to that anchored cover, so that her water also made a circle.

For good or ill, Kim's plan was now in effect.

The surging waters merged on either side, coursing down the tunnel. The water was cool but not unbearably cold. The currents swept into the goblins, fore and aft, shoving them back. They were too surprised even to swear effectively. Suddenly they were fighting for their footing— and their lives, because they were not anchored.

The waters quickly filled the tunnel, pushing violently outward. But a level of air remained trapped at the top, having nowhere to go. Kim held Bubbles up so she could breathe it, while breathing it herself. Nada's face was close to hers, and she did the same. The best place to be was in the center, where there was no unified current, just the chaotic backsurge.

Soon the goblins were gone. They had been swept out in both directions, helplessly. Where they went Kim didn't care; they hardly deserved any good breaks.

"Close hatches!" Kim cried.

The merfolk turned the disks the other way, screwing

them back into their niches. It was hard work, but they had leverage. They got them closed, and the spraying water was cut off. The roar of it subsided, and the currents calmed.

Nada's human head glanced around. "That was well wrought, Kim," she said. "You won the challenge. I didn't think you would figure it out in time."

"It was a close call," Kim admitted. "If Bubbles hadn't called my attention to the second portal, I don't think I would have seen the answer." She kissed the dog's wet ear, and Bubbles wagged her tail as well as she could in the water.

"Now, let me see," Nada said. "I can slosh through water and hold on better in human form. We're all females here except Cyrus, and he's a merman, who has no concern about nakedness as long as he is in his natural form."

"True," Cyrus agreed. "I do not wish to offend, but my interest in creatures without tails is small."

"So I will change." Nada became human, a splendid figure of a bare woman. "In any event, it is all right, because I'm not wearing panties at the moment. Now I believe I can find the way out, by following the old naga signals." She started half walking, half swimming along the flooded tunnel.

Cyrus looked at Merci. "Now, there's what I call an interesting creature," he said. "From head to tail."

Merci returned his look with similar candor. "I feel the same."

Then the little light flashed over Kim's head. "You're both in the same water—and not having trouble!"

Both merfolk were startled. "How can that be?" Cyrus asked. "I can't stand salt."

"And I can't stand fresh," Merci said. "This water is brackish, which makes it uncomfortable, but I can stand it."

"I agree," he said. "I can stand brackish water, though it is not my delight."

"The salt and fresh water mixed," Kim said. "So it's all brackish now. Half and half. Now the twain can meet."

"The twain can meet," Merci said, approaching Cyrus. "Maybe we can make it, in this water." She put her arms around him.

"Maybe we can," he agreed, kissing her. Several little red hearts appeared, floating around them. Their tails twined together.

Nada turned back. "Don't make it here! Wait for the nuptials."

The kiss broke and the hearts faded. "Of course," Merci said, blushing.

"Certainly," Cyrus agreed, embarrassed. "The proprieties must be observed."

"Too much was already being observed," Nada remarked.

Kim was privately slightly vexed. She knew that part of the propriety related to her: they considered her at age sixteen to be a borderline case, and were careful to honor the Adult Conspiracy. She had been curious about just how merfolk did make it. Still, it was nice that the merfolk had discovered how to relate to each other.

She set her face forward and followed Nada. There was no sign of the goblins, who must have been washed right out of the tunnels, perhaps to some lower level where they were trying to figure out what happened.

The water slowly sank, so that it was waist deep, then knee deep. The tunnel widened, and more cross-tunnels appeared, all similarly flooded. There was a sound of falling water, suggesting that there was indeed a drain somewhere. The tunnel would be dry again in due course. They needed to get out of it before that happened, because it was only the water that kept the goblins out.

Nada led them to another spiral, this one going up. The water was left behind. That was a relief for Bubbles, who definitely preferred land to water. The two merfolk had to change to legs and don clothing from Kim's pack, while the others turned their backs. Finally they climbed out through a hole.

They were on the south side of the Gap Chasm. And there on the beach was a small wooden boat. "Merci could have brought that across to us, if we had only known it was there," Kim said, chagrined.

"Why, so I could have," Merci agreed, surprised. "I have known about that boat for ages."

Kim almost inquired why Merci hadn't told her about the boat, but she knew the answer: she hadn't asked. This was the game, where the Player had to figure things out. Kim had inquired about a passage, and Merci had answered. Kim had not asked about a boat. A raft, yes, but not a boat. She had missed the obvious.

"Well, Nada and Bubbles and I have to be on our way," Kim said. "I guess you'll want to stay here, Cyrus, with Merci. When you want to get together with her, all you have to do is find a place where a river meets the sea and the water mixes, or maybe there's a freshwater spring under the sea where there can be a similar effect. I'm sure you'll figure it out."

"I am sure we will," Cyrus agreed. "I thank you, Kim Mundane, for bringing me here. You have indeed solved my problem."

"And mine," Merci agreed. She turned to Cyrus. "I know where there is a freshwater spring by the shore. I would love to show you more tail."

"I am eager to see it," he said. They kissed again, then waved farewell and walked eagerly down along the beach, arms around waists.

"So the adventure resumes," Kim said, with mixed feelings. She was glad for the merfolk, but also envious of their happiness. She knew that she faced a horrendous trek though the jungle, where she might encounter anything at all. It was the nature of the game.

13
VIRUS

Dug blinked in the bright light as they emerged from the vole hole. Sure enough, there was solid jungle all around.

He turned to Jenny. "Now this is the game," he said. "And I understand we're somewhere near the lair of Com Pewter, the evil machine. And that I have to settle with him before I can get much farther. So do you know of a fairly direct, safe path there? I want to get this over with."

Sammy jumped down and scampered along a faint path that seemed to appear only after the cat found it. "Wait for me!" Jenny cried, chasing after him.

"There's a path," Sherlock agreed. "But are you ready for the machine? I understand those things can really mess up folk who don't know how to handle them."

"For sure! Maybe I need to think about this a little more."

"Sammy, stop!" Jenny cried. "He's changed his mind!"

The cat stopped, losing interest in the path. The others caught up to him. The path where the cat had been was clear, but ahead there seemed to be nothing but brambles, briers, and branches.

"Maybe a slightly indirect route," Dug said, smiling. "Maybe passing a place where there is something I need."

Sammy resumed motion. This time his pace was slower, so that they could keep up, and it curved more. But the oddity of the path remained: there didn't seem to be any until the cat found it.

They came to a large field filled with weird plants. "There's something here you need?" Sherlock inquired with a lifted eyebrow.

"There's sure to be," Dug said. "So I'll just start looking for it."

"If you tell Sammy exactly what it is, he'll find it for you," Jenny said.

"I don't know exactly what it is but I hope to know it when I see it," Dug said. "Why don't the two of you get some rest while I look? This may take a while."

Both Jenny and Sherlock looked perplexed, but Sammy didn't. In fact, Sammy elected to join him in the search.

Dug stepped into the field. He saw that the assorted plants were in rows, and each had a little sign identifying it. That ought to help!

The first plant he looked at had a number of light cones, each looking suitable for ice cream. Or, as it was in Xanth, eye scream. Sure enough, it was labeled CONEFLOWER. But that wasn't what he needed.

As he squatted to look at the next, he developed an itch in an awkward place. He straightened up and faced away from the others, so as to be able to scratch it inconspicuously, but the itch had gone. So he squatted again—and the itch returned. The closer he leaned toward the plant, the worse it got, making him fidget something awful. Then he saw the sign, and understood: COCKLEBUR.

As he moved toward the next, which seemed to be a clump of grass, something chafed in his trouserleg. He looked down and saw a number of long arrow-shaped thorns in it. He pulled these out, carefully, and resumed motion—only to have more strike him. He looked at the sign. No wonder! This was arrowgrass.

Then his clothing seemed to get tight around the joints. Suspecting the next plant, he squinted to see its sign from a distance. Sure enough, it said BINDWEED. Next to it was a KNOTWEED, which he avoided.

Now he came to a nicer section, passing BUTTER-WEED, MILKWEED, and CANDYTUFT. Those would do with a meal, if there weren't enough from other sources.

Then he encountered a more awkward section, spying LOVEGRASS, VIRGIN'S BOWER, BRIDAL WREATH, and MATRIMONY VINE. Near those was a TWIN-FLOWER. Obviously this was what a woman needed if she wanted to reproduce more rapidly. Just send such a flower to the stork depot, to let the stork know how many to deliver.

The next section was animalistic. There was a CAT-TAIL, KITTENTAIL, PUSSYTOES, DRAGONHEAD, HOUND'S TONGUE, and SQUIRRELTAIL. Then full creatures: BEE PLANT, BUTTERFLY WEED, CHICK-WEED, DUCKWEED, GOAT GRASS, MONKEY FLOWER, and OYSTER PLANT. But none of them were what he needed.

Then there were assorted sewing plants: PINCUSHION, NEEDLE AND THREAD, THIMBLE BERRY, LEATHER FLOWER, and HEMLOCK. That last was evidently what women wearing long skirts used to prevent the hems from unraveling so that they stepped on them. There was a warning: it shouldn't be taken internally, lest it lock up the innards.

The next section had an emaciated SKELETON WEED, a bright SHOOTING STAR, a WALLFLOWER, and a PAINTBRUSH slopping a new color on it.

Then came some seed plants: STICKSEED, TICK-SEED, and BUGSEED. Sammy was inspecting the last closely. "Yes," Dug murmured, harvesting some of its seeds. "That may be what I want." He put the seeds in his pocket and went on, because he did not want to draw attention to the nature of exactly what he wanted.

Then he came to an ugly section: CHEATGRASS, POVERTY WEED, SNEEZEWEED, TUMBLEGRASS, and CHOKE CHERRY. He managed to sneak past those without suffering too many afflictions.

But what followed was worse: a patch of STINKWEED. He had had enough trouble with the stink horn to know the danger of this, so he intelligently moved right on to the SMARTWEED and then wisely to SAGEBRUSH.

The last plant in the row was labeled CRYPTOGRAMMA. This was very puzzling; he just couldn't figure it out, so he left it alone. It was also called ROCK BRAKE, but he couldn't tell whether it stopped big rolling stones or broke them up into pebbles.

He walked back along the second row. There were endless wonders there, but he paid them less attention, because he already had what he had come for. Then he saw a group of MONIAS: old, middle-aged, young, and new. This might be even better! So he took a New Monia flower and set it in a buttonhole.

He returned to the others. "Did you find what you wanted?" Sherlock inquired.

Dug coughed. "I think so."

"You okay, man? Sounds as if you have some congestion."

"I'll be all right," Dug said, trying not to hack. He hadn't realized that the flower would take effect so quickly. But of course things could be instant, in this magic land. He would just have to suffer through.

Sherlock and Jenny had fixed a good meal, but Dug did not have much appetite. He felt feverish and weak, and his breathing was getting difficult. But he pretended to be normal. He had a reason.

They finished eating and moved on, following the leisurely paths Sammy found. Dug had to struggle to keep moving. "Listen, there's something wrong," Sherlock said. "Ever since you looked through that garden patch, you've been stumbling as if you're sick. What happened in there?"

"Nothing I can tell you," Dug said hoarsely. "Just let me be."

Sherlock exchanged one long glance and two short ones with Jenny, and let it drop. The long glance bounced on the ground and shattered when it was dropped, but the short ones survived intact.

But when Dug staggered, stumbled, and fell, Jenny took action. "You're my responsibility," she said. "Because I'm your Companion. I will get in trouble for not guiding you well if you lose because you are too ill to continue. We must find a healing spring. That will make you well."

Dug was now too sick to protest effectively. He knew that what she said was true. But he also knew that he had to persevere, or he would lose again to Pewter. He could not tell them why, lest the evil machine learn of his words through some spy, and be prepared to foil his ploy.

Sherlock made a travois from wood and vine, softening it with pillows. He lifted Dug onto it, and hauled him along that way. Jenny had Sammy find the nearest spring. She wasn't able to clarify its particular type: it seemed that to the cat, one spring was much like another. She was able only to establish that it not be a regular ordinary water source. It had to be a magic spring.

As it turned out, there was one not too far away. They reached it, but were cautious. Dug heard them discussing it, though he was now too tired to join the dialogue.

"We have to be sure it's a healing spring," Jenny said. "Because there are different kinds, such as love springs and hate springs. It will be worse than nothing if we dose him with the wrong kind of elixir."

"But how can we tell, without trying it?" Sherlock asked. "We don't want to taste a love spring or a hate spring either."

"We certainly don't!" she agreed. "No offense to you. Because a love spring isn't just romantic; it leads immediately to a violent summoning of the stork. That would be a violation of the Adult Conspiracy, because I'm still a child."

"We don't want to violate any conspiracy," Sherlock agreed. "But inaction isn't any good either; we have to test the water somehow. Could we just sniff a little, so all we get is a mere suggestion?"

"Maybe that will be all right," she agreed doubtfully. "Let me try it first. Then if I start getting romantic, or whatever, you run away."

"Those springs must be potent," Sherlock remarked.

"Exactly."

So Jenny got down and sniffed the spring. "Oh, I feel young!" she exclaimed.

"Well, you *are* young. What kind of spring is it?"

"Not a love spring," she decided. "I don't love you or hate you. But I do feel changed."

"So maybe you've been healed of whatever was bothering you," he said reasonably. "This must be the one we want."

"Maybe. I'm not quite sure. There's something odd about it. You better sniff it too, and see what you think."

Sherlock got down and sniffed. "Wow! I feel two years younger!"

"You look a bit younger too," she agreed. "Is it healing you?"

"No. I have a sore toe, and it's still sore."

"Maybe you should dip your toe, and see if it heals."

"Good idea!" Sherlock removed his shoe and dipped his sore toe. The skin turned fresh but did not actually heal.

Then they paused while an insect flew down to taste the water. But the insect turned into a grub.

"It must be a transforming spring," Jenny said. "It changed into another kind of bug."

"No, it reverted to its earlier form," Sherlock said. "Insects hatch from grubs. It's their youthful stage—" He broke off, realization coming.

"A youth spring!" Jenny cried. "This must be the Fountain of Youth! Nobody knows where it is, and we stumbled on it by accident!"

"Sammy didn't stumble on it," he reminded her. "He was looking for a magic spring."

"That's right. And what a spring he found! But it isn't the one we want. Dug's only a year older than I am, really; he doesn't want to be any younger."

"You're fifteen?" Sherlock asked. "I thought you were a child."

"I am a child, by game definition. But outside the game I'm sneaking up on adult status, and actually I know the secret of the Conspiracy. Maybe I look younger to you, because I'm an elf; I'm smaller than a human girl my age would be."

"That must be it," he agreed. "Well, none of us need this elixir, so we'd better move on. It's an irony, though; a lot of people would give their fortunes to drink from this."

"People are funny," she agreed.

Dug wanted to tell them to mark the place carefully, so they could find the spring again, because the knowledge would be invaluable. But his breath was so short he couldn't speak.

They resumed their search, following the cat to another spring. Dug caught a glimpse of it before Sherlock laid the travois flat on the ground. The spring was round, with a quilted surface, as if the waves lacked the energy to ripple properly. This time when Jenny sniffed, she turned over and lay down on the water. "It must be an ether spring, putting you to sleep!" Sherlock said, horrified.

"No it isn't," she replied. "It's a bed spring. Oh, I could just lie here forever and sleep." Indeed, she was floating on the soft water. It was one big water bed.

"Don't do that!" He bent down and picked her up. He carried her away from the spring, until she recovered enough to stay away.

"I guess you're right," Jenny said sadly. "This is not the

time to rest. But it sure was the most comfortable bed I ever felt."

So they moved on again. Dug faded out, feeling delirious, so didn't know how long it took to reach it. But it was definitely later in the day.

Jenny sniffed it. Faint stars appeared in her eyes. "Oh, guest stars," she said, smiling. "I love them." Then she turned to look at Sherlock. "In fact, I love—"

"Get away from there!" Sherlock cried. "That's a love spring!"

"Much better than a hate spring," she replied dreamily.

"Get away!" he repeated firmly.

"Anything you say, you handsome creature." She moved languorously away. "Wouldn't you like to carry me again?"

"Not this time! You just breathe the air away from the spring for a while until it wears off."

Reluctantly the elf girl did so. Dug had never had reason to question the black man's decency, but if he had, this scene would have resolved it. He was getting just enough of a whiff of the spring to understand that it would be extraordinarily easy to take advantage of a situation.

So they set off for yet another spring, as the day waned. Dug hoped the next one wasn't a hate spring, because then Jenny and Sherlock might come to hate him, and leave him to expire alone.

As the sun set, they came to it. Jenny sniffed. "I think this is it!" she said, excited.

"You're not trying to trick me into tasting a love spring?" Sherlock asked.

"Dip your sore toe."

He did. "Hey—it healed!"

They brought some of the water to Dug. With the first drop on his lips he began to feel better. He swallowed, and felt better yet. He inhaled the vapor, and his lungs began to clear. This was definitely the healing elixir.

But his chest did not heal quite all the way. He knew why: he was still wearing the New Monia flower, and it was still sending illness into his lungs. He could have been better long ago, if he had just thrown that flower away. But he refused. He had to wear it just as if it were harmless.

"I'm better," he announced. "But I'd better take some of this elixir along, just in case of relapse." He dipped a small bottle in the spring, filled it, and corked it. It was amazing how sick he had felt, though he knew this was all pretense; an effect of the game couldn't touch him in real life. It certainly had seemed real, though.

It was now dusk. They foraged for food and camping materials, and set up for the night. There was no regular camping place here; evidently they had wandered from the normal route of the game. But if anything happened, they could heal quickly, because of the spring.

Dug thought he had been resting while the others worked, but now he discovered how tired he was. He sank into blissful sleep.

In the morning they resumed their trek, heading for Com Pewter's lair. At first they had to pick their way through thick jungle. Dug wondered why, since it seemed to thin in a nearby valley. Then he saw a dragon feeding on something, and realized that the easiest route was not necessarily the best. Sammy Cat was leading them the safe way—which was where the dragons weren't foraging. His encounter with the Gap Dragon had been more than sufficient to teach him respect—and that had been merely a steamer, not a firebreather.

They heard a companion. There ahead was a clearing, and in the clearing was a giant spinning object. "What's that thing doing here?" Dug demanded.

"I think that's the Big Top," Jenny said. "It's part of another story. I don't think we had better mess with it."

Dug was learning to take such warnings seriously. "We leave it alone," he agreed.

Now they were able to use some of the paths; Sammy Cat seemed to feel these ones were safe. They came to another area of commotion. It seemed to be an enclosed field, with many animals confined. "The stock market," Jenny explained. "It's full of charging bulls and bears. It's not safe for ordinary folk to enter. People get trampled there all the time, and wiped out."

Dug nodded. Literal bulls and bears. It figured. The Mundane version was scary enough, he understood; he didn't need to mess with this one.

They also bypassed a big shopping centaur. Dug didn't even ask.

At last they approached the region of the evil machine. Dug remembered how easy it had been to reach it, before, using the shortcut. But now they were in much better control. He would not be blindly stampeded into Pewter's cave.

This time he was able to appreciate how cunningly this particular trap was laid. The shortcut to success had indeed been a shortcut, for an innocent who didn't ask where it went or whose success it meant. It had amounted to an enchanted path, safe from other hazards, lulling him into false security. Then the invisible giant had come, scaring him into the one seemingly safe place—which was the worst place.

Dug felt his lung congesting. He quietly took another drop of healing elixir, and felt better. The New Monia flower remained bright and firm, the color of diseased lung tissue with spots of congestion; it was still trying to do its job. That was the way he wanted it. But he was really glad that Jenny had insisted on finding the healing spring; that made all the difference. Now, if his devious and punnish plan jest, uh, just worked . . .

He had a spot decision to make. Should he be wary of the giant, and sneak in to confront Pewter by surprise? Or pretend to be spooked in the usual fashion, so that the evil machine did not realize what Player it was at first? He decided on the latter course; that would be easier, and would surprise Pewter just as much. Perhaps more, because it would seem that this was a new victim being driven in. A surprised machine was more likely to make a mistake, and that was what Dug wanted. Pewter was dangerous, but the game required that he could be beaten, and surprising him was surely the best strategy.

In fact, Dug had a different Companion now, and a fellow traveler. If Pewter saw them first, he would be sure that this was a different Player. He would probably figure that it was Kim, and so would be prepared to freak her out, rattling her and making her fail to think of whatever her winning strategy might be.

"Um, friends," Dug murmured. "Before we go on, there's something I must explain. I met up with Pewter before, and got skunked. I got kicked out of the game, and had to start over, with different paths and challenges. That's why I'm being so careful now. He's got a slick routine to drive folk into his cave, and then he changes reality to whatever he wants it to be. Now, Sherlock, this isn't your responsibility, so maybe you should wait here until I settle with him, one way or the other. But I think you're stuck for it, Jenny, being my Companion."

"Yes," Jenny said. "It's my job to warn you to stay away from Pewter. But I know you can't do that, because you have to beat him to cancel out what happened before. So I'll try to help you. But once we're there, I won't be able to do anything, because he'll just change my script. You're the only one who can stop him, and I don't know how you can do that. Sammy won't be able to help against him, either."

"Right. It's always the Player who has to handle the real crunch. If it's a game challenge. My illness wasn't supposed to be part of the game, so you and Sherlock got me out of it." He paused. "By the way, if I didn't say thank you before, I'll say it now. I really appreciate what both of you did for me during my illness, and I'll try to repay you some way."

"I just did what I'm supposed to," Jenny demurred.

"You'd have done the same for me, if I got sick," Sherlock said.

"I know that. But a False Companion might have just let me be, washing out. And there are plenty of folk who would have figured it was no skin off their noses. So both of you really helped me, and I hope I can turn in a good performance report on Jenny, or whatever it is, and I hope we'll find the ideal place for the Black Wave."

"Let's get on with the action," Sherlock said gruffly. Dug could see that the man wasn't much for compliments, and he liked that.

"Okay. So Jenny and I will head in just as if we are surprised by all of this, and let the invisible giant drive us into the cave. One thing you can do for me, Jenny, if you will: you lead the way into the cave, so that Pewter sees you first. I want him to think it's Kim, until the last moment."

"You do have a plan," she said appreciatively.

"I do. It may not work, but I'll give it the old college try." He turned to Sherlock. "If I lose, I won't come out of that cave. But if Jenny calls the Demon Game Master, and explains how you got stranded here because of the Player, maybe he'll tell you where to go. A place for your Wave, I mean. It's worth a shot."

"Don't worry about that," Sherlock said. "I'm coming in with you. I want to see this dread machine."

Somehow Dug wasn't surprised. Sherlock hadn't backed off from anything yet. "Okay. If you want to follow Jenny in, it'll really surprise the machine. Then I'll appear, and try to polish him off with my sneak play."

"It's sure got me fooled," Sherlock said. "You've just been really sick, and you still don't seem all the way recovered despite that healing water, yet you're eager to get back into the fray."

"Maybe I'm just a crazy teenager," Dug said, smiling.

"Crazy like a fox, maybe."

"Foxes aren't crazy," Jenny protested. "They're pretty smart. Like wolves." She looked momentarily pensive.

No one commented. They walked out into the path leading by the cave.

Soon there was a shuddering of the ground. Trees crashed in the distance. "Hey, there's a meteor crashing!" Sherlock said.

"No, that's just the giant. I think he won't actually step on us. Remember to spook when he gets close."

There was another crash, and a giant footprint appeared. "No problem!" Sherlock said.

They spooked. They ran down the path, away from the approaching giant steps. The mouth of the cave appeared, and they scooted into it just ahead of the last footprint. So far so good.

Jenny ran ahead, toward the dim light of the interior chamber. Sherlock followed. "Good thing we found this cave," he called. "That monster almost squished us."

"It's Com Pewter's cave!" Jenny cried. "Quick, we must get out of it!"

There was a pause. Then she spoke again. "No, we must go on inside."

Dug, hanging back, smiled. Pewter had written a change on his screen.

"I don't like the look of this," Sherlock said. Then: "But maybe it's okay."

Dug moved quietly toward Pewter's chamber, where the two were now standing.

"But Sherlock's not the Player!" Jenny protested. "He's just a fellow traveler."

Dug saw a big question mark on the screen. Pewter had been caught by surprise! He had assumed that Jenny was escorting a Player, and that Sherlock was that player. Exactly as Dug had hoped. The evil machine's circuits had to be in turmoil. Now was his chance.

He strode boldly forward. "No, I am the Player," he said. "I have come to stop your clock, you crock of refuse."

The screen flickered. DUG MUNDANE! ERROR!

"No error, capacitor face. I fought my way back, just so I could settle your metallic hash."

YOU COULD NOT HAVE. NOT WITH YOUR COM-PANION.

"Well, I did! And I changed Companions along the way. Which you didn't anticipate, did you, screen-for-brains?"

CHANGE PROGRAM. ADAPT FOR SMART-POSTERIOR MUNDANE TEEN. RECOMPILE. The screen went black while the recompilation proceeded.

Dug didn't give it the change to complete its operation. "And here's how I'm going to do it, you nutty and bolty contraption. On my return route I picked up the Germ of an Idea and here it is." He brought out the bit of fluff and dropped it on the machine.

REJECTED! the screen printed desperately.

"And a bugseed," Dug continued relentlessly. "That'll put a bug in your program, for sure."

REJECTED! The screen was flickering.

"And here's the piece of resistance," Dug said. "Pardon my French." He lifted the flower from his buttonhole. "My third offering to you, which you can't refuse, because you've already rejected my first two." He held the flower above the screen. "A New Monia posy. That will give you a virus, for sure." He dropped it.

A VIRUS! NONONONOOOO ...

"Tough turnips," Dug said cruelly. "He who lives by the pun, dies by the pun. You've been infected, wirebrain. In other words, YOU LOSE."

The screen went crazy. Characters and symbols flowed across it in weird patterns. Then the words GENERAL SYSTEM FAILURE appeared. Then the letters fell from the words and collected in a pile at the bottom of the screen. The screen faded into black.

"Let's get out of here," Dug said, satisfied. "This pile of junk has nothing for us."

They walked out through the passage. Sammy was happy to show the way. "What kind of logic was that?" Sherlock inquired. "What's this rule about not rejecting three things?"

"Computers are logical but not sensible," Dug said

smugly. "In Pewter's state of confusion, it seemed to make sense. But I probably could have taken him out anyway with the New Monia, just by throwing it at him. Because a virus is a virus, and that one was good and potent. You saw what it did to me."

"That flower!" Jenny exclaimed. "I should have realized!"

"That's why I made it seem like just a decoration," Dug said. "I figured if you didn't catch on, Pewter wouldn't either—until I told him. In Mundania a living virus and a computer virus are two different things, but in Xanth they have to be the same. So I punned him to death."

"That was brilliant!" Sherlock said.

Dug smiled. "Elementary."

The giant was nowhere to be seen. Of course that didn't mean anything. But he wasn't heard, either, so they proceeded along the path unmolested.

"I think you're going to do well in this game," Jenny said.

"Maybe, maybe not. I just make it a point to learn from my mistakes. My first mistake was having eyes only for Nada Naga. My second was not taking puns seriously. So I dumped Nada, and now I'm playing the game to win. But the truth is, I'm just in it for the challenge and the fun now. I think this is a great, if foolish, adventure."

"Well, your next challenge should be the Good Magician's castle," Jenny said.

"One thing nagging me," Sherlock said. "Maybe nothing."

"Nothing's nothing here," Dug said. "What's your point?"

"You mentioned Nada Naga. I can see why you found her distracting. So did I. But there was something funny about her."

"Well, she's a princess," Jenny said. "They tend to be sort of reserved. Except for Princess Electra, who wears blue jeans."

"It's not that. She's a lovely creature, and a good lady.

But there was something about her. When you said how a False Companion would just have let you be sick, something nagged at me. I finally figured it out. Nada would have let you go."

"No she wouldn't," Dug said. "I'll never forget how she fought to help me douse the censor-ship!"

"The what?"

"That was in my first game session. The one I wiped out on with Pewter. But that was my doing; Nada was in my corner all the way, except when I tried to sneak a peek at her panties, and even then she welcomed me back. I know she's human under the princessly mantle."

"Certainly she is," Jenny agreed. "She's a good person. She was willing to marry Prince Dolph, despite not loving him, because he loved her and her family needed the liaison with the human folk. Then she got in trouble with the gourd realm, really by accident, so now she's serving her time with the demons, in this game. Same as I am. But she always does her best, and she's always nice."

"I'm sure she is," Sherlock said doggedly. "I could see that myself. Maybe that's why I picked up on the wrongness. It was as if she felt guilty for something. Something relating to you, Dug. I saw it when she looked at you, when you weren't looking at her."

"She has no cause to feel guilty about me," Dug said. "I was the one who tried to sneak a peek at her body. She had warned me not to, but I—" He shrugged. "I was young and foolish. She never did anything wrong."

"Of course she didn't," Jenny agreed. "She would never do anything wrong. The very notion would tear her up." Then her eyes widened. "Oh, no!" she breathed.

"Right." Sherlock took a breath. "So how would she react if she maybe got selected as a False Companion, the second time around?"

Dug was stunned. "It could be different each time, couldn't it! She could be True the first time, and False the second time. Still, it's hard to believe that she could—"

"She wouldn't exactly have a choice. She had to play by the rules of the game."

"I remember now," Jenny said. "She was the one who suggested that you exchange Companions. Could it be because she didn't want to be False to you, Dug?"

Dug's mind was spinning. Suddenly little things were clicking into place. Why had Com Pewter been so sure that he couldn't fight his way back, with his Companion? Maybe because the evil machine had known she was False, just waiting for the perfect opportunity to wash him out. Why had Nada been reserved in little ways, when she had been more open before? Her attitude *had* subtly changed, as if she were possessed of some secret sadness. Exactly as would be the case if she were required to turn traitor to the one she had before been pledged to help.

The more he pondered it, the more certain he became that it was true. Nada was a False Companion. She had not tried to torpedo him, because he wasn't far enough along to make it really count. Too soon, and he would just come back in another game and take another Companion, or take her again, when she wasn't False. So she would wait, hoping that he would wash out on his own. But if he didn't, and was about to win the prize, then she would arrange to betray him, making him forfeit his victory.

Now that he knew this, he could anticipate that betrayal, and reject her advice at the critical time. If she said the left fork had the prize, he could take the right fork. The key was in judging just when she was going to pull her act of betrayal. Forewarned was forearmed, but it would still be tricky.

Still, it hurt to know that she was now his secret enemy. He had given up on trying to see her panties, but had hoped to win her favor. Now that was impossible. "Brother!" he muttered. "She's like another virus, lurking to destroy the one she's with."

"Good thing you switched Companions, eh?" Sherlock said.

"I didn't switch for that reason," Dug said. "I didn't

realize—" Then he got the point. "Kim! Now she's got the False Companion! She's in trouble!"

"It means she'll lose," Sherlock agreed.

"Unless she can play again, and get back into it. But by that time I may have won the prize. It's not fair."

"So?" Sherlock inquired.

Dug came to his decision. "So I'm going to find her and warn her, or take back my False Companion! I'm not going to let her take the fall for me."

"You'll have trouble finding her. You'll likely have to go off the game routes."

"I know. It'll be rough. Not right to put you through that. So I guess this is where we part company. I'm sorry we didn't find any good places for your folk to settle. But maybe you can go down to the Good Magician's castle and ask him. Jenny can tell you how to get there, I'm sure."

"Forget it," Sherlock said. "I'm not leaving you yet. I just wanted to be sure you'd say what I thought you'd say."

"But this is no longer the game, really," Dug protested. "If I mess up, I'm just out of it. But if you get in trouble, your people will suffer. You've got more at risk than I do."

"More to gain, too. How do we know where I'll find a good place? It may be in the middle of some area you never were slated to cross. I might as well take a look at it. And a party of three can travel better than a party of two."

"Especially when one gets sick," Dug agreed, relieved. "Glad to have you along, then." He turned to Jenny. "Where do you think they went, and where can we best intercept them?"

"Sammy will know," she said.

The cat jumped down. "Wait for me!" Jenny cried, dashing after him.

They were on their way.

$$\overline{14}$$

FOUNDRY

K im was sweaty-hot, stinging-scratched, and worn-
out fatigued. This might be a game, not quite real,
but it felt distressingly real right now. Bubbles
Dog did not seem much better off, though she didn't complain. "Oh, we'll just have to rest," Kim said.

She found a spreading tree with wide ridged roots radi-
ating out. She sat down, leaning back against the trunk,
and pulled the dog into her. "What did I get you into, Bubbles?" she asked rhetorically. "You're old; you don't want
to struggle through wilderness like this! Maybe I should
have left you in that floating bubble."

Bubbles whined, her tail dropping low.

Kim hugged her. "No, I couldn't have done that! You
needed someone to adopt you, and I guess I needed a pet.
I never had a dog before. I'm glad I found you."

A huge serpent appeared. Its head changed, becoming
human. "Oh, there you are," Nada said. "I thought I'd lost
you."

"We're just so tired," Kim confessed. "This perpetual

jungle! Are you sure there isn't some easier route to the Good Magician's castle?"

Nada's face was unreadable. "There may be. But there are complications. The direct route would require us to cross the Kiss-Mee River, and though it has now been restored to its original friendly contours, that can be awkward."

Kim thought about swimming through Kiss-Mee water. There could indeed be complications! Would they be kissing water, fish, or each other? If she were still traveling with Dug she might have risked it. "Better avoid that," she agreed.

"So I have been trying to find a path north of Lake Kiss-Mee," Nada said. "But I am unfamiliar with this region, so it is difficult."

Kim was beginning to miss Jenny Elf and her cat Sammy, who could find things. He would have found them a safe, walkable path. As it was, they just had to struggle through. Still, it seemed harder than it had to be.

Then she spied something through the trees. It was a cloud in the sky, but not a rainy one. It might even be smoke. Was it true in Xanth, as in Mundania, that where there was smoke there was fire? And where there was fire, could there be civilization? Travelable paths? Anything seemed better than this endless jungle!

Kim hauled herself back to her feet. "Let's investigate that smoke," she said.

"I'm not sure that is wise" Nada demurred.

"Why not?"

"It may be a smoker dragon."

Ouch! Kim hadn't thought of that. Then her impulsive nature got the better of her. "But it might *not* be a dragon," she said. "Let's go see, carefully."

Nada shrugged, which was impressive in her natural form, and slithered out in the direction of the smoke. Kim and Bubbles followed.

Before long it was apparent that the smoke was coming from the chimney of a little house in the wood. "If that house is made of candy, I'm going to be a mite suspicious," Kim muttered.

It turned out to be a normal house, with wooden walls and a thatched roof. Still, that did not guarantee that its occupant was friendly. But Kim was so tired that she did the easy thing: she hoped for the best. She approached the door and knocked, while Nada waited nearby in serpent form.

The door opened. A woman stood there. She was absolutely repulsive. She opened her warty face. "Yes?" she said in a voice like gravel in a gearbox.

Kim glanced down at Bubbles. The dog hadn't barked. That suggested that this woman was not a menace. She might even be a decent person, under all that piled-on ugliness. "I'm—I'm a traveler, looking for an easy route to the Good Magician's castle," Kim said hesitantly. "I wondered if—"

"Why, you poor girl," the woman graveled. "You look so tired and hungry! You must come in and have a bit to eat!"

Kim glanced again at Bubbles. Still no objection. She decided to trust the dog's judgment. "Thank you," she said. "I'm Kim. This is Bubbles. May she come in too?"

"Of course, dear, if she's housebroken."

Kim realized that she didn't know about that. "I—" she started doubtfully.

"Oh, that's all right; I'll clean it up if there's a problem. I'm Ma Anathe. I love to have visitors, but I receive so few."

They entered the house. It was larger inside than outside, which was possible in a magic land. It was neatly arranged, and clean.

"Let me serve you some gruel," Anathe grated, as if rocks were caught in a grinder. "It is simple, but all I have."

"I'm sure it will do," Kim said doubtfully. She took her place at the wooden table.

Anathe set a wooden bowl of gruel before her, and another down on the floor for Bubbles. The dog lapped hers appreciatively, once again reassuring Kim. So she took the wooden spoon and tried a cautious sip—and it was good. It definitely was not gruel and unusual punishment.

"Now, about your trip to the Good Magician's castle," Anathe graveled. She seemed to have only those two tones: grate and gravel. "You must get on the enchanted path—"

"I can't," Kim said apologetically. "I'm—I'm a Player in a game, and I have to take my chances."

"Oh, so that's why you are so far into nowhere!" the woman grated. "That's why you are visiting old Anathe Ma! You're desperate."

Kim considered her response. Some diplomacy was in order. "It is true. But if I had known how nice you are, I would have visited anyway."

"That's sweet of you to say," Anathe said sourly. "I don't know much about this game, but I know better than to interfere with demons. If they say you can't use the enchanted paths, then you had best avoid them. That means you will have trouble crossing Kiss Mee."

"Yes," Kim agreed. The gruel was making her sleepy. She saw that it had the same effect on Bubbles, who was going into a dognap.

"Unfortunately that will route you past the foundry," Anathe continued. "The centaurs may be difficult. They don't like strangers there."

She continued to talk, but Kim was just too tired and sleepy to listen. She put her head on the table and slept.

She woke to the sound of Nada Naga's human voice. "What have you done with her? I warn you, if you have hurt her—you're not one of the game challenges, so you have no call to—"

"Hush, woman!" Anathe granted. "Your friend is just sleeping. How could you let her get so tired? And her poor dog, too—that animal is too old for prolonged adventure."

Kim was about to raise her head, to reassure Nada. But

something made her wait. She had not chosen Nada as her Companion; Dug had. She had gone along when he offered to trade, but she had never been quite sure this was legitimate. So while Nada certainly seemed to be a nice person and a competent Companion, Kim had just the slightest guilty tinge of doubt about her. Would Nada do the same job for her as she would have for Dug? So she was curious how Nada would react when Kim seemed to be in trouble.

"Did you give them a magic potion?" Nada demanded. "The demons won't like it if—"

"No potion!" Anathe graveled. "Just good, simple gruel, with a tiny drop of healing elixir. It was all I had. They were both ready to collapse when they came here. I couldn't let them go on like that. If you're supposed to be helping them, you should be ashamed."

Nada stroked across the chamber to the table. "Kim! Are you all right?"

Now Kim lifted her head. She felt somewhat refreshed. It had indeed been good gruel. "I'm all right. I was just so tired, I must have fallen asleep."

"Are you sure?" Nada herself look unsure.

"Yes. Anathe is very nice. Her gruel is very good." Kim reached down to pat Bubbles, who was now also awake. The dog wagged her tail.

Nada did a visible reassessment. Then she turned to Anathe. "I think I owe you an apology. I assumed—"

"Don't bother," the woman grated. "I understand. Everyone thinks that I must be as evil as I look. It is why I live alone."

"Appearances can be deceptive," Nada agreed awkwardly.

"Yes. Few would believe you are a serpent woman."

Now Nada was startled. "How did you know that?"

Anathema smiled. The effect was horrendous. "There are old pine needles in your hair, but none on your clothing, so you weren't rolling on the ground. You must have been in another shape. A werewolf would have walked over the fallen needles, but a serpent would be right down in them. I knew that a lovely young woman like you would not be guarding a person unless she was sure of her power. I have heard about the naga folk. You must have been in serpent form, and just changed."

"True." Nada brought out a comb and ran it through her lustrous gray-brown hair. Several needles fell out, as well as some bits of thread. "There are those who see me in serpent form and are horrified."

"At least you can change your form."

Nada nodded. "You have no magic to compensate?"

"My talent is making good gruel."

There didn't seem to be much help there. "Well, thank you," Nada said. "We must be on our way."

"Yes. I was just telling Kim the route. You must try to get past the foundry without aggravating the centaurs."

"We shall try," Nada said.

"But how can we repay you for the gruel?" Kim asked, standing.

"The pleasure of your brief company was enough," Anathe graveled. She bent down to pat Bubbles' head, and the dog wagged her tail. Then, in a murmur only Kim could hear: "Be watchful, girl; I fear something is afoot."

They left, and resumed their travel west. There was a path from the house, which made it much easier. Kim continued to feel better, as if the gruel had a developing effect as it was digested. Bubbles, too, was more alert.

Then Kim realized something. The dog had accepted Ma Anathe's pat. She had shied away from all others before, except for Kim herself. Bubbles had been right that the woman was not evil, and the dog even liked her, in her nondemonstrative fashion. That was most interesting. Especially since Bubbles was just as cautious about Nada as she was about anyone else.

And Anathe Ma had warned her about something. Kim might have dismissed it, but she trusted the dog's instinct. Anybody Bubbles trusted enough to receive a pat from had to be taken seriously. But what should she be watchful for? She didn't know, and probably Anathe had not known either; it was just intuition. But it aligned with Kim's own. Something was subtly not right.

All she could do was follow the advice: to be watchful. That she would.

The path wound along through the forest as if it had not a care in the world. Sometimes it made a straight rigid backbone, while at other times it practiced sinuous curves. It flirted with a big tangle tree, but stayed just out of reach. Once it set a couple of muddy puddles for unwary feet.

Bubbles hesitated, looking nervous. Kim was learning the signs; the dog was shy about most people, especially strangers, and barked when there was danger. She ignored most objects, but distrusted those that were unusual. So there must be something unusual here.

She saw a patch of flowers beside the path. But they were strange, even for Xanth. They were grotesquely ugly, and they smelled worse. Yet she recognized them as roses. They had the general configuration of roses, but somehow gave the opposite impression. Perhaps that was because they were the color of barf with the smell of puke. Beyond them were regular roses, pretty and sweet-smelling; only one circular patch was ugly.

Kim paused. Could this be a garden cultivated by Anathe? But the woman did not have an ugly house or personality, and her gruel had been good; why should she have ugly roses? There must be some other explanation.

Then she saw a single small chip of wood in the middle of the ugly patch. It looked like a fragment of the heart of pine, the kind her dad had used to start a fire in the fireplace, because it had so much clotted sap that it burned like a torch.

Suddenly it clicked. "Reverse wood!" she cried. She stooped to pick it up.

"Be careful!" Nada exclaimed. "That could be dangerous!"

"Not to me," Kim replied. "I'm a Mundane. I have no

magic. As far as I know, reverse wood reverses magic, not mundane things."

Nada looked doubtful, but did not protest. Kim picked up the chip, and sure enough, it did not hurt her or change her perception. But the roses that had been in its vicinity were already changing, becoming as lovely as the ones beyond the range of the chip. They were magic blue roses, with chocolate perfume; the magic had been reversed by the wood.

She held the chip down for Bubbles to sniff. The dog evinced no fear of it; apparently it had been the reversed roses that had bothered her. She was evidently Mundane, like Kim, so that chip didn't affect her directly.

That sent Kim into a brief spell of wondering. If Bubbles was of Mundane origin, how had she gotten into that floating bubble? Mundania did not have any magical trash disposal. Well, maybe sometime she would learn the answer.

Kim tucked the chip into a pocket. She was sure it would come in handy, in due course. After all, this was the game; things didn't happen just by accident. Maybe a dragon would try to toast her with fire, and the wood would turn it to cool water. The chip was surely the key to an upcoming challenge.

There was a dim sound ahead, but it grew brighter as they approached it. It sounded like metal being pounded.

They came to a cabin formed from knotted trees. "That's an ogre den," Nada said, alarmed.

Kim had had more than enough experience with ogres. She looked for a way to bypass the cabin. But again the jungle closed in thickly, making it impossible to deviate from the path. They would have to chance it. "Maybe those ogres aren't looking for trouble," she said with faint hope.

"Peaceful ogres? That's an oxymoron!"

But Bubbles wasn't barking, and that was a positive sign. As Anathe had shown, not all ugly folk were bad. Anyway, the way she was being channeled here suggested

that it was another challenge. So she would just have to
handle it. Watchfully.

The sound turned out to be an ogre pounding centaur
shoes. These were not like people shoes; they were
U-shaped bits of metal. Sparks flew up with each blow,
and the metal turned red-hot. There was no forge; the
ogre's blows were so hard that the heat came directly from
them.

Kim wanted to try to sneak past without the ogre notic-
ing, but knew that the game would never let her get away
with that. Sure enough, in a moment the ogre looked up
and saw her. "See she!" he roared.

But Bubbles didn't bark, so Kim stood her ground. In a
moment an ogress came from the house. Or was she an
ogress? There was something exceedingly odd about her,
and in a moment Kim realized what it was: she wasn't
ugly. She was at worst ordinary. No fangs. No hairy nose.
Just a reasonably homely countenance. Kim had heard of
only one un-ugly ogress in Xanth, but this one wasn't she.
Was it possible that there were two of them? What was
ogredom coming to!

The ogress looked at Kim. Simultaneously, Bubbles
growled. That meant trouble.

The ogress did not seem threatening. She smiled and
stepped toward them. But Bubbles whined and hid behind
Kim.

Was this the danger Anathe had warned her about? Was
the pretty ogress smiling to cover some sinister plot? What
could it be? The woman was making no threatening ges-
tures.

Nada Naga stepped in front of Kim. "Stop there,
ogress," she said firmly.

But the ogress didn't stop. She just kept smiling and advancing. Nada, annoyed, strode forward to intercept her.
"What are you up to?" Nada demanded.

"I just want to touch you," the ogress said, extending
her hand.

"Why?" Nada asked, with understandable mistrust.

"I just have to do it," the woman said. Then she lunged forward, and her hand touched Nada.

Immediately Nada changed. Not to serpent form; she became ugly. In fact, she was as hideous as Ma Anathe. The ogre woman, in contrast, became radiantly beautiful.

"Oh, ugh!" Nada cried, realizing what had happened. She changed to serpent form, but that didn't help; she was an ugly reptile.

Kim now had some understanding of the threat. But she didn't care. "Hey, change her back!" she cried, advancing on the ogress.

"I can't," the ogress wailed. "I want to, but I can't. It's my curse."

"What do you mean, you can't?" Kim demanded. "If you can enchant a person, you can break the enchantment, can't you?"

"No I can't. It is my talent to make others ugly. To take their beauty for myself. I have to do it; I can't stop myself. And it ruins me, because no ogre will marry a pretty ogress. Father has been trying to get me married off for years, but every time I start to get suitably ugly, some pretty girl comes along and ruins it." She broke into tears, which was a decidedly unogrish thing to do.

Kim's mind was chugging along with a high compression ratio. Was this the challenge? If so, there was a way to handle it. Suddenly she knew what that way was.

"Take this," she said, bringing out the chip of reverse wood. "Touch her again."

The beautiful ogress took the chip, confused. She poked a lovely finger at the serpent, as if afraid it would get bitten off. Nada, realizing that Kim was onto something, remained still, and allowed herself to be touched.

Suddenly the serpent was beautiful, and the ogress was mediocre. The effect had been reversed!

"Oh!" the ogress exclaimed, delighted. "What fine magic! What is it?"

"It is reverse wood," Kim explained. "It reverses the effect of your magic."

"You mean that with it, the ones I touch will become pretty while I turn ugly? Oh, this will change my whole life! I must have it. What do you want for it?"

"Oh, I just found it by the path," Kim said. "You can have it. But I can tell you something you might like to do. There is a woman in a house to the east who is very ugly. She—"

"Yes, Anathe Ma! I have always envied her ugliness."

"Touch her with the chip, and her ugliness will be yours."

"Oh, I will!" the ogress cried. "Father, I must run. But when I return, I'll be truly ogrish!" She ran off down the path. Before long the ogress would be phenomenally ugly, and a kind old woman would be beautiful. It seemed fitting.

Kim picked up Nada's clothes and put them in her pack. Nada continued in serpent form, as there was a male in view.

They paused by the laboring ogre. He ignored them. Bubbles did not seem unduly distressed, so Kim figured he was not a threat to them. She had the feeling that there was more here to be gleaned. This work must be connected to the foundry, and she would have to pass the foundry.

The ogre was doing impressive work. His centaur shoes were minor works of metallic art, and were surely a great help for those centaurs who required them. But what was there here that might help her handle the foundry?

The ogre pounded. A hot fragment of metal tore free and spun into the ground almost by Kim's feet. She stepped back, not wanting to be burned—then reconsidered, and stepped back to where she was. She picked up two sticks and used them to pick up the cooling metal. It was almost in the shape of a crude key.

A key. Could be. Just as the chip of reverse wood had helped solve a problem, this might help solve another. When she encountered that problem. She had the answer; now all she needed was the question. Maybe.

She found a heavy leaf, and set the key in that. Then she folded the leaf around it, and put that in her pocket where the reverse wood chip had been. "Thank you, ogre," she said.

"Girl some welcome," he grunted, continuing his labors.

Kim walked on, satisfied. She had the feeling that she was making progress in the game.

But had she taken care of the thing Anathe had warned her about? She wasn't sure.

Once they were beyond the ill-kempt view of the ogre shoemaker, Nada returned to human form. She was completely lovely again. There was no doubt of this, because she was bare. Every charm practically scintillated. Kim gave her back her clothing, stifling another surge of jealousy. Oh, to look like that! "I think I found a way to thank Anathe for her kindness," she said. "Now she will look as nice as she is."

"I'm just glad you had the reverse wood chip," Nada said. "I have no desire to be an unbeautiful beast."

Neither did Kim. But magic wasn't going to make her beautiful. She would always be a distinctly ordinary girl. In and out of the game.

They moved on. There was a sign ahead: FOUNDRY. "I hope this is the last challenge before we reach the Good Magician's castle," Kim said. "I like Xanth, but I'm getting tired of constantly exercising my brain and body."

"It has been wearing for me too," Nada said. "No offense."

"How did you get to be a Companion?" Kim asked. She had read the Xanth books, but couldn't remember that detail. "Did you volunteer?"

"No, I committed an indiscretion in the realm of the gourd, and was required to pay for it in this manner. Jenny is serving her year for the Good Magician, having done a favor for a friend."

"Well, at least you get to stay in Xanth. Dug and I have to leave, when our games are over."

"But you can return to play again."

"Yes. But it's not quite the same. I wish I could live here all the time."

"All Mundanes do."

They crested a hill, and there in the next valley was the foundry: a huge building surrounded by centaurs. Many of them were lying down; others were standing, but seemed uncomfortable.

They approached the nearest centaur cautiously. "If I may inquire," Kim inquired, "what is going on here?"

"We are all foundering," the centaur replied, pained. "Is that not evident?"

"I guess it is," Kim said. "I suppose this is because of the foundry?"

"This, too, should be evident."

"But why did you come here, if it is so dangerous for you?"

"We came to attend CentaurVention, of course. But a random cursor passed, and dropped a cursory curse, rendering our Vention Center into this awful foundry. Now we are unable to get away, because of our tender feet."

"There's an ogre making centaur shoes to the east," Kim said. "Would those shoes help you to walk?"

"Certainly. But none of us can hotfoot it over there, and in any event, there probably are far too few shoes for us. What we need to do is nullify the cursor's curse. Then the foundry will be gone, and we will not need shoes."

"I am sorry to learn of your distress," Kim said. "But I am not sure what I can do about it. It's really not my problem."

"Have no concern. When you attempt to pass the foundry, as you must to proceed along your route, you too will founder. Then it will be your problem also."

Kim considered that. This definitely sounded like a challenge. She would have to rise to it. "What do you think I can do about it?"

"Since you have not yet foundered, you might be able to find the natural antagonist to the foundry, which of course is the lostwet."

"Of course," Kim agreed. Puns were serious business in Xanth. "The lost-wet would cancel out the found-dry."

"Precisely. Then we would all be free of our founder."

Kim decided to test the extent of this challenge. "On the other hand, I might avoid the whole thing by going back the way I came, and seeking another route south."

"You would have to cut cross-country through the impenetrable jungle," he pointed out. "I suspect you would find that very tiring. Then you would encounter the Big Top, the Gnobody Gnomes, and Com Pewter. I suspect you would rather accept a ride from one of us, bypassing all those hazards."

Kim saw the way of it. "I suspect I would," she agreed. "Where do you suppose I might find the lostwet?"

"There is a lost wax trail to the south which ought to lead there."

"Lost wax?"

"It was lost in the process of casting the foundry curse."

She should have known. "I shall follow that trail," Kim agreed.

They turned south. Bubbles soon sniffed out the smell of wax. It looked as if a huge vat of melted wax had spilled and flowed and cooled and solidified, forming the path. This would be known as the lost wax process. Now it had hardened so that it was easy to walk on.

At the end of the trail of wax was a small lake. The wax seemed to have flowed out across the surface of the lake, cooling, and finally formed a thin wax seal over it. The seal was very strong, so that they were able to walk out on it without falling in the lake. It was transparent, so that they could see right down to the bottom of the lake.

This seemed to be a flat expanse. At the near end was a smooth slope, while at the far end was a portal, similar to the ones she had used to let the water into the naga tunnel. In the center of the portal was a small keyhole.

Kim brought out the key she had saved from the ogre's work. It was now cool and firm. Could this be the key to that lock? This was the game; it was bound to be the proper key. So she would have to put the key in that lock, and open that portal. Beneath it should be the lostwet.

But how was she going to get the key there? She could see the keyhole, but the transparent wax was so hard that she couldn't scratch it, let alone poke a hole in it. She was being tantalized by a goal so near yet so far. "Do you know anything about this?" she asked Nada.

"I knew there was a challenge here, but not its nature," Nada confessed. "I don't know anything about wax."

It figured. The Companion's job was to get the Player safely to the challenges, but not to solve them. So Nada had braced Anathe when it seemed that the woman was interfering with Kim, but was no help in fathoming this riddle.

"Do you have any idea, Bubbles?" Kim asked.

The dog wagged her tail and started sniffing the waxed surface. Kim wasn't sure that Bubbles had really understood her question, but the dog obviously wanted to be helpful.

In a moment Bubbles stopped. She had found something. Kim checked, and saw a tiny hole in the wax. Maybe she could get her finger into it and pull the wax up, making an access to the water.

But her finger wouldn't fit; the hole was too small. And anyway, the wax was so strong that she would need a keyhole saw to cut through it, and of course Xanth didn't have such machines. So what good was the hole?

Then she considered the key again. It was just small enough to fit through that hole. But if she put it through there, she would just lose it in the lake, being unable to retrieve it. That seemed even more pointless than her other options.

But this was the game. There had to be a way. She just had to figure it out.

Kim strained her brain, but could not squeeze out any useful notion. The key was here, the lock was there, and never the twain could meet, it seemed. Unless—

The light of an idea flashed over her head again, but

dimly, because she wasn't sure she had the right clue. It was only half a flash, really. She had played with a puzzle in a book once, in which a string passed through small holes, and something had to be transferred from one loop to another, when it was too big to fit through the holes. The trick had been to manipulate the string, passing it around the object and through the holes, until the puzzle could be solved. Here she had a key, and a keyhole, and a small hole leading to the wrong place; was there a way to get the key to the keyhole indirectly? She didn't have any string, and string wouldn't do the job anyway, but maybe the principle applied.

She lay down on the wax and peered through it, studying the situation. Now she saw that there were a number of bugs running around on the bottom of the lake. They looked like ticks, the kind that had to be kept off people and dogs, but these had to be water bugs, or at least capable of living in water. There were letters of the alphabet on their backs, identifying them. They didn't seem to be doing anything, just moving back and forth in semicircular paths, as if they were pendulums. All of them faced the same way, as if they had fled from the locked portal. When they moved, they didn't turn left or right; they skittered sideways, maintaining their orientation. Every time they reached the end of a semicircle, they clicked. Click-click. That struck Kim as odd behavior, even for such odd creatures.

Pendulums. Clicks. As in big clocks. Making ticks and tocks. So they *were* ticks, Xanth-style. Kim had read how the Good Magician Humfrey in his youthful days had lived on a tick farm, growing ticks for clocks, and had a real problem when the ticks mutated and made mischief. She remembered how aggravating the cri-tic had been. Could it be that some of those errant ticks never had been run down, and here they were? Just waiting to accomplish something?

The other half of her idea flashed. Maybe she could get

them to move the key for her! To take it to the lock she couldn't reach. If only she could figure out how to do it.

She held the key in her hand. Suppose she dropped it through the hole, and simply asked the ticks to move it for her? But why would they bother, even if they understood what she wanted? She had to have some way to encourage them. And there had to be a way, because this was the game.

If they were ticks, where were the tocks? All the bugs were the same; there didn't seem to be any tocks. Where did the tocks come from? She hadn't read of any tock farm. Actually, in a clock, a tock was just the other side of a tick. So were tocks really ticks turned over? If so, there were really tocks as well as ticks.

This was crazy, but maybe it made punnish sense: ticks might not help her, but tocks might. If she could just get them to turn over. The ticks were all facing away from the portal and its keyhole, but tocks might face toward it. So maybe they could take the key the right way.

What could she lose? Kim put the key to the hole in the wax. It dropped through and plinked on the floor of the pool.

Immediately the ticks changed their behavior. They stopped swinging aimlessly, and started advancing on the key. But Kim realized that they would push it the wrong way, away from the lock. She needed tocks to push it the right way.

"Tick-tock!" she cried. But the ticks ignored her.

She realized that nobody would respond to a general call. If someone called "People-smeople!" she would ignore him too. But if someone called her by name or description, she would react.

"Fran-tic!" she called. No tick responded. "Fantas-tic!" Still nothing. "Gigan-tic!" The ticks continued toward the key, and the first one was beginning to push the key off toward a trench Kim now saw some distance beyond. If it fell in there, it would never be recovered!

She was getting nowhere, and she couldn't remember

any more of the ticks she had read about. Then she realized that she had it backward: Humfrey had dealt with all those ticks. She had to address those ticks that had escaped his notice.

She strained her brain. She saw a tick that was somewhat dusky, as if spoiled. Its letter was N. "Necro-tic!" she cried.

The tick paused. She had identified it!

"Necro-toc!" she said. And the tick turned around and faced the other way. She had done it!

"Necro-toc, push the key!" she called.

The tock skittered sideways and reached the key. It made little clocks, rather than clicks, as it moved. It braced its head against the key and pushed. The key moved toward the lock. Kim had found out how to do it. She would get a lick at the lock.

But other ticks were coming to push the other way. One got placed squarely before the key, and it came to a halt. Then a second tick lined up before the first, and the key began to slide back.

Kim saw that one of the ticks seemed a bit doubtful. Its letter was A. "Agnos-tic" she cried, and it paused.

"Agnos-toc. Push the other way!"

The tick turned around and pushed from the other direction. Now it was two to one, and the key resumed motion toward the lock. It was getting close. "Go, go, go!" Kim whispered fervently, urging her team on.

But another tick crowded into the space left by the Agnos-toc, and pushed the other way. So it was two to two, and the key stopped moving again. Then a third tick arrived, making it three to two, and the key started moving away again.

The third tick was not very active itself, but it seemed to stir the other two up, and they pushed harder. Its letter was C. Suddenly Kim recognized it.

"Cataly-tic!" she cried, and it paused. "Cataly-toc!" It turned around. "Push the key." It pushed.

Now the Necro and Agnos tocks were revitalized, becoming very active. The key moved so rapidly that the other ticks could not catch it, and at least it reached the keyhole of the lock. They pushed it in, and then pushed it around so that it turned. There was a loud clock! sound, and the C fell away, leaving the (c)lock. The lock opened.

The water swirled into it. Kim realized that it was like the lock of a canal, handling water. The water would be held there until it was moved on to the next lock.

As the water drained from the pool, the thin wax covering it lost its support. It collapsed, and the three of them had to scramble to get off it before getting dunked.

The ticks and tocks and fragments of wax swirled into the lock along with the water. Soon there was just a dry depression there. They walked down into it. It seemed to be nothing but a fairly level region. Where was the lostwet?

Bubbles paused to sniff something. Kim looked. It was a blinking little square or oblong, so small Kim would not have seen it if the dog had not called her attention to it.

She picked it up. It seemed to have no mass; it was just a tiny manifestation she could balance on the tip of her finger. What could it be?

Then she understood. "It's a cursor!" she cried. "We had to get rid of the water—to get the wet lost—in order to get it. It's the cursor that made the foundry and then got lost in the wet. With this we should be able to reverse the damage it did."

Both Nada and Bubbles looked doubtful, but neither argued. Kim marched out of the lost pool and back onto the lost wax trail, balancing the blinking thing on her finger. They followed.

She reached the place where the centaurs had foundered. "I got it! I got it!" Kim cried, brandishing her blinking finger.

Heads turned to look at her. The male centaurs frowned. The females blushed. What was the matter with them? Centaurs were notoriously unflappable.

Then Kim realized what was wrong. She seemed to be

making a signal with her finger. It might not have the same meaning in Xanth as it did in Mundania, but it could hardly be considered polite.

She straightened out her other fingers. "I have the cursor," she explained. "The one to nullify the curse, I think."

"Of course," the nearest centaur replied. "Put it on the foundry."

Kim walked on to the foundry. As she got closer, her feet started to hurt. Her shoes felt too tight. She wanted to get the weight off. But she knew what it was: she was foundering. All she had to do was nullify the curse, and it would go away. So she gritted her teeth and walked on.

The pain got worse, until it felt as if she were walking on acid-soaked pincushions. She couldn't stand it any more. She had to stop.

But now she was close to the foundry. She held up her finger. "Take this!" she cried, jabbing it toward the building. The cursor flew off and struck the foundry wall.

There was a flash. Kim blinked with the brightness of it. As her eyes cleared, she saw that the building had changed. Now it was the Centaur Vention Center. She had done it!

The centaurs got up and trotted in. "Now we shall give you and your Companion your ride to the Good Magician's castle."

"Thank you," Kim said, gratified. She knew she had managed to win another challenge.

15
TALENTS

D ug ran after Jenny, who was running after Sammy, while Sherlock followed them all. Jenny knew enough to hold on to Sammy when telling him to find something, but she kept forgetting. She was after all a child, Dug remembered; he had to make allowances. Certainly her little cat's talent was useful.

The trouble was that the paths the little cat took were not necessarily suitable for people. They soon got tangled in brambles, burrs, and thistles. "Stop, Sammy!" Jenny cried. "We can't keep up with you!"

The cat stopped. Jenny picked him up. She was about to ask him to pick out an easy and safe path for them to follow, when she paused.

Dug and Sherlock were pausing too. They had blundered into an odd section of the forest. It wasn't that the trees were different, just that their arrangement was odd. Instead of being randomly scattered, they were growing in lines and curves, as if part of some huge ornamental garden. A garden cultivated by a giant, perhaps.

"I think we should quietly move away from here," Sherlock murmured.

Dug agreed. He did not like the look of this. He turned back the way they had come.

But there was a commotion back there. Something was following them. "Oops," Jenny said. "I think maybe we're somewhere we shouldn't be."

"My sentiment exactly," Dug said, reversing course. He led the way to the side, trying to avoid the thing behind by going at right angles to its motion. But he came up against a massive hedge of woven trees. There was no way through it, and the thorns on the trunks made it impossible to climb up and over. "In fact, I think maybe we're in another challenge." It was the last thing he wanted. He didn't care about the game at the moment; he just wanted to intercept Kim so he could warn her that she had a False Companion who would betray her at the key moment. The longer it took to catch up to her, the greater the risk of her betrayal.

He walked beside the dread hedge, seeking somewhere to hide. But the hedge curved around, herding him toward the center of the tree garden. Meanwhile the thing closed in from behind. There seemed to be no escape.

"All right, already," Dug said. "I'll face it!" It had not been fear of bodily harm that had driven him to hide, but fear of delay. He wanted to skip the game for now, until he could warn Kim, and maybe exchange Companions back so that the liability would be his instead of hers. It was the right thing to do.

They stood and waited for the thing. And Dug was surprised again. Because it wasn't a monster, it was a pair of horses with riders. And a foal. A halfway handsome man rode the stallion, and a lovely woman rode the mare. The man wore a sword. But the oddest thing was the metal. Each horse had heavy chains wrapped around its body. What was going on here?

The man spied them. He waved. "Hi, there, friends," he

said in a friendly fashion. "What are you doing in the Garden of Talents? I thought it was closed to the public."

Appearances could be extremely deceptive, in Xanth. But Dug saw nothing to be gained by being too defensive. This just possibly barely might be a chance encounter. So he told the truth. "I am Dug. I am playing in a game. This is Jenny Elf, my Companion, and this is Sherlock, who is looking for a place for his Black Wave to settle in peace. We strayed in here unintentionally, and wish only to leave it behind."

"The game?" the man asked, his brow wrinkling.

"The demons are running it," Jenny explained.

The woman took an interest. "Then it must be fun." She turned to the man. "Let's learn more of this, Jordan."

The man was amenable. "Okay." He jumped down from his horse, while the woman floated down. He strode forward. "I'm Jordan the Barbarian. My talent is to heal quickly. This is my wife, Renee. Or Threnody, if you like that better. She's half demon. These are our friends the ghost horses: Pook, Peek, and Puck." The stallion, mare, and foal nodded their heads in turn when named, showing that they understood human dialogue.

"Oh, I know of you," Jenny said. "I learned about it in centaur school. You came from more than four hundred years ago, in Xanth's history, and met Threnody—"

"In the year 677," Threnody said. "We had a small misunderstanding, but later we got together again."

"In 1074," Jordan said. He counted on his fingers. "Eighteen years ago. We've been happily exploring the wilderness ever since. And whatever." He pinched Threnody's well-rounded bottom.

"There's a certain charming naturalness about barbarians," Threnody said, smiling as she kicked his shin. "They're so ill-mannered."

"And a certain sexy mystery about demon women," Jordan agreed. He tried to pinch her again, but this time his hand seemed to pass through her body as if it were smoke.

It occurred to Dug that the two were well matched. Jordan liked a woman who was mysterious and sexy and had certain demonly qualities, and Threnody/Renee liked a man who had few human restraints. She probably didn't give him any trouble about seeing her panties, but she could prevent him from handling her flesh when she chose.

"The demons are running the game," Jenny said. "It's for two Mundanes: a girl who won a prize, and—well, I'm not sure how Dug got in."

"Pirated copy, probably," Dug said. "I should've asked. My friend who wanted my girlfriend got it."

"Pirates, eh?" Jordan said, interested. "They're like barbarians."

"I'm from Mundania," Dug said. "I'm just visiting Xanth, playing the game. But right now I don't want to play it, I want to intercept the other player, Kim, so I can—"

"Wipe her out!" Jordan said, pleased.

"Not exactly. I really don't care about the prize. But—"

"But you like the girl," Threnody said. "So you want to catch her and make like a barbarian." She pinched Jordan's bottom.

"Uh, not exactly that, either," Dug said, privately intrigued by the byplay between the two. "I maybe did something that's going to wipe her out, and I have to warn her before it happens. So it's fair."

"Fair?" Jordan asked blankly.

Threnody nudged him. "You know about fairness. It's in the *Barbarian Handbook*. Page 432, Footnote F."

He looked sheepish. "I guess I didn't read that far. Barbarians aren't much for books."

"I quote: 'If all else fails, try fairness. Fair women can be very appealing.' "

He brightened. "Oh. Sure. All I need now is a fair—"

He broke off, because she had just drawn a knife and cut off his mouth. Jordan looked surprised. Then he fetched out a big handkerchief, mopped the blood, and gave her a reproving glance. Already his mouth was healing. New lips were growing to replace the lost ones. Well, he had said that his talent was fast healing. He had meant it literally.

"Anyway," Dug continued, refusing to act as shaken as he was by this incidental demonstration, "I just want to get on away from here and on my way. But the big thorny hedge is stopping me. Do you know any way past it?"

"I could phase through it," Threnody said. "I can become demonically insubstantial when I choose. But I don't suppose that will help you much."

"That hedge usually doesn't bother us," Jordan said. He lisped a bit, because his mouth had not yet grown back to full size and flexibility. "But probably you can't get by it. You see, it grows only when it wants to catch someone, and then it grows in a circle, so they can't get out. You have to find a magic talent to get out."

"That's a game challenge!" Dug said. "How could you have encountered it, if you're not part of the game?"

"Threnody told me we might have a bit part to play in a game," Jordan admitted. "I guess this is it. Maybe it will relieve the boredom of being stuck with one woman."

Threnody lifted her knife, but this time he caught her hand, then kissed her with his new-formed lips. Dug doubted that Jordan was really bored.

"Well, then, can you tell me how I find a magic talent? I'm Mundane; I don't have any magic of my own."

"Sure. There's a box of talents in the center. You can't miss it. Only there's a catch."

"There's always a catch," Dug agreed wearily.

"You have to pick out talents blindly. You have to use a talent at least once before you can put it back and take another."

That didn't seem like much of a catch, so Dug knew it couldn't be the whole story. "What's the catch to the catch?"

"Hey, you're thinking like a barbarian!" Jordan said with approval. His mouth was now almost the way it had been before. "Never trust any civilized person. The catch is you don't know what talent you've got, so you'll have trouble using it."

"But it will take forever to guess, without a hint," Dug protested.

"There's a hint," Threnody said. "It's a list of fifty talents. You can check them off as you identify them. If you use up all fifty, there'll be a new list. If you get one that will enable you to escape the garden early, you won't need to return it; it will fade out in a day or so anyway."

So that was it. If he were lucky, and quick to fathom his luck, he could be on his way rapidly. Otherwise he might be stuck for hours. Or days.

Dug turned and walked to the center of the glade. Sammy jumped down to show him the way. The others followed.

"May I pet Puck?" Jenny asked, approaching the ghost foal. "He's so cute."

The chained foal approached her, agreeing to be petted. "Why are they wearing those chains?" Sherlock asked.

"That's the way ghost horses are," Jordan said. "Without their chains they'd fade out. It's the chains that hold them in this realm."

"Wouldn't it be kinder to unwrap them and let them go?" Jenny asked.

"Then what would we ride?" Jordan asked sensibly.

Sherlock and Jenny didn't argue. They evidently realized that there was not too much point in discussing gentle social concerns with a barbarian.

Dug came into the central glade. There was the spellbox. It was circular, with a flat top. Behind it was a billboard, titled 50 SPELLS.

There did not seem to be any opening in the top. But Dug was getting used to the ways of magic. He touched the top with his hand, and sure enough, his hand passed right through it, disappearing beyond, as if the top were a sheet of liquid paint. His questing fingers caught something. He drew his hand back, hauling out the thing—and his hand was empty. But he felt subtly changed.

The others were watching him. "Do you have a talent?" Jenny asked.

"I have something," he said. "I suppose it's a talent. But I don't know which one."

"You can read the list, and try them in order," Sherlock suggested.

Dug read the list:

1. Change Color of Anything.
2. Change One Food to Another.
3. Null Taste.
4. Alter Smells.
5. Make Objects Adhere.

The talents seemed straightforward and harmless. "Okay, how does a person make his magic work?" he asked.

"I have to get injured before mine works," Jordan said. "Then it's automatic."

"I just will myself smoky," Threnody said. "And solid again. It's slow, but it happens. It's not really a talent; I simply partake of some human and some demon nature."

"I just hum," Jenny said. "Anyone who isn't paying attention enters my dream."

Dug hadn't realized that Jenny had a magic talent of her own; he had assumed that it tied in with her cat. "Okay, I'll will something to change color." He looked around. "That stone there: turn pink."

He concentrated, trying to turn the stone pink. Nothing happened. "No luck," he said. "So it's not that."

"Are you sure?" Jenny asked. "Maybe you have to call it 'anything.'"

"Okay." He addressed the stone. "I dub thee 'anything.' Now turn pink."

Again, nothing happened. "So I'll try the next." He fished in his pocket and found a few nuts left over from his last snack: two M's, one N, one O, and three P's. He lifted the P-nut. "Change to a marshmallow," he ordered it.

Nothing happened. "Maybe it's a marshmallow in the shape of a P-nut," Sherlock suggested.

Dug tasted it. "No, it's still peanut-flavored." He glanced at the list. "So now I'll null its taste." He concentrated, then tasted it again. It remained P-flavored. So he tried the next: "Make it smell like a rose." With no success. "Then make it adhere to my finger." He touched his finger to it, but there was no adhesion.

He sighed. "This is apt to be tedious." He read the next five talents:

6. Change Water to Vapor or Ice, and Back.
7. Make Raw Food Cooked.
8. Sense When Someone Is About to Die.
9. Call Up Small Intense Gusts of Wind.
10. See Through Objects.

"We have any water?" Dug asked.

Jordan had a flask. He poured a bit out, and Dug tried to vaporize or freeze it, but without success. Then he tried to cook the P-nut, with no luck.

#8 brought him up short. "How do I tell when someone's about to die, if no one *is* about to die?"

"I can slay someone for you," Jordan offered cheerfully, drawing his sword.

Dug would have laughed, but he had the eerie feeling that the man wasn't joking. "No thanks! That talent wouldn't help me get out of here anyway, so I'm just going to assume this isn't that. I'll try the next, and see if I can call up a small, intense gust of wind."

"That's not magic," Sherlock said. "I can do it naturally." He bent over.

"That won't be necessary," Dug said quickly, though he was strongly tempted to laugh. Jordan didn't worry about temptation; he burst out with a rich ho-ho-ho!

"That's another way of doing it," Sherlock agreed.

Pook, the ghost horse, didn't bother to laugh. He simply let fly with his own loud gust of wind.

"Thanks, folks," Dug said. "But I'm the one who has to break the, uh, make the wind." He concentrated, but no other wind stirred.

Next he tried to see through objects. He couldn't. "Just as well," Jenny said. "You might have looked through Threnody's or my clothing and seen our panties."

Dug hadn't thought of that. He bit his tongue so as not to laugh, knowing that they took such things more seriously than he did. "Right. Close call."

He addressed the next five talents:

11. Make Others Mute.
12. Extinguish Fires.
13. Heal Cuts & Abrasions.
14. Resist Bad Dreams.
15. Reverse Someone's Sex.

"Okay, in order," Dug said. "Do I have a volunteer to become mute?"

"Sure, try me," Sherlock said.

Dug concentrated. "Sherlock, become mute!" he intoned. "Did it work?"

"No."

Dug went on to the next. "We'll have to set a fire, to see if I can quench it magically."

Jordan went to Pook and fetched two small stones. He squatted by some dry grass and knocked the stones together. A fat spark flew out, igniting the grass. There was a little fire.

Dug focused on the fire, but he couldn't put it out. So Jordan brought out some marshmallows and began toasting them on the end of a stick.

"Now, can I heal a cut?" Dug asked. "I don't think we should cut anyone to test this! Anyway, we have some healing elixir, which would do the job. Let's skip this one for now."

"No, we can test it," Jordan said. He took his knife and

passed the tip across Threnody's arm, scratching it. "Heal this."

Dug focused on the scratch, but nothing happened. "I think that's not it."

Jenny brought out the healing elixir and dripped a drop on the scratch. The scratch disappeared.

But the next one was worse. "How can I find out whether I can resist bad dreams, if I'm not asleep? And if I were asleep, and dreaming, suppose only good dreams came? It could take a month before I had a bad dream to resist."

"Maybe you could try a bad daydream," Jenny suggested.

"Mare Imbri would never deliver one of those," Threnody objected.

"Who is Mare Imbri?" Dug asked.

"She's the day mare who brings good daydreams," Jenny explained. "She brought Kim the daydream of floating bubbles, and Kim got Bubbles Dog from one of them."

Live and learn. "Well, I'll try to imagine a bad daydream, and see if I can resist it," Dug said. He concentrated, imagining falling into an endless hole. That notion had always scared him, and it still did. "I don't seem to have any special resistance," he said.

But there was no easing the difficulty of the progression. "I don't want to change someone's sex!" Dug said.

"You could change one of us, then change him back," Threnody suggested.

"Who volunteers for that?" Dug asked. He glanced at Sherlock. "You want to be a woman for a minute?"

The man shook his head no. He pointed to his throat.

"That's what I thought," Dug said. "It could be a one-way trip. So I'll just skip this one, for now." Then something registered. "Why did you point to your throat, Sherlock?"

The man didn't answer. He just pointed again.

"He can't speak!" Jenny cried. "The mute talent worked!"

"No it didn't," Dug said. "He said it didn't."

Sherlock pointed to Jordan. "Jordan said it," Threnody said.

"Well, I thought it didn't," Jordan said. Threnody gave him a disgusted look.

Dug looked at Sherlock. "The magic really did make you mute?"

Sherlock nodded vehemently.

"Well, at least that identifies it. But it's not the one I need. Let's see if I can unmute you." He concentrated. "Sherlock, speak again."

There was no result. It was a one-way talent.

"It should wear off in a few hours," Threnody said.

Sherlock grimaced, not completely pleased.

"Gee, I'm sorry," Dug said. "I guess I'd better not experiment on real people any more."

"I can make you feel better," Threnody said. "I'll give you a gourd-style apology for your inconvenience. She approached Sherlock, took hold of him, and gave him a demonically passionate kiss.

Dug could have sworn that the man's feet left the ground for a few seconds. His eyes rolled back in his head, and a dreamy smile washed across his face. He looked as if he had been anesthetized. Certainly he felt better.

"Renee has that effect," Jordan remarked nonchalantly. "A demoness can make a man deliriously happy, if she chooses. I happen to know."

It was evidently true. Sherlock seemed to be beyond caring about any little inconvenience such as not being able to speak. In fact, he looked as if he would have been speechless even if he weren't already mute.

Dug returned to business. "So I don't need this talent, because it won't get me by the thorntree hedge. All it proves is that the magic does work, and that I have a whole lot of talents to check through." He looked around. "Where do I ditch this mute magic?"

"You just reach back into the spellbox," Threnody said. "It will let go, so you can take another."

"But won't I risk getting the same talents back?"

"No, new talents float to the surface; used ones sink to the bottom. Just don't reach too deep."

Dug reached in, and he did feel something leave him. He caught a new something, and brought it out.

He read the next five talents:

16. Can Merge with Others.
17. Can Re-create Any Sound Heard.
18. Can Create Heat.
19. Can Cause Objects to Levitate.
20. Can Adjust Weight of Things.

"Nuh-uh! I'm not trying to merge with anyone!"

Threnody sighed. "And I was so looking forward to it."

Dug didn't comment, because again he suspected that she wasn't joking. She was opposite to Nada Naga in everything other than beauty.

He tried to re-create sound, but couldn't. He tried to heat something, and couldn't. He tried to make something float, and couldn't. He tried to make a stone become heavier, and failed again.

So he tried the next five:

21. Immunity to Poison.
22. Can Ease Pain in Others.
23. Can Breathe Anywhere.
24. Can Change the Magic of Water.
25. Can Make Trees Fall.

Dug refused to try the first. He wasn't sure how to test the second, until Threnody touched her knife to Jordan's arm, making it bleed. Dug tried to make the barbarian's pain stop, but couldn't. Fortunately it soon stopped itself, as Jordan quickly healed. Dug couldn't test the breathing, because he couldn't find a vacuum or a deep lake to try.

Similarly he had no magic water to change from Hate to Love or Lethe. He wasn't going to mess with the vial of healing elixir they had, just in case it got spoiled. And the trees ignored his attempt to fell them magically.

He ground on through the remaining talents of the list. Nothing matched. "But how can that be?" he asked plaintively. "It's got to be one of them!"

"Maybe one of the ones you skipped," Jenny said.

"Or one of the first fifteen," Threnody suggested. "You didn't test them, this time; you picked up where you left off after the first talent."

She was right. Of course he had to test all the talents each time. Which made the job even more tedious.

Resigned, he tried #1, Changing Color. And it worked: he turned the rock pink.

"Two down," he said. "Only forty-eight to go." He was coming to appreciate how long it could take to test fifty times, for fifty different talents each time. Magic was becoming a lot more tedious than he would have thought.

"Maybe Sammy can help," Jenny said.

"I really don't see how—" Dug started. But the little cat was already bounding to the spellbox. "Wait for me!!" Dug cried, grabbing for Sammy before he fell through the porous lid.

But the cat didn't fall through the lid. For him it was solid. He sniffed the surface, looking for something, then seemed to find it.

Could it be? Dug reached into the box by the cat's nose, and caught the first spell he found there. He brought it out.

Was this the one he needed? But what *did* he need?

He skimmed through the list. Attract Animals. Mimic People's Appearance. Create Light. Darkness. Communicate with Anyone. Repel Dragons. Slow Time. Calm Tangle Trees. Reverse Emotions. Make Fire.

Would that last one enable him to burn down the thorntree hedge? He tried to make fire, but didn't get as much as a curl of smoke.

Make Earth Tremors. Blow Hurricane Force.

Maybe one of those would shake down the hedge, or blow it away. But he was unable to evoke either.

Create Pain. Sniff Danger. Control Animals. Make Others Sleep. Make Invisible Shield. Make Things Invulnerable. Reverse People's Actions. Generate Hatred. Mimic Person's Talent.

"I just don't see how any of these can get me out of here, really," Dug said, frustrated.

Sammy jumped off the spellbox and ran to Threnody, who picked him up.

Dug was learning to pick up on insignificant details. What did that cat have in mind?

Suddenly it clicked. "Mimic Someone's Talents!" he cried. "Threnody can become smoky. If I can make things turn smoky-diffuse, we can get through." He approached the woman. "Give me your talent, please."

"I thought you'd never ask," she said with a dusky smile. She held her hand out to him, cupping it in the air.

He took whatever it was she held. Then he turned to face the thorntree hedge. "Become diffuse," he ordered it.

Then he walked to it and tried to put his hand through it. "Ouch!" He had skewered his extremity on a thorn, but that wasn't the whole reason for his pain. The magic hadn't worked.

Then he reconsidered. That thorn had gone right through his palm and out the other side. It had hurt, but not as much as it should have. His hand was not bleeding.

He touched the hedge again, more cautiously, and this time his hand passed through it with faint resistance, as if the hedge were made of thin gelatin. Or viscous fluid. The magic was working! Threnody's ability to turn smoky was slow, so his was slow too, but in time it did get there.

He turned back to the others. "I have made the hedge pervious," he said. "Thanks to Sammy's hint, and your talent, Threnody. Thank you both."

Threnody stroked Sammy's back. "We were getting bored," she said.

It figured. They knew he would get the talent eventually,

but they didn't want to wait three more days. So they had helped him. Was this cheating? At the moment he hardly cared; he just wanted to get on with the journey, hoping to intercept Kim before her disaster struck.

"Let's go," he said. He walked through the hedge, which was now fully smoky. Jenny and Sherlock followed, and Sammy jumped down to join them. Jenny paused to wave goodbye to Jordan and Threnody, then hurried on.

Beyond was the thick jungle. It was quickly evident that they were not about to make swift progress through it. There was also the smell of dragon smoke, which boded ill for their safety.

But Dug had another notion. "If this talent of Threnody's is safe to use on people, I can make us smoky, and we can move right on through, the way a demon would."

He tried it on himself. Jenny watched, while Sherlock gathered small, thin vines and began weaving them into some sort of pattern. Slowly Dug diffused, until he was able to walk through a tree. "Good enough," he said faintly. "Let me do the rest of you, and we'll be on our way."

Then a breeze came up, and blew him away. He saved himself only by scrambling into another tree, where the wind couldn't catch him. "I'm having a second thought," he confessed.

"Maybe if you did Sherlock and me," Jenny suggested, "and not Sammy. Then he could scamper to intercept—" She paused, realizing that the cat was about to take off. "To do something. And haul us along by a rope. Because we wouldn't weigh much. That should be pretty fast."

"Brilliant!" Dug cried airily. "If you weren't a child, I'd kiss you!"

"I'm only a year younger than you," she said, looking hurt.

Dug realized that the matter of age could be as sensitive to an elf as to a human. Jenny looked little, because she was an elf, but she wasn't. She was a child by game definition only. "Okay, I'll kiss you," he said.

He pulled himself from the tree as the wind died down, and walked over to her. He leaned down to kiss her. But his face passed right through hers. *I wish there were a boy of my kind here.* Then he drew back again, tried again, and did it right, just barely brushing her lips with his own, so that they didn't overlap.

Then he wondered why he should have been wishing for a boy of his kind here. There had been a romantic implication. That was hardly his idea of romance! In any event, there were other human beings in Xanth.

Oh—that had been Jenny's thought, not his own. He had picked it up when his brain overlapped hers. She was an elf of a different fantasy world, unlike the elves of Xanth. Her prospects for romance here were nil, unless she wanted to cross species boundaries. That sort of thing seemed to be more common in Xanth than in Mundania, but still, it was only natural to want the company of her own kind.

Xanth seemed like a land of puns and silliness, but under the surface there were the same real concerns that the people he knew back home felt. This was a solid reminder.

But he couldn't stop now to think through the philosophical ramifications. He had to move swiftly to intercept Kim, so he could warn her of the danger she was in.

"Let me change you," he said to Jenny, who had not seemed to notice his pause for thought. Perhaps she had paused for her own thoughts. "Then I'll change Sherlock, and we'll be on our way."

He focused on her, and she slowly turned diffuse. He tested by touching her hand every so often; when her hand seemed solid to him, he knew she was as diffuse as he was. "Don't let the wind get you," he warned her.

Then he addressed Sherlock. Soon the black man was as smoky as the other two.

Belatedly Dug remembered something. "We should have made a bag, or net, or something to hold us, so

Sammy can haul us. A solid framework, not a phased-out one, so—"

Sherlock pointed to his tangle of vines. He had started work on that even before Jenny made the suggestion, anticipating the need. Because the vines were small, the net was light; it would be possible for the cat to pull it.

But there was a problem. They were too diffuse to handle the vines. Their hands passed through the vines without contact.

Dug pondered. "I wonder just how versatile this talent of Threnody's is?" he asked. "If I can make just our hands more solid, or part of the vine smoky—"

The second idea seemed better. He concentrated on the tail end of the net, making that smoky. He tested it by picking up the end, while his hands passed through the lead harness. Then he worked his way forward, changing it partway. It was possible!

They put their legs through holes in the pattern, and strung it around themselves. It spread out enough so that all three of them could hang on without crowding.

Then Dug made the harness end smoky, and Jenny called Sammy, and Dug put the harness on the cat. Once it was secure, he made it solid again, so that Sammy would not simply walk through it when he got going. But the vines connecting to the rest of them were phased out, making them almost weightless. As long as the phasing was in parts of the same vines, they were tight; it was when one thing was phased out and another wasn't that they passed through each other.

"I think we're ready," Dug said.

Jenny spoke. "Sammy, go find Kim."

The cat took off. The net followed, hauling them abruptly forward. They were on their way.

Their separation ended. They were jammed together. The world might seem insubstantial, but they were fully solid to each other. Dug lifted his arms to try to hold the other two off, but it was impossible. "Okay, so we travel together," he said, putting his arms around Jenny Elf, who was right in front of him. Sherlock, beside them both, put his arms around both of them. Now they made a compact, stable mass.

Sammy, under no restraints, chose his own route. He scampered between two close-growing trees. The three of them passed through the trees. He squeezed under a root. They went through it. He found a cat-sized tunnel through a mass of thorns. They went through every thorn. But without getting stuck.

There was indeed a dragon. The thing loomed up, belching clouds of smoke. Sammy zipped under its tail. The dragon whipped around, trying to catch the cat, but was too slow. Instead its talons swiped through the netful of people, without effect. But Dug flinched and Jenny stifled a scream. The dragon, frustrated, blew out a hot blast of turbulent smoke. It surrounded them, making the world dark, but didn't make them choke. In a moment they were out of it, unscathed.

"I could get to like this kind of traveling," Dug said, making an effort at bravado.

Jenny nodded. She was looking a bit motion-sick. Sherlock had done the sensible thing: his eyes were closed. Dug, seeing that, closed his own. Then he just seemed to be floating through faintly rushing water.

As they moved along, Dug thought of something. "Threnody's talent—that was making herself smoky," he said. "But I was not only doing that, I was making other people and things smoky. Can demons do that?"

"I don't think so," Jenny said, surprised.

Dug decided not to question this further, because his conclusion might turn out to be dangerous to their progress. Possibly he had inadvertently wiggled through a small hole in the game program.

After a time they stopped. Dug opened his eyes. They were on a trail—and two centaurs were bearing down on them at a gallop. What now?

"I see Kim!" Jenny cried. "And Nada!"

Now Dug saw. They were riding the centaurs. He tried

to untangle himself from Sherlock, Jenny, and the net, so he could signal them to stop and talk.

Kim was looking one way, Nada the other. Nada saw them; Dug saw the shock of recognition in her eyes. She turned her face away, saying something. The two centaurs galloped faster.

The cat, perhaps concerned about getting trampled, bolted into the brush. The centaurs galloped on past, their hooves throwing up divots of dirt. "Wait!" Dug cried. "I have to talk to you!"

It was too late. The centaurs were already well along the path, and nobody was looking back.

"She's False, all right," Dug said. "She saw us—and made them speed up, so they'd be by before Kim saw us. We'll never catch them now."

"But we know where they're going," Jenny said. "The Good Magician's castle."

"But the cat's tired," Sherlock said. "Going to be hard to catch them now."

Dug looked at him. "Your muteness has worn off! The magic's fading."

"And that means that your ability to diffuse us is about to fade, too," Sherlock said. "Better make us solid while you still can, or we'll be stuck in ghost form."

"Good point!" Dug got to work changing them back to solidity. But he did so with a heavy heart. They were going to have to walk to the Good Magician's castle, and chances were that by the time they got there, Kim and Nada would be gone. And with Nada warned what he was up to, she was likely to betray Kim before he could catch her.

"I'm afraid there's going to be trouble," Dug said heavily. Jenny and Sherlock nodded agreement.

16
GOURD

Kim was glad to be traveling so rapidly, after the slow slogging she had done before. But much as she liked horses, and therefore also centaurs, she would be glad when this ride was done. She didn't have the hang of it; she kept bouncing, and her thighs were getting sore. So she was annoyed when the two centaurs accelerated. "What's the matter?" she asked.

"Nada saw something, and warned us to get past it swiftly," the centaur replied, turning his head. "It looked like a tangle of bodies."

Kim didn't know what that could have been, but was glad not to have encountered it. Still, she would rather have made the decision herself. Nada was maybe just a little bit pushy, forgetting that Kim was the Player. Maybe it came of being a princess. Kim had agreed to exchange Companions only because Dug had wanted to; she really had preferred Jenny Elf. "Well, I guess we're past it now," she said. "So let's slow down again, okay?"

They slowed, and her thighs took less of a pounding. That was a relief. She was able to focus on her own thoughts again. She was making good progress toward her game objective. But she wished she could have associated longer with Dug, in the foolish hope that maybe, by some ill chance, she might have made a small impression on him. She knew he was probably as shallow as the average boy was at that age, and that she shouldn't take much note of the fact that he was handsome. But there it was. If she saw him again, she would try to arrange to stay together longer. Somehow. For what little it might be worth. Maybe another snowstorm would come, and they'd be jammed together again in a tent. Maybe he'd become aware of her, as Cyrus and Merci had become aware of each other. Maybe they would kiss before they parted.

Meanwhile, it was nice having Bubbles for company. She was holding the dog before her, which was sometimes tricky, because Bubbles weighed more than half as much as Kim. The dog could not have enjoyed the bumping any more than Kim did, but she did not complain. In fact, Bubbles was a very quiet, polite dog, undemonstrative. But Kim was learning to read her little signs, the angle of her half-floppy ears, the curl of her tail, her general manner, and the dog's attitude was coming through with increasing clarity. Bubbles just wanted to be with Kim, and to help her in whatever she was doing. Nothing else. It was straightforward, and easy enough to accept.

At one point a shadow crossed the foliage, moving toward them. In a moment Kim saw a small flying dragon. It cocked its head, eying them. Both centaurs unslung their bows and whipped arrows from their quivers, nocking them and orienting on the dragon in smooth, continuous, synchronous motions. The dragon veered away, losing interest. The two arrows went back into their quivers and the two bows were slung back across the centaurs' shoulders, again together. Nobody much, it seemed, fooled with a pair of male centaurs, even if it wasn't an enchanted path.

Kim wondered whether it was mostly bluff. But later her centaur fetched his bow again, nocked his arrow, and loosed it without pause. It transfixed a small ugly creature resembling a lizard with wings. The other centaur never drew an arrow, being unconcerned.

"But that little thing couldn't have hurt us," Kim protested.

"It is a basilisk," the centaur explained. "It was about to look at us."

Kim felt a chill. A basilisk. A winged lizard whose gaze could kill. One swift arrow had stopped it—and the other centaur had been so confident of his companion's marksmanship that he hadn't bothered to react.

No, there was no bluffing in centaurs. They were simply competent, and secure in that knowledge.

In due course the centaurs slowed. "This is the Good Magician's castle," her mount said. "You will have to undertake three challenges to enter it, after which the Good Magician will speak with you. Decent fortune."

"Thanks," she said as she slid to the ground. Centaurs weren't much for overstatement.

Nada dismounted with a certain princessly flair. Then the centaurs were off, not even resting. They had done their job, and were heading home, taking no note of fatigue.

Kim and Nada and Bubbles stood and gazed at the castle. It had a moat, and there was a water monster in it, but the creature was yawning; it didn't expect them to be so foolish as to try to swim across. The drawbridge was down, so that they could cross that way.

Except that there was a giant plum before the bridge, and the fruit had split apart to reveal its huge pit, and the pit had opened, and in the pit was a small bull. The bull looked aggressive. They could not reach the bridge without crossing through the region of the pit, and the bull made it evident that it was inclined to fold, spindle, or mutilate anyone who tried that.

"That's a bull pit," Kim said, catching on to a possible pun. Then she did a double take. "Or a pit bull. Or maybe a bully pulpit. Or bull pen. Or something. I'm getting myself confused. But that's what we have to get past."

"I can assume large serpent form and hiss it off," Nada suggested.

"I don't think that's fair, when it's a challenge, as it obviously is," Kim said. "I have to figure out a way to handle it myself." That was true, but it wasn't the whole story. Kim didn't want to accept Nada's help on it; she wanted to prevail by herself.

"As you wish," Nada said, shrugging.

Kim looked around. There was always a way, both in the game and in the normal castle challenges. But all she saw was what looked like a big pillbox. It was probably a military one, because on the side was written FIGHT.

Bubbles walked over to sniff the box. She was mildly curious about everything, with her curiosity being satisfied by a sniff. But this did show one thing: the box wasn't dangerous. Kim followed, lifted the lid, and peered in. There were hundreds of pills, bouncing frantically around. What did this mean?

After a moment she realized that the pills were fighting. Each one was trying to bash any other it encountered, perhaps trying to crack it and pulverize it. That must be why the box said FIGHT on the outside: it was full of fighting pills. But how did this relate to what she had to accomplish?

Well, maybe she could find out. She reached in and swooped out a fighting pill.

The thing was a handful! It banged back and forth in her hand, and expanded in size if not in ferocity. It didn't hurt her, because as it grew it became softer. She hung on, first to its body, then to an end, and finally to a corner as it got to be almost as big as the dog. It was no longer a pill, it was a pillow! And it was still fighting, buffeting her arm, the side of the pillbox, and anything else it could reach. What a scrapper! She didn't dare let it go, because then it would surely be whamming her worse.

Something percolated through her mind. Fighting pillow. Fighting pills. Pillow fight. Pill fight.

The familiar light flashed above her head. She could indeed use these pills.

She swooped her free hand into the pillbox and caught as many fighting pills as she could. It was a struggle to hang on to them. She ran across to the pit bull. "Take this!" she cried, throwing the fighting pillow at him. "And this!" She threw the expanding handful of fighting pills.

The big pillow and small pillows attacked the pit bull with enthusiasm. Wham, wham, wham, WHAM! They needed no anchor; they were able to do their whamming without support. The bull, confused, tried to fight back. He managed to gore the big pillow. Feathers started flying out, adding confusion to the scene. But as the large pillow lost its stuffing, the smaller ones grew to size, their buffeting becoming harder as they did. The bull was entirely distracted.

"Let's go!" Kim cried. She and Bubbles and Nada ran across the plum pit region, and the pit bull didn't even notice them. They left the action behind and got on the drawbridge.

And stopped. For there in the middle of the bridge was a stool, and on the stool perched a pigeon. The stool was covered with bird droppings. In fact, it *was* a bird dropping—an amalgamation of droppings that had mounded into that shape. It stank.

As soon as the pigeon saw them, it flew up above the bridge and dropped another dropping. And another. In fact, droppings fairly rained down around the stool. "Nyaa, nyaa!" it squawked. "I'll bomb you with stools, and your smell will make the castle shut you out. You can't get by me." It dropped another dropping, in the shape of a small stool.

"I can't pass under that dirty bird," Nada said, wrinkling her nose. "It wouldn't be princessly. It thinks it's a harpy." Bubbles, though no princess, seemed no more eager.

"A stool pigeon!" Kim exclaimed, disgusted. She didn't want to get soiled either.

So what was the cleanest way to get past this obnoxious

creature? She looked around, but saw nothing but dung on the bridge. She looked out across the moat, but there was only the moat monster, looking on with amusement. She looked back the way they had come, but saw only the pit bull, still fighting pillows. One pillow, instead of whamming the bull, seemed to be trying to press the bull down, without much effect.

A pillow pressing down. A down pillow.

Kim ran back, grabbed the pillow, and zipped away before the bull could round on her. She threw the pillow at the pigeon.

Sure enough, the pillow landed on the bird and held it down on the giant stool. The pigeon couldn't fly up to bomb them. "Yuck!" the stooled pigeon squawked.

They picked their way through the mess and to the far side of the moat. But the end of the bridge was blocked by a pile of melons. One large melon was bossing the others. "Honey, move over here," she said, and the addressed melon moved over, displacing the other melons, which rolled around before settling down. "Honey, get up on the bridge." The other melon rolled up on the bridge.

Kim stood and watched, trying to fathom the pun. Those looked like a particular type of melon—

"Honeydew!" Kim exclaimed. "Telling the others what to do. And they're so busy doing it that we can't get by the pile of them."

Now she knew the problem. But what was the solution?

Kim looked around again, but this time saw nothing to help. In fact, there was no longer a retreat across the bridge, because the pigeon had succeeded in pecking the down pillow apart, and the down was dropping into the moat. The pit bull had succeeded in goring the remaining pillows, and they too were expiring. So whatever there was that could help, had to be right here.

Bubbles was cautiously sniffing the nearest melons. That didn't necessarily mean anything, but sometimes Kim got notions from watching what the dog did. Could there be anything here for her?

She peered at the constantly shifting pile of melons. They were of different types. Buried almost out of sight was one whose name she couldn't quite remember. But it was suggestive. So she cudgeled her brain and forced it out: cantaloupe. It was a ripe cantaloupe.

And that, perhaps, was her answer. If she could manage to play it right. It was an excruciating pun, but of course she would never have entered this game if she had wanted to avoid that sort of thing.

"Honeydew, there's a cantaloupe in your pile," she said boldly.

The honeydew paused in her stream of directives. "Yes, I know. I'm trying to get rid of it, so I can elope with my honey."

"You think it means can't elope," Kim said. "But it doesn't. It means an incantation of elopement. It's In the Pile, a Cantation of Elope. It's been trying to help you all this time, and you've been refusing to listen."

The honeydew was speechless for a moment. But she recovered quickly. "Then let's elope!" she cried. "Honey, do it now!" And she rolled away from the bridge and around the castle. All the other melons followed her.

"That may be quite a ceremony," Kim murmured appreciatively. "You might say a melon-choly occasion."

Now the way was open. Kim had navigated the last of the three punny challenges. She marched ahead and up to the main gate of the castle.

The door was closed. She lifted a knuckle and knocked.

In a moment the door opened. There stood a pretty young woman of about eighteen, whose hair matched her brown shoes and whose eyes matched her pink dress. Kim was a bit startled by the eyes. "May I help you?" the girl asked softly.

"Um, yes. I'm Kim. I'm playing the game, and I've come to see the Good Magician Humfrey, so I can find out where to find the prize."

"Of course," the girl said, smiling. "Is anyone with you?"

Kim was slightly annoyed. "Of course. Can't you see them?"

"No." The girl looked apologetic. "I'm sorry; I should have told you. I am Wira, the Good Magician's son Hugo's girlfriend. I am blind."

Suddenly Kim felt about two feet high. She had made a pushy, smart remark about sight! She felt herself blushing. "I, uh, they're, uh, Nada Naga, who is my Companion, and Bubbles, my dog."

"Oh, a real dog?" Wira asked. "We don't see many of those here. Our castle dog Canis Major is away right now. May I pet her?"

"I, uh, she doesn't like strangers much," Kim said, feeling worse.

But Bubbles was already stepping forward, wagging her tail. Wira stooped to pet her on the head, and the dog accepted the pet.

Kim was amazed. This was only the second time she had seen Bubbles take to a stranger. "You must have a way with animals," she said.

"It's my talent," Wira said. "I am sensitive to things, and can tell how they are. Animals like me." She straightened up. "But I must not delay you. I will take you to Ivy."

"Princess Ivy? I'd love to meet her. But my business is with the Good Magician."

"Ivy has taken over his appointment book," Wira explained. "It is too hard for the several wives to keep track, since they're always in and out. Ivy will know when he is scheduled to see you."

Oh. Once again Kim had embarrassed herself with an ignorant remark. She shut her mouth and followed Wira, and Bubbles and Nada followed her.

They came to a chamber with a desk and book. There was a young woman, marking items with a pencil. She looked up. "Yes?"

"You're Princess Ivy!" Kim exclaimed, forgetting herself again. "What are you doing as a clerk?"

Ivy smiled. "You must be a Player."

"She is," Nada said from behind her. "Hello, Ivy."

"Nada Naga!" Ivy exclaimed, delighted. She jumped up with unprincessly haste and went to embrace Nada. "I haven't seen you in months!"

"I'm serving my time for sipping red whine in the gourd realm," Nada explained. "This is Kim, the Player I am Companioning."

"She needs to see the Good Magician," Wira added.

"Oh, of course. Let me see." Ivy went back to the book. "Yes, that's an hour from now. That will give you time to clean up and have a bite to eat."

"I'll take them to MareAnn," Wira said.

"MareAnn?" Kim asked.

"She's the Good Magician's Wife of the Month," Wira explained as she set off down the hall without hesitation. She evidently knew her way around the castle, so was not inhibited by her lack of sight. "She was his first love, but his fifth and a halfth wife, because she wouldn't marry him early. She can summon equines."

"Oh. Yes," Kim said, remembering. She had read about that, just as she had read about Wira. Now she remembered that Wira had been put to sleep by her family, because she wasn't much use to them. Fortunately she had met the Good Magician's family in the dream realm, and they had rescued her. Somehow what she had read didn't register readily here in real-seeming life. The people she was meeting were far more impressive than those she remembered from books.

MareAnn was in the kitchen, baking animal cookies in the shape of horses. Cookies might grow on plants by the banks of the With-A-Cookee River, but elsewhere it seemed easier just to bake them instead of making the long trip to fetch them from the river. MareAnn was a pleasant older woman who seemed not at all out of the ordinary. Yet Kim had a vision of her as she was in her youth, with lovely brown hair and eyes matching the manes and tails of the unicorns she could summon then, with marvelously formed legs because of all the equine-back riding she did. She had met and loved Humfrey when they both were in their teens, in fact when they were even younger than Kim was now, sixteen. But MareAnn had been determinedly innocent, so the unicorns wouldn't leave her, and refused to marry Humfrey though she loved him. It had been such sweet sorrow. Kim saw her riding, her hair flung out behind, a tear on her cheek, as she left Humfrey to be King of Xanth. Humfrey had married a de-moness instead, but it was always MareAnn he loved.

Kim snapped out of it, aware that others were looking at her. "Oh—I guess I was daydreaming," she said, embarrassed again.

"Of course," MareAnn said. "Mare Imbri is here. She brought you a daydream. She tells me she also brought you the dream of the disposal bubbles."

Kim almost thought she saw the outline of a small black mare behind the woman. "Yes. It was the strangest thing, turning real at the end. That's how I got Bubbles, my dog." She petted Bubbles. "Just now she showed me how it was when you were young. You were so beautiful and nice!" Then she realized that she had committed yet another gaffe. "I mean, not that you aren't now—"

"My dear, I am happier now than I was then," MareAnn said. "Even though I can no longer summon unicorns. The other equines still do come to me, though." She petted Mare Imbri, who perked her ears forward. The horse *was* there, though invisible.

Then Mare Imbri glanced elsewhere, and abruptly bolted through the wall and away. Someone else had a daydream coming. Kim felt a twinge of envy for that person.

There was a garden behind the castle with toiletrees that helped them get cleaned up and back in order. They returned to find the cookies on the table, along with a coiled chain. "What's this?" Kim asked doubtfully.

"A food chain, of course," MareAnn said. "A ghost horse brought it in. Just break off any link you want."

She should have known. She dimly remembered that ghost horses wore chains wrapped around their bodies, which they could rattle to distract and frighten living folk. It hadn't occurred to her that such chains might be edible.

They broke off links and chewed on them, and the food was good. Each link was a different texture and flavor. Some were like vegetables, some like breads, and some like meat. As a general rule, the vegetables were at the lower end of the chain, and the meats at the upper end. Kim broke off a link at the very top and gave it to Bubbles, who found it quite intriguing.

After the meal it was time for the appointment with the Good Magician. Wira showed them the way up the winding stone stairs to the gloomy cubbyhole the Magician called his own. Kim realized that it made sense for the blind girl to do this, because the lack of light did not concern her. She could find the Good Magician in complete darkness.

And there he was, almost hidden behind a monstrous tome. "What do you want?" he demanded grumpily, evidently irritated about being disturbed.

"This is Kim, the game Player, Father Humfrey," Wira said. "She has an appointment."

"Oh." He glanced at Wira and the barest hint of a flicker of the corner of a smile brushed by his glum mouth. Kim realized that he really liked the girl, though he labored gnomefully not to show it.

"I have a Question," Kim said. "But I don't think I can pay for it. I mean, you require a year's service for an Answer, but I'm Mundane, and can't stay in Xanth that long."

"It is part of your Companion's service," Humfrey said. "It has been factored in. Ask and be done with it."

Just like that! But suddenly Kim realized that this too was a challenge. The obvious question was where the game prize was to be found. But she had lost much of her interest in that, about the time she met Dug. Now she wished she could ask about something that didn't concern the game. But of course that was out of bounds.

Or was it? She didn't *have* to go for the win, did she? Why not play the game her way, and if she lost, at least she had expressed herself. She pondered a good two-thirds of a moment, then asked: "How can I get what I most desire?"

Humfrey turned the pages of his tome. "D," he muttered as he did so. "Demagogue, demon, depraved, descent, desire. Ardent, bestial, confused, decayed, foolish . . . most. Ape, baboon, canary . . . human. Player, game. Female. Young. Kim." His forehead added a wrinkle. "Now, that is interesting." He glanced up at Kim. "Your greatest desire changed recently."

That was one comprehensive reference tome! "I suppose it did, sir," she confessed meekly.

"No matter. Go to the realm of the gourd. You will find it there."

Bubbles wagged her tail.

"The gourd?" Kim asked somewhat blankly.

"That is the realm of dreams, accessible by a certain variety of gourd," Nada said. "I can find one for you."

Kim had known that. Her blankness was because she could not see how the realm of dreams could possibly help her do anything but dream, when what she wanted was a better reality. *The Book of Answers* must have slipped a cog, or whatever it did. Maybe that was because this was a computer game, and only so much could be programmed into it. The game would naturally assume that her most ardent desire was for the game prize. It was foolish to expect the game to know or care anything about her real life or feelings.

"Thank you, sir," she said, trying not to show her disappointment. "I will visit the realm of the gourd."

Humfrey's nose was already buried in the tome. He had tuned her out.

As they went back down the stone steps, Wira spoke. "The Good Magician's Answers may seem cryptic or unsatisfactory at first, but they are always correct. I am sure your greatest desire will be found in the realm of dreams. Mine was."

"Thank you," Kim said. But her doubt remained.

"Magician Grey Murphy brought in three fresh gourds yesterday," Wira said. "We have them in the guest room."

"You knew yesterday that someone would need gourds?" Kim asked. She was not impressed so much as resigned. Obviously the Good Magician had a standard Answer lined up for game Players, and that was to direct them to the next stage of the game. Kim had now explored much of Xanth, except for the gourd. It made sense that she explore that too. How could the game know that though her body would continue going through the motions of the quest, her heart had been foolishly diverted? Only an idiot would go to Xanth for anything but laughs. Unfortunately she was that idiot.

Wira showed them to the guest room. Sure enough, there were three gourds lying on mattresses. "You must hold hands as you look into the gourds," Wira explained. "Otherwise you will not find yourselves in the same region."

"How did you get into the gourd world, being blind?" Kim asked.

"There are other ways. When I was put to sleep, I was in a coffin, and its magic let my soul drift from my body and join the souls of the others of that realm."

So when Wira was put to sleep, it had been a lot like dying. Kim could think of similar cases in Mundania.

She looked at Nada. "You really don't have to join us in this," she said. "I know what the dream world is like."

"I insist," Nada said with a peculiar expression. Had Kim not been distracted by her own private concerns, she might have wondered what was on the Naga princess' mind.

They lay down on the mattresses and held hands. Kim was in the middle; her left hand held Nada's right, and her right hand held Bubbles' left forepaw. Then Wira turned Kim's gourd around so that the peephole was toward her.

Though she was blind, she seemed to know exactly what she was doing. Kim realized that it made sense to have Wira here, because it was impossible for her to be accidentally caught by the gourd.

Kim looked into the peephole—and abruptly found herself standing in a gloomy field near an even gloomier cemetery. Oh, no! This must be the section of the dream realm reserved for the walking skeletons. She could handle it, but she would have preferred to be in a candy garden or the pasture of the night mares.

In a moment minus an instant Bubbles appeared beside her. "Oh, Bubbles!" Kim cried gladly. "I never thought to ask whether you wanted to come here. But I'm glad you're with me." She petted the dog, who licked her hand.

Then Nada Naga appeared. "Oh, the graveyard shift," she said. "That is not my favorite."

"Mine neither," Kim agreed. "But maybe we don't have to deal with the skeletons. This is just our starting point. The prize may be somewhere else."

"Defended by a challenge," Nada agreed. "The most rigorous one." There was something about the way she said it that made Kim a trace uneasy, but she couldn't fathom why. Nada had been a proper Companion throughout, though somewhat reserved. That was to be expected of a princess.

"Well, then, let's look elsewhere," Kim said. It seemed to her that the Good Magician's Answer, all-purpose as it might be, was not a great help, because she knew that the realm of dreams was as big in its fashion as all the rest of Xanth. The prize could be anywhere at all. But of course this was the game, so there would surely be a hint for her to pick up on.

But as they started to walk away from the cemetery, a skeleton spied them. "Hi-yo!" it called, hailing them. "Are you looking for something?"

Kim realized that if her route lay through the cemetery, the game would not let her avoid it. So she turned back with resignation. "I am a Mundane playing the game. I am looking for the prize."

The skeleton seemed somewhat taken aback. Its general configuration indicated that it was male. "Oh, I had understood you sought what you most desired," he said.

Kim was startled. "That is what I asked for," she admitted. "But how did you know that?"

"Oops, I slipped," he said. "I was not supposed to tell you what I knew, only to guide you to the challenge. I am painfully sorry."

The light flashed over Kim's head. "You are Marrow Bones!" she exclaimed.

The skeleton was chagrined. "How did you know that?"

Kim had to smile. "I saw you as one of the prospective Companions, and I suspect you folk have to work at other chores if you're not chosen. So you must be working here, in your bailiwick, as it were."

"You are correct, of course," he agreed. "But I was supposed to assume another identity for the role. I hope you will excuse this irregularity."

"I am happy to," Kim said, feeling better. "I feel as if I know you, having read about you before."

"That is nice," Marrow said uncertainly. "I do know Princess Nada Naga, of course, ever since we met when she was a child of eight."

"I was actually fourteen," Nada said. "I had to pretend to be eight. Prince Dolph was really disappointed when he found out."

"I think it worked out for the best," Marrow said. "Electra seems a better match for him, no offense."

"No offense at all," Nada agreed. "I never was able to relate very well to younger men."

The skeleton turned to the dog. "But I do not believe I know this one."

"This is Bubbles," Kim said. "She's my dog." But as she spoke, she felt a wash of regret. She really liked the dog, and it was going to hurt to have to leave her behind when she finished the game and returned to Mundania.

She realized that the dog was just another game character who would revert to her normal life once this chore was done. Still, she wished it could be otherwise. She trusted Bubbles in a way she did not quite trust Nada.

"Well, I'm afraid our show will not be very effective, since you recognized me," Marrow said. "It is supposed to be a challenge of fear, but fear does not work well when the basis of it is known. I am not quite sure what to do."

"No problem," Kim said. "I'm not eager to rush on with it. Let's sit and chat for a while first."

"But this is not game protocol," Nada protested.

"To bleep with protocol," Kim said. "If I can't have my heart's desire, I might as well enjoy the adventure." She plumped down on the nearest gravestone. Bubbles lay down by her feet. "Marrow, just how did your kind come about? I'm sure you did not evolve as skeletons from the outset."

Marrow sat on another gravestone. "It is a somewhat degenerative story. I am not sure you would relish it."

"Try me and see." Kim was enjoying the prospect of messing up the all-knowing game a bit. Maybe she would even ferret out a hole in the program.

"Very well. Long ago, before the Night Stallion tamed the magic of the gourd realm, human beings who looked through the peepholes of the hypnogourds would be trapped, not knowing the secret of breaking the spell, which is simply to have a friend break the contact of the eye with the peephole. Thus many of them were forever trapped here. They would remain alive in the dream realm, no matter how wasted their physical bodies became, so long as their eye socket oriented on the peephole. But their dream bodies would waste away, reflecting the condition of their physical bodies. So in time the gourd realm became inhabited by zombielike figures, and finally by walking skeletons. Each was horrified by his or her appearance, and the appearance of others. I have to say that they were somewhat enamored of their flesh, especially those portions of it that distinguished their male and female attributes. That was not the worst of it; the gourds are living vegetables, and when a particular gourd sprouted and dissolved, the person trapped by it would be released. At this state, however, this meant death. So the folk within the gourd faded out at that point. This was all they had to look forward to: captivity, emaciation, skeletonization, and finally disappearance.

"But one day a male skeleton and a female skeleton held a dialogue, and fell in love despite their grotesque appearances. Their minds were compatible, and it was their minds they loved. But when they came to love each other, they found each other's body less repulsive. They experimented, and discovered the skeleton key, and made a skeleton child. It was not easy, because they had to borrow bones from their own bodies, and this made it harder for them to function. Nevertheless, their accomplishment was phenomenal, because for the first time they were able to reproduce their kind—as animated skeletons. They had found love and familyhood within the gourd. They hastened to tell other skeletons of this, and others managed to make their own offspring. They did not tell the little skels that they would soon fade out of existence; that knowledge was too cruel. Instead they took pleasure in the innocence of the little ones, making a facsimile of heaven within hell. They adapted their histories to the gourd setting, and developed new myths to replace the old. They tried to explain everything in terms of the dream reality, so as to spare their children knowledge of the terrible truth.

"But they had accomplished more than they knew. Two things happened. First, the little skels did not fade out when their parents did; they did not derive from Xanth or fleshly creatures, and so did not cease to exist when gourds rotted. For the gourds are merely apertures; they convey the minds of their captives to the dream realm, much as an eye conveys the image to the mind. The folk of the dream realm are not in the gourds themselves any more than the images are stored within the eyeballs. So a new species had been created within the dream realm. Second, the little skels grew. They did not do it by eating, for they lacked digestive systems and neither imbibed nor excreted, if you will excuse the vulgar terms. Instead they found stray bones scattered around and added them to themselves, becoming larger. When the surviving parents realized this, they were generous with their own bones, knowing that these bones would only be lost when their possessors faded out. So there was suddenly a large supply, and the skels prospered and grew more rapidly. In time there came the first generation of dream realm adults: folk who had never known the outer realm, and to whom it was merely a repulsive alternate world peopled by flesh-clad parodies of skels. They became proud of their own heritage, and their own offspring believed that this was the way it had always been. They were no longer limited to human skeletons; there were now assorted animal skels, existing the same way. All of us learned how to disassemble and reassemble our bones, so as to form strings of them or other shapes. This was convenient when we needed to navigate high cliffs or other hazards. We came to regard ourselves as the most versatile of creatures, with some justice.

"Then the Night Stallion came, and organized the dream realm, and sent out the night mares with dreams crafted to punish those sleeping folk who deserved it. It turned out to be a considerable market; it was amazing how many living folk had guilty consciences which earned them bad dreams. As the dream business prospered, fancier dreams were crafted, and the call went out for specialists to craft them. Some gourd folk became carpenters, and some artists, and some sculptors, making the settings and scenery. Some became organizers and directors, coordinating the efforts of others. Some became writers, scripting the scenes. And some became actors in the scenes. The realm of the gourd had assumed meaning."

Marrow Bones paused. He shook his skull. "So it remains, for most of my kind. But accidents of fate and magic caused me to get lost within the gourd, until I was rescued by Esk Ogre from the dread outer realm. I discovered that the fleshly folk, though repulsive, were not as horrible as we had believed, and in time I came to accept them as they were, flesh and all. In fact, I came to prefer existence outside of the gourd; it was a different and often fascinating world. Later Grace'l Ossein was expelled from the gourd, because she had interfered with a bad dream she believed was wrong, and I came to know her, and she came to know this realm. Now we are both satisfied to live externally, and we have two offspring, Picka Bone and Joy'nt Bone, in whom we delight. They are content to exist in this realm, too."

"That's fascinating," Kim said. "But I understand that you skeletons don't have souls. How can you exist out here without them?"

"This is a problem," Marrow agreed. "We are trying to acquire souls for ourselves and our children, but souls do not grow on trees." He tilted his head, indicating that this was to be considered a humorous remark. "Supposedly it is possible for mortal folk to share their souls, giving half away, and they then regenerate. But so far we have found none willing to do this. We fear that in time those of us who exist in the outer realm will fade, much as our distant human ancestors did within the gourd." He shrugged, and his bones rattled. "However, this is by no means your concern. You must try to win your game, and I must try to prevent you from doing this, abiding by the rules of the game."

"Yes, I suppose that is true," Kim said. "I wish there were a better way." She sighed. "Well, let's get on with it. What's next?"

Dug stared down the road. He knew there was no chance to catch Kim now; the centaurs were simply too fast. But he was not about to give up. Guilt drove him on. "We'll just have to walk toward the Good Magician's castle, and hope to catch her before anything happens," he said.

"Nada's really a nice person," Jenny said. "I'm sure she's very unhappy about having to be False."

"Nevertheless, she is now the enemy," Dug said. "What I want to do is catch up to Kim, tell her the danger, and trade back. Then you can help Kim win her prize, and I'll—well, I don't know what I'll do, but at least I won't feel like such a heel."

"But you didn't know about Nada when you traded," Jenny said. "It isn't your fault she's False."

"Doesn't matter. It's not right to let Kim get washed out, when it was supposed to be me. I feel guilty."

"I like your attitude," Sherlock said.

"So do I," Jenny said.

"It's just a routine attitude everyone should have. What

I need now is to find the fastest way to the castle. Which I guess is simply hotfooting it south."

Dug's pack was sitting a bit uncomfortably, after the wild ride in smoky condition. He took it off, and discovered to his surprise that it was a pretty golden color. It wasn't gold, just gold-colored as if it had been painted. "Look at this," he said, surprised.

"It changed color!" Jenny said. "It's pretty."

"But how did it happen?" Dug asked. "I was wearing it, so I didn't see it happen. Did either of you?"

They both shook their heads no. It was a minor mystery. However, Dug didn't trust mysteries. Not in this treacherous game. Little things could signal important developments.

He opened the pack and took out a somewhat squished sandwich—and it too was painted gold. Yet he was sure it hadn't been, a moment ago. He touched a spare shirt—and saw it change color. "I'm doing it!" he exclaimed. "Everything I touch turns to gold!"

"Uh-oh," Sherlock said. "I heard about King Midas. That's one mean curse."

"But the stuff isn't solid gold," Dug said. "Just gold-plated. See, this shirt's still flexible, it's just changed color. And the sandwich's still soft; the wrapper's golden, is all."

"It still does seem like a curse," Jenny said. "Maybe you shouldn't touch anyone else until you know how to stop it."

"I'd love to stop it," Dug said. He concentrated on not changing color, and touched another item in the pack. But it turned golden anyway. He walked to the side of the path and touched the leaf of a tree. It too turned golden.

He realized that this could not be random. He had not done anything special in the last few minutes, so didn't think he had invoked any magic. He hadn't picked up a stink horn, for example. So why should this spell be on him?

He stared at the golden pack. Gold-plated pack, actually. It had been gilded. It was gilt.

Gilt. That sounded like guilt. And one thing he was feeling now was guilt. He had said so.

He groaned. "I'm being victimized by a pun," he said. "Gilt by association."

"But we don't feel guilty," Jenny said.

"Gilt. G I L T. If you associate with me, and I touch you, you'll be gilded. Gold-colored. Gilt. Gilty. Someone's made it literal."

"Then you should be able to stop it," Jenny said.

"Maybe now I can." Dug stood and faced the forest. "I deny any gilt by association," he declaimed. Then he touched another item in his pack. It did not change. "Ha. I neutralized the pun."

"Curses," someone muttered. "Foiled again."

The three of them passed a glance around. None of them had spoken.

There was a swirl of air, like a small whirlwind. It became smoky, then solid, taking the shape of a well-proportioned woman, scantily clad.

"Metria!" Jenny exclaimed. "What are you doing here?"

Dug remembered that there had been a lady demon among the choices available for Companion. This would be her.

"Two things," the demoness said. "I'm investigating your chaos."

"My what?" Dug asked.

"Confusion, disorder, misapprehension, ferment, jumble litter—"

"Foul-up?" Dug asked.

"Whatever," she agreed crossly. "What are you doing with the wrong Companion?"

"We traded," Dug said. "I decided that Jenny Elf was better for me than Nada Naga."

"But the challenges were pitched for Nada!"

Dug wondered whether that was good or bad. "You mean that she could have helped me through better—or that she couldn't?"

"Oh, I don't know. Just that Grossclout had it figured

one way, and you were playing it another. Using the cat to find your way through. Zilch only knows how the other player's been doing with the serpent woman."

"So is there a rule against it?" Dug asked.

"Not exactly. Nobody thought anybody'd be fool enough to pull a stunt like that."

"So what's the problem?"

The demoness fidgeted. "It's just not steak."

"Not what?"

"Encounter, converge, intersect, unite, connect, join—"

"Meet?" Dug could handle puns when he had to.

"Whatever. It's just not meet to change things around like that. Now I have to recomplicate things."

"You mean I'm doing okay, so you're going to mess me up?" Dug was bemused. He wasn't even trying for the prize. He just wanted to undo the mischief he had inadvertently caused.

"Approximately," the demoness agreed.

"Wait half a moment," Jenny said. "Metria, did Professor Grossclout tell you specifically to interfere with Dug's progress?"

"What's it to you, waif?"

"I'm Dug's Companion. It's my job to steer him past unnecessary confusions and complications, so that he won't think he's in some other game where that sort of thing is supposed to be standard. You strike me as exactly that kind of mischief. What exactly did Grossclout say to you?"

The demoness fidgeted. "He said to investigate, and use my judgment."

"He meant to judge whether Dug was in some unwarranted trouble, because of the mixup," Jenny said. "He's not, so all you have to do is go back and report that all swell."

"All what?"

"Bulge, grow, increase, billow, bloat, inflate—"

"Hey!" Dug protested.

"I mean surfs, seas, waters—"

"Wells?" Metria offered.

"Yes. Only the other way around: swell."

"Oh, you mean that everything is satisfactory."

"That's what I mean," Jenny said evenly. "In your own imitable fashion. So you can now buzz off and tell him that. No more turning his guilt literal, or whatever else your demonly fancy conceives. He is not for you to play with, Metria."

Dug saw that Jenny was trying to do her job. Obviously the demoness would only interfere with whatever he was trying to accomplish. He liked the elf's attitude.

Metria pondered. She glanced at Dug, then at Sherlock. Her garment flashed translucent, not quite showing her panties. Assuming she was wearing any. "But these are such interesting men. I think I'll stay and investigate some more."

"But you have to go back and report to Grossclout," Jenny reminded her.

"I have to use my judgment. My judgment is that I should hang around a bit more." For an instant she assumed the form of a woman being suspended by the neck until dead.

"But you aren't supposed to interfere with my legitimate Companioning."

"But Nada Naga's supposed to be his Companion," Metria pointed out. "You're not his legitimate Companion. You're Kim's."

Jenny turned to Dug. "This is likely to be trouble," she said. "Fortunately her attention span is not great. If you ignore her, she'll go away after a while."

Metria smiled. "Yes, ignore me, Dug Mundane." She stepped into him, her clothing disappearing.

Dug expected her to be smoky, but she was completely solid. He realized belatedly that she was not half demon, the way Threnody was, but full demon. She could change instantly.

Metria squeezed against him. Not only was she nude, she was voluptuous. She reached up and drew his head down for a kiss. "You should have chosen me to be your Companion," she murmured. "I could have made your life deliriously exciting."

He realized that it was true. He had taken one look at beautiful Nada and chosen her, but now he saw that the demoness could make herself just as shapely, and she had no princessly attitude to counter it. He probably should have chosen her. He might not have gotten far in the game, but he would have enjoyed the distraction. He was now appreciating first-hand (first-mouth) what Sherlock had when he had gotten kissed by a demoness.

"Still could," she added, sliding her bare front across his clothed front as she inhaled. He realized that it was no bluff. Innocent was not a term anyone would ever apply to this creature.

However, at the moment he had a different mission. He had to catch up to Kim and warn her about her False Companion. So he steeled himself to ward off the demoness' allure. "Forget it," he said. "Maybe some other time, you infernal creature."

Right away he realized that he had blundered. Metria's mouth curled into a frown, and then on into a fanged, tusked muzzle. It snapped at his nose, but was insubstantial as it closed. Dug was startled but unhurt.

Then the demoness faded into air. "I'll be back," her words came.

"Oh, mice!" Jenny swore. "I told you to ignore her, not to insult her. Now she'll be seriously mischievous."

"She was getting hard to ignore," Dug said defensively.

"All she was doing was getting in your way."

"She was hard to ignore," Sherlock said. "A child wouldn't understand."

Jenny shrugged, obviously not understanding what appeal there could be in a lusciously shaped bare demoness who wasn't wearing panties. Dug was glad for Sherlock's support.

They set off south. But soon they encountered a huge

gray donkey. "Well, now," the creature said. "Are you the three folk the demoness said are looking for trouble?"

Already the mischief of a demoness scorned was manifesting. This was obviously no ordinary equine. In fact, he saw that it had a whole bundle of tails. Dug thought fast. This was really just another kind of challenge: how to turn mischief into something positive. "No, we are the three folk who are *in* trouble," he said. "We're looking for a way out of trouble. She must have misunderstood."

"Hee haw haw!" the donkey brayed. "That's for sure."

"In fact, what we need to get out of trouble is a ride," Dug said. "A fine animal like you could do us a big favor."

"Hee haw! I'm the Ass O' Nine Tails. I can give you a ride anywhere. But you'll have to listen to my tales."

Dug glanced at the other two. "Seems fair to me. Can you take us to the Good Magician's castle?"

"Hee haw! That I can. Hop on."

Dug congratulated himself, internally. He had succeeded in converting a menace into an asset. A genuine ass-et.

Jenny looked doubtful, but didn't protest. That meant that she had concluded that the giant ass was not dangerous to ride. So he helped her mount, and then climbed on behind her, and Sherlock climbed on behind him. There was generous room for all three, as well as Sammy Cat in front of Jenny.

The Ass started off. "Hee haw! I have nine tales, of course," he said. He flicked up the first of his tails. "First I will tell you about the Deadly Night Shade and the Kith of Death. It seemed that a certain shade of the night was lonely, having no kithing kin. So he decided that nobody else should have kithing cousins either. He became the deadliest night shade of all."

At first Dug found the tale interesting. But after a while it palled, because the Ass was great on de-tail but not on plot. He told how the shade killed one cousin after another, using his deadly kiss, until all the kith were dead. There it ended. There was no resolution and no justice, just continuous killing. Dug realized that the Ass's memory was a good deal better than his originality. Yet he realized that he had seen many similar stories on TV back in Mundania.

"Then there is the tale of Rubella and the Fool Moon," the Ass continued as soon as the first story expired in dullness. He told how Rubella kept fooling the moon, adding a measly pockmark on the moon's face each time. After an hour or so of the narration, the moon's whole face was pocked and cratered, but the moon was too foolish to learn how to stop Rubella. Again, there was no point; it was just one pock after another.

Then there was the tale of the Fait Accompli and the DeOgreant. Fait set out to weaken the ogres by eliminating their powerful smell. She used a special roll-on gunk to deogreize each ogre in turn, until no ogre had a strong smell. Unfortunately she accomplished nothing, because the ogres remained horribly strong and still crunched bones at a great rate. The bulk of the tale was concerned with a description of each of a hundred or so ogres Fait dealt with.

Then there was the tale of Michael Velli and the Crow Bar. Michael set out with devious cunning and no ethics to ruin the crows' favorite hangout: a bar where they could drink themselves silly on corn squeezings. He did this by informing each crow separately that the bar was closed. When, after another hour of narration, he had told each of about three hundred crows this, the bar was indeed closed for lack of patronage. Michael was very pleased with his connivance.

Dug wasn't. He was lulled to sleep by the dullness of the tales, while the huge Ass plodded on.

He woke amidst the tale of Mother Hen and her sons Vim and Vigor. Exactly what kind of a trial these cocky youngsters were to Ms. Hen he was never to learn, because he realized that they were approaching a castle. The party had arrived, thank goodness.

"The Good Magician's castle!" he exclaimed, waking

Jenny, Sammy, and Sherlock, who it seemed had been just as bored as he with the endless tales. They slid down to the ground, flexing the dullness out of their legs.

"No, this is Castle Roogna," the Ass said, surprised, flicking several tails.

"So it is!" Jenny said, recognizing it. "There's the orchard and the zombie graveyard."

"But we were supposed to go to the Good Magician's castle," Dug protested.

"By no means," the Ass demurred. "I was going to Castle Roogna."

"But you agreed to take us to the Good Magician's castle!" Dug was adding annoyance to his confusion.

"Hee haw! You asked could I take you there, and I agreed I could. I did not say I would, and you did not ask me to. So I came here."

Dug realized that he had been had by the Ass. There had been no definite commitment. It had been, as it were, a handshake agreement, not worth the paper it was written on. And the Ass had told them such continuously dull tales that all three of them had fallen asleep and been unable to correct the route when it went wrong. Jenny Elf would have recognized the wrong direction, and acted to correct it. Certainly Sammy Cat could have found the way to the right castle, had he too not been lulled into sleep. But nobody could have remained awake for the whole of that barrage of asinine tales. Dug felt like a fool moon, and a real country rubella, being the victim of this fait accompli.

The Demoness Metria appeared. "Oh, too bad," she said silkily. "I see that your Companion has let you down, and allowed you to be delivered to the wrong castle. How unfortunate, when you could so readily have had a more competent Companion." She inhaled again, allowing her full blouse to turn translucent, not far from Dug's face.

"Hee haw haw!" the Ass brayed gustily.

Jenny looked as if she were about to speak a word not properly in the Juvenile Lexicon. Dug saved her the trouble by taking action he knew he would regret. He swung a fist at the demoness' face.

Naturally his hand passed right through Metria's head without resistance. Then she stepped into him and planted a too too solid kiss on his mouth. Then she faded into smoke and drifted away on the nearest vagrant breeze. She had had her revenge.

Dug realized that he had lost this challenge. Fortunately it had not been a game challenge, just the mischief of a jealous fantasy female. There was no point in belaboring it; he'd just have to get back on track and get where he was going. And hope he wasn't too late.

"What's the fastest way to the Good Magician's castle?" he asked.

"Be sensible, man," Sherlock said. "She's there already. You need to figure out where she's going from there."

"He's right," Jenny said. "And the best place to ask is Castle Roogna."

"You figure the king will know?"

"Oh, we shouldn't bother King Dor about this," Jenny said. "I was thinking—well, I can't say right now, but maybe it will work out."

Dug looked at her curiously. "You can't say what you expect to happen?"

She fidgeted. "It's a special situation. I'm doing my best, really I am."

Dug looked at Sherlock, who shrugged. There was no question that Jenny meant well, but was she competent? Dug couldn't see how this could concern the dread Adult Conspiracy she was so concerned about, and couldn't think of any other reason for her to be evasive. But if she did have a worthwhile notion, he needed it. "Okay. Lead the way."

Jenny gladly obliged. She led them by assorted fruit trees to the moat, where the huge horrendous moat monster eyed them. "Soufflé!" Jenny exclaimed. "What are you doing here?"

The monster hissed.

"Oh, you're here to baby-sit the twins? Where's Electra?"

The monster hissed again.

"Oh, she and Dolph are off visiting the Isle of View? What would they be doing there?"

"You know he can't tell you that!" Sherlock said.

Jenny was abashed. "That's right, he can't!" She faced the monster again. "This is Dug, who is a Player in the game, and this is Sherlock, of the Black Wave. They're friends."

Soufflé Serpent nodded and swam back across the moat. Jenny led the way over the drawbridge. Dug wondered whether she had made up the dialogue with the monster, who had perhaps recognized her by smell and accepted her.

Then he saw two little children, hardly more than babies, in pink bassinets at the edge of the moat. The monster was indeed watching them.

"But is that safe?" he asked. "That monster could gulp them down in an instant."

"As safe as anywhere," Jenny said. "Nobody will bother them with Soufflé on guard. They like him, and he likes them. He hasn't had much chance to play with royal children recently."

Dug could appreciate why not. "I gather that Electra is their mother? Who is she? I seem to remember you saying something about blue jeans on a princess."

"Princess Electra is Prince Dolph's wife. She was caught by a curse meant for a princess and slept for much of a thousand years until Prince Dolph kissed her awake. Now she *is* a princess, so maybe the curse knew what it was doing. The twins are Dawn and Eve. When they get old enough to talk, Dawn will be able to tell anything about any living thing, and Eve will be able to tell anything about any inanimate thing."

"Those are good talents," Dug said.

"Yes, they are Magician-class talents. Such magic runs in the royal line."

They came to the main door. It was open. Dug wondered at this easy access to the leading castle of the land. But with a moat monster on guard, maybe it made sense.

A young woman appeared. She had jade-green hair and aqua-green eyes. "Hi, Ivy," Jenny said.

"I'm Ida," the woman said.

"Oh, I keep confusing you two!" Jenny turned to the others. "This is Dug, who is in the game; I'm his Companion. This is Sherlock, who is a member of the Black Wave." Then, after a pause: "This is Princess Ida, Ivy's twin sister."

Dug was taken aback. He didn't know what to say to a princess. Fortunately Sherlock did. "Nice to meet you, Princess. We met Princess Nada Naga before."

Dug realized that he hadn't thought of Nada that way, despite being frustrated by her princessly liabilities. Why should he be abashed here, when he hadn't been with Nada?

"Oh, yes, she and Ivy are best friends," Ida said brightly. "I am here to learn the ways of princesses, because I didn't know I was one, until recently. What are you here for, Sherlock?"

"I'm looking for a place for my people to settle. I figure there's bound to be somewhere where we're needed."

"Oh, I'm sure there is," Ida agreed brightly. She turned to Dug. "I did not know that Castle Roogna was participating in the game. Why did you come here?"

"I was an ass," Dug said. "I mean, I let an ass fool me into going to the wrong place. Now I just have to believe that there is some way to do what I have to do."

"Oh, I'm sure there is," Ida said, exactly as she had with Sherlock. She seemed to be a very positive person.

"That's wonderful!" Jenny exclaimed.

Dug and Sherlock looked at her. "It's wonderful that the Princess is being polite to us?" Dug asked.

"Oh, princesses are always polite," Ida said. "She means that she's glad that both of you will succeed in your quests."

"No offense, Princess, but how can you know that?" Sherlock inquired.

"It is my talent," Ida explained. "The Idea. When I have an idea, it comes true. But it has to originate with someone who doesn't know my talent. Neither of you knew."

"You mean that just our telling you our hopes will make them come true?" Dug asked doubtfully.

"That's the way I hoped it would be," Jenny said. "Now we'll just have to see how these things happen."

Sherlock glanced at Dug. "This as weird to you as it is to me?"

"At least," Dug said. "I didn't even say what it is I have to do. It's not winning the game, it's warning Kim in time. And I still don't know how to reach her. But I guess there's a way."

"There is; I'm sure of it," Ida said. "But come in; I didn't mean to keep you standing here." She turned and led the way into the interior.

Dug wondered whether things were really as positive as others chose to believe. But this was a magic land, so maybe things were magically positive.

They came to a central chamber where a man was sitting. He stood as they entered. "Ah, these must be the folk I am looking for," he said, smiling.

"I'm sure they are," Princess Ida agreed.

Sherlock seized the moment. "If you're looking for neighbors—"

"As a matter of fact, we are," the man said. "We would like several hundred men, women, and children to colonize the fringe of Lake Ogre-Chobee and keep it civilized. We are too busy with our plays to take proper time with it. But most other Xanthians are too busy with their own pursuits to tackle a chore like that." He paused. "I'm Curtis Curse Friend, here on a recruiting mission."

"The Curse Fiends—uh, Friends are all right," Jenny murmured. "They have a long history."

The man glanced at her. "So do the elves. But I never before saw one your size."

"Do you care about the color of those men, women, and children?" Sherlock inquired cautiously.

"Of course. We prefer that they not be green, because they would get lost in the vegetation as well as getting confused with the chobees swimming in the lake."

"Well, we have several hundred black people up in the isthmus who are looking for a home. But it's quite a journey this far, what with the Gap Chasm and all, and I believe Lake Ogre-Chobee is farther south. It could take some time for them to get there."

"Do you care about cursing?"

Sherlock looked at him sidelong. "Do you curse without cause?"

"Only to protect ourselves, or to clear rubbish." Curtis paused. "I trust you realize that we are talking about explosive magical curses, not harpy talk."

"Right. No fowl language. We feel about curses the way we do about arrows: we don't want them hurled at us from ambush. We just want to mind our business and get along with our neighbors."

"We have a way for you to travel," Curtis said. "We have some magic bubble jars we traded for. Each bubble will hold one large person, or two small ones, and will float safely to the destination named for it. It would take about one day for a string of bubbles to cross Xanth."

Sherlock stuck out his hand. "I think we got a deal."

Curtis took it. "I was sure we would." He brought out a little bottle "Oops, this one's almost empty; there's only enough for two bubbles left." He fished in his pocket for another.

"May I have that one?" Jenny asked. "I know someone who could use it."

Curtis shrugged and gave it to her. He brought out another for Sherlock. "This will make several hundred bubbles, if used carefully. Simply blow a bubble with this bubble-ring, and have a person step into it in the first minute before it sets. Then tell it where to go. Don't touch it from outside until it gets there. We'll have a man waiting at Lake Ogre-Chobee to pop the first one; after that you can handle them yourselves."

Sherlock turned to Dug. "It seems that my quest is done. I'll be going back to the isthmus with this bottle, as soon as I know you are okay."

"I will blow a bubble to carry you to the isthmus, as soon as you are ready," Curtis said.

"You might as well go now," Dug said. "You have been a great help to me, and you don't owe me anything."

"No, I want to see it through. If my solution was here, yours must be too. We just have to find it."

"Well, we might ask a magic mirror," Jenny suggested.

"I will fetch one," Ida said, hurrying off.

"That's one nice young woman, even if she is a princess," Curtis said. "I came here to explain my mission, hoping that the answer would be here, and she was very positive. I had this idea that maybe I'd find some colonists today, and she agreed. She must have known you were coming."

"*We* didn't know we were coming here," Dug said. "It was an accident." Then he remembered how the Demoness Metria had tricked them. "I think."

Ida returned with an ordinary mirror. "Ask this," she said to Dug. "You don't have to rhyme, but it helps."

Dug pondered rhymes. "Mirror, mirror, in my hand— where is Kim in this land?"

A picture formed: a green melon. That was all.

"She's in a melon?" Dug asked, perplexed.

"That's a gourd!" Jenny said. "She's gone to the hypnogourd. Oh, that's an adventure."

"I've heard references to some kind of gourd," Dug said. "But how can a person be in one?"

"It's a whole nother realm," Jenny explained. "You just look in the peephole, and you're there. I'll go with you, and Sammy will find Kim. But I warn you, this will be a weird adventure."

"Weirder than what I've seen already?" Dug asked disbelievingly. "Weirder than having a nine-tailed ass make an ass of me?"

"Much." She looked at Sherlock. "So I guess you don't need to wait any longer. We'll get gourds here, and that will be it."

"You sure?" Sherlock asked.

"Oh, yes. Obviously the prize is in the gourd realm, so she'll either win it or lose it, and her game will be over."

"Okay." Sherlock extended his hand, and Dug shook it. "It's been great knowing you, Dug, and if you're ever traveling around Lake Ogre-Chobee—"

"I'll drop by," Dug said, suddenly sorry to see the man go. "I just want to say—"

"I know." Sherlock wasn't any more for emotional display than Dug was.

"We do have gourds in a garden near the castle," Ida said. "We shall bring three in for you and Jenny and Sammy."

"Thanks," Dug said. His mouth felt dry.

18
PRIZE

K im looked around. The place she least wanted to
enter was the boneyard, so this was surely where
the prize was hidden. So she nerved herself and
marched forward.

Bubbles stayed right with her, nervously close. The dog
shared her apprehension about this place. Kim knew that
there really wasn't anything to fear from bones; they were
dead, so were no more dangerous than stones or chips of
wood. Even with magic they shouldn't be fearsome, because they formed into characters like Marrow. In any
event, this was the dream realm, where nothing was truly
physical. A dream, in a fantasy land, in the game, which
was all imaginary to begin with. Still she felt a supersti-
tious chill. She was glad she had Bubbles and Nada for
company.

Marrow had disappeared, but she knew he would turn
up again, and in a guise intended to repel her. She braced
herself for the show.

Meanwhile the landscape was bad enough. It was dark,
and growing darker. A monstrous gibbous moon emerged

from behind a cloud—and the moon was bone white, with bony pocks. In fact, it looked like one big bone. That very word, gibbous, had always made her flinch, though she knew that all it meant was rounded, more than half full. It had nothing to do with gibbons, which weren't bad animals anyway. But the moon was always gibbous when something awful was going to happen, such as a poor girl getting murdered or a vampire striking.

"Careful," Nada murmured.

Kim looked. She had almost walked into a pool, because she had been looking at the moon instead of where she was going. The water was dark and looked almost slimy, as if pus had oozed into it and turned it to jelly. Ugh! Where had she gotten a notion like that?

There was something under the water. Kim peered—and saw bones. And perhaps pieces of attached flesh. As she looked, they seemed to move. Double ugh! She averted her gaze and walked on.

They crested a hill and saw a sinister valley. In the most dismal depths of it squatted a truly ugly castle. The moon, by the alchemy of this region, was now setting behind that edifice, illuminating it so that every facet of its misshapen structure showed clearly. There was of course a moat, and high ramparts, and a portcullis, and turrets and embrasures. But somehow instead of seeming delightfully medieval, it seemed frightening.

As she got closer, Kim saw that it was worse than she had thought. The castle was not made out of wood or stone; it was made of bones. Big bones framed the front gate, and little bones filled in the crevices, and sharpened bones topped the walls. A rotting flag hung from a spire, showing a skull and crossbones. The portcullis was actually a giant skull with pointed fangs.

"Maybe the prize is not in there," Kim whispered.

But the moment she tried to turn away, she discovered that there were palisades encroaching from either side, channeling her in toward the castle. She looked directly back, and saw a foul fog swirling up over the crest of the hill, rendering visibility zero and harboring who knew what. If she tried to go back through that fog, she would probably stumble into the corpse-filled water. There was no place to go but forward. Of course.

The closer she got, the larger the castle seemed, until it loomed impossibly high. The big bones seemed to have been carved by a cleaver to fit their assignments, and the smaller ones seemed to have been chewed on. Some were split lengthwise. This was the kind of castle a brute ogre would fashion when in an ill mood.

The fluid of the moat looked even worse than the pond water. Even Bubbles shied away from it. Something stirred within its noisome depths, but Kim didn't care to see what it was. Instead she scrunched up most of her remaining nerve and set foot on the bone planks of the drawbridge. One of them rolled under her foot, causing her to lose her balance and almost pitch into the murky water.

She righted herself and took another step—and another bone rolled, trying to send her off to the side. So she got down on her hands and knees—and felt the slickness of the surface of the bones, as if they had only recently been stripped of their flesh. She gritted her teeth and moved forward—this time feeling a string or something. She looked, and saw it was a tendon, not quite separated from the joint. Triple ugh!

She made it across the moat, with Bubbles crawling along beside her. She stood on the bone pavement, which seemed to have been formed of hipbones embedded in bone fragments, and gazed at the awful entry. Would that giant fanged upper portcullis jaw crash down on her as she tried to enter? Surely it would; that was what it was for.

She heard something rumble behind her. She jumped and looked back. The drawbridge was lifting! Gross tendons were hauling it up until it was vertical, leaving no escape from the castle. Now she really couldn't change her mind.

"Everything about the place seems to be one-way,"

Nada noted. "The fog, the fencing, the bridge. You aren't allowed to change your mind."

"It's victory or defeat," Kim agreed. "And I guess victory is better."

"Of course it is," Nada said warmly. "What is the point in playing the game, if not to win the prize?"

What use to explain about human feelings to a princess? "I suppose so," Kim agreed. "But I sort of liked just being in Xanth."

"You will be able to return. And with the magic talent you win as the prize, you'll be able to play longer and better."

Kim realized that she was right. Since she couldn't have her true heart's desire, she might as well have the prize. "Yes. Let's get on with it."

She took a step toward the portcullis. Bubbles whined. Kim stopped. As far as she knew, the dog had no magic. She wasn't like Jenny's cat Sammy, who could find anything. That didn't mean that Bubbles wasn't worthwhile, just that her reactions to magic effects might not be wholly accurate. Still, she generally had reason for her concerns. "What is it, Bubbles?" Kim inquired, putting a hand on the dog's back.

Bubbles looked up at the deadly fangs of the portcullis, and her tail dropped low.

Oh—naturally the dog did not want to enter the mouth of a monster!

Kim took another step. Bubbles yelped as if someone had trodden on her tail.

"Something's wrong here," Kim said. "You think that big mouth is going to close on us?" As she said it, she realized it was true: that was what a portcullis was. A gate that came crashing down to shut out intruders. Maybe down *on* them, if they moved slow. "It *is* going to come down on us! It's one more way to be wiped out." A wipeout here would be just as final as a wipeout in Xanth proper, even if this was the dream realm.

"It must be," Nada agreed. "Maybe there's another way into the castle."

They walked to the side, but the moat quickly closed in, squeezing the ground out until there was no break between the water and the bonewall. There was no other entry.

"So it has to be the portcullis," Kim said. "Maybe we can put a block on it, so the fangs can't come down on us."

But there was nothing to use as a block. "Maybe we can climb the wall to a window," Nada suggested. "I can climb in serpent form."   ·

Kim tried to get a handhold on a projecting bone, but it was slippery, and there was no good bone to grab above it. Even if she could climb the wall, Kim knew she would grow faint before she reached any height, and probably fall off. And how could the dog ever climb it? So that was out.

She sighed. "I think we'll just have to go through the main entrance. I'll bet it has to be fast. And right together, three abreast. That portcullis has to take a moment to get started. So it should crash down behind us."

"It should," Nada agreed.

They lined up. "Ready, set, go!" Kim cried, and they took off.

They crossed the line of the gateway—and the portcullis came crashing down. Wham! the fangs plunged into the floor at their heels. The retreat was closed. But they had made it through unscathed.

Only then did Kim wonder what would have happened if they had not been in perfect alignment. Suppose the dog had lagged behind, and gotten trapped outside? Or, worse, chomped? Suppose the dog had run ahead, and triggered the drop too soon, so that it crunched the two people? This had been a very risky ploy!

Kim resolved to be more careful from now on. She looked ahead, and saw a dark hall leading into the center of the castle. Its walls were polished bones, tightly interwoven. She wasn't sure how bones could be woven, but these were. There was barely enough light for them to see.

Well, the hall must lead somewhere. Kim started to walk down it—and Bubbles whined.

Magic or no magic, she was coming to trust the dog's judgment. There was something fishy about this passage.

Kim looked around. There was a chink in a corner, and a bone fragment on the floor beneath it. In due course some skeleton crew would come by and use bone paste to fasten the chip back into place.

Bubbles went over to sniff the fragment. That didn't mean anything; the dog sniffed everything. It was her way of getting acquainted. But it reminded Kim that there was always a way through, in the game, and usually a hint about that way through. That fallen chip of bone was the only unusual thing here. Was it a hint?

Kim went to pick it up. It seemed quite ordinary. She tried to return it to its place in the wall, but it wouldn't stay. She didn't have any paste with which to fasten it there. She couldn't make the repair.

Then she thought of something else. This was Xanth, and one of the commonest forms of magic here was illusion. Things could seem to be what they were not. Or could not seem to be what they were.

Kim took the chip of bone and sent it sliding down the hall. The floor was smooth, because the bones were shored by plaster or cement. It was like sending a puck down a shuffleboard alley.

Then the chip disappeared. Kim smiled. "I think we've found what's wrong with this hall," she said.

She got down on her hands and knees again and crawled carefully forward. Bubbles joined her. When she came to the place where the chip had disappeared, she reached forward—and felt nothing. The floor was gone. There was a pit there. The floor looked continuous, but it was illusion, covering the trap.

Kim nudged up to the edge and felt deeper. There

seemed to be no bottom to the pit. It would have been a bad fall, probably a wipeout.

But how was she going to get across it? Kim pondered. "I'm going to gamble," she said. She fished in her pack and found a spare pair of socks. She separated them, and rolled each one up into a ball. Then she tossed one ahead about four feet. It landed and rolled on along the hall, finally fetching up at the entrance to the next chamber. "So there is a continuation," she said, satisfied. "No more invisible pits. She tossed the second sock about three feet. It, too, landed and rolled.

But Kim couldn't reach across the pit; her questing fingers found nothing. So it couldn't be much under three feet. Still, three feet was jumpable.

"This is like the portcullis," she said. "We'll have to jump. But I think we can do it singly." She removed her pack and set it at the edge of the pit. "This is where the jump starts. I'll go first." She looked at the dog. "You wait." She hoped Bubbles would understand.

She walked to the front end of the hall. Then she ran down it, reached the pack, and leaped. She landed cleanly and slowed to a stop.

"Now you, Bubbles," she called.

The dog ran down the hall, leaped at the pack, and landed where Kim had. She was old and solid and barely made it, but her spirit was there.

"Now mark the place and toss over the pack," Kim said to Nada. "Then jump over yourself."

In this manner they traversed the hall and came to the central chamber of the castle. It was huge. Portals opened out around it in about nine directions, and more opened out from the balcony levels. In the center was a big ball of bright red string.

As they stepped into the chamber, the door to the passage slammed shut with a bone-rattling jar.

"I think I have this figured," Kim said. "Somewhere in this castle is the prize. I have to search to find it. And any door I pass through will be closed after me, so I can't go back. But maybe some of those chambers have several doors. So I'll mark my trail with string, so I'll know if I've passed that way before. If I find the prize before I lock myself into a dead-end chamber, I'll win."

"There must be dangers along the way, too," Nada said. "Judging by what we've seen so far."

"Yes. So this will be dicey. But winnable if I'm smart enough and lucky enough." Kim considered as she went carefully to fetch the string. "Bubbles, you're the most cautious about danger. You lead the way." She wasn't sure the dog would understand, but it was worth a try.

Bubbles sniffed around, then headed for one of the portals. She paused at the entrance to the chamber, waiting for Kim.

Kim tied the end of the string to a projecting bone and strung the line out behind as she went to join the dog. "Okay, Bubbles, you lead, but be careful."

The dog entered the chamber, but did not proceed to the center. She went to the side. As she did so, something came down from the high ceiling. It swung back and forth. It was a pendulum. A big sharp-edged bone on a long tendon, and it crossed the full chamber. But it shouldn't be hard to pass, if they timed it for when it was at one end of the chamber.

Then a second pendulum came down, with another knife bone. It swung opposite to the first, reaching the other end, so that there was no chance to pass; both ends were covered. However, when the two sharp bones were at the edges of their swings, it should be possible to run through the center.

And a third pendulum descended, timed to swing across the center while the other two were outside. But maybe they could pass a bit to the side, opposite that third, while the first and second were still out. And a fourth, going opposite to the third. Now everything was covered. The chamber was a crisscrossing pattern of swinging bones. There was no clearance at the edges; the blades almost touched the walls.

Nada shook her head. "I think we had better try another chamber."

Kim turned back—and saw that the door had quietly closed behind them. Again, they couldn't retreat.

"Maybe we could leap over them?" Kim asked. But then she realized that the swinging tendons were almost as dangerous as the sharp bones. They could catch a person, and tangle her, so that one of the other knives would swing back and cut her apart. The only safe course was to avoid the pendulums entirely.

Already Kim's eyes were glazing. No matter where she looked, a pendulum was passing or about to pass. There just seemed to be no way to cross safely.

Yet there had to be a way. If she could just figure it out. Some way to get through without blindly gambling.

Kim shut her eyes, closing out the bewildering array. There were only two sets of pendulums, swinging oppositely. While one set touched the edges, the other passed the middle. She judged that each single pendulum took two seconds to complete its swing from one side to the other, and that a person needed one second to get safely across the covered zone. With just two pendulums, that second would be available in the center or at the edge. But with the four, only half a second. Not safe.

She opened her eyes and studied the pattern again. This time she looked at one edge, and counted seconds. She discovered to her surprise that a blade came near one wall every second, not every half second. How could this be?

She sketched a diagram in the dust of the floor, and realized that she had made an error. Each single pendulum did take two seconds to swing across—and two more to swing back. That was a four-second cycle. So four pendulums reduced it to one-second cycles. She could make it! She had almost allowed herself to be dazzled by the crisscrossing blades, so that she was ready to give up when she didn't need to.

"Okay," she said. "We'll go through singly. It's going to be close but possible."

"But those blades—" Nada protested, alarmed.

"Are passing any given spot at one-second intervals, I think. So all we have to do is pick a spot, like maybe the center, and dash through there right after a pair of blades has passed. In fact, I think the thing to do is aim for the crossing blades. They'll be moving out of the way as we come, and the other two will just be starting in. So it should be clear for that second."

Nada still looked extremely doubtful.

"I'll go first," Kim said. "And this time I'll carry Bubbles, but I don't know how to explain to her how to time it, and I don't want to risk any confusion. Then you can pass, carrying the ball of string. Come on, Bubbles." She squatted, put her arms around the dog, heaved her up, and stood herself. Oh, Bubbles was heavy! And how did the game make her feel that weight, when this was all just animation on a screen? It didn't matter. She just had to be sure not to lose her timing.

Kim went up to the crisscrossing blades. She felt the breeze of their passing. She started counting, timing them. "One, two, one, two," as the first and second sets of pendulums passed the center. Then she retreated a step, nerved herself, and lumbered across, trying to time it to come just barely after "two."

She made it. She lowered the dog to the floor, feeling faint. She didn't like such nervous business!

Nada timed it similarly and came across. Whereupon the four pendulums slowed, stopped, and withdrew into the ceiling. "Just like 'The Pit and the Pendulum,' " Kim remarked. No explanation, no follow-up, they just quit when they got outsmarted.

They went to the next chamber. This one had a pit across its center, too wide to jump. There was a ladder-bridge formed of bones on the far side, that evidently could be lowered in the manner of a drawbridge. On the near side was a length of cord hanging from a ceiling beam. That was all.

Kim pondered the situation. She should be able to use

the cord to snag the ladder and pull it down across the pit
so they could cross. But the cord was firmly tied, and
would not come loose. She might cut it—but she could not
reach high enough to cut off enough to use for this purpose. She might grab hold of it and try to swing across the
pit, but she was afraid it wasn't strong enough to hold her
weight. That also prevented her from trying to climb it to
the beam; it could break anywhere, ruining it. So what use
was it?

Then her lightbulb flashed. She removed her pack,
which was not heavy enough to break the cord, and tied it
to the end. Then she swung the pack across the pit, getting
the feel of it. It banged into the upright ladder. She swung
it again, this time to one side, and it swung around behind
the ladder, hooking it, and snagged. But the ladder did not
fall.

Now she was in trouble. The cord was out of reach.
How could she get hold of it?

Then she took her ball of string. She lofted that up over
the near end of the cord and caught it. The string was not
heavy, but it was strong enough to pull the cord down just
within reach of her hand. Then she pulled on the cord until
the snagged pack brought it crashing down across the pit.
Now they could cross.

The next chamber was worse. The moment they tried to
enter it, the ceiling started descending and the floor as-
cended. Both surfaces had knife-pointed bones sticking
out. Pity the poor person who tried to scramble through
there!

When they backed off, the floor and ceiling stopped
moving, then retreated, ready to trap the next unwary person. Kim wondered why they didn't just keep going until
they met halfway up and closed off the chamber.

Could that be a clue? Could it be that the way wasn't
closed until the person was actually caught between those
jaws?

She took her pack and set it on the edge of the chamber

floor. The floor rose, and the ceiling dropped. Just before they crunched the pack, Kim pulled it away.

She ducked down and peered under the floor. It had been pushed up by a column of bones. She could see right by that column to the next chamber. There was her way through—*under* the floor!

Then the floor dropped, because there was nothing on it. The route disappeared.

She returned the pack to the floor. "Nada, take this off just before it gets crunched," Kim said. Then, as the floor rose, she ducked down and scrambled under it. "Come on, Bubbles!" she cried.

Nada seemed startled by the suddenness and daring of Kim's action, but she recovered in time to grab the pack.

"Now hurl it across to me," Kim said. "Before the floor subsides. I'll use it from this end to raise the floor for you."

The next chamber had a bone stair whose steps moved down when stepped on, so it was impossible to make progress. Kim finally managed to fool it by facing backward, so that it thought she was trying to walk down, and carried her back to what it thought was her starting place, the top.

In similar manner they wended their way through one chamber after another, avoiding any where the red string already crossed, until they were high in the castle. There seemed to be only one chamber remaining. Beyond it they could see a glowing golden chest. That had to be the prize!

But the intervening chamber had a sharply sloping floor, slippery slick. Anyone trying to cross it would be dumped into one of this castle's patented bottomless pits. What was the way through?

Kim gazed out the bone window. She saw that she was now three stories up, overlooking the lifted drawbridge. The landscape was just as gloomy as before. So why was she staring at it?

She analyzed her motive. She was foolishly hoping that the other Player, Dug, would show up. Because this was really the last chance, if she were to see him again. She had no idea where he lived in Mundania, so would be unable to locate him there, even if he had any slight interest in her.

Then she saw something on the horizon. Someone was coming along the dreary path! It was a small figure, chasing a smaller animal. That must be Jenny!

"Dug is coming," Kim said, excited.

"I can assume serpent form," Nada said. "I can grab onto a post with my teeth, and you can swing across on my tail."

"Sammy Cat must have found the way," Kim said. "Now they'll be here too."

"You must act quickly, before Dug gets your prize," Nada said.

But Kim dallied, watching the approaching trio. She saw the ugly fog roiling up behind them, herding them, and the palisades funneling them in toward the castle.

Then she did something absolutely foolish. She fished in her pack for a hankie and waved it out the window. Just as if she were a maiden in distress.

And Dug saw it! "Kim!" he cried faintly.

She thrilled to the sound. "Dug!" she called back.

"Wait right there! Don't do anything!"

What lovely words! "I'll wait," she cried gladly.

"What are you doing?" Nada demanded. "The prize is within your grasp, and you're letting him catch up?"

"Yes," Kim said dreamily. "I like him, and I won't get a chance to see him once the game is over. So if we can talk, if he's interested—"

"All he wants is to get the prize," Nada said.

"He can have it," Kim said. "I just want to exchange phone numbers before we leave the game. I was afraid he wouldn't get here in time."

As she watched, the little group below charged to the castle. The drawbridge was up, but that didn't stop them. Cat, elf, and young man plunged into the grimy moat and swam across. Apparently there wasn't a moat monster, or else Sammy knew that it was on the far side of the castle at the moment and couldn't get them. What an act of reckless daring!

"I was mistaken," Nada said grimly. "I believe he wants more than the prize. He wants me."

Now they were at the base of the wall. The cat still led the way, finding a section to climb, digging his little claws into the softening bones. There seemed to be handholds there that weren't closer to the drawbridge. In fact, it looked as if there were an inset ladder, making it much easier for them to climb the wall, avoiding all the hazards of the interior. Dug followed the other two, hauling himself along.

He tilted back his head, and saw her peering down. "Kim! Don't move from that spot! There's something I have to tell you!"

He wanted to tell her something. He was interested after all! "Oh, yes," she breathed. Then something registered. She turned back to face Nada. "What?"

"He chose me as his Companion because he liked my looks," Nada said grimly. "He wanted to see my body. But he was too sneaky about it, and almost got put out of the game."

"Yes, so he lost interest," Kim agreed. "But I'm not a princess, and—"

"By this time he will have learned that the Companions, too, are a challenge. A Player may do anything with a Companion he desires, if he is able to find the correct way. It is a matter of approach. If he treats his Companion with proper respect, he can earn her respect. He can force her cooperation, with the right words. So if he has found the appropriate manner to approach me—"

Kim suffered a sudden flare of jealousy. Dug could get at this beautiful, luscious princess? What the hell would he want with a nothing girl like Kim, then? "The prize—and you?" she said, appalled.

"I have no way to prevent it," Nada said seriously. "If he gets you to trade back Companions, and if he knows the key dialogue. So you must act swiftly, before he gets here. I will not be able to advise you, if you trade."

Kim, torn by doubt, gazed down again from the window. The cat was almost there, with Jenny not far behind, and Dug close behind her. "What do you want, Dug?" she asked.

"Nada!" he gasped. "I must trade her back from you, because—"

"Oh!" Kim cried, her lingering hope dashed. He was just another selfish, careless, horny teenage boy. She was tempted to throw her pack down on his head, but it wasn't handy. She turned away from the window. "Let's go for the prize, Nada!"

Nada immediately assumed serpent form and slithered from her clothing. She lunged at the bone beam above the tilting floor, and caught it with her teeth. Her body slid down across the floor, but in a moment she curled her tail up for Kim to grab.

Bubbles whined.

Kim hesitated. Was something wrong here? It occurred to her that she should have to solve the riddle of the chamber herself, rather than letting her Companion solve it for her. Yet she could appreciate why Nada did not want Dug to recover her as his Companion.

She glanced back, hearing something. The cat appeared in the window and jumped to the floor. Jenny Elf's head was next. "Wait, Kim!" Jenny cried.

Of course Jenny now served Dug, and would help him do whatever he wanted to do. Even if that meant getting herself traded back. Jenny could not be trusted while she was Dug's Companion.

Kim caught hold of Nada's tail, bracing herself for the sliding swing across the slanted floor. Would she be able to catch hold of the far edge and haul herself up to the golden chest?

Bubbles whined again, her tail curled all the way under her body. The dog was really upset. "Don't worry, Bubbles," Kim said. "I'm not leaving you. I'm just crossing to the prize." But now she wondered: what would happen to the dog, when Kim won and left the game?

Suddenly she was overwhelmed by realization. "Oh, Bubbles, I don't want to leave you!" she cried, dropping Nada's tail so that she could hug the dog. "But how can I take you with me? What will become of you?"

"You *can* take her," Jenny said. "There's a way."

"A way?" Hope flared.

"I have a jar of bubbles. Like the one you got her from. I can give it to you, if you take me back as your Companion."

It was another ploy to make her trade! Furious, Kim caught Nada's tail again and stepped into the slanting chamber. She was starting to swing down—

Then Dug was there, tackling her around the waist before the serpent could take her weight. The elf had distracted her just long enough to get caught!

"Let me go!" Kim cried, struggling to twist out of his grasp so she could swing across. Half her body was hanging over the edge, while Dug's arms were wrapped around her thighs and waist. If she could just wriggle free—

But he hauled her back and into him, using his strength to make her captive. "Kim!" he cried. "I've got to tell you—"

"I don't want to listen!" she cried, letting go of the serpent's tail so she could flail at him with her hands. "I was willing to let you have the prize, but no, you had to—"

"I don't care about the prize!" he said, pinning her arms. In any other circumstances she would have been glad to have him hugging her this close. "You can have it! I know that's what you came for. All I want is to tell you—"

"That you want Princess Nada Naga for more than just guidance!" she finished for him. "Oh, I hate you!"

He looked surprised. "No, I only want to talk to you, to save you from—"

"Me?" Foolish hope flared again. "It's me you want?"

"Yes. To explain—"

"Oh!" she exclaimed, overcome with opposite emotion. Her feelings were swinging like a pendulum. "Really?"

"Really. I was afraid I wouldn't be able to catch you before—"

"Oh, yes!" she cried. She lifted her head and kissed him hard on the mouth. It was the most wonderful sensation. "I feel that way about you, too, Dug! My number is area code Tee zero zero, 447-4377. What's yours?"

He looked confused. "I—I mean, I had to tell you that Nada's a False Companion. She was about to drop you down the hole. You can trade back, and Jenny will help you get the prize. It wasn't right to let you get torpedoed by what was meant for me."

She was stunned. "You—you came to warn me?"

He let her go. "Yes. I was afraid I wouldn't reach you in time. I'd never forgive myself if you lost your prize because of me."

She realized that it was true. There had been little things about Nada, and the way Bubbles had reacted—of course she was a False Companion! Dug had done the natural, decent thing, when he figured it out. He could nullify Nada, knowing her nature. But he wouldn't bother, because he wasn't even trying for the prize. Maybe he'd just experiment, to see how far the princess would go before he got washed out of the game.

And Kim had assumed that it was something else. She felt the great-grandmother of all blushes washing over her face, turning it glaring red. She covered her face with her hands. "Thank you," she said in as controlled a voice as she could manage. "I will—I will trade back Companions."

"Good," he said. He caught Nada's tail with one hand. "Let go, Princess, and I'll haul you in. Unless you prefer to drop down the hole you meant for Kim."

The serpent let go of the beam, and Dug did haul it in. Then he turned his back. "Change and get dressed. I don't care if you shove me in the hole; you are my Companion now, and you can't touch Kim."

Nada changed, becoming a naked woman, getting quickly into her clothing. Kim suppressed a surge of jealousy for her splendid proportions and complexion.

"Now I will help you," Jenny said. "I have found a bubble maker that can make two bubbles. You can use the first bubble to float safely across. Then you'll be able to use the last bubble to go home." She showed the jar.

"Why, that's a regular bubble mix," Kim said. "Children use them to blow soap bubbles."

"No, these are magic bubbles, big enough to hold people. Sherlock is using them to carry the Black Wave to Lake Ogre-Chobee, where they will settle as neighbors to the Curse Fiends—I mean, Curse Friends."

"I'm glad that worked out," Kim said. "Those must be the same type of bubbles I found Bubbles in." She patted the dog.

"Yes. They are used to carry people or things where they want to go. So they are just what you need now."

"No," Kim said firmly. "I must find my own way to the prize." For one thing, it gave her something to focus on, so that she could try to forget her chagrin at her misunderstanding of Dug's motive. "I thank you, Jenny, but I want to do this myself."

"That's good," Jenny agreed.

Kim studied the situation. The floor tilted so sharply that a fly would barely be able to cling to it. The space was too wide for her to jump. She saw a notch where the floor would fit if it were level; evidently it was hinged. Maybe the last Player had stepped on it and been dumped when it swung down.

She reached down and around, finding the edge of the tilting floor. Sure enough, her hand found its underside. She pulled—and the floor came up. She was swinging it back to its proper position! It was surprisingly light.

In a moment she had pulled it level and clicked it into place. But she knew she couldn't trust it. How could she make sure it would support her weight?

"Go across it, Dug," Nada said. "You can still win."

"You disgust me," Dug said. "First because you are False; you're still trying to make me get dumped. Second because I wouldn't take that prize anyway; it's Kim's to take. She deserves to win that prize."

He really was a decent person, Kim knew. If only—

She cut off the thought. She felt around the notch—and found a swinging bone that would lock the floor into place. Now it could be used.

She looked at Dug. "I don't need that prize either," she said. "If you would like it, you can have it."

"You can take it, Dug," Nada said. "She doesn't want it."

He shook his head. "You know, we don't have the right attitude about this game. We're supposed to be scrambling madly for the prize."

Kim had wanted the prize. But that desire had faded after she met Dug. Now that she had thoroughly embarrassed herself in that respect, what else was there but the prize? "I suppose somebody should take it," she said. She stepped out on the chamber floor, half expecting it to give way and drop her into the hole. But it remained firm.

Kim paused and looked back. Dug was standing there, watching her. Nada was facing away, her head hanging. Jenny was about to follow Kim. There was something wrong here, but Kim couldn't figure out what it was. There was an expectancy, a tension, as if all hell were about to break loose. What was going to happen, and who knew it?

She started to turn back toward the prize. Then Nada moved. The woman flung herself toward the notch, with its fastener-bone. But Sammy Cat leaped there first, covering it. And Dug tackled Nada much the way he had tackled Kim before. The serpent princess was brought up short of the bone. "Get on across!" Dug cried. "Before she—"

Kim jumped forward and picked up the prize box, just as Nada became a huge serpent. Kim opened the box as the serpent slithered out of Dug's grasp and toward her.

Kim reached in to take the little globe inside as the serpent's head came up to knock the box from her hand.

Her hand glowed, painlessly. The globe had disappeared. The serpent saw the glow, and fell as if struck.

I am your Talent, a voice said in Kim's head. *I am the Talent of Erasure. When you return to Xanth, you will be able to Erase anything you choose. Try me now.*

Unsure how this applied, Kim reached out and stroked her hand across a section of the wall, as if erasing chalk on a blackboard. The wall disappeared behind her hand, showing the sky beyond the castle wall.

She stared. "Anything?" she asked.

Anything, living or inanimate. Use me wisely.

Wisely! She didn't want to use this at all! This was a destructive talent.

No, you may cancel my effect by reversing the stroke. Use the back of your hand.

Kim stroked her hand back across the open section, with her palm toward her, and the wall reappeared, except for one sliver her hand missed. Still, this power frightened her. She didn't want to be forever erasing innocent things!

Then she got smart. She willed the talent to turn off, then stroked her hand back across the wall. Nothing happened. She willed it on again, and touched the wall with one finger. A finger-sized hole appeared. She willed it off and stroked her backhand across the hole. Nothing happened. She willed it on and made the same reverse stroke. This time the hole filled in. She had it under control. This was a tool as well as a weapon, a talent of phenomenal power, when she learned to use it properly. But for now she didn't want to use it at all.

She returned her attention to the others. Nada had reverted to her normal form, that of a serpent with a human head, and was sobbing. "I didn't want to do it!" Nada said. "I didn't want to be False! But I had no choice."

"But why did you try to be False to me, when you were Dug's Companion?" Kim asked.

"Because he wanted you to win."

Kim looked at Dug, who nodded. But she wasn't satisfied. "There's got to be more of it than that. What aren't you telling us?"

To her surprise, Nada answered. "It really doesn't matter, now that the issue has been decided. I don't have to be False any more. I will tell you the whole truth."

"What's gone before was a half-truth?" Dug asked.

Nada smiled, becoming beautiful again. "Not even a quarter-truth, Dug. The Demon $E(A/R)^{th}$ was trying to take over this land from the Demon $X(A/N)^{th}$. They made the decision in their normal fashion: they gambled. They set up the game, and chose characters. If $X(A/N)^{th}$'s Player won the prize, he won the wager. If $E(A/R)^{th}$'s Player won, he did. But Earth used a devious ploy: he sabotaged his own Player, and arranged for him to have a False Companion when he returned. Then he had the two Players exchange Companions. In this manner he thought to ensure that $X(A/N)^{th}$'s Player lost, even if $E(A/R)^{th}$'s Player did not reach the prize first. It would be at least a tie, requiring another game to settle the issue. When that ploy failed, because of the willfullness of Earth's Player, the False Demon made me act."

Kim was too surprised to speak. But Dug did. "What would have happened if the other Demon had won? If I had gotten the prize?"

"The magic of Xanth would have been lost, and it would have become just like Mundania." More tears squeezed from Nada's eyes. "Oh, I'm glad I didn't succeed! It was the most horrible thing! But I had to do everything I could to make you lose, Kim. I'm so mortified!"

Kim found her voice. "There was a whole lot more riding on this than I knew! Xanth without magic—" She couldn't finish.

"More than I knew, too," Dug agreed. "I just wanted to play fair." He looked at Kim. "Well, you better get on home with your prize. I guess you'll be a Sorceress next time you play."

"Yes, you must go," Jenny agreed. "The game is about

to fade out, and we Companions will return to our normal pursuits."

"But what will become of Bubbles?" Kim asked. "I can't just leave her here!" She sat down and hugged the dog.

"Then take her with you," Jenny said.

"I can do that? I can take her to—to Mundania?"

"She's a Mundane dog."

"But in Mundania she'll die in a year or so," Kim said. "She's old. Here in Xanth she can live, because of the magic. I don't want to condemn her to death because of my own selfishness." Because she realized that that was the case: she wanted Bubbles with her.

"Save the second bubble in the bottle," Jenny said. "When you can't keep her in Mundania any more, send her back to Xanth. To one of the folk she likes."

"Like Ma Anathe," Nada said. "Or Wira."

Kim felt a great relief. "Oh, I'll do that! Oh, Bubbles, I can keep you with me!" Bubbles licked her face.

"I hope you can forgive me," Nada said to Dug. "I would much rather have been your Fair Companion, as I was the first time. If you will accept my apology—"

"What, a gourd-style apology?" he asked, smiling.

"Yes." She put her arms around him and kissed him passionately.

Kim, despairingly jealous, could only busy herself with her own business. She brought out the bottle. She found the little blower, and dipped it in the fluid. She brought it out, capped the bottle, and blew. A bubble formed. It expanded, until it became large enough for both girl and dog. She and Bubbles stepped into it. "Take us home," Kim said.

The bubble lifted. It floated to the castle wall, and through it. Kim had only an instant to look back, to see Jenny Elf waving goodbye. Then they were out floating over the landscape and leaving the bone castle behind.

The scene faded, and the chamber in the Good Magician's castle appeared. There lay Bubbles, Nada, and Kim herself, looking into the peepholes of the gourds. The bubble settled over the girl and dog, and the two of them merged with their other forms. When the bubble lifted, only Nada remained there.

They floated out the window and high into the air. Xanth spread out below them, then was lost under a screen of clouds. There was a shudder.

The scene changed again. Kim blinked. She was sitting in her room, before her computer screen, which had gone blank. She was out of the game. Back in reality.

It had all been the game. Now she had to face the mundane grind of schoolwork and dullness. Who would believe the adventure she had had? They would say it was just a game. As if her feelings didn't count. She felt an overwhelming grief.

Something nuzzled her hand. She looked down. There was Bubbles!

Kim got down and hugged the dog again. "Oh, Bubbles, I asked for what I most desired—and I got it! It was you, to keep!" Somehow the magic had reached out of the game, and given her this.

Yet that was not quite true. There had been another thing she wanted. But what was the point in brooding about that? In or out of the game, she remained just a plain girl.

The phone rang. Startled, Kim answered it.

"Now, don't hang up on me, Kim," a familiar voice said. "It's Dug. I know I made a real ass of myself. I've been good at that, recently. But I figured I might as well go whole-hog, or whatever pun fits. I'm really sorry about what happened—I mean, when you said—and I never picked up on—"

Kim felt the flush coming to her face again. "That's all right, Dug. I shouldn't have—"

"I mean, I've always been stupid about girls, which is why I'm out a girlfriend now. But I was really out to lunch on that one. So I called to apologize, and—"

"There is no need," Kim said. "I was the one who made the mistake." Her face was burning.

"And when you kissed me, I almost freaked out."

Would he never give over! "I—I—" Kim said, trying to find some way to get away from her shame.

"But you know, I'd be a fool to judge by one kiss," Dug continued relentlessly. "So if you can forgive me for being a blockhead, I'd like to try for more. Like maybe a gourd-style apology. That is, I mean—well, how about a date? So we can start really getting to know each other, you know, to be sure it's not just a fluke. I mean, I don't know anything about you, really, except that you sure can kiss, better than Nada does, and you're real! And—oh, come on, Kim, give me a chance! I can be an okay guy, once you get my attention, and you sure did that. Is it a date?"

"Yes," Kim breathed, realizing that she had after all gotten all of what she most desired. Dog *and* boy. The Good Magician *had* known!

AUTHOR'S NOTE

This novel was phrased as a game because I had the notion for the Xanth Game of Companions, but lacked expertise to fashion a computer game. I'm a writer, not a programmer. So I did it my way, showing how the game works, and LEGEND is making the game. You may have noticed that after a while the setting of the game seemed real to the players. The first step was refocusing the eyes to get a three-dimensional effect. This is not magic; it's something that can be done by a Mundane outfit called STARE-E-O, making a flat picture become three-dimensional without colored glasses or anything, just the effort of refocusing the eyes. Impressed by this, I incorporated it into the game. The second step, of believing in magic—well, that's more difficult, but perhaps some players will be able to manage it, and reap the rewards thereof. There is hope for anyone who found this novel becoming real while reading it.

Real people seldom enter Xanth. Jenny Elf and her cat Sammy came to Xanth three novels ago, when the Mundane Jenny was hit and almost killed by a drunken driver.

The real Jenny continues to improve, slowly, learning to sit without support and to stand briefly in her wheelchair. She has been in a special school, but hopes to return to regular school in due course. She is using a computer. Now a real animal has arrived: Bubbles Dog. Bubbles was originally adopted by a neighbor, who named her, while we had her sister Tipsy and her cousin Lucky. We wound up keeping her, and we didn't feel right about changing her name, though we weren't keen on it. Tipsy died of cancer in 1988, and Lucky of old age in 1991. We did not want to leave Bubbles alone outside, so we tried letting her into the house—and she turned out to be a perfect house dog. So at age twelve she changed her status and became closer to us, and we really liked her constant company. But larger dogs don't live as long as small ones, and she was over seventy pounds; we knew she would not live much longer. Indeed, just before her thirteenth birthday, while I was writing this novel, she died. The shock was considerable, because we had come to know and like her so well. She was a mongrel, but a really nice dog, and she had fitted so well into our lives. So I brought her into Xanth, where she can live the life she could not continue with us. In effect, I put her in the bubble, where Kim could find her. I don't need to tell you what Bubbles was like, because you know her from the novel.

Just before I started this novel, our horse Blue died, almost thirty-four. That was another shock, because we had had her fourteen years and she was the model for Mare Imbri. So it seemed fitting that Mare Imbri conduct Bubbles to Xanth in the form of a daydream that turned real. They were together in life; they are together in Xanth. Our house and our pasture seem empty now, but in our fond thoughts our friends remain. No, we're not looking for more pets. After a quarter century of having them, and being tied home because of them, we are now ready to relax and travel a bit. Then we'll see.

Between the last Xanth novel and this one another interesting thing happened. Jenny Elf had an iris flower named after her. You see, I had a letter from Thom Ericson, who breeds irises, inquiring whether it would be all right. So now Jenny Elf exists outside of Xanth, too, in the form of her unique flower. I asked Thom whether he had another flower, and the result was another: the Janet Hines Iris. You see, Janet Hines is a reader of mine who is in a sadder state than Jenny. She was not hit by a drunken driver, but by a devastating disease which slowly deprived her of her mobility and her sight. Now she is paralyzed, and can not talk, so she communicates by blinking her eyes, though she is blind. Like Jenny, she retains her mind, but not much use of her body. In 1991 I visited Janet and talked to her. She could respond only by blinking and smiling. But she was glad to know about the iris, and she likes to listen to my novels. I have loyal fans. She, too, is now learning to use a computer to facilitate communication.

I learned to my chagrin that I had gotten the name of a character wrong: Dana Demoness, Humfrey's first wife. How can that be, when she is a fictional character? Because the one who corrected me was Asia Lynn, who had suggested her. So next time she shows up in Xanth, she will make a point of correcting it: she is really Dara Demoness.

The talent of erasure Kim won was suggested a couple of novels ago by Stephanie Erb. I don't know when or whether Kim will show up in a future novel, but if she does, that's going to be some talent. She'll be able to erase the lock on a door, so she can get in, or erase part of a river so she can walk across dry, or erase an attacking monster. Kim herself, winning a prize in a talent contest, was suggested by Dawn Baker. But Kim's romance with Dug was her own idea.

I have half a slew of pun and notion credits, so will jam them into this paragraph in roughly the order they appeared in the novel, though sometimes I collect several under one name: self-popping popcorn, caramel corn—Jane Goulon; vocal cords—Vickie Brockmeier; electrici-tree—Joshua Ping; Stu-Pid—Stuart E. Greenberg; another demon trying to take over Xanth, deadly night shade, Miss Fire, guest stars—G. Beardwell; censor-ship—Mark Lord; Fairy Nuff—Carolyn Baxter; Ice Queen Clone—Adam Maule; strawberries and bull-frog—Cliff Hicks; lipstick—Jackson Chin; winged unicorns from *Spell* love spring breeding—L. K. Law; maidenhead with a hymen—Richard K. Reeves; Kiss-Mee made Kill-Mee by pulling the S's straight—David H. Zaback; fabric plant—Dawn Baker; Bec on Call—Rebecca Worrell, Curse Fiend history, skeleton history—Erin Schram; dream becomes reality, and vice versa—Dawn Baker; Black Wave—Princilla Claiborne; Black Smith—Randolph A. Crawford; humble pie—Rich Montgomery; useful bubbles—Derek Adams; pun-gent—Jon Morrison; roc-ettes—David Karty; money talks—Alyson Victoria Dewsnap; Germ of an Idea—Rose Platt; Lake Champagne—Mat Cannington, Alicia Littich, Heather Miller; box kite—Rhys-Michael Silverlocke; hiquigems—Verna; odd plants from coneflower to rock brake—John E. Ericson, PhD (Posthole Digger), who claims that all of them grow in Western Colorado; Com Pewter catches a virus—Najan Mughal; ogre girl's talent of ugly—Tamara Lynn Bailey; reverse wood to modify talent—Jonathan Carter; the three ticks: Necro, Agnos, and Cataly—Cindy Shipley; fifty talents—Matt Evans; pit bull, pillow fight, down pillow—Jeremy Lucash; stool pigeon, toiletrees—Dramon K. Hayes; honeydew—Tamara Lynn Bailey; cantaloupe—Jeremy Lucash, Aaron Wikkgrink, Travis Kincher; food chain—William S. Fisher; gilt by association—Gerald Lim; Ass O' Nine Tails—Mickey Bagala, Justin Studebaker, David Haley; Fool Moon—Rich Montgomery; DeOgreant—anonymous; Crow Bar—Dan McDonald; Mother Hen—Richard K. Reeves.

There were more puns and talents offered, but I was unable to use all of them in this novel. Some related to characters who didn't show up here. I will try to use them next time. I should also say that if certain regions seem to resemble counterparts in the Mundane state of Florida, such as Tallahassee (the tall hassle grove)—well, you probably just imagined it.

And to forestall the barrage of questions I may otherwise receive: yes, this Xanth novel has a new publisher. That doesn't mean that the prior Xanths are inferior, just that in the dreary world of Mundania these things happen. Those who want to buy any of my novels by mail order, or subscribe to my quarterly newsletter, can call 1-800 HI PIERS.